THE KEY TO SKANDOS

A MAGICAL TALE OF ADVENTURE AND LOVE

WILLIAM A. PRATER

Ordering Information:

Prime Seven Media
518 Landmann St.
Tomah City, WI 54660

Printed in the United States of America

Table of Contents

CHAPTER 1

Once, upon a time...

In the Britain of long, long ago, life for the poor was extremely hard; all were obliged to serve. To tend cattle or labour in the fields from dawn to dusk; rewarded with but their lives, a hovel; barely sufficient food for themselves and their children, nothing for elderly relatives.

Nor had they peace when the day's toil was done. Knowing ghastly ghouls, spirits and vampires were abroad, they lay cowering in terror throughout countless hours of darkness, none daring to move until the dawn of a new day and when all might venture forth in safety once again. For these sad unfortunates it was a life without hope, without joy; miserable beyond compare. There was no one to whom they could turn. No higher authority, no people's champion, no justice.

But far, far to the east lived a powerful magician whose name was Zildus. Highly respected, Zildus was renowned for kindly deeds although still relatively unknown in the west. Apprenticed to an academy founded centuries earlier by Breethan the Mysterious, his influence spread, and he was eventually acknowledged the finest, most powerful sorcerer in the land.

By and by, Zildus engaged two apprentices, Wegglar and his distant cousin Fular. Not in the least surprising, given his impeccable credentials, Zildus proved a highly-talented teacher. Tackling his role with wisdom, energy and enthusiasm, Zildus explained, schooled, tutored and trained, until the young novices' abilities were almost the equal of his own. Both graduated with honours; students were students no more. Zildus was both happy and sad. Wegglar adopted the title 'Wegglar the Wizard' and Fular became known as 'Fular the Witch'.

Magical Law decrees that wizards, sorcerers and witches should have territory of their own unless married; it was written. Zildus was master in the east. Wegglar and Fular, therefore, moved to the west. Wegglar was ambitious, wanted his own castle, yet needed to accumulate sufficient wealth. But he was a patient wizard. Pending that day, he practised his art from caves among the hills above Makklis. Fular was unpretentious, didn't fancy a castle anyway, castles were *far* too cold and draughty. She took up residence at Than-Gol, pro tem, in a fortified lodge rented from Zildus.

During initiate years, Wegglar and Fular became extremely close, kissed and cuddled a great deal and contrived to spend as much time together as duty, studies – and Zildus, would allow. The couple seemed destined to one day unite in a life-long partnership – or so it was thought. But from the moment they became magicians in their own right – for reasons that Zildus never could quite fathom – they constantly bickered and quarrelled; hurled lightning-bolts at each other across the Cherzil plain– generally at night, rendering it a frightening, noisy and dangerous place to live.

At that time, western regions were controlled and dominated by feudal barons and war-lords, created landowners by a warrior king as a reward for, and to whom they swore allegiance. Such was their power they overran the country, plundered and pillaged and seized titles by force. Simple foresters, herders and farmers were robbed of their heritage; regardless of the fact they had worked the land since settlements first became established centuries earlier.

The regime was inflexible and cruel, indifferent to the welfare of those held in subjugation. Severe punishment was meted with impunity to those who dared question the authority of heavily-armed, well-disciplined militiamen, trained in the control and exploitation of peasant labour.

These troops exercised almost limitless power over those they supervised but were themselves controlled by fear, subject to instant decapitation if found guilty of the slightest dereliction of duty. They received ample food and excellent accommodation in return for unswerving obedience and loyalty, therefore few beheadings were necessary. Those who *were* given the chop from time to time served as an excellent deterrent to those who might otherwise have been tempted.

But *nobody* was immune from the demonic depravity which ruled whilst the sun was at rest. All were fearful of the happenings of the night, when the air was heavily impregnated with unrest and foreboding, a dreadful aura which permeated the hearts of all, slave and captor alike.

For harpies flew with impunity, to snatch a sleeping baby from the crib, or take one aloft alive and screaming when abandoned by a mother no longer capable of caring. It was widely believed such hapless mites were doomed to suffer unspeakable deeds at the hands of Demons, Goblins and Sprites until, finally, they would either be eaten alive or else otherwise cruelly sacrificed.

Even the King – reputed to fear no man, beast or spirit, was obliged to defer to the necromancy of the night. During daylight, however, the castle was his home, his haven, his sanctuary. Surrounded by servants, protected by loyal guards, his security was never in question.

With the coming of Wegglar and Fular, however, life became increasingly impossible for the unfortunate king, whose residence lay plumb, smack bang in the centre of the Cherzil plain. The howls and shrieks of demons and fiends were one thing, the advent of lightning-bolts and thunder-crashes quite another, proving just about the last straw… it simply couldn't go on. Tired and irritable, the King summoned Courtiers; ye Royal Soothsayer, ye Lord Chamberlain:

'Gather together ye wisest in the land,' he roared, 'I am undone. Mine head acheth, mine eyes groweth dim. Render unto me peace and quiet 'ere long – or I'll have the lot of you boiled in oil.' He gave them just twenty- four hours to come up with a solution!

The discussions raged till midnight, alas without result. Nobody – except one, had a clue.

'I have an idea, kind sirs,' the scullery-maid cried, fearing for her job should the castle be closed.

'Hush, child,' the Soothsayer said sharply, 'hold thou thy tongue, for thou knowest nothing.'

'Hold on,' the Lord Chamberlain frowned, 'thou knowest nothing either. Give the wench a chance, gadzooks. Any idea couldst be better than none. Go ahead, girl, what say thou?'

The maid blushed and curtsied:

'Call unto Zildus the Magician,' she said, 'for did'st train Fular *and* Wegglar the Wizard. They are cause of the trouble, 'tis said. Should'st not Zildus, therefore, determines the cure?'

'Egad,' the Lord Chamberlain said, 'thou could'st be right. Here, taketh my ring for reward.'

An emissary was appointed, forthwith dispatched to the east. He carried a document: 'By Royal Command, an Invitation', addressed to Zildus the Magician. Couched in terms calculated to ensure the Sorcerer's interest, the emissary had little difficulty in persuading Zildus to accompany him to Cherzil for an urgent, immediate, right royal audience with the King.

Several audiences later and after much hard bargaining, the monarch appointed Zildus to a new, specifically-created post: 'Sorcerer Royal', with a brief to rid Cherzil of sufficient noise, demonology and witchcraft to restore the tranquillity of the night, in return for which the enchanter would benefit from royal patronage and a fortune in precious metals and stones. The deal was to include the Bez Mer Chalice, a powerful symbol of togetherness.

Zildus drove a hard bargain. The Bez Mer Chalice was not only beautiful, it was priceless. Skilfully fashioned a thousand years earlier by craftsmen of a bygone era; a drinking vessel of purest gold, inlaid with diamonds, rubies and sapphires, part of ye Royal Treasure.

The Chalice comprised of two drinking-cups which could be used separately or, if placed base-to-base would become as one. With a quarter turn left with inward pressure and a half turn right, the two united by means of a cleverly-contrived locking system. It then became a single drinking- cup, identical when inverted no matter which half was uppermost.

Its offer desolated the King, but he chose well. Zildus was undoubtedly the magician for the job! Setting about his task with vigour, and by dint of brilliantly-contrived magical spells and incantations, night disturbance around the castle at Cherz soon diminished and all but disappeared.

Zildus visited former protégés, first Wegglar, and then Fular.

Zildus explained that he had been appointed specifically to restore tranquillity by the King:

'Tis right be done,' he informed Wegglar. 'The King is powerful. It does not do to get up ye Royal Nose. I shall cast spell upon spell,' he declared, 'banish hence all Demons, Spirits and Banshees, prevail upon ye Harpies and Dragons to move elsewhere.

'All this I shall do 'ere long. But ye War of Attrition between you and Fular must cease forthwith. She also will be told, forsooth,' he added quickly, when Wegglar seemed angry at the mere mention of her name.

'Let me further explain,' Zildus then said. 'My magical spells will unite to become one, the most spectacular, most powerful, most dangerous sorcery of all. Just one thunder-bolt from either of you would'st blow the entire country into another dimension – not necessarily the nearest, either. Normal life – including the King, the people, the weather, most birds and animals wouldst remain, but everything nasty – including you and Fular – wilt catapult into the middle of next week!'

'How so, dear Zildus?' asked Wegglar. 'What mystical enigma dost imply?'

'Parallel Worlds,' his mentor replied, tapping his nose. 'Prithee listen and I shall explain.'

The sorcerer proceeded to enlighten his eager listener – in part! Parallel worlds surrounded the planet, Wegglar learned. Of labyrinthine passages and complex portals through which such worlds may be accessed, the keys known only to those sufficiently schooled to use them. Zildus explained one of the peculiarities.

On one world in particular – Skandos, the time relationship between it and the real world was so different as to be almost impossible to calculate; a full year within equated to a matter of minutes without. But this would not be apparent to those on either side of the portal unless passing freely to and fro and was therefore of little or no consequence. It was extremely interesting, nevertheless.

'So you see,' Zildus finally said. 'We magicians must stick together. To do otherwise would'st encourages disaster.' Wegglar nodded, sagely, but Zildus hadn't finished:

'In return for your cooperation, I shall fund the building of your castle. Do we have a deal?'

'Egad, yes,' Wegglar agreed. 'But watch out for Fular, Zildus. Prithee don't hold your breath.'

'Have no fear,' Zildus assured him. 'Fular shall toe ye line. She's good natured, actually.'

Indeed she was – in return for living rent-free for twenty-five years. Zildus thought it a bargain.

The King was delighted – until the second night following his grateful words *and* parting with a treasure chest so valuable it defied imagination. Woe and alack, his delight was short-lived. An hour after of settling down to slumber he awakened, satisfaction transformed into wrath. An out-of-season hurricane: shrieking winds, torrential rain, thunder, tempest and lightning. Groggily, Fular awoke. Without a second thought, assumed Wegglar was up to his old tricks. She let fly and, not to be outdone, so did Wegglar. It was *horrendous, awful, catastrophic!* A series of monumental explosions crashed through the air, the night sky turned deep purple: stars disappeared. Violent tremors rocked the ground; fearsome creatures took to the air. Bedlam!

Across Cherzil, however, night sky remained the night sky; rent asunder by lightning bolt after lightning bolt. The crashing crack-boom of thunder shook the castle from rampart to dungeon, reverberating and rattling the hills until well after dawn.

The King went potty, even angrier when, despite his summons, Zildus failed to put in an appearance. Come daylight the castle was searched, but Zildus was nowhere to be found. His quarters were empty; bed not slept in. Zildus the Magician had seemingly grabbed the booty and legged it. His Royal Mightiness was livid, apoplectic. He ordered an immediate proclamation.

Zildus was stripped of his title; Royal Patronage withdrawn. Zildus was Guilty of Treason, of Criminal Deception, Crime against ye Kingdom. Zildus was a magician, but popular no more.

The King retired to his chambers: devised new tortures to guarantee return of Royal Treasure. (Plus several innovative, extremely painful means of depriving the errant sorcerer of his life). To ensure none of these measures were overlooked through unforeseen memory lapse, the King dictated details to his Scribe, and personally saw to it his wishes were properly recorded.

Anger and disappointment caused the King to overlook one very important fact: Zildus was Master his Art. Not for nothing had the wily magician studied and practised. For not only was he able to come and go as he chose – by means that only he was privy, he was also cognisant of recent events, and right up to speed apropos royal annoyance at his supposed failure.

Few who were knowledgeable would doubt Zildus was indeed Principal Sorcerer in the land. Fewer still would provoke his displeasure, despite the magician's well-known kindliness.

Little more than an hour after dawn, when the sun was but a few strides into the sky, the Monarch was rendered incapable, moments before Zildus materialised before his very eyes. With no option other than to listen, the King's eyes softened to reflect his understanding, as he learnt that Zildus spent the night visiting an ailing elder, preventing him from knowing about – much less stopping – the local disturbances.

Released from immobility, His Majesty graciously acknowledged the royal rage had been somewhat premature and offered an assurance the matter would be rectified without delay.

He therefore relented: Zildus' title was restored, together with ye Royal Patronage. For after that one, astonishing, truly devastating storm, peace and tranquillity returned. No more Banshees, Dervishes or Devils. No Harpies, no Goblins, Gremlins or Dragons. No more howling winds or lightning bolts, no more crashing of thunder, no more – anything. It was *eerily* quiet.

Zildus came and Zildus went – but neither Wegglar nor Fular were anywhere to be found. Strangely, the caves of Wegglar bore no signs of habitation and the home of Fular lay empty. It was almost as if neither witch nor wizard had ever existed. It was *inexplicable*, to say the least…

Time passed. Ever solicitous, Zildus kept a fatherly eye on his former pupils – he was a kindly sorcerer. He made sure – discreetly, of course – that they were settled and comfortable, not suffering undue hardship or homesickness by virtue of isolation from the real world – not that they had any choice in the matter.

It was a form of poetic justice – in a manner of speaking. For theirs was a closed domain within the boundaries of which they could live their lives and hurl thunder-bolts with impunity; where they might practice the ancient magical arts without hurt or annoyance to others.

Zildus' self-appointed task bore no reward other than the satisfaction of caring about his protégés, even if they must remain unaware of it. He did an extremely good job. He built extensive locks of enchantment into the portal, with safeguards too intricate for those untrained to unravel, even should they cooperate one with the other and pool magical resources.

The task was fraught with difficulties; never before attempted. No tried and tested formulae. No ancient precedent, no clues. Strenuous weeks were spent creating and testing experimental incantations until, finally, by means of the Bez Mer Chalice, he succeeded.

The magician made several trips in and out of *Skandos*, not only to test and confirm the efficacy of each system, but to install a substantial supply of basic provisions sufficient to sustain the new residents for two or three earthly years, for no plant or animal within that world was adaptable for use as human food. Should either Wegglar or Fular have wondered from whence it came, neither said so. Perhaps they thought it was down to providence or possibly even 'Magic'.

Three decades later, curious to discover whether Wegglar and Fular had yet resolved their differences, Zildus again visited *Skandos*, was saddened to discover the pair still quarrelled. Zildus did notice, however, that Wegglar's head was magnificently adorned with a tall, pointed hat; whilst as an aid to transportation Fular habitually straddled a broomstick. As a tribute to the banished pair, Zildus introduced both items into magical code, eventually to become standard throughout the profession.

Hoping against hope that Fular and Wegglar would one day become reconciled, the charitable wizard secreted one half of The Bez Mer Chalice in the domain of each without either's knowledge and by so doing, created an opportunity for them to discover The Final Key, which might one day be activated by the penultimate catalyst, the seed of which he thoughtfully yet discretely placed outside Skandos.

Zildus tirelessly employed his magical skills to combat evil and banish malevolent spirits with no small measure of success. His fame spread across the land and he retained the post of 'Sorcerer Royal' throughout the reign of the King and that of his successor, during which the people were released from serfdom – due largely to Zildus and years of unstinting effort.

Eventually, at the age of one hundred and seventeen, his life's work done, the sorcerer returned his magic staff and book of spells to the Academy of Breethan.

As he prepared to relinquish his distinguished mortality he rested content, secure in the knowledge that the provisions he so thoughtfully placed in Skandos would eventually become exhausted – compelling the wayward pair to combine skills in order to find food, and that providing they set aside their differences for long enough, they would eventually unravel the secrets of the portal and be free to return to the world without unhindered. After all, he mused, it was never his intention that the wayward pair should suffer permanent banishment, even though their predicament was largely of their own making and richly deserved…

CHAPTER 2

Bessimer

The little fellow's eyes glistened, his lower lip trembled. He felt betrayed, unhappy, abandoned. Clearly unused to leaving mother's side, he was reacting to her departure on finding himself in the care of a stranger, after a leave-taking which brought both he and his parent close to tears.

'Come along, my dear,' the headmistress said, 'let's go and meet the other little boys and girls.' She had many years of experience in dealing with such matters and her firm, kindly manner persuaded him not to cry, as she led him by the hand and into the classroom. It may also have helped that she bore a passing resemblance to his mother. For Miss Jamieson was also young, pretty and smelt faintly of roses. He was soon at ease and found he was enjoying himself, thoughts of tears forgotten, on his very first day of full-time education.

At mid-morning break, little more than an hour after introductions, the latest pupil was awarded his nickname – perhaps predictably – by the very first boy he approached in the playground:

'Hello, please, would you like to play with me?' he began, timidly.

'Who do you think you're talking to?' the boy demanded, 'soppy little new boy – what's more I know your name,' he went on, 'it's not just Bessimer, it's Bessimer George Collinson, so there.' Bessimer was obviously upset by the unexpected response, prompting the boy to gleefully press home his advantage:

'Why don't you get yourself a *proper* name? Sissy, sissy, you're not really a boy, bet you're a girl… Bessie!' The boy found it amusing. He grinned, smirked at his own cleverness and shouted, 'Bessie! **Bessie!**' and then, at the top of his voice, 'BE————*S S I E!'*

Bessimer was taken aback. His face fell, as the implication behind the taunt struck fully home. Gritting his teeth, however, he steeled himself to angrily retort:

'I'm *not* a girl, I'm a boy. You can call me *George* if you like; it's my middle name, anyway, but **don't** call me *Bessimer* – or I'll tell everybody you're nothing but a horrible, sneaky little twerp. And I'm *not* a rotten sissy, so there!' He was, understandably, extremely indignant.

'Sissy, sissy, Bessie; Bessie wessie, diddums,' his tormentor persisted, hooted gleefully and scampered off round the corner cackling his head off, clearly unrepentant.

The exchanges had brought him dangerously close to tears, but Bessimer manfully went after him, hoping to reverse the insult, but the boy had simply melted into the throng. He may not have been able to put it in so many words, but Bessimer George Collinson desperately wanted to convince his classmate – and everyone else who overheard the jibe – that his preferred name was 'George', the new 'handle' was misguided, intensely disliked and, therefore, utterly gratuitous – but it was, alas, far, far too late.

For Graham Beswick – the boy who so rudely responded to Bessimer's tentative and friendly advance, had done so exceedingly loudly in one of the most public places of all, the playground. Bessimer George Collinson was sentenced thereafter to be known as 'Bessie', to schoolmates and contemporaries alike – at least and until he became sufficiently proficient at fisticuffs to have his preferences in the matter respectfully heeded.

And yet, seven years on and despite innumerable battles because of his name, Bessimer's prowess in the noble art remained singularly unimpressive, thus ensuring continuing usage of the highly-disliked and decidedly effeminate-sounding moniker.

Of course, grown-ups – such as the vicar, parents, teachers and the like – used his given name freely, but he held his parents principally responsible for imposing and perpetuating the misnomer in the first place. Indifferent to his many and vociferous protestations, they doggedly persisted with 'Bessimer', whereas he was convinced that were 'George' adopted in lieu, the hated feminisation would eventually become abandoned and the teasing would automatically cease.

Albert Harold Parsons, however, deferred to Bessimer's wishes from the first day they met. He was of about the same age as Bessimer and obligingly addressed him as 'George' and loyally continued to do so. Inevitably, the two became firm friends and became almost inseparable.

Bessimer George Collinson had abundant love and regard for his parents, excepting only in the matter of his name; perceived by the boy as an unnecessary and deliberate cruelty, inflicted solely because his uncle (father's childless brother Leonard) had brainwashed his parents into believing the ancient family style (Leonard's middle name) should be preserved into future generations.

Further years were to pass before Bessimer was to discover another reason – a very strange and important reason – for bearing his unusual name. A clue – of sorts, emerged when he was about eight. Window- shopping one day, Bessimer was drooling over the display in the window of Maria's Cake Parlour, hungrily wondering what he should buy with the last of his pocket-money. Albert stood at his side. He too was hungry but stony- broke, a mere onlooker. He wasn't seriously concerned however; no matter what Bessimer might choose, there would always be a share for him.

At that very moment, perhaps by coincidence, while the boys' attention was held by a tray of delectable-looking, crunchy pork pies, a schoolmate happened by on his bicycle. Spotting the friends, he shouted: 'Hey Albert, Hey Bessie' and then, louder still, 'Hey, Bessie. Doing some shopping for Mummy, then?'

Neither turned ignoring the sarcasm. Stung by their indifference and intent on gaining recognition, the lad opened his mouth, filled his lungs and bellowed at the top of his voice:

'BESS-I-MER, BESS-I-MER!' Cackling at his imaginary cleverness, the boy continued on his way; failing to observe the extraordinary consequence of pronouncing Bessimer's name, twice in succession. At precisely the repeat of the second syllable whilst the friends' eyes were fixed firmly on the pies, the tray and its entire contents flickered pale-green, turned hazy – and abruptly vanished! Simultaneously, Bessimer's hands – which, like his nose were in contact with the glass – appeared to vibrate and tingle. He glanced down in alarm; only to discover his fingertips were also green, similar to that surrounding the pies, whilst emitting a faint but distinct crackling. He hastily snatched his hands away. The crackling ceased, the aura disappeared – and yet the tingle remained.

Albert was equally astonished as Bessimer: 'Did you see *that?*' They gasped in unison. Utterly bewildered, with popping eyes and hugely concerned, they faced one another in alarm:

'Hey, George, look. Somebody's half-inched the flaming pies. Crikey, must be magic.'

'Yeah, but what about my hands, they still tingle.' Cautiously, Bessimer flexed his fingers; relieved to find all five still in working order. Abruptly, the tingle ceased much to his relief.

Albert nodded. 'Yes, George, I did. Oo 'er how weird.' A look of fear came into his eyes.

'Crikey, someone's left a gold coin where the pies used to be! Whoever was behind it was certainly no thief, that's something, I suppose. Come on, let's get out of here,' he proposed, 'I reckon the flipping place is haunted.'

Bessimer was not of a mind to disagree. Hunger forgotten, the boys hastily departed… not that they didn't discuss the incident at some length, desperate for a satisfactory explanation. Eventually, they were forced to admit failure and give up, and by tacit agreement and to avoid the almost certainty of embarrassing ridicule, they steadfastly thereafter kept quiet about the incident.

Approaching their teens, Bessimer had grown into a healthy, sturdy youngster. Brown haired, grey-eyed and intelligent, his regular features complimented a polite and friendly manner – beyond doubt an extremely nice young man. His principle interests – football, cricket and fishing – were shared in equal part by Albert, fair-haired, blue-eyed, loyal bosom pal; similar in stature and nature.

Until this time, neither paid anything other than cursory attention to girls – silly creatures, who didn't appreciate football, cricket or fishing; played with soppy prams and equally soppy dolls. Girls, therefore, were of little or no consequence – at least as far as *they* were concerned.

But, latterly, of about the same age, fair-haired, hazel-eyed and vivacious, Constance 'Connie' Cartwright began to appear rather more in the scheme of things, especially where Bessimer was concerned. For some time she contrived to cross his path as often as she could, rather more frequently than by mere coincidence – after all, her home was nearly a kilometre from his.

Initially, the attraction was somewhat one-sided, but Connie was not only delightfully pretty she was persistent and extremely single-minded. Reticent at first but despite himself, Bessimer felt flattered by the attention and made no protest when she habitually used his first name in full.

He found himself increasingly in her company, but not at the expense of Albert, despite his friend's well-known fancy for the girl. Connie was agreeably disposed towards Albert, but made it clear she preferred Bessimer and was not romantically interested in anyone else. The three accepted the situation for what it was and became firm friends, which led Connie to occasionally participate in activities formerly considered essentially male.

The friendship deepened, rather more so where Connie and Bessimer were concerned, and this somewhat lopsided situation remained virtually unchanged for almost a year. One fine autumn day however, not long after all three celebrated thirteenth birthdays, the trio set off by bicycle for an afternoon's fishing on the river Weaver, a couple of kilometres or so from their homes in Nantwich, an important market town in Cheshire.

After an hour or so, bored of catching 'tiddlers' and seeking a change of fortune, Albert left Bessimer and Connie to their own devices and went to try his luck for pike in a backwater, some two hundred metres or so downstream.

Bessimer openly ogled Connie. She looked stunning; the most desirable creature he had ever clapped eyes on. Perceptively turning her head, Connie neatly intercepted his look and with shining eyes she parted her lips and smiled. It wasn't long before two rods sat on unattended rests as nature guided the pair into each other's arms, putting into practice something of the theory relative to boy/girl relationships which they eagerly set about exploring with ever-increasing fervour. Twenty bliss-filled minutes slipped by unnoticed before Albert returned, by which time the couple were sitting demurely side by side apparently intent on fishing. He made no comment but couldn't fail to have noticed the faint flush to Connie's cheeks; nor the frequent glances exchanged between the pair or two rapt expressions that had nothing whatever to do with fishing...

Later that evening in a farmer's field close to where the three spent the afternoon, a second extraordinary event took place, unseen by humans, surpassing even that of the disappearing pies...

C H A P T E R 3

Through the Portal

Beyond doubt the night was breathtakingly beautiful. The full disc of a harvest moon shone with iridescent brilliance against the backdrop of a sky inlaid with millions of scintillating points of light coming from stars of countless galaxies; a vision of opalescent luminosity akin to newly-minted sovereigns against the dark velvet of a jeweller's tray embellished with myriads of tiny diamonds.

Intent on the succulent grasses upon which they fed, noses a-twitch, ears alert for the slightest hint of danger, a couple of dozen rabbits munched away contentedly three or four metres from the meadow boundary, with the warren entrance inside an adjacent wood. The animals appeared as black outlines in relief against the darkening grassland, some two hours after the sun finally disappeared below the horizon.

Scarcely a breath stirred the grasses, what little there was prevented the scent of downwind predators from alerting the rabbits. Taking full advantage, virtually invisible against the hedgerow along which he crept, the wraithlike figure of a dog-fox stealthily stalked his prey. Once within striking distance, the hunter fixed unwavering eyes on the nearest bunny, flattened to the ground and gathered his haunches in readiness to pounce.

A couple of kilometres from the field, Constance stirred in her sleep. The girl smiled as memory reprised the events of the day. Her lips parted and she spoke aloud as she dreamed:

'Bessimer, Bessimer, oh Bessimer,' she murmured, softly, 'oh Bessimer, I think I love you.'

He was about to spring. An eruption of pastel-green light flickered across the meadow accompanied by an eerie crackling. In an instant all the feeding bunnies vanished whilst the startled fox flattened and drew back his mask in a snarl, perceiving that not only his intended prey but *all* of the furry delicacies in the field had mysteriously disappeared. Frustrated, bewildered and supper less, he bad-temperedly slunk away.

Elsewhere, the subject of the girl's thoughts was also asleep in bed. He too moved restlessly but didn't awaken, not even when his arms tingled and pale-green light shone momentarily from beneath the sheets. With a barely perceptible crackle the light was gone…

The following morning Connie paid rather more attention to her appearance than usual. She brushed her hair with exceptional enthusiasm and applied the small amount of makeup she wore with unusual care. Once breakfasted, with shining eyes and a spring in her step she tripped lightly down the path to meet Bessimer, gallantly waiting to escort her to school.

The couple greeted one another with obvious pleasure and set off hand in hand. Chattering animatedly and totally engrossed, they not only failed to call for Albert but passed his house without so much as a sideways glance. Poor neglected Albert: he emerged and fell in behind, pensive and deep in thought, deeming it wiser and prudent not to intrude. By the time Bessimer and Connie reached school they had arranged to meet in the gym at lunchtime wanting to be alone together once again, intending to return home after school via a circuitous route through the woods. No thought of Albert even entered their heads nor did he form any part of their plans.

Differing timetables decreed Albert saw nothing of his friends that morning but at lunchtime, when neither appeared at the usual rendezvous, he chanced to spot Bessimer entering the gym closely followed by Connie. It took no great feat of perception to conclude he was now 'odd man out' despite years of unswerving loyalty. No explanation or apology, no giggle of embarrassment – no nothing. Grumpily, Albert sulked.

When classes ended and the pair went off together – still without a word or even a text, in a fit of pique and totally out of character Albert set out to follow, keeping well back to avoid detection. He reached the woods barely in time to glimpse Bessimer glance back prior to disappearing into a coppice hand in hand with Connie. *They're heading towards the canal, taking the towpath route home,* Albert mused. 'Cor, Penny Plinkers!' he exclaimed, 'that way's at least a kilometre further.' *No time for Hanky- Panky* (he smiled at the thought) *else they'll never be home for tea.*

Realising he may have been spotted he quickened his pace to make sure they didn't double back in an attempt to shake him off. But even as he reached the spot where they disappeared, a cry of alarm – almost a scream, came from within the trees.

Was Connie in danger? Instantly protective, adrenaline flooded his veins. He heard a shout for assistance, unmistakeably Bessimer's voice: 'Help! Help! We're caught and it won't let go.'

Not for a moment did Albert hesitate; his reason for following the pair forgotten. He snatched off his cap, shoved it in his pocket and, throwing caution to the wind rushed to the rescue as fast as his legs – and thick shrubbery – would allow. He didn't have far to run – about fifty metres, or so, before he blundered into a clearing.

He stopped dead, eyes popping. Bessimer and Connie were indeed in need of help; securely trapped by writhing, tentacle-like branches reaching from within a clump of bushes. Entwined face to face, they had evidently been surprised and pinioned whilst locked in embrace.

Albert took it in at a glance, continued his headlong rush and skidded to a halt beside his friends. Unhesitatingly, he reached for the nearest entrapping branch.

The moment his fingers were within touching distance, the offending appendages retracted, releasing the sweethearts from bondage, leaving them shaken but otherwise unharmed. Wringing their rescuer by the hand, Bessimer was first to express his grateful thanks:

'Gosh, thanks, Alby. Crikey, that was weird. Good job you came along when you did; we might easily have been stuck till the middle of next week.'

'Yes, thanks, Albert,' Connie sweetly echoed, reinforcing gratitude with a peck on the cheek. 'I was ever so frightened when that tree thing grabbed us; it was so tight it was beginning to hurt.'

Albert shrugged. 'It was nothing really. I saw you leaving school and was trying to catch up. But if you must know,' he suddenly blurted, 'I wanted to know why you've been avoiding me.' Connie and Bessimer exchanged guilty looks. Bessimer hastened to explain.

'We weren't trying to avoid you, you silly sausage. We just wanted to be alone for a while.' Connie said nothing, blushed crimson. Gallantly, Albert attempted to spare her feelings:

'It's not *that* important,' he murmured, 'no harm done. I just hope we go on being friends.'

'I'm sure we will,' Bessimer assured him. 'And so am I,' Connie echoed, happily.

The trio exchanged understanding looks, realising there would *always* be occasions when sweethearts would seek to be alone. That apart, Albert would *never* be excluded.

The incident, therefore, was considered closed.

Youth, if nothing else, is resilient. Friendship intact and harmony restored, they set about examining the thicket – but cautiously and from a distance. It *seemed* innocuous enough, much the same as any other bush – except when Connie and Bessimer advanced too close. When they did, clutching branches shot out and curved towards them, which Albert's close proximity seemed to repel. Should he reach out, the threatening arms would stop, reverse and bend the other way. It was extremely curious and the three tested and re-tested the phenomena several times before setting off to walk the rest of the way home together. They didn't get far. Eighty metres or so give or take.

They emerged from the trees to find themselves confronted by an obstacle: a huge, seemingly impenetrable wall around five metres high, stretching completely to the horizon in either direction.

The friends were nonplussed. These were woodlands they had played in for most of their lives, extensively explored and knew thoroughly. Never before had they encountered a barrier or restriction of any kind, neither here nor anywhere else.

'Where the dickens did *that* spring from?' Bessimer wondered. He was much intrigued and moved a pace or two closer for a better look.

'Don't know, maybe they've built a new "Nick" since we were last this way,' Albert ventured. A frown creased Connie's brow:

'I hope it's nothing to do with that dreadful bush,' she shivered perceptively.

'Nah shouldn't think so,' Bessimer said, intending to reassure but somehow lacking conviction.

Albert moved alongside Bessimer. Walls had no means to entrap, after all and he was equally curious, keen to establish just exactly how it was constructed. There was no evidence of mortar; therefore joints between the blocks were virtually invisible.

He ran speculative hands over the surfaces, curiously warm to the touch, unlike conventional building materials. He seemed puzzled; scratched his ear, rubbed his chin – and wondered.

'You know,' he began, 'there's something strange here. See how smooth they feel, nothing at all like normal blocks.' Connie held back. Without conscious reason, she was reluctant to become involved any further. But Bessimer nodded as he conducted his own examination, subjecting the edifice to an even closer scrutiny. Curiosity led him to test the surfaces for himself:

'Yes, Alby, I see what you mean. It *does* feel unusual – sort of warm, bit like Polystyrene.' He began absently tracing the 'joint' around the nearest slab with a forefinger. Instantly, the wall changed colour, from beige to pale-green, and a nimbus of similar hue sprang into being. Bessimer froze, alarmed – but even more cautious.

Albert jumped as though stung, while Connie – believing Bessimer to be in danger, reacted with equal swiftness. Instinctively, she rushed forward to try and protect him, shouting:

'Bessimer, Bessimer, *oh Bessimer,* for goodness sake, do be careful. What's going on?'

There was a tremendous, ear-splitting 'crack!' which made them jump. Shocked motionless they could only gape as the wall shimmered briefly and an aperture the size of a dinner-plate appeared. Then, faster than the eye could follow, accompanied by a quavering, high-pitched whine, the breach burst, rapidly expanding into an orifice around two metres in diameter. Through it, they caught a glimpse of scarlet trees silhouetted against an ominous, purple sky and as they gaped in disbelief, the halo flared into incandescent brilliance and enveloped them, sparkling, flashing and crackling with vibrant intensity, at the same time pulsing a strange tingle throughout the whole of their bodies. Incredible as it may seem, the sensation intensified until reaching a mind-numbing crescendo, peaking as they shot through the breach with tremendous force; crashing to the ground in a tangled confusion of arms and legs amid clouds of orange-coloured dust.

As they climbed to their feet, winded and bewildered, the portal silently diminished – reminiscent of an old fashioned camera-lens iris – to finally close with a soft but ominous 'thud'.

The light faded and was gone. Once again the wall presented an impenetrable barrier: to all intents and purposes they were stranded. Understandably, perhaps, three normally garrulous youngsters were rendered speechless – temporarily at least. Bessimer was first to recover:

'C-crikey, wh-what happened, where the heck are we?' he uncharacteristically stuttered. Seeking inspiration, he turned to his friends, first Connie and then Albert. Both shook their heads. Dazed and uncomprehending, battered, bewildered, neither seemed able to respond.

Viewed from the 'wrong' side, the wall presented a totally different appearance. No longer influenced by sun and sky it was shades darker, a sort of dusky maroon. It appeared significantly taller, although it still extended in either direction as far as the eye could see. Which way was north? Which was south? None had the foggiest.

Beyond the horizon thunder rumbled. Distant lightning etched pale fingers across kilometres of purple, leaden sky. There was little wind; the very air possessed a sense of 'wrongness'.

A far-off, mournful wail resembling the cry of a wolf but pitched considerably higher had the friends' hackles rise; they shivered, involuntarily and turned in the direction of the sound. Some two kilometres distant, soaring above rising terrain cloaked with a forest of red, a menacing black shape wheeled and turned… *a flying dinosaur?* Was it coming this way? Briefly it glided, in relief against the sky until it swooped and disappeared behind an upwards-clutching tangle of vermillion branches… the friends breathed a collective sigh of relief, although the impression of stark, unimaginable horror chilling their bones was far more terrifying than anything encountered in the wildest of nightmares – but, clearly, this was no dream!

The youngsters were well advanced for their ages though still in early teens. And whilst unable to view such a potentially dangerous situation with anything approaching equanimity, each nevertheless displayed a remarkable degree of composure – well, almost.

Connie thrust her hand in Bessimer's who reciprocated with a silent, comforting squeeze. Albert shoved his hands in his pockets and sucked breath across his teeth, whistling tunelessly. He seemed about to speak – but thought better of it. It was down to Bessimer to come to terms with their astonishing predicament. Notwithstanding unease he looked about with considerable interest, but decided to reserve judgement until the situation became clearer, continuing to hold Connie's hand, quietly reassuring.

She was pacified at first but as minutes ticked by, worry returned and she became increasingly anxious. Releasing his hand she clung to his arm, seeking more by way of comfort. To combat her mounting fear, he smiled reassuringly and retrieved her hand for yet another comforting squeeze:

'Don't worry, sweetheart,' he said, 'we found the way through, didn't we?' When she hesitantly nodded Bessimer confidently continued: 'Then it stands to reason we'll jolly-well find the way back. Trust me, you'll see.'

'Oh, Bessimer, I hope you're right,' she breathed, apparently comforted.

'In any case,' the girl stoutly declared, 'as long as I'm with you I'm not the least bit frightened.'

'Good girl,' he chuckled, approvingly. Still smiling he turned to Albert:

'What do you reckon, Alby? Explore – or set about finding a way back?'

Connie tensed; expression again of alarm. Bessimer appeared not to notice, but in tune with her unease, Albert discounted Bessimer's display of bravado. In any case he had little doubt as to what they should do next – assuming they *had* a choice, that is.

'Well, Be— er, George,' he advised, firmly, 'get that flaming door unlocked – if we can. We need to know how and why it opened; maybe where the rotten wall came from in the first place.' Albert had almost called Bessimer by his first name – not that he seemed to mind. He offered no reply and his frown indicated he remained every bit as perplexed as ever.

'It opened just after the green light came on.' The interjection came from Connie.

'Yes, that's right, it did.' Albert was quick to confirm. Thoughtfully, Bessimer returned to the wall stretching out a tentative hand:

'Maybe *this* is what it needs to open it?' he began, hurriedly interrupted by Connie:

'For goodness sake, Bessimer,' she tutted, again alarmed, '*do* please be careful.'

'Don't worry, Connie – and please don't fuss. We've got to keep trying, haven't we?'

Her face fell. 'I'm *not* fussing thank you very much,' she retorted, 'I'm watching out for you.'

'Sorry,' he said, contrite, 'I didn't mean it like that. I've a gut-feeling the wall opens when touched so I'm going to try touching it again. Cheer up. We might be on our way home in a minute.' Experiencing little of the courage he was trying to convey, and whilst Albert and Connie anxiously looked on, Bessimer attempted to replicate his movements prior to the wall changing colour and when nothing happened, repeatedly rubbed, poked, prodded stroked and scratched. Sadly, too little avail. The wall remained massive, impenetrable, bleak – and stubbornly blank. Eventually, after what seemed an eternity, probably no more than five minutes, he stepped back, shoulders slumped, dismayed and close to despair. 'It's no use,' he grumbled, unhappily, 'I've tried and tried and nothing seems to happen.' It was pure defeatism and Albert frowned:

'Hold up, George,' he cautioned, 'we're not beaten yet. Tell you what,' he suggested: 'You just tried circling a block with your *right* finger, clockwise as before, right?' Bessimer nodded.

'Yes, I did; right – clockwise, what of it?'

'Well,' Albert replied, impatiently, 'how about using your *left* finger and go *anti*-clockwise? We came through one way and need to reverse the procedure, so try backwards, eh? Worth a shot don't you think? Come *on*, George, hurry up, I want to go home. *Do* something; get us out of here.' He was impatient, hopping; fizzing and buzzing. Thus pressured, Bessimer felt unable to refuse.

'OK, Alby, keep your shirt on. I'll give it a whirl.'

Squaring his shoulders he stepped forward and extending his *left* forefinger; outlined one of the blocks – albeit gingerly, cack-handed and awkward – anti-clockwise. The instant his finger had travelled full circuit the wall glowed and the halo reappeared, exactly as before. Although hoping for such a reaction, Bessimer was nevertheless startled. He smartly whipped his hand away, although steadfastly standing his ground. Behind him, Albert nudged Connie, winking to avoid further alarm. 'Better keep close,' he warned, jokingly; 'or we might both be left behind.' For all his affected jocularity there was more than a hint of seriousness in his steady blue eyes.

The light remained. Drat, no aperture. Bessimer stepped back – the light went out. Crumbs! He experimented: No light, move forward. Circle clockwise with finger – nothing; anti-clockwise, light… fascinating. Connie and Albert looked on equally intrigued, and Bessimer repeated the process – but, still no doorway. It seemed appropriate to confer, long established practice for friends in times of trouble; homework problems or a minor scrape; one would usually come up with a solution. Albert opened the batting:

'Well,' he began, 'this is weird and no mistake. Wonder if anything to do with the S.A.S. or Secret Service, maybe,' he speculated, 'or just magic of some sort?' He scratched his head.

'Can't be magic, that's just a load of old codswallop,' he jeered. 'But you're on the right track, George, I'll be bound. There's little doubt about it, you've definitely rumbled the sequence.'

Bessimer mustered a smile: 'I think so too but *something's* missing because the gateway didn't activate. Whatever we've overlooked, well *that's* the bit we're short of. How about it, Alby, old son?' he asked, 'any bright ideas?'

'Offhand I can't think of any,' Albert admitted. 'How about you, Con? You spotted the doorway after Bess – er, George opened it.' He glanced across apologetically. Bessimer grinned:

'Call me "Bessimer" same as Connie,' he said, 'I honestly don't much mind anymore.'

Connie chimed in, 'About time too, you old fusspot,' she chirruped, squeezing his hand. 'It's a *lovely* name, and you should be proud of it – what's more it suits you right down to the ground.'

'Well, OK,' Albert said, 'thanks. But that was a one-off, George. Slipped out and I apologise. But about the wall? Oughtn't we to be getting home; it must be nearly teatime.' It was a moot point. Conversation petered away and practically ceased – until Connie piped up again:

'You two give it more thought. I'm hungry, tired – and oops, I need to spend a penny.'

Possibly out of respect for Connie's privacy the significance of her remark failed to register. Neither replied but unilaterally returned to the wall – to make yet another important discovery. Simply by approaching the light sprang into being – *without Bessimer so much as lifting a finger!* A quick experiment confirmed it. The light was actually sensitive to Bessimer's mere presence.

Connie fidgeted, feeling abandoned and left to her own devices; nobody paying her attention. She glanced about; espied bushes with spiky blue flowers and leaves a bilious yellow. *Oh, well,* she thought. *A bush is a bush and I really have to go!* Leaving the boys to their experiments, she slipped away from the wall, unobserved. A full half minute elapsed before Bessimer chanced to glance behind – to realise that Connie was no longer behind him.

'Hey!' he exclaimed. 'Where's Connie? Connie! Connie!' he shouted, 'where are you?'

'I'm over here behind the bushes,' she called back. 'Won't be a minute.'

'OK, but hurry up,' he sighed with relief, 'the pesky doorway might open any second.'

His words and the return of green light coincided. There were sounds of movement from behind the bushes, a short silence, loud rustling – and *voices!* One was Connie, the other – deeper in timbre, most definitely was not. Connie again, loud and emphatic:

'No, I will *not!* I'm staying here – and that's *that!'* There was a distinct *whoosh!* They froze – an ear-piercing shriek, unmistakably

Connie. And then, clearly terrified: 'Help! She's taking me. ***Bessimer, Bessimer...*** H – e – l – p!'

The light intensified, the bright-green halo appeared, flared into dazzling brilliance accompanied by a thunderous 'crash!' Again a plate-sized aperture sprang into being; the same inexplicable tingle as before. Neither seemed able to move; dazed by noise, dazzled by light, completely and utterly bewildered.

The familiar whine returned, rising to a screeching crescendo. Just as before, the breeched wall expanded into a large, circular opening. A glimpse of green fields, familiar woodlands and, with scarcely a moment to draw breath, Bessimer and Albert were propelled back through the orifice by forces too powerful to resist; thrown breathless to the ground, powerless to move as the portal contracted at lightning speed and closed with a final, heart-stopping 'thud'.

Fit and healthy, fortified by the resilience of youth it took only moments to recover from the cacophony of sound and clamour of transposition. Bessimer blinked, flicked hair from his eyes and clambered to his feet. He cast about: blue sky, green grasses and trees – all *normal*! Without doubt they were back, Bessimer and Albert, that is – but what of Connie? His face fell as he helped Albert to his feet.

'*We've* made it, Alby,' he said, relieved yet unhappy, 'but somehow left poor Connie behind.'

Albert brushed uselessly at soil and grass-stains on his trousers. He too was distressed:

'S-sorry, George,' he blubbed, 'it's my fault. You were busy. I should've been watching out for Connie. I warned her to keep close but the light distracted me. I didn't even realise she was missing...' He broke off, gasped. 'What's happening? The wall, it's flipping-well vanishing.' Bessimer spun, his jaw dropped; face a picture of amazement, bewilderment – and grief. The barrier was fast losing substance, wavering, dissolving and, in a blink of an eye, was gone.

'Connie, Connie,' he shouted to an empty field, trees – and the banks of the canal.

'Whoa, calm down,' Albert soothed, 'it's not as bad as you think. Yes, the barrier's gone but we'll find it again, you'll see.' He grabbed for his mobile, checked the screen and scrolled to Connie, hit 'call' but was immediately switched to voicemail. 'No good,' he reported. 'No signal, too far from town, but I thought it worth a try.' He patted Bessimer's arm.

'I know you're worried, so am I. It's my fault, you were busy, I should've have been looking out for her.' Bessimer smiled, wanly. 'I'm sorry too, got carried away. But it's *not* your fault, if anybody's it's mine. She's *my* girl friend; I should have taken better care of her.' He stood sadly, recalling Connie's cries for help – and the heart-wrenching fear in her voice.

'Let's agree to differ,' Albert grunted. 'Come on, better get cracking and set about getting her back.' A handshake and with no further ado they sorrowfully began to search.

For more than an hour they traipsed, desperately seeking the barrier. It began to drizzle. They were hungry, tired and cold, but still persevered. Another hour passed, by which time they were soaked to the skin, bedraggled, miserable and hungry. As leader, Bessimer finally called a halt.

'That's it,' he declared. 'We'll call it a day. We need food, a bath and a good night's sleep. We'll skip school tomorrow and rescue Connie before the day is out, you'll see.'

Meanwhile, in a strange, frightening and frequently dangerous world far beyond the barrier...

CHAPTER 4

The Keep of Fular

The Keep of Fular, a fortified stronghold built of Skandovian sandstone, stood on a small plateau in the foothills of Bortzin Mountain where natural attributes especially suited: designed, built and occupied for many years by the practicing magical woman known as Fular the Witch.

Modelled on a towered lodge at Than Gol, her one-time home, the edifice is moated to the front and amply protected by overhanging cliffs to sides and rear. Immediate vegetation is sparse and the ground slopes gently away for around two hundred metres, becoming heavily afforested thereafter. A unique, enviable situation rending unobserved daylight approaches virtually next to impossible.

The view from uppermost windows and roof extends across many kilometres of scarlet-topped forest until the terrain rises sharply to where a steep cliff incorporating an enormous cave provides both lair and take-off for a Brerb, the winged predatory monster of Skandos, a voracious beast that preys on all but the smallest of creatures that venture within range of its lair.

High in the mountains, a freshwater spring – augmented by ice-cold glacial melt and seasonally by torrential rains – meanders and cascades the slopes, ultimately to become a tributary of the river bisecting the forest below. Across the plateau the stream passes close to the witch's domain, where a cleverly-engineered culvert maintains the level of moat water and provides the Keep with fresh water throughout the year. Calculated by Skandovian almanac, the Keep took five years to construct and has enabled the witch to live in comparative safety and comfort ever since.

In her prime at an earthly age of twenty-eight, Fular remains strikingly handsome. Winsome, slender and mysterious, with luxuriant, long black hair – once likened to the lustre of a raven's wing – an oval face and finely-textured complexion, her isolation from the world without served only to add the mystique of maturity with little signs of aging. Forever beautiful, she once inspired desire and admiration amongst many of her youthful contemporaries and, more especially, her handsome colleague, Wegglar, whose primary interest turned to passion and developed into love by the time they were mid-way through magical training.

These days, however, her contempt for Wegglar was scarcely improved by knowing the man she once loved lived tantalisingly close, yet remained largely unpunished for destroying that love through churlishly rejecting her most cherished wish. They spoke little. Several means of communication were readily and permanently available, none activated until the provisions placed by Zildus eventually became exhausted and they were forced to cooperate in order to survive.

'Wegglar, thou niggardly Philistine, curse thy knavish ancestors. Once weazel always weazel, thou miserable wretch,' Fular muttered, as she followed the movements of the wizard through the eyes of her familiar. (She was perfectly aware Wegglar might similarly be watching her).

The witch's frustrations were temporarily forgotten, however, when the young female arrived in Skandos, a unique opportunity to satisfy a long- standing ambition and negate something of the sadness that had lain dormant within her heart over so many frustrated and miserable years. Her new-found pleasure manifold; interference she would not tolerate, of that she was determined and Fular was not at all pleased the girl's companions had somehow contrived to return. Irritation deepened when she perceived the man-children were intent on opposing her, turned to anger when they not only evaded the Brerb, but sent her ballistic when Wegglar disregarded magical ethics and intervened, foiling her carefully engineered plot for permanent removal. With the girl safely ensconced within the Keep, no further threat would have remained; opposition impossible. Magical lore forbade others of the profession from active opposition within the boundaries of another's domain, it was written, leaving her to pursue her life and that of her companion in peace. Fular's muttered tirade concluded, plaintively:

'Why dost meddle in matters not thy concern?' She directed a volley of thunderbolts towards the wizard, more to make a point, if truth be told, than to cause actual damage or do him physical harm.

Constance Cartwright meanwhile, languished in a locked room high in the Keep with no alternative other than to wait for rescue, eternally hopeful Fular might have a change of heart, relent and set her free. She repeatedly consulted her mobile, but there was nothing resembling a signal and the battery was in the last throes of exhaustion. Annoyed at not having charged it the previous evening, she returned it to her pocket in disgust. With time on her hands she reflected:

A quirk of fate; an inopportune call of nature; an irresponsible move away from Bessimer, Albert and relative safety; the subsequent bizarre flight from the barrier – dreamlike, unworldly and unreal. She prowled her cell, vainly seeking means of escape; decidedly a *horrid* cell. Nor was it furnished – apart from a pile of itchy, scratchy furs. Bleak, unfriendly – decidedly! The only light came from a single window set up near the ceiling, far and away too high to even peer through…

Thinking of home, mother and father; a comfortable bed and Bessimer – yes, *especially* Bessimer – brought a lump to her throat and tears to her eyes but she bravely blinked them away. She drew comfort from knowing Bessimer would also be worrying about her; no doubt striving manfully to come to her rescue.

Although hoping against hope rescue was imminent, immediate prospects were far from rosy. Connie sighed, disconsolately; pinched herself to confirm it wasn't a dream and cast her mind back to the barrier and the moment she straightened and the beautiful, but strangely dressed woman appeared as if from nowhere watching her with blatant curiosity:

'Who are you and what do you want?' she demanded – and blushed, remembering her delicate situation. Hastily, she bent and adjusted her clothing. *Surely it wasn't polite to stare – even here!*

'I bring greetings, pretty maid. Fear not for I mean no harm,' the woman had said. 'I am Fular; long have I awaited your coming. But come; visit with me the Keep nigh Bortzin where fine food, drink and comfort abound.' Fular smiled, engagingly. She truly was beautiful.

At first Connie was tempted. The woman *was* hypnotically persuasive and compelling. But commonsense prevailed. Why on *earth* should she accompany a complete stranger?

'No, I will *not*,' Connie told her, firmly. 'I'm staying right here – and that's *that!*'

'Come,' the woman wheedled, 't'would makes Fular exceeding happy. Come, fly with me.'

'Not flipping likely,' Connie retorted. 'On your bike, missus. With you I'm going nowhere. My friends are over there so clear off or I'll call them. Anyway it's late. I've got to be home for tea.'

Unfortunately, Fular's grasp of Connie's rather graphic second refusal was equally immediate. The more unfortunate, perhaps, the witch was none too pleased – as she swiftly demonstrated. A slender woman but astonishingly strong, she grabbed Connie by one arm and pulled her from the bushes. There was scarcely time to call for help before her feet left the ground and a rush of wind confirmed the evidence of her eyes – she was actually *flying* and at a furious pace. She *still* found it hard to believe. That she had been uplifted and whizzed through the air by the mysterious woman called 'Fular'. Connie remained, as yet, unaware that the brilliant flash and booming explosion moments into the flight marked the instant the boys were ejected back through the barrier…

The journey was no less frightening for its brevity. Within minutes she found herself dumped in a heap in front of a large orange-coloured house at the foot of a huge mountain. Dazed and confused, she rested a moment before climbing shakily to her feet. She felt giddy she recalled, whilst the woman – her captor, she rightly supposed – stood watching impatiently. To Connie's dismay Fular seemed entirely different, no longer the kindly lady who appeared at the barrier. She seemed agitated – afraid, almost. Poor Connie was at a loss to understand:

'Where am I? What is this place? Why have you brought me here?' she gasped, trying desperately to recover her wits. But her croaks of protest seemed only to infuriate the more.

'Pretend not the innocent child,' the woman snapped, angrily. 'How knewest prevail Bez Mer? Art also witch? Explain – and reply true,' she snarled, 'else thy future assuredly depends. Fular shalt sorely punish should'st offer false tongue. Speak wench. Try not further my patience.'

The woman's garbled speech had Connie fuddled – as if she wasn't confused enough already. She couldn't understand or even guess what the woman was on about. It was all too much.

'I d-don't know what you mean, Fular,' she had faltered and shook her head, helplessly. 'Please let me go. I don't understand. I've never even heard of "Bez Mer", truly I haven't.'

Fular's eyes turned black. She drew back her hand as if to strike – but Connie refused to flinch:

'Don't you *dare*,' she shouted, defiantly. 'Hit me and you'll be sorry. My friends will soon be here, you'll see. I'm not frightened of you anyway. I've already told you I know nothing about this stupid "Bez Mer". Why won't you believe me? Let me go, Fular – please.'

'Thou shalt stay till truth be told,' Fular declared unmoved, then delivered a bombshell: 'Thy companions art returned the world without,' she taunted, 'and can'st not aid. Assuredly, by Breethan thou shalt remain. Cast spells if thou wilt,' she sneered, 'Fular shalt ever prevail.'

Without another word Fular grabbed Connie and frog-marched her through huge double doors into the building, up stone stairs and along a flag-paved corridor. She stopped and opened a substantial timber door set flush in solid stonework… *an upstairs dungeon? Oh, oh!* Angry, still not speaking, the woman manhandled Connie inside and slammed the door.

Connie remembered only too well how her heart sank at the sound of bolts ramming home, the click, clunk, click of receding footsteps, the ensuing silence – the fear, the injustice, the *loneliness*! What had she done to merit kidnap, punishment, threats and pitiless incarceration? What's more at the hands of a woman she increasingly suspected to be a real live *WITCH!* That breathtaking flight, so bewildering she couldn't be certain what exactly *did* take place

– although the recollection of zooming through the air remained vivid enough.

What was the time? How long since she, Bessimer and Albert arrived in this terrible place? Connie glanced at her watch: three forty-six; it must have stopped. The second-hand moved, stopped, moved, stopped… she shook it – nothing improved. Curiously she watched, waited until it moved again then counted, slowly – *one, two, and three.* On reaching a count of one hundred and eighteen the hand advanced a second… once in almost two minutes? Drat, the battery must be flat and would have to be replaced. Connie sighed; another irritation to be put up with.

Her parents would worry – and there was the added anguish of being parted from Bessimer. The thought that he and Albert were back the other side of the barrier was almost impossible to bear.

Just as she was beginning to think nothing worse could possibly happen, the feeble light through the window flashed and flickered; there was a distant rumble of thunder and the cell was suddenly plunged into darkness. Forlorn abandonment pervaded every atom of her being.

It was all very well telling herself to be brave and all would come right in the end. It didn't prevent her eyes from welling over; nor from fumbling to the furs and throwing herself down, sobbing as if her heart would break. Scalding tears of abject misery went streaming down her cheeks – but there was nobody, neither to comfort her nor heed her distress. Poor sweet Connie; she sobbed and she sobbed and she sobbed until, eventually, she cried herself to sleep….sleep, blessed sleep, the ultimate anaesthetic!

Fast asleep, she was dreaming of home; failed to hear to hear the bolts slide back, the door creak and the rustle of clothing when someone entered the room. For a moment or two Connie slept on

– until an inner sense warned her she was no longer alone. She opened her eyes – groggily at first, coming awake with a start with the discovery she was being subjected to intense scrutiny by the witch, whose expression was now curiously tender. But was it a ruse? Was Fular playing mind-games? Or was she still angry? Connie was stricken with panic.

Scrambling to her feet, she backed away until brought up short by the wall – not that the witch made any sort of move, hostile or otherwise. She merely stared, silent, unmoving – impasse?

Eventually Fular did move. She held out a jug, said: 'water', and motioned Connie to drink. Why so friendly all of a sudden? Connie was, understandingly, deeply suspicious:

'How do I know you haven't poisoned it?' she demanded, 'I wouldn't put it past you.' Fular started shaking her head but Connie wasn't finished. 'What is this place?' she challenged. 'Why did you bring me here? Why have you kept me locked up? You're a witch – aren't you?'

'Greetings, Konnee,' her captor began. 'Verily Fular be witch and by magical means thy name dost know. But in equal truth would'st harms thee not.' With that the witch sipped from the jug and again offered it to her captive. Reassured, Connie accepted and drank, gratefully and thirstily. For some reason Fular suddenly seemed friendly – nothing like the hag who had virtually dragged her into this cell, thank goodness – kindly and much more like the lady of the barrier.

Connie wondered about her speech, curiously middle ages English, she supposed. Not difficult to understand and surprisingly easy on the ear. Thirst quenched, she perked a little.

It was daylight; earlier fears fast receding; maybe it was time she should assert herself. Fular *appeared* amenable but it wouldn't do to be overly cocksure. But she *would* stand her ground:

'If you didn't mean me harm, why did you bring me to your rotten dump? I want to go home – now!' she demanded, vehemently. 'Let me out. I'm hungry and badly in need of a bath.'

The witch seemed startled – puzzled, almost, but didn't answer. Connie followed up her attack:

'Let me go,' she repeated. 'Let me go or I'll scream till somebody hears and rescues me.'

Fular evidently understood perfectly. Her placatory expression disappeared to be replaced by one of implacable determination. She wagged a forceful forefinger:

'Thou entered Skandos to become companion,' she announced, sternly, 'nor shall depart 'ere Destiny grants Fular release – as signs hast long foretold – when cometh the Advent of Bez Mer. But come, refresh and break thy fast with Fular.' Her dark eyes twinkled. She even managed a smile as she continued: 'When entirely at ease, mayhap Fular shalt explain more.'

The prospect of a wash and something to eat was appealing, persuading Connie to bide her time. Fular took her by the hand. Having already experienced the witch's strength, Connie knew better than resist as she was led from the chamber back down the steps, along several passages to an inner courtyard thence to a stone outbuilding equipped with washing and toilet facilities. Once Connie was inside Fular bolted the door and departed; leaving no opportunity for escape.

But by now Connie wasn't overly bothered; the sting of ice-cold water was exhilarating and by the time Fular returned Connie felt alive, alert and enormously cheered, much more her usual self.

'Yes, thank you,' she replied, chirpily, in response to Fular's 'Art refreshed, Konnee?'

She allowed herself to again be taken by the arm, across the courtyard along a cloister to a patio, where an iron pot hung from a trivet above a glowing fire and a faint breeze wafted the tantalising aroma of stewing rabbit – Connie came close to drooling, she was extremely hungry. Still holding Connie, Fular paused to stir the pot before leading the girl into an adjacent room furnished with a rough-hewn table and a matching wooden bench. The table was bare apart from a water jug, platters, a pair of hand- hewn beakers and a couple of crudely fashioned wooden spoons.

'Wait here, Konnee,' the witch instructed, taking platters from the table to return outside.

Alone and unrestrained, Connie saw an opportunity to look about. She had already decided to escape given reasonable opportunity, but a glance confirmed the doorway to be the only exit and as Fular was outside tending the cooking, escape was out of the question for the time being. A short while later, the witch returned bearing platters of delectable-smelling stew. She placed one on the table for herself the other in front of Connie and motioned her to eat.

'Pray join with Fular and partake, Konnee,' she said, 'is exceedingly good.' Without further ado the witch bent her head and started to eat… Fair enough, Connie thought. Hesitant at first, she took a tentative taste, and then another. The stew was delicious; the tastiest she'd ever experienced. Thoughts of escape temporarily forgotten Connie proceeded to put it away as fast as possible. There was a goodly amount and it took time, but Connie did the meal full justice to be sure. By the time she finished scraping the platter and licking the spoon clean she finally felt replete.

Sighing with satisfaction, her thoughts returned to escape. Glancing through the door, she was trying to estimate the whereabouts of the main entrance and the possibility of finding the doors still open, when the level of light in the dim interior darkened further and a terrifyingly grotesque creature materialised at the entrance. The witch seemed unconcerned, whereas Connie averted her eyes and tried her best not to scream. It was a *Manikin*, with huge, staring red eyes which seemed to glow menacingly in the gloom. The creature possessed an incredibly large, hairless, misshapen green head – curiously reminiscent of a squashed cabbage – with projecting lumps of tissue positioned to approximate eyebrows, a nose shaped like a melon, trombone-shaped orange ears and a ponderous, corpulent body clad in a brown loose-fitting top and matching pantaloons, beneath which protruded a pair of large, six-toed feet clad in rough sandals. As if this were not enough, the being possessed a cavernous, toothless mouth surrounded by thick, jet-black lips: a nightmare apparition that had Connie cringing in shock, horror and disbelief – and little wonder. When the entity advanced into the room and began shuffling towards her she screamed, stuffed her fist in her mouth, jumped to her feet and backed away until brought up short by the wall. Disturbed by the kerfuffle, Fular looked up, angrily:

'Sit thee down, silly wench. Hush, for 'tis but Gimnal, mine Grobbelin and faithful Familiar.' The newcomer came to an abrupt halt, turned towards the witch back again to Connie, 'eyebrow' raised in a strange parody of quizzicality – and, horror of horrors, it actually spoke:

'Greetings, Konnee. Konnee give Gimnal Choklit?' it wheedled, adenoidal and child-like.

Connie grabbed the wall for support. 'Oo-er, it can t-talk,' she gasped, practically speechless herself. 'And it knows my n-name as well,' she stuttered. 'Cor, crikey, I must be going barmy.'

'Choklit, Choklit,' the grobbelin begged, with outstretched hand. Connie steeled herself.

'I'm s-sorry, Gimnal, I don't have any ch–chocolate,' she managed but with an effort.

The interchange further irritated Fular; she gestured towards the table and snapped:

'Again doth instructs thee sit; assuredly wilt punish should'st further disregard.'

Connie's unease had scarcely lessened because of the Grobbelin's vocal ability but, just as he, she also nurtured an instinctive fear of Fular. Obediently, she sat, suppressing a desire to glare defiance, determined not to be intimidated. But she was curious:

'Er, excuse me, Fular,' she began, hesitantly, 'but how does Gimnal know about chocolate?'

The witch looked up, treated the Manikin to a withering look (he cringed) and acidly replied.

'Did'st pilfer, vile thief, from provender brought hence,' she declared. 'T'was many moons ago, addict since, art Gimnal. Give none his better good, forsooth, else brains doth surely addle.' Having delivered this rather garbled explanation, the witch dismissively turned away, signalled a command to the grobbelin – one he clearly understood.

Connie watched curiously as he lifted one foot and spun through 45 degrees to face the wall – yet, strangely, his body appeared not to move. His obedience – whilst odd, had little effect on his longing for chocolate, it seemed.

'Allbut give Gimnal Choklit, Dzorj give Gimnal Choklit,' he scrounged, from the corner of his enormous cakehole. 'Why not Konnee give Gimnal Choklit?' To say Connie was astonished was putting mildly. She was stunned; but the grobbelin hadn't finished. 'Konnee not give Gimnal Choklit, Konnee not friend.'

Never mind the chocolate, Connie thought, excitedly, what exactly *had* the horrid creature said? She longed to question him, but refrained for fear of upsetting Fular. *Was it possible? Yes, it was.* Unlikely as it seemed there seemed little doubt. The manikin had named Albert and her darling Bessimer. *Were they coming to her rescue?* Her heart did a back-flip. *What did the grobbelin know? How did he know? This place gets crazier by the minute.*

The witch, however, took not the slightest jot of notice. She pointed, snapped her fingers, and barked:

'Wilt now Weem for Fular? Tis time, forsooth.' She closed her eyes, raised both hands and chanted: 'Cringle crangle, burlap blue. Weem yon wall and show me through.' She repeated the rhyme over and over and abruptly stopped.

Connie's hand flew to her mouth – oh, oh! *The wall – it was changing. Oh gosh.* It was difficult not to cry out but somehow she managed. She sat, transfixed, as the wall transformed through just about every colour of the rainbow: First to beige then orange then pink and then red. White and then blue, indigo too, cerise and purple and finally blue. *It was like a nursery rhyme in colour.*

Connie suppressed a giggle. After all, this was serious business. Spellbound, she watched the blue wane and fade, the wall briefly shimmer and dissolve into total transparency. What began as solid wall had evolved into something resembling a patio-sized window, but without a view and bereft of glass. *Crumbs! It's like giant television,* Connie murmured, fascinated. Her perception did her credit. No sooner had the thought entered her mind than Fular again signalled the grobbelin.

Gimnal lifted one foot, began pivoting on the other. Slowly he increased speed, gyrating like an oversized top, faster and faster, his body a blur; Fular chanted a succession of words, strange words, harsh guttural words – almost Germanic. What they meant, Connie hadn't a clue, but one phrase was repeated, over and over. *A'och Veem,*

A'och Veem, A'och Veem. Connie supposed – correctly, in point of fact – that Fular was speaking Gimnal's native tongue. Did 'Veem' mean 'Weem'? It didn't matter. Whatever 'Weem' meant was a mystery, anyway.

Abruptly, Gimnal vanished. Micro-seconds later the 'screen' illuminated showing a bleak featureless hilltop with a scattering of bushes but precious little else, silhouetted in relief against the purple sky. Connie couldn't help herself. She gasped with astonishment. How on earth? Was it – magic? The answer was blindingly apparent: *Yes* and *yes* again. Fular was *definitely* a witch – and little doubt about Gimnal, either. Here stood a magical companion, a real live *Familiar.*

Connie's explosive gasp served little purpose other than to distract the witch. Her black, piercing eyes flashed. She was angry again. 'Do not *dare* interrupt Weem,' she snarled. 'Did'st not hears Fular bid thee hush, stupid wench? Come; return thy room this instant or wilt's lock you in the dungeon.' With that, she grabbed Connie by the wrist and rushed her from the room. Given no opportunity to protest, Connie was manhandled to her cell and bundled inside. It was something of a shock, poor Connie. A loud bang as the door slammed, a rattle of bolts, receding footsteps and silence, she was alone once more.

But she collected her thoughts, dusted herself down – and actually *smiled.* The reason, simple: *Fular's Familiar.* Good old Gimnal had let the cat out of the bag. *Bessimer and Albert were back!* She sighed, rapturously happy. It was true – really, really true. Connie could feel it in her bones.

Elsewhere, Fular was glaring angrily at those who dared oppose, portrayed faithfully via the eyes, ears and mind of Gimnal, her Familiar. As she watched, the striplings were climbing to their feet, having been transported to the hill with the aid of Wegglar (through magical means, she was perfectly aware). She cursed – a *witch's* curse:

'Assuredly art weazel, vile meddler,' she hissed, 'a plague on thy magic, forsooth.' Her wrath was justified. The long, difficult and dangerous journey would have taken days for her youthful enemies to accomplish on foot, ample time in which to prepare her defences.

She gesticulated angrily and clapped her hands: *'Fiddle de faddle, loud buzzing on wing. Chase mine foes, with noises and sting,'* she intoned, uttering a long, guttural incantation ending with strangely persuasive chuckling sounds – almost as though calling to pets. Seconds later the boys on the viewing wall were rolling over and over down the hill, trying to dodge dozens of vicious-looking 'insects' clearly in hot pursuit. Fular cackled with glee.

'Zimble, my beauties,' she crowed. 'Zimble they right back to Wegglar.'

Meanwhile Connie languished. But, unlike her first sojourn in Fular's 'nick', she wasn't in the least bit despondent. It was simply a matter of waiting, she thought. That she would be rescued she had little doubt. She would still do a bunk of course, given reasonable opportunity but found it difficult to imagine how. She filled in time by reprising the astonishing succession of events since leaving school hand in hand with Bessimer, telling herself that few of the events could possibly have been accidental, and strove mightily to fathom a reason. The happenenings themselves provided very few clues – at least, so far as she was able to tell.

The review highlighted anomalies, however; such as Fular's assertion she was brought to this place – Skandos, she called it, as her companion. So it wasn't just by accident then? What had she meant by: 'nor shall depart ere Destiny grants Fular release – as signs hath long foretold – when cometh the advent of Bez Mer…' or words of similar ilk? Was it the intention to keep her here, year on year; a prisoner at the whim of a lonely old woman? If so was Connie expected to meekly acquiesce without even *trying* to escape? Should the answer to either be 'yes', she told herself, grimly, the old hag was certainly in for a surprise. She suppressed an irrational impulse to giggle when it occurred to her that 'Bez Mer,' when slurred and pronounced slowly, sounded remarkably similar to 'Bess-i- mer'. It was just too silly…

Connie pondered the significance of the 'caring' expression on Fular's face when she awoke to find the witch was watching. Or had it been, perhaps, merely a figment of her imagination? She questioned the witch's trustworthiness. Fular promised to explain things further but had so far told her nothing of significance. Why had she been so hastily bundled from that socking-great 'television' – just as it was starting to get interesting? *Hm*, she thought, *Fishy!*

Of course, paramount to the matter of escape was the whereabouts of Bessimer and Albert. The idea they might abandon her was inconceivable. Never mind that witch's poodle, Gimnal. He *had* dropped a broad hint, but so what? Had the boys *really* succeeded in returning? You bet, and were busy mounting a rescue this very minute. She took comfort from the thought. Her heart told her that help was at hand; she could almost *sense* Bessimer's close proximity.

What was the purpose behind that astonishing wall? How come Gimnal disappeared? Were both somehow inter-related; the mechanism whereby Fular conducted her spying? She had, after all, revealed it was through Gimnal she had discovered her name was 'Konnee'. Back to the reason she was bundled from the room. Was it to prevent her witnessing some other fascinating event for which total privacy was required? Or was there another, far more sinister explanation? She gave up. Time would doubtless provide an answer. What about time? She pulled out her watch, still stopping and starting. Three fifty-seven? 'Pah!' she snorted, and consigned it to her pocket. Who needs a watch, anyway? Clock watching? That's a workplace preoccupation whereby time is *guaranteed* to pass more slowly.

She commenced pacing, stopping occasionally to rest. Alternating between the two, sometimes alert, sometimes trying to sleep. But when darkness returned, preceded by that warning flicker of lightning and grumble of thunder, Connie fell asleep, curled among the furs in the foetal position.

CHAPTER 5

The Return

As they trudged the canal bank heading for home, Albert repeatedly consulted his watch. He huffed irritably, removed the offending timepiece from his wrist and shook it vigorously. Puzzled, he said, 'I reckon we went through the barrier around three forty-five and were blown back just after four or thereabouts. What's the time by yours? It must be well after tea time.'

'I suppose,' Bessimer replied, absently. Hastily, he corrected himself.

'Sorry, Alby. I was thinking about Connie. What did you say?'

'I asked you what the time was,' his friend replied, shortly.

Bessimer dutifully looked at his timepiece and then did a double-take.

'Blooming thing must have stopped,' he declared. 'It's still going but says three fifty-seven.'

'That's weird, practically the same as mine. That's more than coincidence if you ask me.'

'Maybe it was the barrier mechanism,' Bessimer suggested. 'Most watches are sensitive to magnetic fields as you probably know. Maybe we were gone longer than we thought, so what?'

'Nuts,' Albert muttered, lost for words. 'Something's not right,' he declared. 'Watches might stop but brains go on working – at least mine does.' He held his timepiece to his ear:

'Yours isn't the only one still ticking,' he announced. 'So is mine.'

'Fancy that,' replied Bessimer, sourly. 'Come on, stop gabbing willya. I want my flipping tea.'

It was well after six when they arrived home to encounter considerable parental flak. Worse still, Connie's mum was also hovering, flustered and ready to pounce. As neither could account satisfactorily for her daughter's absence, Mrs Cartwright straight away telephoned the police.

'Sorry, officer,' Bessimer said later, much distressed. 'I can't tell you anything I haven't already told Connie's Mum.' He took a deep breath nevertheless, and plunged. 'We were walking home – the long way round by the canal, and Connie needed to spend a penny – you know what girls are like. So while Albert and I waited she went behind some bushes. She called out something we couldn't quite catch; I shouted back, she didn't answer.' He looked up. The officer nodded.

'Well,' Bessimer resumed, tiredly, 'it was quiet; she wasn't making a sound so I called again...' His face crumpled – but he somehow recovered. 'We went to look, but s-she wasn't there,' he faltered. 'We searched for ages, up and down – got soaking wet, but couldn't find her. That's why we were so late getting home,' he manfully tried to explain, by now dangerously close to tears.

The policeman was demonstrably sympathetic and did his best to reassure Bessimer.

'All right, young fellow, that'll do for now,' he said, gently. 'Your friend Albert told us pretty much the same story. We needn't trouble you anymore tonight, but we might need you to come to the Station in the morning.' He turned to Connie's mother, now wringing her hands, anxiously.

'There's little more we can do tonight, Mrs Cartwright,' he said. 'No doubt there'll be a search mounted first thing in the morning and we'll keep you informed.' And to Bessimer:

'Get yourself off to bed, Master Bessimer. You look as if you could do with a good night's sleep.' Stooping, he patted the distressed boy on the shoulder. Bessimer smiled, wanly, his eyes reflecting nothing but sadness.

'Thanks, but I doubt if I'll sleep,' he said, nevertheless climbing to his feet and making for the door. 'I'm really worried about Connie – she's my girlfriend, you know,' he said, half over his shoulder. 'Wherever she is no matter what; no matter how long it may take, Albert and I are agreed, we'll go back there and we'll find her – and, with a bit of luck we'll find her tomorrow.' For all his fatigue, he sounded *very* determined.

'Don't get under our feet,' the policeman warned – alas, to thin air. Bessimer was already through the door and halfway up the stairs…

'Today's the day, no question,' Bessimer declared. Albert expressed similar sentiments. They were heading in the direction of school, having met as arranged at Bessimer's gate. Connie's absence was keenly felt and having a profound effect on the boys; converting the usual happy-go-lucky trek to school into a morose methodical plod, more in keeping with a funeral cortege.

'This won't do,' Bessimer suddenly declared, lengthening his stride. 'Shake it up, Alby,' he said, 'I'm not going home without Connie and that's that. We've a heck of a lot to achieve,' he added. 'Come on, let's sort out a plan and get cracking. Are you with me?'

Albert snorted. 'Soppy question,' he retorted, quick as a flash. 'Course I am, you daft wuzzock. Why the heck shouldn't I be?' He was more than a little indignant. 'And slow down, blow you,' he grunted, struggling to match Bessimer's pace. 'Let's get everything into perspective,' he puffed. '*First* we sort the plan, and *then* get your flipping move on. *That's* the way forward, surely?'

Bessimer stopped in his tracks, stunned, almost as if struck by lightning:

'Cor, Penny Plinkers,' he gasped. 'I've just figured it out. The other side of the wall… it's, it's a *different world!* That's why the sky's purple, the trees red. That weird bird-monster, and all that. And if there's a time difference, on top of everything else, it could explain why we went through at three forty-five and came back seconds later, yet were gone for at least twenty minutes; the reason our watches went up the creek. Mine's OK now, by the way, how's yours?' Albert's eyebrows shot skywards.

'Perfect,' he confirmed, and whistled. 'You could be spot on, George,' he ventured, 'in which case why are we standing here gossiping? Connie's stranded alone in that dreadful place with an awful monster on the loose. Our task is to get back there and start looking for her, don't you think?'

'That we should,' Bessimer agreed, 'but we might spend a fair bit of time achieving it. Come on, Alby, let's go shopping – pop, crisps and chocolate – lots of chocolate. Connie will be *starving.*'

'What about that plan?' Albert insisted. 'We can't go off half-cocked; we still have the police to consider. We're supposed to keep out of their way, aren't we? That copper last night seemed OK but his mates might be nowhere near as friendly. We could end up in the nick if we're not careful.'

'Not a snowflake's chance in the Sahara,' Bessimer laughed. 'They have to catch us first.' He tapped his nose: '*We* know the woods, the canal – the whole area, backwards.' He smiled. 'Don't worry; it'll be fun dodging them. In any case, they won't be looking for us; they'll be looking for Connie. Some coppers are pretty smart, but most are not. I reckon they haven't a hope of finding her. But *we* will, never fear. Come on Alby,' he urged, 'let's be getting to those shops.'

Half an hour later, with bulging satchels and well-stuffed pockets – sans two weeks' pocket money – tiptoeing, ducking and weaving, Bessimer and Albert made steady progress. They crossed fields, traversed a stream, sidled through thickets, sneaked along hedgerows, scampered and froze and then froze again. They heard voices a time or two – a glimpse of blue uniforms now and then, but never were they challenged, not once were they seen, not ever, all the way to the canal.

But where was the wall? There lay the canal, the towpath, a barge and bargee – but no barrier. They conferred: 'We're either missing something or doing something wrong,' Albert declared and Bessimer entirely agreed.

'Yes, and I think I know what. *Procedure*, that's what. Stick to what we did yesterday. Which means we approach the canal via the woods, the clearing, and the bush that grabbed me and Connie – except poor old Connie isn't with us today,' he couldn't help but sadly add.

'I know just how you feel,' Albert said. 'I miss her too, you know.' It was a sobering thought.

'If you're right,' he went on, 'and you usually are,' he added, 'what if nothing happens without Connie present?'

If Bessimer was shocked by the hypothetical question he didn't show it, merely replying, 'Then we keep on trying until something *does* happen. Don't be such a defeatist, Alby, it doesn't suit you.'

'Sorry,' Albert apologised. 'You probably think me a geek. Only I just wondered…?'

'Think nothing of it,' Bessimer returned. 'Come on, mate, we're wasting valuable time. Let's get cracking, find Connie and get her out of that crazy place. She'll be going potty.' By tacit agreement they took time out to consider. But in a moment, Bessimer's eyes widened and he stopped, brow furrowed in concentration. There he remained, deep in thought for a full two minutes, when his face cleared and he actually smiled:

'It – it's a *sequential trigger*,' he blurted. 'We have to do *everything* exactly the same as yesterday, not just messing about with the bush, but by synchronising the time factor as well.' Desperate for something – anything by way of a further clue, he challenged his memory:

'*Ye gateways fain parallel. Tis the Advent of Bez Mer*,' he murmured, from a seed buried somewhere deep within his subconscious. He shook his head to collate his thoughts and smiled.

'There you are, sorted,' he grinned. 'Starting at three forty-five, we do exactly as we did yesterday, *including* shaking hands with that bush.' When Albert gaped, dumbfounded, Bessimer obligingly added: '*And when portal art lit, fain thy signal*,' he intoned. '*Calleth thou twice upon Bez Mer…*'

Albert battled his way from mental fog, dismissed astonishment and snapped out of daze.

'What one earth *are* you rabbiting about?' he gasped. 'Where the dickens did *that* come from?'

'Don't look so surprised,' Bessimer chuckled, 'it was a piece of cake, really. I started to wonder for a bit and the answers just came. It's as if I've known all along. And I'll tell you something else,' he averred, confidently, 'if you haven't cottoned on. I trace round a block after the green light appears, then to open the portal my name is pronounced twice. Albert gaped, clearly flummoxed.

'How in blazes did you work that out?'

'Wasn't that difficult,' Bessimer admitted, truthfully. 'Cast your mind to when we were at the wall. Just before we went through – and again when we came back, Connie called my name twice. Tell you what,' he mused, 'there's something else; makes sense now I come to think of it. Remember looking in *Maria's* window when we were younger? When that tray full of pies vanished while we were still weighing up the goodies?' Although Albert nodded, he still seemed puzzled. 'Yes, I remember,' he said, 'but I don't see the connection.'

'Simple,' Bessimer told him. 'That twit on the bike, John Lewis. He shouted my name – twice. *Now* do you remember?' Albert regarded him in astonishment, as if seeing him in a different light.

'Fancy sussing that,' he said, 'I've often wondered. Good thinking? Inspirational, more like.'

'Know what "inspirational" means?' Bessimer drawled, amused. Albert laughed, delightedly. 'Not really,' he hooted, 'but it sure sounded good.' Bessimer cuffed his ear, well naturedly.

The return to the woods and making it to the clearing proved trouble-free. No police were in evidence, no sign of searchers; morning activities had either been suspended or discontinued. In point of fact the police had been inundated with reports, alleged sightings and other so-called 'information', and most policemen searching for Connie had already diverted to a different area.

'Come on you old fraud, we've time to kill. Let's do something about coffee.'

'Couldn't we just hole up amongst the trees? We'd be in position, ready to go.'

'Better not,' Bessimer decided, 'we've shopping to do – or have you forgotten?'

'Oh,' said Albert, chastened. But, not to be outdone, he piped up again.

'Yes, we need chocolate, crisps and plenty of pop, but we haven't any money, then there's our lunch to be paid for. Can't shop *or* buy lunch without money,' he griped – and added, sotto voce, 'not even *you*, clever clogs.' Bessimer sighed: Albert could sometimes be *very* tiresome, but he *was* a staunch and loyal friend.

'What I have in mind is really quite simple' he said. 'We pop to the Post Office and draw some of my savings, mosey to school and nip in through the back. Spend some time in the library then mingle with the crowd when it's time for nosh. You know, make as if we've been there all along. Lurk behind the bogs until the end of lessons and stroll out through the gates as usual.' Pique forgotten, Albert's face cracked into a delighted grin: 'Should have guessed, I suppose,' he chortled. 'You've thought of just about everything. Doubtful anyone's likely to think twice…?'

'We're doing something wrong,' Bessimer worried, 'we must be. That's four times into the clearing and no sign of the rotten bush.' He glanced at his watch: 'I make it three thirty.'

'Don't panic,' Albert advised, 'there's bound to be a reason. Let's think it through, sensibly and logically.' He too checked his watch: 'Timing's OK,' he confirmed, 'mine's the same.'

'I know what *is* different,' Bessimer grumped, sadly, 'we haven't got Connie with us.'

'Shouldn't make two pence worth of difference,' Albert remarked. 'But *you're* the expert, George, it's *your* show so it's down to you, I guess.' Bessimer sniffed, rather pointedly:

'*Tell* me about it,' he snorted. 'Some pal you are. What happened to good old teamwork?'

'That's enough of that,' Albert rejoined. 'Don't be so touchy, I was only making a point. I'm in just as deep as you and I'll help in any way I can — as you very well know. I got the distinct impression this morning you knew *exactly* what to do. That's what you implied, anyway.'

Bessimer managed a wan smile: 'Touché, Alby. I suppose I deserved that,' he said, ruefully. 'Sorry,' he went on, apologetically,

'I really am. I dare say you thought I was being cocky – and before you say a word,' he added, 'I can assure you I wasn't. Fact is, Alby, the knowledge – the key to the portal, call it what you will – sort of came to me, just as I said it did.'

There was no doubting his earnestness or his sincerity. 'I don't know how, I don't know why,' he declared. 'The only thing I do know is that I want desperately to rescue Connie, and for that I need help – yours of course, Alby, my very best friend.' He held out his hand:

'*Will* you help, Albert, please?' Ignoring the outstretched hand, Albert grabbed his friend into a bear hug: 'Course I will,' he choked, almost overcome, 'and don't you ever doubt me either.'

Bessimer was equally affected; eyes glistening, stricken silent by the lump in his throat. It was a poignant, moving moment; strengthening the bond between the two even further.

Whether by accident, chance, destiny or divine intervention, their second attempt was timed to perfection: The start of an adventure with obvious potential for danger, in an incredible, alien place where survival of the one might depend on the fortitude, grit and determination of the other...

'Hang on, the trick is to replicate yesterday *exactly* – excepting for Connie, that is,' he couldn't help but add. 'We go into the trees, you wait out of sight and I go into the clearing alone. As soon as the bush grabs me, I'll shout and you rush to the rescue, just as you did yesterday. OK?'

'Sure,' said Albert, 'sounds reasonable, but we'd better be quick; might be running out of time.' Bessimer checked: three forty-three. Instinctively he *knew* they would succeed. *Nothing* could alter that, it was written: 'Don't worry, it's OK,' he said, calm and unfazed. 'Come on, let's get to it.' Albert hesitated, seemed suddenly doubtful but obediently followed Bessimer into the trees.

'Help, help,' Bessimer bellowed, a minute or so later. 'Albert – the bush – help, it's got me!'

'Hold on, George. Be right there,' Albert roared back; he burst into the clearing at a gallop. Tentacle-like appendages clutched Bessimer, one across the throat. He was red-faced; struggling.

'Get me l-loose,' he gurgled, espying Albert and evidently distressed. 'It-it's *hurting* me.'

Unhesitatingly, Albert rushed to Bessimer's aid. He made a grab for the branch – which true to form duly retracted, leaving Bessimer free but on this occasion ruefully rubbing a sore neck.

'Thanks Alby,' he said, gratefully. Eying the motivational shrub with distaste, he edged away.

'There wasn't even a *sign* of it,' he complained, gesturing towards the bush. 'I was looking around and it just grabbed me from behind.' He shivered: 'good job you were handy.'

'No worries,' Albert chirruped. 'We're in business, George. Come on, let's find that barrier.'

'Suits me,' Bessimer said, warily skirting the bush. The pair went out of the trees at a run.

Lo and behold, the barrier! There it was just as before. Tall, wide, looming – inviting almost. Bessimer wasted no time. With Albert in tow he literally galloped to within reach of the wall. The pale green light appeared: 'So far so good,' he muttered. He knew the procedure: select the nearest block, reach out to touch it, trace its outline – *clockwise*, mind, and *Bingo* – or so he hoped.

'Here goes. Nothing venture – or so they say,' he breathed. He placed his forefinger in position and traced round the block, self-consciously proclaiming, 'Bessimer, Bessimer,' but without result. He tried again, this time louder: *'Bessimer, Bessimer'* and, louder still: ***'Bessimer, Bessimer'*** – but alas, still no portal. Dismayed, frustrated, increasingly anxious and with Connie's rescue at stake, he turned and appealed to Albert.

'It isn't flipping working, Alby, What am I doing wrong? What shall I do? Oh, corks. What about Connie?' The pale green light still glowed; everything in place yet something was missing – but what? Albert scratched his head, equally puzzled. But in a second or two his face cleared as he realised the answer and blurted:

'I've got it, quick, circle the block again.' Catching on, Bessimer obliged. The instant his finger completed a full three hundred and sixty degrees, Albert bellowed: *'**Bessimer! Bessimer!**'*

Instantly the wall changed colour, the nimbus surrounding Bessimer expanded to envelope them, dazzlingly brilliant. There was a thunderous 'Crash!' The wall shimmered; a hole appeared – the embryonic portal at last. With no time to prepare, breathtakingly violent, the by-now familiar, whine and tooth-scraping crescendo and the orifice exploded to full size – and boom, they were through, spread-eagled on dusty ground, ears ringing, decidedly battered – but not blue.

'Whew, nearly as much fun as a smack with a wet haddock,' Bessimer complained, but with a delighted grin. He picked himself up and stooped to assist Albert. 'That was pretty smart. How did you guess what to do?' Albert grunted. 'Got lucky, I suppose,' he modestly declared. Bessimer thought otherwise: 'Pull the other one,' he retorted, 'I reckon you sussed it; somebody other than me has call my name out, so why not admit it?' Albert looked sheepish:

'We-ll, yes,' he confessed, 'that's right. But I didn't want to crow,' he explained. 'It was your gun, you found it loaded and cocked it – but *you* can't pull the trigger. Which means,' he hesitated then plunged: 'you can't get back by yourself. If we don't find Connie – or something nasty happens to me – you'll be stuck in this forsaken place forever.'

'But we *will* find Connie, never fear – and nothing's likely to happen to you,' Bessimer confidently declared, careful to add, 'not while I'm around, anyway. We act as a team, remember.'

Albert seemed relieved. 'Yes, and just as well. Cos without you I can't get back either.' He grinned. 'I watch your back; you watch mine – is that it? Makes us quits, in a manner of speaking.' Such blatant plagiarism earned him a rather quizzical look, and then:

'Yup,' said Bessimer solemnly, 'it sure does.' The adventurers regarded one another steadily; wordlessly, *los amigos* briefly clasped hands. While they were talking the portal diminished and silently closed. The boys scarcely noticed.

Whoo- ah- oo– oo, it came, a long, keening, haunting cry. They both stiffened.

H-wee- oo– ar- oo, the wail again, but this time softer, less distinct and fading rapidly.

They stared across scarlet-topped forest towards the hills beyond, but saw nothing.

'It *sounded* like that big dragon thing,' Bessimer ventured.

Albert nervously brushed orange dust from his clothes. 'Sure did,' he agreed, 'I'd forgotten about it to be perfectly honest. I wonder if it really *was* a dragon. Mightn't it have been a pterodactyl or something similar?'

Bessimer sniffed: 'Jurassic, *boracic*, whatever. Whatever this place is it isn't prehistoric. I prefer dragons thank you very much. Dragons don't go *whoo whoo* and only exist in mythology.'

'Yeah, right,' growled Albert, 'but that was no myth, it was a monster no matter *what* you call it.' He mustered a grin. 'Let's agree to disagree. I vote we stay as far away from it as possible.'

'I certainly won't argue with that,' Bessimer concurred. 'Come on, let's get looking for Connie.'

'Whoa, hang on a minute, before galloping off half-cocked don't we need a fresh plan of action?'

It was Bessimer's turn to look embarrassed. 'Oops, I wasn't thinking straight. Finding Connie is one thing, finding the way back quite another.' He scratched his chin:

'Ah, I know, we need a landmark. How about the wall?'

'Could be,' Albert replied. 'Better check it out from a distance – but carefully mind; stick together and avoid unnecessary risks,' wisely advocating caution.

Facing the wall, the chums linked arms and commenced pacing backwards: *One, two and three…* At a count of twenty – roughly eight metres, they reckoned – the wall disappeared to be replaced by the canal and the woods beyond. Two steps forward and there it was again. Bessimer's face fell. *Some landmark*, he thought. He raised a questioning eyebrow; it was Albert's call, after all.

'Yes, we really do need a landmark,' his pal concurred, 'and it's obviously not the wall. But before we do anything or go anywhere, I suggest we learn something about the place. I vote we stay put and have a jolly good look round. The wall is handy; we know the formula and,' he muttered, sagely, 'if the going gets rough, we could easily up and scarper.' The implication was obvious; a sobering, solemn reminder of the overriding possibility of danger.

'Connie!' Bessimer exclaimed, connecting the issues. 'She could be in danger. If only we knew.' The reality was all too apparent. Albert was right. There was much to learn and untold dangers yet be encountered, in this strange, alien and unfamiliar world… but was it so unfamiliar? He sighed, took another long, hard and penetrating look around – and wondered!

CHAPTER 6

Grobbelin

The landscape remained every bit as unprepossessing as they remembered; red-topped outlandishly purple sky, curiously-textured orange-coloured ground, nightmarish shrubs and patchy, grass-like verdure – dingy and brown, with crimson-coloured trees just about everywhere. This presumably indigenous flora was surreal, garish and unearthly; grew singly, in pairs and in groups of up to a dozen or so, the largest concentration on rising ground some two or three hundred kilometres from where they stood.

The chums were reminded of the strange flying animal. Neither spoke – they didn't need to. With the barrier at their backs they felt reasonably safe, secure in the knowledge that escape, if need be, was comfortably within reach; a false premise, as events were later to show.

But wait! Some two or three hundred metres away, across bleak, uninspiring terrain something stirred. Dun-coloured, creeping stealthily from behind a thicket, it was obviously an animal of some kind, but what? Bessimer nudged Albert: 'What do you reckon, Alby? – oh, look, there's another.' They watched, fascinated, as more and more kept appearing.

'Ten, I make it,' Albert said, after a while. Squinting, he corrected himself. 'Well, no, eleven,' he declared, this time with finality.

'Looks like they're feeding,' Bessimer observed. 'They're chomping on that brown-coloured grass-like stuff anyway. Seems there's nothing to worry about; just harmless herbivores."

Supposing these were rabbits in a Cheshire field? At a cursory glance they might be. But bunnies have long pointy ears and little white scuts, not green, swivelling antennae and brushes like a fox, four legs – not six; hop, skip and scamper but not creep. Heaven forbid a rabbit should act or look anything like one of these...

The relationship between the two was long established. Albert invariably deferred to Bessimer; born leader but never overbearing. The role came naturally and he was always at pains to consider Albert's feelings, often at his own expense. Theirs was a remarkable friendship, tailor-made for just such an adventure. In Albert's eyes just about everything seemed dangerous and unreal, whereas Bessimer – often startled but rarely alarmed, viewed each and every revelation with equanimity; relying on inner conviction and a curious sense of destiny. It was almost as if he'd been here before. He hadn't, of course, yet that strange feeling of familiarity persisted. Maybe he had dreamt about it? He had no idea.

Albert yawned, stretched and sat down. Bessimer followed suit and after a while, reached in his pack for a chocolate bar. He sniffed it, twiddled it, thought better of it and returned it whence it came. 'I think I'll save it,' he decided, sadly, 'especially for Connie.'

Albert forbore to comment, instead asked: 'How about a drop of pop?' He unzipped his haversack and withdrew a bottle – *Lemonade*, the label said. Viewed in yucky, plum-coloured daylight it was more in keeping with blackcurrant juice – but it tasted OK. He proffered the bottle:

'Fancy a swig, George?' Absently, Bessimer accepted and took a couple of swallows. The friends continued scanning terrain, tacitly vigilant, even when seated. Before long, Bessimer's eye was drawn to the colourful bushes from behind which Connie had disappeared.

'Those shrubs over there, Alby.' He pointed. 'They look like Connie's bushes.'

Albert agreed. 'Yes,' he said, 'the ones with spiny blue flowers and ghastly yellow leaves. What of it?'

'Stay here a minute,' Bessimer said, 'and keep a sharp look out. I'm going over for a look.'

'What on earth for?' Albert questioned, to which Bessimer replied: 'I'm fed up with just sitting. We've nattered, had a breather but decided nothing. Neither of us has the remotest idea what we should do or where we should go. Any clue might be helpful. Maybe I'll find one where Connie disappeared, seconds before we were whizzed back through the portal.'

Albert seemed likely to demur but logic demanded he should agree – but advocated caution:

'If you intend going by yourself I'm not at all keen. We agreed to stick together, don't forget.'

Bessimer shrugged: 'It's only a few metres away and we can easily maintain voice contact.'

'Well, OK then – but don't be too long.'

'Back in a flash,' Bessimer chirruped. He jumped to his feet, crossed the intervening space at a run across and disappeared. 'Can you hear me?' he shouted.

'No problem,' Albert yelled in return.

'See anything? What are you doing? Hurry up; I'm getting nervous now you're out of sight.' Bessimer promptly reappeared. Albert heaved a sigh of relief. 'Find anything?' he called.

'Scuff marks here and there,' Bessimer replied, 'nothing of any consequence.' Returning to the barrier he grumped, 'But we had to start somewhere and I simply *had* to take a look.'

'OK, but what next?' Albert returned, equally shortly. 'Where the heck do we go from here?'

'I haven't the foggiest,' Bessimer admitted, spreading his hands.

'There is *one* thing though,' Albert eventually ventured.

'Go on, I'm all ears,' Bessimer replied.

'So I see,' Albert retorted, an insult Bessimer chose to ignore. Unabashed, Albert continued by pointedly stating the obvious: 'We need a landmark – agreed?'

'Of course,' said Bessimer, puzzled. 'There'll be no exploring until one is established. Why, do you have one in mind?'

'Well, I *have* been looking,' Albert told him, sarcastically, 'and the obvious choice is that clump of yellow and blue spiky bushes – Connie's. There are odd ones and bunches of twos and threes all over the place, but her clump is far and away the biggest. Look around, see for yourself.' Without answering, Bessimer straightway resumed his own survey, scanning back and forth, up down and across until he was satisfied there were indeed very few alternatives.

'I guess you're right,' he eventually conceded, 'but whether we'll be able to pick it out at a distance-?' He shrugged. 'I'm not at all sure.' Albert forbore answering and changed the subject:

'You know, there's something else that's bothering me. I could have sworn I heard voices just before Connie disappeared. Events moved so quickly I'll admit to being confused. *Was* she talking to somebody, George, or did I imagine it? Were those voices for real, I'd like to know?'

'Well, I heard them too,' Bessimer confirmed, 'so I guess they must have been real. But don't ask me to explain the how, why's or wherefore's,' he shrugged, 'because I really haven't the foggiest… but whoever Connie was talking to had an unusually deep voice,' he recalled, a moment or so later.

Albert latched on, eagerly: 'Yes, that's right; they jolly-well well did.'

'In which case, take it as read,' Bessimer concluded for him. '*Somebody* was talking to Connie and take that as definite. We've no idea who but I'm sure we'll find out – pretty soon, hopefully.'

'I certainly hope so,' Albert grunted, 'because whoever it was knows more about Connie's whereabouts than we do… and it wasn't some flaming bloke either, because Connie distinctly shouted – and I quote: "she's got me", unquote.'

'Yes, and that means there's somebody else beside you, me and Connie in this awful place.' The implication was far-reaching. Again the friends fell silent, subdued and contemplative.

Without warning, a flash of lightning flickered across the sky; an ear- shattering crash of thunder followed and a consequential long, continuous rumble reverberated and echoed from distant hills. Simultaneously, the pale gentian daylight flickered briefly and winked from existence.

Two gob-smacked friends found themselves in almost total darkness, wondering what on earth was happening and how best it should be dealt with. Nonplussed, they stood in stunned silence until the penny suddenly dropped – at least for Albert it did, for he was first to comment:

'Corks, that's flipping torn it,' he grumbled. 'Rotten night-time already.'

Smiling ruefully into the blackness, Bessimer put it rather better:

'It was sudden admittedly, but what else do you expect when the sun goes bye byes? Complaining won't help, that's for sure.' He added, 'That we won't be exploring today is equally true. We've no option but to stick it out and just make the best of it.' Albert wasn't in the least impressed and proceeded to say so.

'Lousy rotten dump,' he whinged. 'Night without warning; no twilight; no sunset either for that matter – assuming there *is* a sun, that is, and as for daylight, you can hardly call it daylight,' he jeered. 'Weird, purple gloom more like. Whoever heard of daylight switching itself off anyway? Surely that can't be normal?' Having sounded off, he subsided, still muttering to himself.

'Tell me about it,' Bessimer chuckled. It was an apt, neat expression that said it all.

'Come on, park your tail,' he commanded, flopping down. 'The ground's hard and dusty but better than nothing. You never know we might even manage a spot of kip.'

'Some hope of *that*,' Albert sniffed. 'How long since *you* last slept on the ground?' He lowered himself down, at pains to avoid Bessimer who, wisely, forbore to respond.

Out of the darkness a loud, keening wail disturbed the silence: *whoo- ee- oo—oo, whoo- oo- ee*. The sound was unmistakable, enough to make the blood run cold. It was the monstrous aerial dragon-creature, it had to be.

Two pairs of eyes cast skywards, seeking desperately to pinpoint the location. Suddenly – dazzling brilliance! Twin beams scythed the sky a short distance ahead, seeking, probing, scanning and then – horror of horrors, swivelled to bathe the friends in light almost the equal of daylight. Mesmerised, like rabbits in the headlights of a truck, the boys seemed rooted to the spot. The wail increased to a shriek; a dark shape loomed – ***Danger!***

'***George, look out!***' Albert bellowed. As if galvanised by his voice, the creature swooped. Albert shouted again, '***George, the barrier. Jump for it, George.*** **Don't argue, just jump!**'

Youthful, lightning-fast reflexes had the friends rolling into the lee of the barrier which, happily, reactivated, bathing the boys in that all-too- familiar glow when, with a Banshee wail remarkably like a cry of frustration, the aerial predator banked sharply and climbed away, soared onward for a couple of hundred metres where it extinguished those extraordinary hunting orbs, leaving two intended victims safe in the lee of the barrier, where they crouched, shaken but otherwise unharmed. The thrusting *hiss, whoosh, hiss* of powerful wing beats diminished into the distance.

'Do you know, George,' Albert coolly remarked, 'we came close to becoming that nasty wee beastie's supper.' His carefully modulated tone belied his bravado; Bessimer wasn't fooled.

'Whew, yes and but for your quick-thinking, we might well have been. I was absolutely petrified to be honest, scared half out of my wits. Good job one of us was in decent working order.'

Albert giggled. 'Oo, you do say the nicest things,' and he cackled until he almost wet his pants.

Bessimer hesitated. Was it perhaps emotional release or was Albert simply nipping hysteria in the bud? He didn't know; it would be churlish to ask. Albert most probably had saved *both* their lives. He reached for and patted an unresisting shoulder. 'Feel better?' he asked, gently.

Albert responded, laconically: 'Yes, mate – and thanks,' loosing off a final, convulsive hiccup.

Bessimer unbuckled his rucksack and shrugged free. Not without difficulty he manipulated the stiff, unyielding canvas to roughly the shape of a pillow, lay down and tried it for comfort.

'Wotcha doing?' Albert inquired.

'Rucksack, pillow, spot of kip,' he was advised. 'Join me?'

'Good idea,' Albert said, 'but I fancy supper first. Couple of choccy bars, crisps, swig of pop?'

'Choccy *bar*,' he was told firmly, 'you horrid little greedy-guts. We've limited supplies with no idea how long they must last. Half a bar; split a bag of crisps – that'll keep us going, surely.'

'I suppose,' Albert conceded, and again changed the subject. 'This is a nightmare place and no mistake. I reckon finding Connie will prove a darn sight more difficult than we imagined. Let's face it, getting just this far has taken us long enough.'

'Pre-zactly,' Bessimer assured him, succinctly.

'Surprisingly,' Albert mused, changing the subject yet again, 'I can just about make out the barrier thicket.' Shading his eyes, he squinted, attempting to estimate and triangulate distances.

'We need to return here should we run into trouble, but just how critical this spot is in relation to the barrier is hard to say.' Seeking answers, he went on to speculate: 'Without a datum point it's impossible to say but we certainly won't be going home if we can't find it – and, moreover, it could come in jolly handy should we be attacked by that monster again.'

'I agree. Tell you what. How about an experiment? I need a leak, anyway.'

'Go on,' Albert replied, patently curious, 'I'm listening.'

'OK,' said Bessimer, 'I'll pace the wall, counting aloud, and you shout "stop" the instant the green light goes out. That'll tell us all we need to know without the risk of losing touch.'

'Sure, why not?' Albert readily agreed. 'Get yourself going, already.'

Bessimer duly began pacing. On his sixth stride, *the glow winked out.*

'Won't be a minute,' he called; relieved himself and retraced his steps, repeating the manoeuvre in the opposite direction with exactly the same result.

As a further experiment, they changed places, but in Albert's case the light failed to extinguish. Finally, it was established. The controlling factor was Bessimer. Within closely defined limits, his presence and his alone served not only to reveal the barrier, but to prime, cock and activate the portal as well. The concept was astonishing; no less the magnitude of the task which lay ahead. Bessimer felt truly humbled.

'Blimey, Alby, who'd have thought?' he said, hushed with awe. 'But at least now we know although I must say it's still hard to believe. The light, the portal – everything; they only work for *me*, but to be perfectly honest,' he added, thoughtfully, 'I rather suspected that might be the case.'

'Well,' said Albert, 'now you jolly-well know for sure.' He peered into the gloom.

'Another thing's certain, come to think of it' he adduced, 'we're stuck here for the night.'

'Foregone conclusion, I guess,' replied Bessimer, 'but we're not doomed to spend it in total darkness.' Buoyed by optimism, he perked up. 'Not all bad, maybe a sign of better things to come. Be great to rescue Connie by lunchtime tomorrow and be home in time for tea, wouldn't it?'

'You wish,' Albert retorted, and grimaced into the gloom. He wasn't in the least bit optimistic. Emulating Bessimer's example, however, he shaped his rucksack into a make-shift pillow.

'I'm pretty well fagged-out,' he yawned, 'ready for forty winks; but that flying whatsit was *really* scary – supposing it tries again? We'd better keep an eye out. How about taking turns?' A wise precaution; memories of a rushing monster with outstretched talons remained all too fresh.

'Just what I was thinking,' Bessimer said. 'Rock-on, Tommy, go for it. I'll take first watch.' Sitting with his back to the barrier he peered into the gloom, grimly determined. Gratefully, Albert settled down and at long last and within minutes succumbed into fitful sleep.

But it *had* been a long, tiring day. There was nothing to be seen and Bessimer's straining eyes soon faltered and his eyelids drooped. He dozed, exhausted – for how long was anybody's guess.

A shape drifted closer. What was that, a noise from out of the darkness? With a guilty start, he snapped awake, groaned and rubbed his eyes in disbelief; did a double take and looked again.

'Cor, Penny Plinkers,' he gasped, 'I *must* be dreaming. It's a rotten nightmare.' He pinched himself to be sure and then nudged Albert urgently. 'Wake up, Alby, we've a visitor.'

'Wassermarra, wodda yer want?' Albert mumbled, still half asleep. 'Leave me be.'

'Wake *up*,' Bessimer insisted. 'It-it's **weird**. Hurry, we're being watched.' He grabbed Albert's shoulder and shook it. 'Come on, look lively. It's green with huge, staring red eyes.'

That did it. Albert sighed, opened his eyes and heaved himself into a sitting position.

'What the blazes are you on about?' he snarled. 'I was dreaming about a lovely big plateful of steak, egg and chips…' Then he too did a double take and clutched at Bessimer's sleeve.

'Crikey, what the spiff is **that**?' he gasped.

'Like I already said,' Bessimer said, sharply, 'we're not alone. *Now* will you believe me?'

The boys found themselves confronted by a large, caricature-like creature a couple of metres away. Pastel green, it glowed in the dark and appeared to float, almost as if unsupported. As an apparition it was certainly unusual although not, in the boys' eyes, particularly frightening. Besides luminescent red eyes, the being sported a cabbage-shaped head, orange, trombone-shaped ears, a large melon-shaped nose and a cavernous, black- lipped toothless mouth – and that was just for starters. The body, still somewhat indistinct, possessed a sort of in-built luminosity. To the boys' way of thinking this in itself was spooky enough. Fascinated, they watched as the being drifted closer, bringing fully into view a grotesquely corpulent torso. The newcomer edged even closer and – to their utter astonishment – it actually spoke:

'I bid greetings, earthlings. I Gimnal, Grobbelin of Skandos,' it began. 'By what names are ye?' High-pitched and nasal, its childish voice seemed somehow curiously appealing.

'This place is full of surprises,' Bessimer muttered in an aside, 'gets dafter by the minute.' Poking Albert ungraciously in the ribs, he asked, 'Will you answer or shall I do the honours?'

'Don't look at me,' Albert responded, hastily. '*You* saw it first, *you* do the talking.'

'Mr – er, Gimnal,' Bessimer began, 'I am George; my friend here is Albert. We came to rescue our friend, a girl called Connie. Have you seen her by any chance?'

'Dzorj, Allbut,' the creature mimicked, in fractured, accented, barely passable English. '*Dzorj* give Gimnal Choklit, *Allbut* give Gimnal Choklit?' it whined, singsong-fashion.

Pale streaks of light flashed the sky. Thunder rumbled; the purple overcast reappeared; not instantly, as from day to night, but strangely disorientating nonetheless.

Bessimer blinked owlishly, temporarily confused. He quickly recovered however and returned to the question of Gimnal and Connie's whereabouts but, to his dismay, the manikin had contrived to vanish. It didn't make sense. Not without reason and not for the first time, Bessimer rubbed his eyes, in danger of doubting his own senses. First it *was* and then it *wasn't*. Was it an apparition, visible only at night? But did apparitions talk? Maybe he *had* dreamt it? – Surely not. Irritably, he turned to Albert.

'That's queer,' he began, 'he vanish—' but was interrupted. 'Tee, hee, hee,' came an inane cackle from somewhere behind Connie's thicket. *What the heck…?*

'Here I be, Dzorj. Coo-ee. Dzorj give Gimnal Choklit?' the humanoid begged, directly in front.

'So *there* you are,' Bessimer exclaimed, in surprise. 'We thought you'd gone.'

The creature bobbed twice, raised one foot, pivoted through ninety degrees – and again vanished.

'Now *that's* what I *call* a party trick,' Albert chortled.

'Oh, my giddy aunt,' Bessimer blurted, scratching his head, 'how the heck does he do *that*?'

'Coo-ee. Here I be, Dzorj' – from ten metres to the right. 'Choklit?' the grobbelin whined.

This time Bessimer almost lost it. 'Stand still, blow you,' he said, crossly. 'I need to talk to you.' Albert stifled a giggle – just, and only with an effort. *Brilliant; hilarious, better than the pictures!* Two unblinking red orbs again confronted them: the manikin thrust out a hand, expectantly:

'*Now* maybe Dzorj give Gimnal Choklit?' he declared, triumphantly, 'Gimnal *like* Choklit.'

Bessimer sighed. 'You're not short on bottle, I'll give you that,' he sighed in abject surrender. He produced a bar of Dairy Milk and tentatively offered it.

In the blink of an eye, the hominoid snatched the delicacy and whizzed it into his cavernous cake bin, whole and complete with wrapper. A slurp; chomp, twist, a look of heavenly bliss – and zip! it was gone.

Having successfully exploited Bessimer's generosity, Gimnal switched his attention to Albert.

'Allbut give Gimnal Choklit?' it begged, shamelessly.

Quick-thinking Albert put his hand in his pocket – but artfully paused. 'Maybe, Gimnal,' he said, 'but first we need help and information.'

The grobbelin stared fixedly but didn't reply. There was a long silence. Two anxious boys – and a creature of indeterminate origin, ability and intention – regarded each another speculatively.

Seen in daylight the visitor was rather more substantial than his night- time image suggested. For one thing, that extraordinary head – still green, they observed – no longer glowed, totally disproving an initial impression of disembodiment. Indeed, it sat firmly on a rotund, singularly corpulent body – and, clad entirely in brown, would be practically invisible at night if unlit!

The hominoid was a little more than a metre in height, they guessed, measured from the soles of large, six-toed feet to the top of that enormous, cabbage-like, completely hairless head.

Unbidden, by means of a comical side-to-side rocking motion, it swayed closer. Its unworldly features – vaguely humanistic, they realised – included folds of skin above ruby-coloured eyes the size of saucers, shaped and positioned to approximate eyebrows. It possessed ears – of a sort; large, swivelling, trombone-shaped and bright orange. Not beautiful by any standards – except perhaps to another similarly equipped. Nor was it comical, quite the opposite in fact. It appeared to possess all that was needed to emulate human facial expressions – and Gimnal was quick to learn, as they were soon to discover. Expression does not merely complement, it can often replace the spoken word, as they were also later to discover. There followed a long silence.

At last Gimnal spoke. 'First give Gimnal Choklit?' he insisted, eying Albert, calculatingly.

Albert was shrewd. Maybe the creature was chocoholic — it seemed likely, in which case he had no intention of surrendering what might prove an advantage. Chocolate didn't grow on trees!

'Not flipping likely,' he retorted. 'Perchance art crafty gnome. Information first, if you please.'

The hominoid put on an incredible display of annoyance. He puffed his cheeks, blazed his orbs like incandescent fog-lights and jiggled from foot to foot, positively radiating indignation.

'*Gnome!*' he screeched. 'Callest *Gnome*, thou knavish poltroon? Thou dost try patience, forsooth. Foul creature from beneath I be not. As told afore I Gimnal, Grobbelin of Skandos. Gnomes speak untrue, dig tunnels; eat cooking rock,' he roared, 'not proper food like grobbelins.'

'Oops,' Bessimer intervened, 'he seems *ever* so annoyed. Quick, do something. Bung him a choccy-bar for heaven's sake before he ups and blows a gasket.'

Albert hesitated. 'Hang in there a minute, George; he's most probably bluffing.'

'He sure doesn't like gnomes,' Bessimer said in an aside. 'Maybe you'd better apologise.'

Albert nodded. 'Sorry, Gimnal, I meant no offence,' he said. 'I had no idea you didn't like gnomes but we really do need help. OK, I'll give you more chocolate — just *one* bar, mind, but tell us where Connie is and I'll give you two.'

Almost as quickly as they arose, Gimnal's hackles subsided. He hesitated, but challenged:

'Hokay? Dost hokay means Allbut wilt — or Allbut wilt not?' He swivelled his optics and rubbed his tummy. 'Konnee; Choklit?'

he wheedled. At further mention of Connie, Albert relented — albeit reluctantly. 'OK means wilt,' he conceded. Aiming for cooperation, he proffered a single bar of chocolate flake. Bessimer nodded his approval.

The greedy creature was nothing if not consistent. Unhesitatingly, he grabbed the confection and manoeuvred the corners of his mouth into the semblance of a grin — or so it seemed. In any event and in a flash, into the cavernous dustbin went the chocolate, wrappings included. Perhaps it was his party piece — or maybe not? But he went 'br-r-r-p' contently, just the same.

He *sounds* chuffed enough, Bessimer thought, privately amused. *Alby, you're doing just fine!*

'Now then,' Albert resumed, 'I'd say we struck a bargain. I've kept my part, now it's your turn. You've scoffed two whole bars of chocolate after all. *Are* you going to help us or are you not?'

Gimnal shook his ponderous head. 'What seeks thee of Skandos?' he demanded, abruptly.

'Why dost seek Konnee?' He jiggled closer: 'Dost intend harm? Speak true. Art buffoon?'

Albert flushed: *Bouncy little horror,* he thought, angrily. *Buffoon indeed. I'll show him.*

'Buffoon?' he retorted. '*You're* the buffoon, you little green twit — what the heck is Skandos?'

The hominoid glared, turned brilliant pink and seemed likely to explode. '***Skandos***?' he squealed, gesticulating, angrily. '***This*** be Skandos, thou disaffected dolt. *Thou* art assuredly buffoon.' His eyeballs flashed, he jiggled, bounced up and down and repeated. 'Why dost seek Konnee?'

Recognising a potentially explosive situation when he saw one and realising they would be sunk if the grobbelin scarpered without revealing Connie's whereabouts, Bessimer hastily stepped in.

'I'm *sure* we've already told you,' he explained, 'Connie is our friend. We just want to find her.'

He eyed the grobbelin, wonderingly. 'And if you mean this *place* is called Skandos,' he blurted, 'then we really didn't know. We're truly very sorry, mister – er, Gimnal.'

The manikin reverted more normal pastel green and positively beamed – or so it appeared. In any event the corners of his mouth ascended and stayed there. He simply *radiated* pleasure.

He puffed his chest and tapped it. 'I Gimnal,' he again announced, 'Grobbelin of Skandos.' Rocking from foot to foot and pointing to each in turn, he demonstrated his communicative skills:

'Me Gimnal, you Dzorj, him Allbut,' he declared, smugly. Gesturing far and wide triumphantly, he concluded, 'This be *Skandos*, the world within; my world where thou art but strangers.'

'Thank goodness *that's* sorted,' Albert sarcastically muttered, earning himself a frosty look.

'Can it, Alby,' Bessimer warned, quietly. 'Don't rock the boat; I think he's going to help.' Albert sniffed, pointedly, but said nothing. Bessimer might well be right – he usually was.

'Choklit, Dzorj. Dzorj give Gimnal Choklit?' the manikin demanded, nothing if not consistent.

'OK,' Bessimer agreed, 'just one, mind, but only when you've told us where Connie is.'

'Konnee that way,' the hominoid declared, pointing towards the hills, 'many leagues hence.'

'Well, thanks,' Bessimer replied, 'it'll do for a start,' ignoring the outstretched hand. 'Where, exactly and how do we get there? Is there a path or something?' Gimnal shook his head.

'First, give Gimnal two, three, nice Choklit.' His elocution, whilst creditable, indicated a wider grasp of English than hitherto displayed.

Surrendering – with a shrug, Bessimer handed over a third and final chunk of delectable bribery.

'Remember,' he said, sternly, 'this one is positively your last.'

'Hokay,' the artful manikin agreed, tossing the delicacy into his rapacious cakehole. 'Swift' was hardly the word for it – supersonic, more like!

'B-r-r-r-p,' he hiccupped, with evident satisfaction, 'Luvverly. *Now* Gimnal help, hokay?'

'Brilliant,' Bessimer beamed, 'I always *knew* you would.' Delighted at the creature's change of heart, optimistic the rescue proper of Connie could finally begin, he dug Albert in the ribs.

'What do you reckon, Alby? Good news or what?'

Albert was equally enthusiastic – but curious. It occurred to him they might have further need of the grobbelin, in which case maybe he could be bribed with something other than chocolate? Supplies were limited and the speed with which Gimnal caused an entire bar to disappear, whilst novel, was somewhat alarming. The importance of conserving stock couldn't be overstated; who knows how long it might have to last?

'Great stuff, George, you played a blinder.' He clapped his hands to applaud the grobbelin – who smirked knowingly. Albert seized his opportunity.

'You obviously like chocolate,' he said, 'but we don't have much. What else do you like to eat?' Gimnal regarded him quizzically.

'Not understand,' he muttered. 'Gimnal only like choklit not eat man- food,' he shuddered.

'Come on, you must like something else. You do eat, surely?'

'Only eat Grobbelin food, Gimnal go home for food once, twice every day.'

'What sort of food?'

'Grobbelin eat griggle,' he replied, 'but Gimnal also like Choklit,' he added, hopefully.

'What's griggle?' Bessimer intervened, curiosity aroused.

'Grobbelin grow griggle in cave,' he explained. Fishing inside his robe he produced a wrinkled, root-like vegetable vaguely resembling turnip and proffered it.

'Dzorj like try?' he invited. 'Only little bit,' he warned, 'too much make Dzorj sick.' Bessimer graciously accepted the offering and cautiously took a nibble.

'Hm, not bad at all,' he declared. 'Here, Alby you try a bit.' Albert hastily shook his head.

'Not right now,' he declined. 'Time is passing and we still need to know where Connie is. Come on,' he told the grobbelin, 'you've had your chocolate, now it's time you earned it. Now, for the last time: where is Connie?'

'First, need stylus,' the creature preened, immodestly? Casting about he spotted a nearby stick, jiggled off to retrieve it and jiggled his way back again.

'Dzorj watch, Allbut watch,' he lectured. 'Gimnal does picture, picture show Konnee.' He tapped the ground and scratched a cross. 'This art here,' he said. Lifting one foot he vanished – only to reappear a good five metres away. 'And yonder be Brerb,' he declared, gesturing towards the hills. He stooped to scratch a crude, distinctly dragon-like outline. Straightening, he trembled.

'Beware ye Brerb,' he warned, earnestly. 'Brerb eat Grobbelin, eat Dzorj, and eat Allbut. Brerb eat vile Brogtin, even eat Gruffle. Brerb eat *everything* – cursed art Brerb.' He shook his head.

'Brerb very big ,very smart; always hungry.' Again he twisted and vanished, materialising again some three hundred metres away. The tiny figure waved two equally tiny arms, appeared to gyrate – and *presto*, was back at the barrier. 'Three leagues hence be Konnee,' Gimnal proudly declared.

The chums conferred.

'I think I've got it,' Bessimer said. 'We're here, the monster — Brerb, he calls it — hangs out over by that hill, around two kilometres, I guess. I gather Connie's a good deal further than that so it's fair to assume we're in for quite a trek. Just how far *is* a league, anyway?'

'Four kilometres or thereabouts, I think, not that it matters. Problem is we *still* know nothing of consequence regarding Connie's whereabouts — not with any degree of accuracy.'

'You're right, Alby. I'll quiz him again,' Bessimer agreed. Turning back to the grobbelin, he posed a further question: 'Please, Gimnal, where exactly is Connie? And how long will it take us to get there?'

'Aha,' exclaimed Gimnal. 'Methinks thou cannot Weem and must therefore Gromp as child. Is not so?' He regarded them with something approaching pity, questioning eyebrow-flap raised.

Bessimer was momentarily baffled but, after thinking for a moment manfully tried again.

'Please, Gimnal. What do you mean by "Weem" — and what is "Gromp"?'

The hominoid shuffled his feet awkwardly, regarding the pals with something approaching incredulity.

'Verily, Dzorj hast little knowledge,' he piped, pityingly. 'Mayhap Gimnal explains?' He lifted one foot, revolved on the other and spiralled down until his body seemed to disappear, leaving his head apparently floating, just millimetres above the ground. He then simply vanished, leaving the soil undisturbed, only to reappear, milliseconds later, two or three metres to the right. He spun twice and again disappeared, re-materialising a split-second later right back where he started.

'This Weem,' he announced, proudly. Turning, he teetered a few paces to the left, spun through ninety degrees and tottered back. 'And this Gromp,' he smugly informed them.

'OK, so we're in for a long walk,' Albert sniffed.

Patiently, Bessimer tried again.

'That's all very well, Mister Gimnal. But you *still* haven't told us where Connie is.'

'Not understand,' the hominoid huffed, shifting from one foot to the other. 'Gimnal get Choklit; tell Dzorj Connie maybe three leagues hence. Canst tell more, knowest not more. Make mistress very angry.'

Mistress, what mistress? Bessimer pounced.

'*You* don't understand? *We* don't understand,' he lectured sternly. 'You say Connie is three leagues away but we need to know more. You promised help so we gave you more chocolate. And what's all this about a Mistress? Why angry? Which mistress? What are you hiding?'

Caught on the hop – literally, the hominoid flashed brilliant pink. His brow-flaps shot skywards, eye-orbs blazing incandescent, he rocked, he swayed and he violently trembled… *Oh, oh!* Neither of the friends had ever witnessed anything or anybody quite like it.

'*Wicked,*' Albert remarked, drily, not in the least bit sympathetic. 'He's flipped his cork. Look, George, he's doing his fruit.'

Bessimer thought otherwise. 'Don't be facetious,' he chided. 'Can't you see the poor chap's scared half to death? But why I haven't the foggiest.'

Albert hung his head. 'Sorry, George. Sorry – er, Gimnal,' he apologised, 'I didn't realise…'

'No worries,' Bessimer said, 'I dare say he won't hold it against you. Fear and anger are equally emotive, easily recognisable in humans perhaps less so in grobbelins.' He turned again to Gimnal and patted his arm.

'Never mind, Gimnal,' he soothed, gently. 'I don't know why but you're obviously frightened. Our mission is to rescue Connie and so we shall. We were hoping you could tell us where she is, how she got there and how to go about finding her. But you've been very helpful and we're grateful. Don't worry, we'll manage, somehow.' Bessimer's solicitude was genuine; born of a growing fondness for the strangely engaging little fellow. Gimnal blinked, soulfully. Large, orange tears welled and spilled… he was actually crying!

'Dzorj art kind, forsooth,' he snivelled. 'Tis rare, such kindness, Gimnal knowest not…' A warning glance: *Alby, hold your tongue, say nothing!* Albert nodded; message understood.

'There, there,' Bessimer soothed, 'don't cry. You mustn't upset yourself.' He patted again.

'*Should* you happen across Connie,' he ventured, 'then maybe you could let us know?'

Gimnal bobbed and nodded. 'Assuredly art kind,' he sobbed. 'Gimnal wilt tells, forsooth.' Child-like, he cuffed his eyes. 'Konnee art with Fular, witch, mine Mistress,' he suddenly blurted. 'Fular hast Keep by Bortzin Mountain three leagues hence as didst truly say. Pray tell not,' he pleaded – and added, tearfully, 'else Fular beat Gimnal severe.' The admission was a breakthrough, the fillip needed to render Connie's rescue more likely and less of a pipe dream. Bessimer smiled.

'Don't worry,' he hastened to reassure, 'we neither of us shall breathe a word.' He was pleased and with very good reason. Triggering the creature's distress had brought about an unexpected dividend – not only Connie's whereabouts, important though it was, but an extraordinary revelation as a bonus. Whether or not

Gimnal's Mistress turned out to really be a witch remained to be seen, but Bessimer had a sneaking suspicion she might be somehow be connected with Connie's disappearance…?

Gimnal's flaring pink subsided to something approaching normal; yet Bessimer hesitated. Although tempted, pushing too hard might re-alienate the hominoid and ruin all chance of further information. Albert also waited, equally anxious; sufficiently wise not to intervene.

The friends exchanged a glance of mutual understanding. And, just for a moment, it seemed, Gimnal had something to add. But instead of speaking he cringed, turned sickly yellow and rolled his eyes, symptomatic of terror regardless of species. Symptoms Bessimer certainly recognised but, unsure how best to respond, he simply watched and waited hoping for the manikin to recover. Hesitation proved costly. Jiggling from side to side, Gimnal began to oscillate, gaining momentum the while. Abruptly, he stopped, lifted one foot, and pivoted on the other…*what the spiff?*

'Wait a moment,' Bessimer blurted, 'you're not thinking of leaving, I hope–' He cut short. For even as he spoke and in the twinkling of an eye, the grobbelin abruptly vanished.

'Well, that's *brilliant,*' Albert remarked, sarcastically. 'The chocolate- scoffing little twerp's upped and hopped it – and, surprise, surprise, he's told us next to nothing,' he caustically added. Bessimer however, although disappointed, was rather more charitably disposed.

'I suppose,' he grunted, 'a bit more information would have helped. But he was obviously frightened and I'm not surprised he hopped it. But we know which way to go; roughly how far, and that Bortzin Mountain is the place to aim for. That's better than nothing, so be grateful for small mercies, as my mother used to say. Be happy, Alby, me old mate, I know I jolly-well am.'

'All very well,' Albert moaned, conceding even if only partially convinced. 'Waste of good chocolate if you ask me, the little green chiseller.' Bessimer emphatically shook his head.

'No, it blooming well wasn't, you old moaner. He was really quite helpful. Come on, look lively. Let's go find Connie, instead of standing gabbing like washer-women, wasting precious time.'

Putting words into action he swung his haversack to his shoulder, and waited impatiently as Albert fiddled with a shoelace before irritably following suit. 'OK, I'm ready,' he finally said.

'Right,' Bessimer replied, 'we head towards that hill avoiding open ground as far as possible. We may need to dive for cover if that monster – Brerb, Gimnal called it – should reappear.' He grimaced. 'So keep a sharp lookout, especially skywards.' The warning was hardly necessary: neither needed reminding that with a Brerb about, they must both be permanently alert.

A final glance to fix the position of the barrier thicket relative to the hilltop – and the probable lair of the Brerb – and the friends finally resumed their quest across Skandos' garishly alien but spectacularly beautiful landscape.

Their departure from the relative safety of the barrier did not, however, pass unnoticed…

CHAPTER 7

So near – and yet so far

Ever watchful when crossing open ground, the chums made the best possible use of what little cover existed when zigzagging between groups of indigenous red trees, until reaching a lightly wooded area, in turn giving way to heavily forested slopes beyond, comfortably and incident free.

Neither spoke but before entering the trees, mutual recognition that the exit to Skandos was now far beyond immediate reach prompted a final look in the direction of Connie's thicket. Much to their relief it remained clearly visible, verifying the approximate position of the barrier.

Once beneath the crimson canopy – where gentian daylight was transformed to a nauseous, purple/red gloom – they found themselves confronted by seemingly impenetrable plants, creepers and shrubs. With little option other than to proceed; they shouldered forward, hands in pockets as a precaution, avoiding dodgy-looking vegetation, carefully skirting several varieties of scarlet foliated trees that were protected by upward-spiralling rows of bony spines.

It was warm and uncomfortable and although bomber jackets made matters worse, they kept them on for the valuable protection they provided against thorns. The going was hard, but progress satisfactory – until flailing tendrils brushed against Albert's face:

'Ouch!' he roared, hand to his hand to cheek and jerking to a halt. 'That hurt. Watch yourself, George. Something just stung me on the chops. Bit like stinging-nettle but a thousand times worse.'

'Bother, that's all we need,' Bessimer groaned, also forced to stop. 'Let's take a look.' Albert obediently turned his head to reveal a livid red weal extending right across his cheek. The injury brought immediate contrition. 'Crumbs, that really is nasty,' Bessimer sympathised. He moistened a handkerchief with lemonade and gently dabbed Albert's face. 'Better?'

'Ye-es, just a bit,' Albert replied, wincing nevertheless.

'From here on in we'd better be a lot more careful, no telling what we might bump into.'

'*You're* telling *me*, cocker,' Albert retorted, sarcastically, 'as if I don't already know.'

'You know perfectly well what I mean. We both of us need to watch it.'

It was here they again heard – and recognised – the mournful wail of a Brerb. The blood-curdling cries seemed to be some way off – but could possibly be attenuated by the trees. A sobering thought. Exchanging uneasy glances both grimaced and involuntarily shivered.

Ten careful, sweaty minutes and around twenty metres later, they heard the unmistakable tinkle and gurgle of running water from somewhere close by.

'Unless my tired old ears deceive me,' said Bessimer with grin, 'That sounds remarkably like a river or a stream of some sort up ahead – and not too far either.'

'Sure does,' was Albert's eager reply. 'Come on, George. I'd give anything for a nice cool drink of water. Pop's all right, but the more of it you drink, the thirstier you seem to become.'

Encouraged by thoughts of sparkling water, the boys tackled the remaining ten metres of ground with renewed enthusiasm, and minutes later emerged from the trees at a run.

They found themselves on the banks of a moderately-deep, vegetation-free brook, whose crystal-clear waters trilled enticingly over a bed of local orange-coloured pebbles and rock. Bessimer unhesitatingly threw himself full-length, gleefully splashed water into his face, cupped his hands and greedily began to drink.

'Hey, be careful, George,' Albert shouted. 'Oughtn't we to check it out first?'

Bessimer looked up and laughed, supremely confident. 'What's to check?' He grinned. 'Not frightened of good old aqua, surely?' He resumed slaking his very considerable thirst.

'All very well,' grumbled his friend. 'It's probably OK but in this place you can never be sure.'

Bessimer sat up, stretched and laughed again. 'Don't be such a scaredy-cat, Alby. It's cool, it's fresh, it's clear and tastes lovely. Anyone with half an eye could tell that simply by looking.'

'What if the witch put something in the water? Serve you right if you turned into a frog.'

'Why, do you think Gimnal's mistress really is a witch? And supposing she is, she doesn't even know we're here, how the heck could she?'

'What about Gimnal? She scares him half to death and he might easily have blabbed.'

'Unlikely. Why admit telling us which way to go; no harm in that surely?'

'Maybe fear prompted him to squeal,' Albert replied, again far from convinced.

'Have it your own way,' Bessimer rejoined. 'Do you want a nice cool gargle or not?'

Still muttering, Albert nevertheless joined his friend at the water's edge and began to drink.

Once finished, Bessimer stripped off, jumped in and bathed. Albert swiftly followed suit. Ten minutes later, revived and refreshed, they forded the stream and resumed trekking through endless undergrowth, breaking free of the endemic, red-topped trees half-an-hour later. Clear of the trees, the tor barely half a kilometre ahead, Bessimer came to a sudden halt and gawped.

A sphere of pearly, shimmering luminescence, pale against the sky appeared as if from nowhere and spiralled down to land just ahead, swiftly resolving into the figure of a tall man clad in a voluminous black cloak and baggy pantaloons, wearing a tall, pointy black hat embellished with a single silver-coloured crescent.

'Oo-er, it's a bloke,' Albert gasped, almost lost for words.

'Bloke, nothing,' Bessimer retorted. 'Bet you a pound to a pinch of pepper he's a wizard.'

'Greetings,' the man boomed, well-naturedly. 'I am Wegglar and who, pray, art ye?' He was tall, bearded and handsome, with an unmistakable twinkle in his eye.

'I am George,' Bessimer replied, 'and this is my friend, Albert.'

Absently stroking his flowing beard, the newcomer regarded them with obvious curiosity.

'Why hast entered Skandos?' he wanted to know. 'Are not aware much danger abounds?'

'Yes, but we came to find Connie, my girlfriend. We believe she's at the Keep of Fular.'

'That is assuredly so. But what means "girlfriend"?' Bessimer reddened; shuffled his feet.

'Connie's female – a girl. Girlfriend is a term used for signifying a female sweetheart.'

'A-ha, so Connie is your chosen for who wouldst forfeit thy life? Verily, art brave. Unless well-accustomed, much peril abides. Have care lest Brerb doth feast thy bones. Beware further, for Fular is dangerous, a witch; oft ill of temper – as doubtless doth know.'

'But we *didn't* know, n-not really,' he spluttered.

The wizard made no comment, waiting patiently until Bessimer recovered his voice.

'Gimnal the Grobbelin…' he began. 'Er, you do know of Gimnal the grobbelin?' When the wizard nodded, Bessimer hurried on. 'Well, Gimnal told us Fular was his mistress and that he's afraid of her. But I'm absolutely certain he'd have absolutely no reason for telling her about us.'

'Verily; Grobbelin are craven by nature, else masters would'st be; fain lackeys be not.'

'He was kind and helpful, but couldn't tell us how to find the Keep of Fular,' Bessimer ventured.

'Could'st – but dare not,' the wizard remarked, with an air of knowledgeable certainty. Moving closer, he produced a small box from a pouch at his waist. 'Wilt sooth in a trice,' he said, reaching to Albert and smearing the injured cheek with a colourless salve. 'Tis plain hast encountered vile Bleshnan vine,' he observed, sympathetically.

'It – it's fading already,' Bessimer gaped. Indeed, the welt had already all but disappeared.

'Thanks very much,' said an astonished Albert. 'Thanks again; it doesn't hurt anymore.'

'Art welcome,' the sorcerer replied, offering the box. 'Take it, lest needs again.'

'Gosh, thanks.' Albert accepted the box with alacrity, carefully stowing it away.

Encouraged by the man's friendliness, Bessimer sought answers to worrying questions. 'Excuse me, sir. What do you know about this – this witch, Fular? Why has she kidnapped Connie? And will Connie still be safe? Albert and I are really worried.'

Wegglar didn't immediately respond. For a moment, he seemed pensive, wistful, almost. But squaring his shoulders he replied, regretfully, 'Tis no secret; Fular once mine dearest heart; kind and beautiful? In truth yes, but t'was many years ago; times hath changed, alas. Beauteous yet, mayhap still of good heart, but assuredly sour in both mind and temper. That Connie is safe without harm is true, though I neither know nor canst say t'will ever be so.'

He turned and pointed several degrees to the right of the hill and continued: 'Verily, close to Bortzin Mountain doth lay your goal, but 'tis far and a dangerous journey.'

'Thank you, but we *have* to go. Connie needs us and will be frightened so far away from home.'

'Wait and behold.' Wegglar withdrew a black cane tipped with a gold star from inside his cloak, tapped the ground twice and pointed towards a small dune some twenty metres away. Orange-coloured sand shifted and swirled to reveal slavering jaws, fearsome teeth and the red-flecked eyes of a lion-sized, dun-coloured creature lying in wait.

'Brogtin,' the wizard remarked, matter-of-factly. 'Mayhap thinks boy makes tasty meal.' He waved his – wand?

Cover blown, the beast snarled and loped away into the distance.

'Methinks Wegglar should help you find Konnee?' the sorcerer suggested, softly. 'By Breethan and mystical means, wouldst gladly transport thee to Bortzin, with Fular's Keep but half a league onwards. Not one step further else Fular wilts enrage.'

Not only was it a tempting offer, it was tantamount to an admission.

Bessimer was curious. 'Before we go any further can I ask you a question?' He suspected he knew the answer but nevertheless needed to hear it for himself.

The wizard smiled and bobbed his head. 'Most assuredly you can, my boy.'

'If Fular's a real live witch, then can you confirm you're a real live wizard?'

Wegglar smiled again and nodded. 'Wizard indeed, live most assuredly. Shall we begin?'

'I thought so,' grunted Bessimer, in an aside. Seeking Albert's approval he posed a question: 'What do you think, Alby? Shall we give it a whirl?'

'If it means avoiding that rotten Brerb,' his friend replied, 'then it's certainly OK by me.'

It was the decider. 'Could you? *Would* you, Mr Wizard? We'd certainly be very grateful.'

Whereupon the sorcerer raised one hand, circled his wand with the other and chanted: *Breethan, Benedicti, Quo Bortzin, nigh peak. Take George; take Albert no further to seek. Convey both thither, this instant by right. Deliver both safely afore this night.*

The image of the wizard faded and blurred, replaced by flashing, brilliant white light and rushing winds. Amber-coloured stars whirled, flashed and flickered and they were enveloped in a pale green nimbus – yet again. They seemed to float end over end with little sense of gravity, and an eerie pallid glow interspersed with twinkles of sparkling light persisted throughout vertiginous floating, tumbling and stomach-churning nausea.

The sensation was short-lived, however, and the pals soon recovered their respective equilibriums, neither actually being sick.

There was no conversation, no sense of time and a sense of limbo persisted throughout. Minutes, seconds – or perhaps mere moments later – coincidental with the return of gravity and with nothing more serious than a slight bump, the light faded and the friends were back on the ground unharmed. Surprisingly – or perhaps not – both landed on their feet.

'Corks,' exclaimed Bessimer, in considerable awe, 'how about that?'

Albert seemed dazed and said nothing.

Conversation was non-existent as they cast about, seeking and probing; instinctively seeking to establish their whereabouts.

Not that it was of much help, but they had been deposited on the slopes of a featureless hillside, fifty metres below a boulder-strewn ridge sharply in relief against an angry purple sky. The ground was rocky and for the most part bare, with only an occasional patch of low, scrubby verdure. Nothing seemed capable of concealing anything large enough to pose a threat.

Away from the ridge, the view was stunning. Accustomed as they were to nature's kaleidoscope of reds, greens, yellows and blues – and every conceivable hue in between – the scene was garish, unworldly and unreal. Notwithstanding, there remained an element of mystical beauty which couldn't be ignored.

A vast expanse of vermilion-topped forest stretched almost as far as the eye could see. Occasional gaps in the canopy were distinguished by the yellow and blue gleam of endemic shrubbery and a meandering gash – probably denoting the route of a river – extended diagonally from the right until merging into the base of an upwards-thrusting, claret-capped hill almost at the horizon. Significantly, it might even be the home of the Brerb, for the distance equated neatly to the three leagues suggested by Gimnal – about twelve kilometres, according to Albert's conversion.

And still neither conversed, each totally wrapt in thought whilst further minutes ticked by.

'Are you thinking what I'm thinking?' Bessimer suddenly blurted. 'Cos if that's where we've just come from, the Keep of Fular and Connie must be somewhere the other side of this hill.'

'Whoa, I'm still weighing it up,' protested Albert, although privately in agreement, 'but I think I'm almost with you. If the wizard's done as he promised, we've little more than a kilometre to go.'

With mounting excitement and a dawning realisation that the first part of their quest might be nearing an end, Albert became visibly cock-a-hoop. He clapped Bessimer's shoulder, gleefully.

'Good old Wegglar,' he chortled, 'his magic sure saved us from one hell of a route march.'

'My sentiments entirely,' Bessimer replied, with a grin. 'Come on, let's go find Connie.' He pointed. 'See those three boulders, up near the summit? Last one there's a dummy.'

'Yippee!' Albert whooped, as the pair joyfully scrambled up the slope, but just short of the target, each let out a shout of alarm, ducked and dodged and instinctively dived for cover. Bessimer's momentum was the greatest and they collided in mid-air and hit the deck in a tangle. Albert attempted to rise, but hastily clapped his hands to his face and remained on the ground.

They came from nowhere: buzzing, swooping, diving and whirling. First one, then another followed by dozens more. Huge insects vaguely resembling bumble-bees but with yellow and red striped bodies the size of golf balls, long, wicked-looking stings and – horror of horror – evil, beady little eyes set in elfin, quasi-human faces.

Seeking cover, the boys desperately scrambled for the boulders, too little avail. Shouting proved futile; the more they tried to frighten them away the more the attack seemed to intensify. There was no let-up; the situation was rapidly becoming untenable; Bessimer was galvanised into action.

'We daren't risk being stung,' he warned. 'These beasties are most probably poisonous. They're out to get us and seem likely to succeed. Come on,' he shouted, 'it's time to scarper.'

'OK by me,' Albert bellowed back. '*Geronimo*! *Let's go!*' Waving their hands, ducking, dodging and weaving they shot clear of the boulders and dived for the hill, stumbling, rolling and tumbling until finally reaching the bottom. Once there, close to the forest margins, although huffing and puffing; bruised and breathless, both were hugely relieved to be safe and in one piece. Miraculously, their attackers had mysteriously disappeared… Mission accomplished?

'I get the distinct impression someone didn't want us to advance any further,' Bessimer remarked, ruefully, once dusted down and recovered of breath.

'Yeah, no prizes for guessing who that might be. It'll be that rotten witch, it has to be.'

A single warning flash: a distant rumble of thunder and in an instant – almost total darkness.

'Blow it,' grizzled Albert in a huff, 'flipping night time already.'

'Could be just the opportunity we need,' Bessimer said. 'What about climbing back up there and making ourselves scarce among the boulders till daylight?'

'What, in pitch darkness? You're off your trolley, kiddo, we'd end up getting lost.'

'Not necessarily. Up is up, my boy, and we could feel our way – crawl, if necessary. No beasties, the witch won't spot us, and we can plan ahead the moment daylight returns. One way or another, witch or no witch, we're going to rescue Connie *and* find the way home.' There was no mistaking his complete and utter determination.

'You betcha,' Albert said, softly, 'we're in this together and nothing's going to stand in our way, but I don't much fancy blundering about in the dark. Crumbs,' he complained, 'it's so black I can't tell which is up or which way is down, much less find the way back up there.'

'Shush, listen. I think I know how to tell.' Obligingly, Albert shushed.

'There it goes again!' An occasional murmur, faint at first, a grunt – and then silence again.

'That time *I* heard something. What on earth was it, d'you reckon?'

'Be quiet, can't you, just listen.'

The sounds came again, but louder. A mournful cacophony of grunts, growls and howls, getting louder by the moment. A gleam of luminescence twinkled within the trees and for Albert, the penny finally dropped.

'I see what you mean,' he said. 'It's coming from the jungle; a right noisy menagerie, if ever there was. Assuming we set off with that din behind us, the hill has to be directly ahead.'

'You've got it in one,' said Bessimer, 'but we do still have a choice.'

'What do you mean?'

'We'll, we obviously need cover of some sort. The forest would do, but judging from that din, I don't much fancy spending a night among the trees.'

'Nor me,' snorted Albert emphatically. 'I'd rather take my chances out here.'

'Then that's that settled. Confound the witch; let's get back up that hill… and, as ever, we stick together,' he added, tucking a precautionary arm in Albert's.

'Come on, let's give it a whirl.' With the forest at their rear, they set off, variously climbing, crawling and scrabbling, pressing ever upwards.

Around halfway, as luck would have it, clouds lifted and a pale crescent moon appeared in a sombre sky and, feeble though it was, provided just sufficient illumination to proceed a good deal more readily. Several more bruises, two pairs of sore knees and one bumped elbow later, persistence finally paid off and they reached the comparative safety of the boulders, settling in the lee of the largest.

'What now?' Albert wanted to know.

'Swig of pop,' Bessimer declared, fishing a bottle from his backpack, 'followed by a spot of shut-eye – taking turns, of course – then blow the witch and everything else till daylight.'

'Sounds good,' Albert replied, 'but what wouldn't I give for a nice warm comfy bed.'

'You and me both,' Bessimer grunted. 'Bags you take first watch. Give me a dig if you feel yourself nodding off – and here's to a decent kip without a greedy Grobbelin showing his fizzog.'

'Hokay, you're the boss,' yawned Albert, far too tired to argue. Battered and exhausted, Bessimer curled into a ball and fell asleep while Albert did his level best to carry out his duty and justify Bessimer's trust. With back jammed against a boulder, despite an aching head and watering eyes he manfully scanned the blackness, alert for the slightest hint of movement. Long dreary minutes passed and nothing stirred…

Myriads of microscopic droplets, odourless and undetectable showered precisely on target. Albert yawned mightily. He began to nod and his eyelids drooped. Recovering with a start he half reached to Bessimer, but his leaden arm refused his bidding and fell back again. Powerless to resist, he crumpled to the ground in an ungainly heap, already snoring his head off.

Bessimer's rhythmic breathing deepened: neither he nor Albert would stir until daybreak. Imperceptible and silent, invisible tendrils gently insinuated themselves between recumbent figures and ground, multiplying tenfold in the process.

In seconds, cocoon-like and defiant of gravity, the pair rose majestically into the night sky and sailed effortlessly through the air to a distant hill where, still fast asleep, they were deposited close to the summit adjacent a group of boulders similar to those from whence they had come. The shroud dissolved as silently as it formed. Neither stirred – not even when twin headlamps scythed the night sky and passed almost directly overhead.

Daylight arrived Skandovian style – noisy, abrupt and unexpected. Albert blinked, knuckled his eyes and stretched. Memory came flooding back. He paled, guiltily; he'd been asleep. *What if they'd been attacked?* But he shrugged. *Why worry? We're both OK, anyway.*

'Hey, wake up, lazybones,' he called, digging a toe in his companion's ribs.

Bessimer awoke with a start. 'What's up? What's going on? Crikey, it's daylight already.'

'Yeah, so it is,' a trifle sarcastically, 'time to wakey, wakey, rise and shine.'

Bessimer shook his head, taking a moment to clear his mind. His face darkened.

'Wait a minute, I distinctly told you to call me, so why didn't you?'

Albert hung his head. 'Sorry,' he said, sheepishly, 'I meant to, but was that knackered I must have nodded off. Still, no harm done,' he parroted, cheerfully. 'We're still in one piece, safe and sound.'

Bessimer frowned. 'No thanks to you, you idle twit. Next time…' He left the rest unsaid.

Albert got up and offered his hand. 'Come on, George, time to get cracking.'

'You bet,' Bessimer replied, rising to his feet with Albert's assistance. 'Connie's somewhere the other side of that hill. I can just picture her face when *we* come knocking on the door.' Trying to imagine what lay beyond, he eyed the boulders thoughtfully. Abruptly, his expression changed. 'You know, Alby,' he said, slowly, 'there's something peculiar about these rocks. I can't quite fathom what but they seem different, somehow. It might be imagination but they seem further apart than they were, even though it was dark at the time.'

Albert stared, first at one, then another and then back again. He too, seemed puzzled.

'Yes, I see what you mean.' He frowned. 'Besides that, several seem a good deal larger. Is someone playing mind games, George, or what?' Casting about, he looked, first this way and then that: at the rocks, the slope leading towards the forest – but wait, it was no longer a forest but woodland. He looked further, searching for the valley, the river, the distant peak – only to realise everything differed from the day before – but did it?

'Corks, that's torn it,' he exclaimed, pointing. 'Look, that's where we left the trees and met the wizard, and there in the distance is the barrier thicket, as plain as the nose on your face.' Although unintentional, his bombshell observation triggered an irritable exchange.

Bessimer pursed his lips, shaded his eyes, squinted and cursed their luck.

'I was beginning to suspect as much. We're practically back where we started.'

Albert flushed, not only with disappointment but with anger and disbelief.

'Blow it, we were within spitting-distance. How on earth did we get back here?'

'By much the same means we travelled there, I suppose.'

'But that was down to Wegglar. Why on earth would he whiz us back again?'

'Who said anything about Wegglar?'

'Who else could it have been?'

'Give you one guess.'

'Oh, Fular, I suppose.'

'Of course it was, who else?'

'Then she must have sneaked up while we slept, but how come we knew nothing about it?'

'How the blazes should I know? You were the one supposedly keeping watch, remember?'

Albert muttered something and subsided.

Patiently, Bessimer allowed him time to consider. 'Might as well be comfortable and have a bite to eat,' he said, flopping to the ground.

'No, you jolly-well don't,' Albert blurted, grabbing his haversack. 'Let's get out of here – and sharpish. Unless I'm very much mistaken we're right in the middle of the Brerb's dinner plate.'

Bessimer didn't argue; just snapped alert. Recovering his belongings he took the lead, intending to find a vantage point from where to observe, reconnoitre and to establish the best course of action for recovering lost ground.

'We'll look for the best route from here,' he said, squeezing through a gap between the boulders. Once through he dropped to his knees. 'Hold it,' he shouted, 'the ground is crumbly and drops away. Stay put. I'll go take a look.' Gingerly edging forward he suddenly stopped.

'Watch out,' he called. 'We're right near the top of a precipice.' He peered over the edge and whistled. 'You were right about the Brerb.

Animal bones everywhere. You'd better come and see for yourself – but be careful.'

Without hesitation, Albert dropped to his knees and inched forward. He was almost there, offering a helping hand when Bessimer yelled in alarm.

'Get back, Alby. The ground is giving way——— arrrgh!' Amidst a welter of shale, he scrabbled frantically – and uselessly – sliding and slithering completely over the edge. The ground rumbled and shook; a sizeable section of cliff fell away.

Albert also began to slide, powerless to stop. His gut-reaction was immediate: 'Help, help – *Gee-or-ge*, **George**,' he shouted, utterly terrified.

There was a sensation of falling; a glimpse of Bessimer; a ledge, a scattering of bones. Landing awkwardly he sprawled full-length; winded, but otherwise unharmed. Casting about, saw Bessimer was also down, lying motionless a couple of metres away. Without thought for his own safety, he crawled to render assistance. Awash with anxiety, he shook his dearest friend by the shoulder:

'George, George,' he panicked. 'Oh, crikey, George, are you all right?'

'Yeah, course I am,' Bessimer grunted, ruefully. 'A touch winded, that's all.'

'Thank goodness for that,' Albert gasped, with relief. 'I thought for a min you were a goner.'

'Nah,' Bessimer replied. 'Tough as old boots,' he lied. Ignoring twinges of pain he manfully craned his neck to risk a glance upwards, was horrified to discover that so much ground had fallen away, two of the boulders were now perched precariously immediately above their heads. Loose shale came clattering down, most skittered harmlessly into the void. Bessimer couldn't help a sharp intake of breath.

'Better watch our heads,' he warned. 'Little bits mostly seem harmless, but one of those whopping-great boulders could quite easily flatten both of us.' He eased into a kneeling position, inching forward until perilously close to the edge, peering outwards and downwards.

'Sooner you than me,' Albert declared with a shiver, digging in his toes for all his worth.

The ledge was narrow, some two metres below the rim, perched above a sheer drop with jagged rocks randomly strewn at the base some twenty metres below. In the absence of suitable equipment descent was out of the question; climbing back impossible. To all intents and purposes they were marooned. A short way to the left the ledge broadened, giving access to an enormous cave and to the right, it narrowed briefly before tapering away completely.

'It doesn't require genius to guess who lives there,' Albert grimaced, with a jerk of his head. 'And if we'd fallen a tidgy bit to the right…?' he added, with a shudder. 'Look how high up we are – and right above those dirty great rocks.'

'Tell me about it,' Bessimer replied, drily. 'But shut it a mo, can't you. I'm trying to fathom a way out of this pickle but as it seems hopeless I'm therefore open to suggestion… well?'

'Haven't a clue,' Albert admitted, glumly. 'Short of a miracle, we're up the creek without a paddle and no mistake.'

'So bring on your miracle. There's no way up and there's no way down – we're trapped.'

The sky darkened; a winged shape appeared in the sky heading in their direction. Closing rapidly it swooped as if to attack. Both instinctively ducked, petrified. Almost upon them, the creature unexpectedly soared up and over the cliff and disappeared from view.

'Missed,' Bessimer gasped in relief. 'It can't get at us; we're too close to the cliff.'

The sound of wing-beats changed pitch and became increasingly louder.

'Hang about,' Albert cautioned. 'Don't count your chickens. I think it's coming back.'

The bird-beast reappeared, heading away, powerfully flapping; rapidly gaining height. It turned, straightened and with wings folded kestrel-fashion powered into a dive. Demonstrating aerial ability borne of years of practice, it swooped, flapped briefly with outstretched talons and settled barely three metres away directly in front of the cave.

Close up it was truly monstrous: huge scaly body; tyrannosaurus-like head, fearsome teeth and jaws. Shuffling sideways with outstretched neck, fangs bared and jaws a-slavering, tasty prey was practically within reach. Belching an almighty gust of foul, foetid breath it screeched with triumph and arched its neck…

Albert shrieked and grabbed Bessimer's arm. 'George. *George.* Quick, get us out of here.'

'Can't,' Bessimer shouted, 'no time. Just duck – and keep ducking. It might get fed up and try somewhere else.' But, unexpectedly, help was close at hand…

'Tee, hee, hee,' a voice tittered from behind…

What here, from out of thin air? Bessimer risked a glance over his shoulder but saw nothing. Busily dodging and ducking, he had failed to notice a pair of luminescent red eyes peering from within a barely discernible opening… until he distantly felt the tap of a hand on his shoulder. He spun as if stung – to be confronted by a grinning hominoid closely resembling Gimnal.

Cor, Penny Plinkers: there's another one of them?

'Come, Dzorj, come, Allbut,' the newcomer beckoned. 'Pray hasten, fain Allbut too. Wilt not enters afore Brerb doth dreadfully rend thee asunder, eat thee and feast thy bones?'

'Cor, not half,' Bessimer chortled. 'Come on, Alby, look lively. The cavalry has arrived.'

Although narrow, it was the work of a moment for each in turn to wriggle through the orifice. Once inside, the screech of the frustrated Brerb seemed strangely inconsequential. Taking care not to bang their heads, the friends straightened and looked about. It wasn't a cave, they realised, rather a narrow rift in the cliffs.

Glowing in the dark, their saviour, the quaint little manikin beckoned. 'Come, Dzorj, come, Allbut,' he piped, with a bow, 'Bulgan will guide the path to safety.'

Bulgan, so that's his name, in the nick of time, too. Did he just happen by or was he sent? Five minutes and eighty metres later the humanoid stopped, stepped to one side and pointed, allowing the friends to emerge, blinking, into broad daylight – and safety…?

Whoo-Whee-Whoo! The cry was unmistakable: **The Brerb**!

'Alby,' Bessimer shouted frantically, 'get back, back into the tunnel. Quick.' He spun on his heel but to no avail. As mysteriously as he had appeared, the Grobbelin had gone… so too had the tunnel. With nowhere to run they cringed; the monster was almost upon them…

'George! *Be-ss-i-mer! Be-ss-i-mer!*' In an instant, they were grasped by an enormous invisible hand and hurled through the air.

A wail of frustration rattled their ears. *Whoo–Whee. Whee-Whoo…* Abruptly, the cries ceased.

Cautiously, Bessimer raised his head; was utterly astonished to discover they were again in the lee of the rocks close to the summit and – to his relief – the winged monster was nowhere to be seen. 'It's OK, Alby,' he breathed in relief, 'the rotten thing's gone.'

Suddenly, and again without warning, everything became blurred and immediately went blank.

CHAPTER 8

What's in a name...?

Spread-eagled, disorientated and traumatised, neither stirred – until a deep, sonorous voice broke into two confused and addled minds demanding immediate attention:

'Tis plain displeased yon Fular be. Whom else would'st banish from whence thou came?'

Bessimer groaned, fighting his way back to reality.

Dazedly, Albert forced his eyes open to discover the tall, familiar figure of Wegglar gazing down at them. He seemed unusually agitated.

'Can Fular's displeasure ne'er assuage? T'was not kind heart a-fear thee by Zimblebugs, even though seldom harms, but to deliberately imperil young innocents' lives? That canst never be.'

'H-hello, m-mister wizard,' Albert stuttered, 'and thanks a bunch. I reckon we owe you.'

Hearing voices, Bessimer sat up, opened his eyes and smiled. 'Gosh, thanks, Sir Wegglar,' he said, gratefully. 'We were nearly done for.'

Wegglar frowned, and pointed to Albert.

'How didst know invoke Bez Mer?' the magician demanded. 'Speak – honest and true.'

Albert scratched his chin uncomprehendingly. 'Huh?' he questioned. 'Bez Mer? What's that?'

Wegglar's dark eyes flashed. He drew himself up and thrust his beard with annoyance.

'Have care, foolish boy,' he growled, 'pretend not the innocent. Thou *didst* invoke and dare not deny. Would'st have Wegglar doubt mine own ears? *How* did you know? Speak, boy!'

Albert shook his head clearly at a loss, compelling Bessimer to step hastily into the breach.

'I *think* I know what you mean, Mister Wegglar,' he began, haltingly. 'It was when Albert called my name. I'm usually known as George – my middle name – but my first is really Bessimer. It's not exactly "Bez Mer", of course, but I suppose it *does* sound a tidgy bit similar.'

For the first time the wizard seemed taken aback. Uncharacteristically his jaw dropped.

'Thou, *thou* art… Bez Mer?' he gasped. 'Whom Fular dares endanger? Cursed be, foul witch.' Whereupon he dropped to one knee and bowed, slowly, deeply – almost reverently.

'No, no,' Bessimer protested, in consternation and with considerable embarrassment.

'It's not "Bez Mer", it's Bessimer; b, e, double s, i, m, e, r. Please, *please* get up, Sir Wizard. I'm not who you think, I can't be. I'm just an ordinary schoolboy.'

Fascinated, Albert made as it to intervene. 'But…' he began, only to fall silent again.

The sorcerer shook his head but rose to his feet nevertheless. He helped Bessimer up, placed both hands on his shoulders and gazed long, hard and deep into his eyes.

Unflinching, Bessimer steadfastly stared back.

Apparently satisfied, the wizard smiled.

'T'was no mere chance thou cometh Skandos,' he declared, 't'was long ordained and writ. By Breethan Supreme, by ancient scribe;

by Zildus the Great; by my life, perchance Fular's too. Methinks "Bez Mer" be your family style. Your father and your father's father perhaps? Most probably *all* thy male forbears, thence generation upon generation. Is indeed not so?'

'Yes, my grandfather and my uncle – my father's brother,' Bessimer blurted, 'they're all named Bessimer just like me.' He was becoming flushed – with embarrassment perhaps?

'A-ha,' Wegglar exclaimed, with evident satisfaction, 'at last dost come to pass. Be not of faint heart, neither of mind nor of spirit, thy coming be long foreordained Thou art assuredly Bez Mer.' He nodded sagely, utterly convinced.

'Oh, so what if I am?' Bessimer protested. 'And what if it is? What am I supposed to do?'

'Tis not yet time,' the wizard admitted, 'but hearken unto Wegglar. Thou entered Skandos by mystic means – as long foretold – and Destiny wilt surely prevail. Wegglar and Fular are also of your world – the world without. Banished in times of peril and dire circumstance, through wondrous and magical intricacies; born of our learned master, Zildus.'

He paused and asked softly: 'Doest fully understand, O Bez Mer?'

'Yes, I think so,' Bessimer replied, 'but I'm blessed if I can fathom what you're getting at. We came to rescue Connie, Albert and me. That's our mission – our only mission. Nothing else matters, but nothing. We won't be put off for a second, not by witches not by wizards – and certainly not by Brerb, Brogtin, or Zigron and all that jazz,' he declared.

Albert smiled and nodded; Bessimer's earnest statement clearly met with *his* approval. Bother soppy Bez Mer and his equally soppy ancestors, rescuing Connie was their first and only priority.

Wegglar hastened to reassure and elaborate without in any way demeaning Bessimer's stated intension.

'Patience, Bez Mer, wilt further explains.' Again he paused, ostensibly to collect his thoughts.

Quick to grab an opportunity, Albert piped up. 'Just a minute,' he said, 'what about me?'

'Thou art secondary of moment, but no less important. How so thy role is far from clear. If *truly* faithful squire – as Wegglar doth perceive – then wouldst better serve and speak when spoken.'

Albert flushed at the reproof but nevertheless subsided, allowing the wizard to continue.

'Magical means,' the sorcerer went on, sadly, 'whilst bounteous give little pleasure. I yearn to return the world without – mayhap Fular too; and the advent of Bez Mer doth promise release.

'Even so, no matter howsoever, events must follow their natural course. Wegglar will guide, protect and watch over, yet at pains never to interfere. Tis soured Fular wilt meddles dost fear…' The sorcerer grimaced, smiled ruefully – and then brightened as he proffered an invitation.

'You shall visit my castle; refresh, partake of vittles and rest,' he declared. 'We shall speak further when at ease. But be not mistaken, for 'tis a sign. Methinks, assuredly, thou art Bez Mer.'

Bessimer shook his head; opened his mouth; thought better of it and decided to hold his tongue.

'Come,' said Wegglar again, 'prepare thyself, Albert too. Bulgan and hospitality doth wait.'

'Bulgan, was he the little fellow who rescued us?' Albert interjected, climbing to his feet.

'Assuredly, t'was mine grobbelin,' the wizard replied, 'cousin of Gimnal, my very good friend.'

'Corks,' Bessimer blurted, 'he's yours then, *another* blinking grobbelin. There's more than one?'

'Indeed,' the wizard replied, 'and fortunately so. How else couldst know of your plight?'

'Blimey,' Albert exclaimed, aghast, 'that's rich. Have you been using him to spy on us?'

Wegglar shook his head. 'Spying? No. Watching, yes,' he admitted. His voice changed timbre.

'Time,' he resumed, 'merits especial care, less ill become should destiny be hastened. By trick of grobbelin and witching wiles, Fular sees and can oft-times hear, as indeed canst Wegglar. Therefore, since grobbelins have ears and be difficult to detect, I shall henceforth address you as "George" as does Albert your honest, true and faithful friend.' He drew himself up, and further declared:

'I fear for your safety afore Bez Mer wilts ever be so. Come,' he repeated, with a smile, 'we shall travel to my castle forthwith.' He raised his wand…

Lightning forked, darted and flashed; peals of thunder went 'boom' and 'crack-crack'. There was no sound; no sense of gravity, neither up nor of down. A sensation of floating end over end. A well-remembered experience was repeating itself. The familiar green aura; a moment of gut- wrenching nausea; a fleeting sense of limbo – a bump; and they were down. This time, happily, with none of the usual side effects.

The boys bounced to their feet and began eagerly looking about, finding themselves in the courtyard of a truly splendid castle. Built of local sandstone, complete with moat, drawbridge and towering ramparts – it apparently had it all.

'Behold,' said the sorcerer, gesturing proudly. 'Welcome to my humble abode.'

'Humble my foot,' Albert remarked, much impressed, 'it's fab, absolutely *massive*.'

'Cor, Penny Plinkers,' echoed Bessimer, 'what a super-duper pad. Did you build it yourself?'

'Partly yes – and partly no,' the wizard replied with a twinkle. 'Designed and planned be true, else by means mystic and mysterious, wouldst believe?' Wide-eyed, Bessimer merely nodded. Wegglar spread his hands and chuckled:

'Better ask no question that begs no answer, howsoever,' he hurried on. 'First refresh and wander at will. Bulgan shall accompany as guide. When familiar, prithee honour my table; join with Wegglar and vittles partake.' For a moment the sorcerer's eyes misted. Shaking his head, he took Bessimer's right hand in his, placed his left on his heart and solemnly averred:

'Mark well, O George, henceforth shalt Wegglar be yours to command. My castle shall be your castle; fain Albert too, forever thy earnest ever faithful, thy companion, thy friend.'

'Crumbs,' Albert giggled, clumsily ruining the moment, 'promotion at last. In that case, we'll have less of the lip in future, George, my boy,' he grinned, punching the air in delight.

'You wish,' Bessimer smilingly retorted. 'Boot on the other foot more like.'

If the wizard was amused, he certainly didn't show it. 'Bulgan,' he called, 'come hither.' From nowhere and in the twinkling of an eye, Gimnal's cousin appeared. The similarities were astonishing – discounting Bulgan's orange head and salmon-pink lips!

The extraordinary being squeaked, *A'och salaam, e Wegglar.* 'What does command, oh master?'

'This is George, my special guest,' the sorcerer declared, pointing to Bessimer. Turning to Albert: 'And here be Albert, companion true. Both shall refresh, take vittles and rest, for this castle shall be their castle; your masters to command – if you value your skin, that is,' he added, darkly. The grobbelin's saucer-sized eyes flared; his gigantic head bobbed in acquiescence.

'First water,' the wizard commanded, 'then conduct, guide and instruct throughout mine domain.' The little humanoid's eyes widened still further when the wizard went on to announce:

'By Wegglar's own hand shalt bedchamber and vittles prepare.'

Impressed by the sorcerer's humility, the grobbelin eyed the dishevelled pair up and down in an entirely different light Without a word, he bobbed, spun and vanished.

Where and how did he go? No harm in asking… Bessimer fidgeted. 'Er, excuse me, Wegglar,' he began, hesitantly; 'can I ask a question, please?'

'Most assuredly,' Wegglar boomed, 'does something be a-troubling you?'

'No – well, yes, in a way,' said Bessimer, apologetically. 'I'm sorry to be a nuisance, but I really would like to know. Please, please tell me, just exactly *how* does Bulgan do that?'

''Tis peculiar to grobbelins; yet Bulgan wilt never explains,' the sorcerer admitted. 'Mayhap the eye doeth deceive? Since no ground be disturbed, methinks the upper part combines with the lower – either by contortion or by illusion – to thus move instantly both thither and thence. Maketh no moment,' he added, sourly, 'since Wegglar hast magic his own.'

'Oh,' said Bessimer, 'I see' – even if little the wiser. 'Some form of time-travel, maybe?'

Forbearing to answer the wizard simply shook his head, effectively closing the subject.

Again as if from nowhere the grobbelin appeared, this time bearing two enormous leather buckets filled to capacity with water; amazingly, none seemed to have spilled.

'Dost Dzorj, dost Allbut wish bathe?' he piped, puffing a little. 'Canst fetch more a-plenty.'

Albert hesitated, brushing ineffectually at his sleeve, but Bessimer jumped at the opportunity.

'Yes please, a bath would be lovely,' he accepted, 'but where is the bathroom?'

By way of answer the hominoid jiggled across the courtyard to where a large stone cistern straddled a shallow gulley. Effortlessly, or so it seemed, he emptied each bucket in turn and vanished, reappearing a second or so later to repeat the process. It was a task with which he seemed entirely familiar for the cistern was filled to capacity within minutes. Proudly, he turned and beckoned.

'Come, Dzorj, come, Allbut,' he called, 'now plenty water wilt fetch drying-cloths.'

'Right ho, thanks,' Bessimer called back, 'be right with you. Come on, Alby… bath–ies!'

Compared with the cool rippling waters of the stream, the contents of the cistern appeared cold, dark and singularly uninviting. Pulling off a trainer, Albert stuck a tentative toe in the water.

'Brrr,' he said, shivering, 'it's freezing. I'd sooner have a *proper* tub – preferably a hot one.'

'Maybe they don't have a bathroom,' Bessimer retorted, already shucking his jacket, 'in which case if it's good enough for Wegglar it must surely be good enough for you.' He laughed. 'Come on, you dirty, smelly little wuzzock. Last one in is a dummy…' Cold water or no, they were still gaily wallowing and splashing when Wegglar returned.

'A-ha, that art indeed much better,' he said, smilingly. 'I go now to prepare supper, but should you need anything – anything at all, call freely upon Bulgan.' He made for the door.

'Thanks, but hang on a minute,' said Albert, 'just how do we do that, exactly?'

'Thus,' replied the wizard. 'Bulgan, come hither,' and the manikin promptly reappeared.

'Hearken unto George, so too unto Allbert,' the wizard commanded, and quickly departed.

The drying cloths provided by Bulgan, although rough, proved adequate. Once clean, dressed, glowing and revived, the chums were finally ready for that promised tour of the castle.

'Bulgan,' Albert called, softly, 'er, um, come here,' without effect… alas, no grobbelin. Impatiently, he tried again: 'Bulgan, *Bulgan*!' he snapped louder, but *still* without success.

'When you asked Wegglar how to summon him *he* said, "Bulgan, come *hither*",' Bessimer quietly remarked.

'Tee, hee, hee,' a voice tittered from out of nowhere, 'what needs, O master?'

'Oh, *there* you are,' sniffed Albert. 'Why the heck didn't you come when *I* called?'

'Did'st call, O Allbut?' he replied, 'Alack and fiddle-me-ray. Bulgan doth beg forgive.'

'Oh, makes no never mind,' Albert snorted testily. 'We're ready to see round the castle.'

'Very well,' the incredible little creature replied, 'Bulgan wilt therefore begins.' Huffing and puffing, sometimes jiggling, occasionally weeming, the hominoid led the way.

The castle was commodious and surprisingly well-appointed. There were galleries, state rooms, dining rooms and a great many other rooms, many containing items of beautifully-crafted, hand-made furniture. There were battlements, towers and courtyards; a moat, drawbridge and a deep, dark dungeon; a huge kitchen equipped with a vast cooking range;

preparation tables, pots and pans, cooking utensils and platters. Courtyard and cloisters, fireplaces – with inglenooks, alcoves and crannies.

In one such corner an ornately-carved chest caught Bessimer's eye. Leaving Albert and Bulgan to chat, he wandered across. Bending closer, he realised there was something unusual about the carvings, more particularly two intricate bosses that seemed strangely offset from centre. He reached out to touch one – and it moved. Intrigued, he nudged – and again it moved. *Strange!* Impelled by more than idle curiosity he pressed them both, first downwards and then sideways. There was a 'click' and the lid swung open.

Awash with curiously he bent still closer, for lying in the bottom was a mysterious object wrapped in a long, shroud-like cloth. Gingerly, he removed the wrappings to reveal a beautiful, jewel-encrusted drinking cup seemingly made of gold…

'Hoy, George! What's that you're sticking your nose in?' Albert suddenly shouted.

Bessimer jumped. 'Nothing,' he called back, guiltily. Hastily, he rewrapped the object and replaced it as found, closed the lid and walked away.

The fascinating tour continued and he put the discovery to the back of his mind. After all, what would Wegglar think were he to discover how churlishly his hospitality had been repaid…?

Next they came to a large carpentry workshop equipped with benches, vices and rack upon rack of assorted tools: Joinery and/or cabinet-making? All that hand-made furniture… *could this be where Wegglar practices yet another of his skills?* They found nothing remotely resembling a bathroom, however… but, all in all – fascinating!

An hour later with tour complete, two hungry boys presented themselves at Wegglar's table. Following several platters of the most delicious stew ever, Bessimer burped, contentedly:

'That was *really* tasty, Mister Wegglar. Er – what exactly was it?'

'Fine plump Coney,' the enchanter chuckled, 'sometime referred to as "rabbit", I believe.'

'Call it what you like; it was yummy,' said Albert, smacking his lips, 'but if that really *was* rabbit then where did it come from? Rabbits rely on grass for food and there's precious little of that here.'

The wizard nodded. 'That is entirely correct. They came from the world without.'

'How did you manage that?' Bessimer asked, curiously. 'Can *you* breach the Portal at will?'

'Alas, I wish that I could,' Wegglar replied, regretfully, and took it upon himself to explain:

'Just as mortals, wizards and witches also need food yet no bird, beast nor plant of Skandos canst eat; to attempt be vile and foul. Zildus – our master – provided provisions a-plenty, year upon year until one day, flour and rice did fail. Necessity determined Wegglar and Fular should combine magical forces or risk starvation – it was no great pleasure, alas. Oftimes since have we brought victuals from the world without, yet good red meat brings none.' He rubbed his stomach, and sighed. 'Man cannot live by bread alone, tis said; in truth an empty gut giveth little comfort.'

'Yeah, right,' interrupted Bessimer, 'but what about the rabbits…?'

Wegglar tugged his beard. For a moment he seemed hesitant, but nevertheless decided to reply:

'In recent days we again united, seeking victuals anew. But twas too little avails…' Again he hesitated.

'Go on,' said Bessimer, by now agog, 'what happened? *What about the rabbits?*'

The sorcerer frowned but nevertheless continued: 'No flour nor bread, yet *some* success did enjoy, for many fine Coney doeth arrive amounting to one full score plus four. I know not how nor couldst Fular explain: Would that she could, for but two remains,' he concluded, sadly.

Bessimer gaped: 'Twenty-four bunnies from out of the blue and neither of you know how?'

'Afraid tis so,' the wizard admitted. 'Reminds years since,' he mused, dreamily. 'No magic entails…' He broke off and crossed to a nearby closet, returning with a standard wooden baker's tray which he placed on the table, turning to the boys, expectantly.

Albert did a double-take whereas Bessimer leapt to his feet. '*Maria's!*' they chorused. Indeed it was; plain to see, stencilled boldly along one edge. Bessimer was first to find his voice:

'Did – did that tray arrive with a couple of dozen pork pies, by any chance? And what about the gold coin that mysteriously appeared in their place?'

Wegglar positively beamed. 'Aha, then you *do* know. But *how* do you know? Pray tell.'

'Albert and I were out shopping.' Bessimer began. 'We were looking in Maria's window when a whole tray of pies suddenly upped and vanished. There were crackling sounds; green flashes and a strange sensation tingled my fingers and ran up my arm. It was so weird it nearly frightened us silly; we were only eight at the time.'

'Didst call upon Bez Mer?'

'No, but a passing boy shouted my name – not once, but twice and very loudly.'

For a moment the enchanter was silent and contemplative. Abruptly, he brightened, offered his hand and smiled.

'I shall doubt thee no more for truly hast come to pass. Thou art assuredly Bez Mer.'

'But what about the gold coin; how do you explain that?'

'T'was simple magic,' the sorcerer confessed, 'no more no less: What goes up must needs come down, equally true in reverse: we of our calling take nothing for free; t'would be dishonest to do any other.'

Bessimer fidgeted. For some inexplicable reason the wizard was dodging the question of the rabbits and was returning – yet again – to the same old theme.

'*Bother* Bez Mer,' he snorted. 'It *might* sort of explain the pies, but what about the rabbits? I don't wish to be rude cos you've been *ever* so kind. But I *still* think you're barking up the wrong tree. Confuse me with Bez Mer if you must, it won't alter a thing. What's in a name, anyway?'

'As I've told you umpteen times already, all we want to do is find Connie.'

The sorcerer smiled secretively and failed to answer… *again, yet why not?*

'Take it easy, George,' Albert piped up, 'don't get your knickers in a twist.' He glanced at the wizard, apologetically. When Wegglar merely nodded and folded his arms, he went on:

'For Pete's sake forget the blinking rabbits. Their acquisition had nothing whatever to do with Wegglar *or* Fular, so don't go harping on. Maybe *nobody* knows the answer – or whatever. Fact is we've been made welcome; provided with a tub, a guided tour and a jolly good supper. Don't know about you, but I'm tired,' he added, rubbing his eyes. 'Now we're safe, how about a spot of beauty sleep? Today seems to have gone on for ever; surely it must be nearly bedtime?'

'Well spoken.' Wegglar nodded, approvingly. 'Assuredly tis correct, night cometh ere long. Resume thy quest on the morrow; I shall gladly assist and protect. Pray summon Bulgan should you have need and now doth Wegglar bid thee good night.'

'OK,' Bessimer conceded, accepting the situation for what it was. But he had one final question:

'Can you help us to the same hill as before?' he asked. 'Half a league from Fular's Keep.'

'Precisely as Wegglar intends,' the wizard chuckled, 'but henceforth shall better prepare.' In a gesture of finality he arose, gathered together the dishes, ladles, beakers platters and spoons; stacked everything on the tray and disappeared through the door.

Having consigned the washing-up to Bulgan, he deferred bed-time and made his way to his private study. Here, he spent time casting highly efficacious undetectable veils of exclusion around the castle, spells so potent little could penetrate without raising the alarm. Grobbelins were smart – but none *that* smart. A Seetelbird, perhaps? Well, possibly, but to the best of his knowledge only one served a human master and that master was he. Fular possessed ample abilities she would never dare use, bound by the same constraints that applied equally to them both. Thus, secrecy for the morrow was assured.

Bessimer was delighted with Wegglar's promise but the wizard's parting remark brought with it a surge of disappointment. Question after question came springing to mind. *What might fate have in store? How much longer before he and Connie were re-united? Would it be tomorrow perhaps?* The question brought a lump to his throat. *Would they succeed in reaching Fular's Keep? What would they do when they got there? What was the place like? Impregnable, heavily barricaded and vigorously defended? Probably, so how would they go about gaining entry? Odds-on Fular would attempt to repel them again – but how? That would depend on how many other nasty tricks were at her disposal and what form were they likely to take, he mused? Just how ruthless could she possibly be?* He shuddered to think. *Was it possible Connie could help in some way? And what did Wegglar mean when he said, 'Henceforth shall better prepare'?* He had no idea…

The boys exchanged glances: 'Will you or shall I?' asked Bessimer. Albert shrugged.

'Bulgan, come hither,' called Bessimer. 'We're tired and wish to sleep. Please show us to our room…'

'Do you know,' Albert said, sleepily, once curled cosily amidst piles of furs, 'after all the weird happenings during the past few days, I thought that nothing would surprise me ever again.'

'So?' grunted Bessimer.

'Well, I was wrong. When Wegglar produced that tray from Maria's I nearly had kittens.'

'Say "Miaou" then, why don'cher and go to flipping sleep.'

CHAPTER 9

Henceforth shall better prepare...

Oblivious to the breeze creaking and sighing through trees and the squeaks, grunts and twitters of nocturnal creatures, the exhausted friends slumbered throughout the night and beyond. Not even when a scything flash of lightening and a distant rumble of thunder heralded dawn did either so much as blink. Nor did they stir when, minutes afterwards, Bulgan materialised bearing water and a couple of rough towels.

'Tee, hee, hee,' he giggled, mischievously prodding each in turn with a six-toed foot.

Both awakened with a start. Albert took one look, turned over and recommenced snoring.

'What the…?' groaned Bessimer. 'Oh, it's you,' he huffed. 'What do you want?'

'Tis time awaken and break thy fast,' the hominoid announced, clearly unrepentant. He nudged Albert again – rather more forcefully. 'Prithee arise, Master Allbut,' he said, impatiently, 'pray arise this instant, my master doth awaits.'

Bessimer sat up and yawned. The presence of the grobbelin served as a reminder of where they were; what they were about and of what still might lay ahead. Stretching luxuriously, he clambered to his feet, whipped away Albert's furs and unceremoniously added his six own pennyworth:

'Yeah, come on, sleepyhead, rise and shine. Today's the day we rescue Connie.'

Moaning and groaning Albert nevertheless complied.

When they were ushered to a ground floor eating room fifteen minutes later, Wegglar was already waiting to greet them.

''Tis a pleasant morning, I bid,' he began with a smile, 'didst sleep well?'

'Yes, thank you,' Albert returned – at least until Bulgan stuck the boot in, that is.'

'Speaking for myself,' Bessimer quickly replied, 'I slept like a baby with a full tummy.' The wizard's eyes crinkled with amusement. Maybe he actually appreciated the simile…

'Pray sit thee down; eat hearty,' he said, generously. 'Thou hast much to achieve this day.'

'Thank you,' Bessimer replied and, without further ado, the pair gratefully complied.

Breakfast consisted of chunks of home-baked bread, dipped in the remnants of the previous evening's stew, served cold, washed down with ice-cold water… simple, but filling. With the meal concluded, the wizard motioned Bulgan to clear the table, led the way to an adjacent room and indicated chairs. Waiting until the friends were seated, he began:

''Tis little doubt thee have questions a-plenty,' he began, 'yet please be patient, I beg. Your mission is just. Wegglar in truth doth understand. Yet hasten not, for haste breeds danger. Prepare well or risk defeat. Beware hidden, deadly flora; lurking beasts; the skills, the jealousy, rage and passion of Fular; beware all these – and more; disregard caution at your peril.'

Bessimer politely raised his hand. 'Sorry, but I've been aching to ask you something,' he interrupted apologetically. 'May I ask you a very important question?'

'Assuredly,' the wizard replied, not in the least put out. 'What is it?'

'Last night you said "henceforth shall better prepare". Does that mean you intend further help in addition to taking us back to that hill – and if so in what way, exactly?'

'What Wegglar says, Wegglar means. Wilt shortly school and explain…' He broke off; his demeanour inexplicably saddened. Collecting his thoughts, he continued:

'Thou must agree to heed instructions and obey implicitly; little doubt you will. Wegglar hast no sons,' he said, regretfully, 'but if ever thus blessed, would that they be as caring as you.

'No part of imparted wisdom may be revealed to others; no incantation or device loaned or otherwise placed at your disposal. Nor may any be used save for personal protection and the safety of Connie. Confide in her if needs be, but always swear her to secrecy. I shall use my best efforts to protect you and wilt gladly allows Fular to engage – even though bodes danger and mayhap cause irreversible harm. Do you fully understand, O George, and will you faithfully so swear?'

'Of *course* I will,' Bessimer replied, 'I promise.'

'And you, Albert, do you also faithfully so swear?'

'You betcha,' Albert responded, earnestly if scarcely grammatically. 'I promise.'

'Good, then we shall begin.'

The enchanter spread a series of finely detailed drawings on the table. He extracted two – one of a Brerb, the other a Brogtin – and shoved them temporarily to one side. Dealing first with plants, he described each in turn, where they were to be found, why and how they should be avoided and if blundered into, what action to take and probable consequences if ignored. Turning to animals, he described characteristics, habitat; the way in which each represented danger and the most effective avoidance technique. His was a captive but enthralled audience: questions were few and eventually he pronounced himself satisfied. Continuing with a lecture regarding Skandos' extraordinary terrain, he concluded by summarising some of the dangers they might yet unwittingly encounter.

'Dost either have question?' Wegglar asked.

'No,' they chorused as if joined at the hip.

'Good,' he said, 'then there's someone I'd like you to meet.' He placed his hand level with his chest and patted his whiskers with the other. The luxuriant growth quivered; there were signs of movement followed by faint rustling. A moment later, the foliage parted and a pair of beady eyes peered forth – only to promptly withdraw again. Wegglar patted again.

'Come, Plebil,' the sorcerer cajoled, softly, 'be not shy; tis time to meet George and Albert.' He held out his hand, pursed his lips and made sucking sounds when the eyes promptly reappeared. A moment later a tiny head emerged and a feathered creature the size of a bat broke free of the restraining whiskers, hopped on his finger and gazed, first at Bessimer and then at Albert.

'Ch-e-ee-p?' it chirruped, questioningly.

'This is George,' the wizard said, pointing with his chin, 'and this one is Albert.'

'*Gee*-o-rge, *All*-but,' the creature mimicked, in high-pitched, distinctly birdlike tones.

'Corks,' Albert exclaimed, in astonishment, 'he can talk.'

'Not "he",' Wegglar corrected, '"She". Plebil is a "Seetelbird" – and Plebil is a lady.'

'Oh, sorry…'

'No matter, I'm sure she will forgive – *won't* you, my little precious?'

'Pr-r-rp – che-e-p, yes, O Wegglar.'

'Now, George,' the sorcerer said, 'please listen carefully. Plebil is a seeing eye. She is clever, obedient and virtually irreplaceable – there are a scarcely a dozen in the whole of Skandos.

'She will come to you at daybreak; accompany when you travel and remain until your journey ends. Her needs are simple; she requires no food – what we eat would be poison and, in the absence of a comfortable beard, will happily repose in a pocket until summoned. Whenever you have need of her services, tap close to your pocket, offer your finger and she will emerge. Point in the direction you wish to travel and simply say "seek". She will fly and scout for danger – she has remarkable, penetrating vision – and will return to inform you of what lies ahead and how far away.

'Her speech is limited but, as you will discover, she has a unique talent for conveying information.

'Should she advocate avoidance, always take care to act upon her advice. Whenever duty allows, offer your finger and convey her to your pocket. Say "thank you" and she will enter, knowing that she may rest. Plebil will return home to roost each eventide – even in total darkness, returning the following dawning, and must always be free to investigate unbidden. For these reasons keep your pocket permanently unfastened. Do I make myself perfectly clear?'

'Gosh, yes,' Bessimer confirmed, regarding Plebil with admiration. Knowingly, she spread her wings to display raven-black plumage reflecting highlights of gold, green and burnished copper.

'Don't worry, I'll take *very* good care of her, she's a real treasure and absolutely *beautiful*.'

'Indeed she is. Now, hold out your finger.' Bessimer complied, whereupon the Seetelbird chirruped once and hopped aboard. She peered quizzically into his face a full thirty seconds. Once apparently satisfied, she blinked owlishly, ruffled and fluffed her feathers a second time and calmly proceeded to preen.

'There,' the wizard smiled, 'Plebil likes you – just as I knew she would.' He scratched his chin, thoughtfully, and then announced, 'You leave shortly; therefore she may remain with you. Offer your pocket as described.'

Clearing his top pocket of paraphernalia, Bessimer did as he was bid. 'Thank you,' he said, whereupon Plebil 'cheeped' contentedly and disappeared within.

'Will she come and sit on *my* finger, Wegglar?' Albert jealously wondered.

'Mayhap, but tis better not. Too many masters wouldst *surely* confuse.'

The enchanter changed tack. 'As stated, you leave shortly, but first – a little magic.' He grabbed at the air and produced two shiny black rods, each thirty centimetres long with a diameter of ten – by simple sleight of hand? Perhaps, equally, maybe not… in any event, Bessimer and Albert were suitably impressed – but there was more. Handing them one apiece, the enchanter smiled gravely. 'Take these and I shall explain,' he said. Stroking his whiskers, he considered carefully before launching into a fascinating and vitally important lecture:

'The hazards of Skandos are many,' he began, 'though Plebil will assuredly prove effective and allow you to continue in relative safety, the wiles of Fular demands a great deal more.' He paused for emphasis.

'As doubtless aware, were we wizards to discontinue the traditional engagement of apprentices from time to time – not unlike my Master, Zildus – the art of sorcery wouldst inevitably disappear.

'I have come to look upon you both with affection and regard; and were you not committed to the rescue of Connie nothing would give greater pleasure than to offer full enrolment as apprentices. But aspirants to the realms of magic needs guarantee total dedication. Long years of study ensue and the craft cannot be lightly entered into…' He paused for emphasis and to allow his words to strike home: but he need not have worried, by this time two pairs of eyes were fairly popping. Obviously his was a willing captive audience and he therefore resumed:

'However and notwithstanding, there will be occasions when you need assistance over and above that which Wegglar canst readily provide, and for this reason it is my pleasure and privilege to offer my humble services for enlisting you both as *Sorcery Initiates* for the remainder of your stay in Skandos. Study will be minimal; abilities limited; powers infinitesimal. Even so an oath must be sworn. Whilst you may *avoid* Fular by means of magic, you must promise *never* to oppose her and restrict your actions exactly as Wegglar shall instruct.'

Summoning the powers of the universe, he drew himself up with outspread arms.

'Wilt thou both so faithfully declare?'

The pals' response was simultaneous, loud and unequivocal: 'Yes, O Wegglar.'

'Having thus declared, do you swear by Breethan, Zildus and the lives of your unborn children to faithfully uphold and honour magical principles; to employ, not for personal gain, but for the betterment of mankind and to render harm unto no man, save those no better deserves? George?'

'I do so solemnly swear.'

'Albert?'

'I do so solemnly swear.'

Wegglar placed a hand on the shoulder of each. Calling upon the Ancients, the knowledge, wisdom and skills of Breethan, Zildus and the infinite powers of the universe, he solemnly intoned:

'By Breethan, quo Astris, thence Zildus, I say. Pass unto George and to Albert this day,

'The knowledge, humility, the wisdom, the way. Sorcerers bold, in truth I now pray.'

Mystical, mysterious knowledge flowed unseen from his fingertips, penetrating deep into the conscious and subconscious of each of the candidates – even although both seemed entirely unaware. Wegglar smiled.

'Your sincerity does you credit; acceptance into Brotherhood is confirmed. I therefore pronounce you *Sorcery Initiates*. Your careers may be short, but may your lives thereafter be long and happy and forever bear fruit. Congratulations!'

Awed by the solemnity of the occasion, it was no great surprise that neither felt able to respond.

'Art not pleased?' the wizard eventually asked, appealing to each in turn.

'Gosh, yes. Thank you, Wegglar,' Bessimer managed, but with an effort.

Albert blinked, almost overcome but manfully squared his shoulders to earnestly echo: 'Yes, thank you, Wegglar. I feel ever so honoured.' He was quick to add, 'And I promise never knowingly to let you down.'

'Spoken like a true companion and worthy initiate,' the wizard said, obviously touched.

'And you *know* you can rely on me,' chipped in Bessimer, not to be outdone.

'Come,' said Wegglar, briskly. 'Time waiteth for no man. There is much yet to be done.'

There followed one final lecture, surprisingly short. The boys learned precisely what they could or could not do; the use of a wand; three basic incantations and four simple spells. In the event of difficulties beyond magical remit, Wegglar laid down specific courses of action.

'Always remember,' the wizard exhorted, 'magic cometh from the heart. Whereas spells be the mixing bowl, incantations – oft but simple rhymes – are as necessary to magic as breath is to life. Incantations tap the mystical powers of the universe and are handed down, generation upon generation. Such incantations are potent; concentrate mind, heart and soul, and must always be delivered firmly, with sincerity and conviction. The wand, on the other hand is powerless by itself: serving merely as a symbol through which to focus and direct magical aspirations. If needs be a pointed finger canst function equally well. Be confident in your ability, for timidity merits disaster and, as Breethan once famously said: "A doubtful magician is a useless magician, ever assuredly likely to fail".'

A session of concentrated practice began, shakily at first, but as confidence grew, each became increasingly successful. Bessimer 'caught on' fairly quickly with Albert running a close second. But Skandos was a dangerous place; Fular a resourceful and formidable protagonist. Wegglar therefore shrewdly encouraged them to combine forces and work together, when success rates improved dramatically. It was late morning before the wizard finally pronounced he was satisfied.

With renewed confidence, bolstered by the backing of Wegglar and their amazing, newly-acquired credentials, the fledgling wizards gathered their belongings and made ready to depart.

After a swift, nausea-free 'flight' with Wegglar's farewells ringing in their ears, Bessimer and Albert found themselves back on the slopes of the self-same hill, roughly a kilometre short of their target – the Keep of Fular. They made a dash for the top where, panting with exertion, they plonked themselves in the lee of the largest of three rocks for a short breather and to take stock.

'First thing,' said Bessimer, having recovered his breath, 'is to suss the lie of the land. I'll nip the other side of the rocks for a quick gander. You stay here and keep a watchful eye out.'

'OK, but don't be long. We've made it this far and I simply can't *wait* to tackle the rest.'

'You and me both,' Bessimer retorted. 'Won't be a min; shout if you run into trouble.'

CHAPTER 10

Nobbled

Elsewhere, not too far distant, an irate exponent of witchcraft was glaring angrily at her screen.

'*Gimnal*,' she screeched, '*fetch my broom this instant*.' Trembling, the little manikin obeyed. Without thanks or gesture of acknowledgement, she snatched it from his grasp and rushed from the room. Pausing for just long enough to throw a coiled rope across her shoulder, she continued her headlong dash up a winding flight of stairs. In the twinkling of an eye she emerged on the topmost battlement, straddled the bewitched accoutrement and pointed the handle directly ahead.

'*Fiddle-de-faddle, flimble and mill*,' she chanted; '*wilt takes Fular that yonder hill?*' What seemed an inanimate object shuddered to life, handle a- tremble – with anticipation?

With a kick of her heels, she shot into the air and hurtled towards her target...

The view had Bessimer gasping. Less than a kilometre across a sparsely-wooded valley at the foot of a lofty mountain stood an impressive, orange-coloured edifice – the Keep of Fular?

'Eureka! Alby,' he shouted, fairly hopping with excitement, 'come and look. I reckon we've found it. That'll be Bortzin Mountain and the building at the bottom Fular's Keep – it *has* to be.'

'Brill,' Albert bellowed back. 'Don't go away; I'll be right with you.'

'There, what did I tell you?' Bessimer chortled, seconds later. 'Look out, Connie, here we come!' He was treated to a massive clap on the shoulder by way of an answer.

Barely visible against a purple sky, a small black dot appeared, rapidly growing larger.

'Hang on a sec,' Albert said, shading his eyes. 'What the heck is *that*?' He pointed.

Bessimer also screened his eyes and focused. What he saw practically stood his hair on end.

'Oh, my giddy aunt, that's all we need!' he moaned. 'A penny gets you a fiver it's Fular.'

Albert's dismay was apparent. 'What?' he blurted. 'Oh, I suppose it must be. How come she knew we were here? Did some kind soul tip her off? But who the heck would pull a trick like that?'

'Never mind the gab,' Bessimer snorted, impatiently. 'Quick, before she sees us!' Suiting action to words, he spun, grabbed Albert's sleeve and practically dragged him the other side of the rocks.

'I doubt she'll have spotted us,' he wheezed, 'too far away. Come on, let's get out of here.'

'How the blazes do we do that?'

'Wegglar's transportation spell, what else?'

'Oh, right, nearly forgot.'

Bessimer cast about. Espying a nearby hillock with a scattering of trees, he withdrew his wand, gripped it firmly and pointed. 'Over there,' he declared, 'that cluster of trees. You can do the honours and *don't* forget to concentrate.' Linking arms to ensure they didn't separate and with eyes fixed firmly on the target, the boys united in magic. Following Wegglar's formulae to the best of his recollection, Albert timidly chanted:

'*Ever bold and have no fear, fain by Breethan takes us there.*' A moment passed but nothing happened. He started again. '*Be bol–*'

'Hold it,' Bessimer gritted – almost dropping his wand. 'For one thing you were chanting in a monotone, and for another you weren't fully concentrating. Go again – and this time as though you mean it.' Without raising his voice, he pleaded: 'Hurry up, Alby, for Pete's sake. If the witch spots us, pound to a pinch she'll nobble us.'

'OK, keep your wool on.' Albert took a deep breath and began again.

'*Ever bold and have no fear, fain by Breethan takes us there…*'

The scenery blurred; in an instant they lifted off and shot into the air.

'Whoopee!' shrieked Albert, delightedly, 'I've done it, it works; we're actually *flying*!'

Feather light, whirling motion; a slight 'bump' – and they were down.

Bessimer commenced scanning for trouble. Not a moment too soon.

High in the sky the silhouette of a woman straddling a broomstick hove into view. Her tall, broad-brimmed hat and flowing robes were a dead give-away. It was the witch – it had to be. As they watched, fascinated, the figure swooped, slowed, rounded the recently-vacated tor and began to circle, obviously searching.

'Quick, into the trees,' Bessimer gasped. 'Hurry up, before she sees us.' As one, they made a dash for cover. Cautiously, they peered from safety; ready – and able, if need be, to move again. The transportation proved successful, so too their ploy to evade the witch – or so it seemed.

Fular continued to circle, ever tighter; each time lower, growing angrier with every revolution.

'Drat and thrice drat,' she snarled. 'Gimnal didst swear they be here. Where they a-hiding? Cursed art Wegglar, thou meddling fool,' she spat.

Eventually, after further fruitless orbits her patience ran out. With a scream of rage, she yanked hard on the broomstick and rocketed skywards. Accelerating furiously she soared, up over the hill and disappeared. Several leagues away, the principal source of her current irritation smiled with evident satisfaction.

'Mayhap *one* day, foolish woman,' he growled, 'thou wilt sit thee down and confer.'

Back at her Keep, talking was the last thing on Fular's mind. She was incandescent; seething with frustrated fury, spitting, snarling and shaking her broomstick like a woman possessed. Bad-temperedly she summoned Gimnal and as was his wont, the hominoid dutifully materialised.

'Yes, O Mistress,' he grovelled, perceiving her wrath, 'dost Fular wish further Weem?'

'No, thou foul, ignoble poltroon,' she screeched, beside herself with anger. 'Fular dost *not*. Wait till told; anticipate not.'

With that she swung the broomstick and let fly. Gimnal attempted to duck but wasn't quite quick enough: the handle caught him squarely across his head. His squawk of pain seemed to infuriate Fular the more. She pounced, retrieved the broom and whacked him and whacked him until he begged for mercy and not until then and only reluctantly, did she finally stop.

'Thou worthless moron,' she berated, 'did thee dare inform me wrong? Mine enemies *not* be at yonder hill and can'st tells not where? Art thou incapable? Can'st Fular no longer rely – or did'st confuse and misdirect a- purpose?'

For all his misery, Gimnal plucked up sufficient courage to vigorously shake his head.

'No, mistress,' he quavered, 'did'st answers faithful and true. Dzorj be there and Allbut too. Perchance Wegglar didst warn of thy coming? If thus be so assuredly tis no fault of Gimnal.'

'Fiddle-de-faddle,' she retorted. 'Wegglar dare not, for fear his powers doth fail. Yon hillock be within Fular's domain, wherein dost hold magical sway; omnipotent and wilts ever thus remain.

'Go. Weem and seek anew. Activate yon wall, find, mark and observe. Weem till dawn if needs be. Cease not afore success else Fular wilt punish severe.' For good measure, she cuffed his head again. He almost fell but managed to right himself. Snivelling in abject misery, he scuttled to the nearest corner, spun once – and disappeared!

The witch's displeasure knew no bounds: she shouted him to return – to no avail. Again she called with no result. She wheedled, cajoled, pleaded and threatened – but still nothing. Maybe the little fellow had suffered punishment enough?… Still cursing, Fular abandoned trying – at least for the moment. Still angry, she decided to deal with him later when he came crawling back to beg forgiveness – as she knew he inevitably would…

'Looks as if she's gone,' Albert observed, after several uneventful minutes slipped past.

'Could be,' replied Bessimer, cautiously, 'but what if the crafty old bat's trying to trick us?' Albert pursed his lips. 'I suppose… Give it another five, d'you reckon?'

'Yeah, better be safe than sorry. If there's still no sign, we'll go grab ourselves another shuftie.' Erring on the side of caution, they waited a full ten minutes.

'Time's up,' Bessimer decided. 'We'll go back to where Wegglar dropped us – and this time, mister, *I'll* do the incantation. Cop hold of my arm.'

Confidently pointing to the selected target, Bessimer boldly intoned and this time the spell performed flawlessly. They were back at the hill in a flash and for a third time they scrambled and scrabbled their way to the top.

'That went well,' Bessimer remarked, mildly, 'all it needed was a bit of practice.'

'Go on, rub it in,' Albert retorted, a trifle testily, 'we got there in the end, didn't we?'

'Sure we did… I was only saying… I didn't mean. Oh heck, I wasn't having a go – honestly.'

Albert seemed sceptical. 'Yeah, right,' he snorted. 'I believe you – but thousands wouldn't.'

'Don't be touchy, be grateful. Transportation is brill. If we stay alert – and we certainly will – the witch will have her work cut out to stop us. We'll be rat-tat-tatting her door before she knows it.'

He dropped to his knees, inched his way to the far side of the rock and waited. When Albert failed to appear he crawled back. 'Come on, Alby,' he urged, 'let's get started. Crouch down and follow me. We've still to suss the lie of the land.'

Albert reluctantly followed, even though something seemed to be troubling him. But when gazing across the valley for a second time, he put doubt to one side and singled out Fular's domain. 'Do you reckon we could make it in one hop?'

'Not a snowflake's chance in the Sahara. Don't you remember what Wegglar said? "Use to avoid, never oppose".'

'Course I do,' Albert protested, 'but transportation isn't *opposition*, surely?'

'Yes, it jolly-well is. Just cast your mind back. We're well inside her boundary – that's why I stopped halfway up the hill. It's shanks' pony from here on in, my boy. We can duck and dive as much as we like, but never *ever* use magic to gain a single step forward.'

'Oh, yeah… I didn't think.' Albert was, understandably, somewhat piqued but crestfallen.

'No matter, we work together. The witch is powerful, don't forget. Suppose we were naïve enough to challenge her magic – and she twigged…?' He paused, dramatically. 'She might even neutralise our spell in mid-air. Alby, I shudder to think! We know she's bitter and twisted, we've had a taste. Then again what if she took it out on Connie? The poor girl's probably having it rough enough already. One false move could make it twenty times worse. Frankly, I'd rather not risk it.'

'OK, 'nuff said,' Albert guiltily replied.

'I vote a spot of lunch,' Bessimer suggested, changing the subject, 'and then get cracking.'

'OK,' Albert agreed. 'We can suss a route and settle on a course of action as we eat.' Without waiting, he returned to the rock, shrugged out of his haversack and sat down. Wordlessly, Bessimer followed suit.

Viewed from their vantage point, Fular's Keep appeared tantalisingly close. Strain as they might, however, establishing anything of real consequence proved frustratingly difficult. That the place was tucked tightly against a perpendicular cliff was blindingly obvious, approach from the rear a non-starter. Furthermore it was well protected on either side. It was just possible to make out a feature resembling a drawbridge; did that mean there was a moat full of water? It was difficult to say. Roughly triangular, three substantial stands of endemic scarlet forest formed a significant barrier between hill and Keep, augmented by a scattering of individual trees and shrubbery. Final approaches were totally bereft of cover – save for a carpet of the ubiquitous brown verdure.

'What wouldn't I give for a decent pair of binos,' Bessimer grumbled, halfway through his second packet of crisps.

'Yeah, me too,' Albert replied, screwing his face in a scowl. 'So much for sorting a plan of campaign. My eyes are watering that much, me choccy bar's gone soggy. I reckon the best thing to do is to concentrate solely on getting within striking distance. What say?'

'Yup, couldn't agree more. There's a fair bit of cover for most of the way. We keep low; zigzag from tree to tree – and anything else that presents itself as cover. Once within striking distance, we'll simply keep out of sight while we fathom the next move. OK by you?'

'You betcha, it's a deal.'

Squinting at the sky, Bessimer glanced at his watch; tapped it – and then remembered.

'Blow it,' he exclaimed, 'still not working properly. How long before dark, d'you reckon?'

Albert pursed his lips: 'Dunno, an hour or so, maybe two. Why?'

'We must be under cover by nightfall, that's why. For one thing Plebil goes off to roost, and for another I don't much fancy spending a night in the open, nor, I suspect,' he added, 'do you.'

'Too right I don't.' Albert grimaced. Calculating distances, he eyed the nearest stand of forest.

'Four or five hundred metres, I'd say, half-an-hour, maybe – three- quarters at most.'

Bessimer climbed to his feet and shrugged into his haversack.

'Right, looks safe enough, but we'd better check first,' he said, and tapped beside his pocket. A faint 'cheep', a rustle and Plebil dutifully emerged. She hopped aboard the proffered finger, stretched her wings, riffled her feathers and cocked her head to one side, looking intently into his face. Bessimer pointed towards the nearest trees. 'Seek,' he told her, gently.

The little bird obligingly spread her wings, flapped briefly – and was gone…

'She can barely speak so how do you expect the poor wee thing to report?' Albert wondered.

'Hopefully, we'll know the answer to that one shortly,' Bessimer returned. 'Come on, stir yourself. I doubt she'll be gone long and we might just as well be ready.'

Albert duly complied. He was fiddling aimlessly with a loose strap when the Seetelbird reappeared, slowed and circled. Bessimer offered his finger and Plebil immediately swooped and landed. Unhesitatingly, she transferred to his wrist, scampered the length of his arm, on to his shoulder and thence his collar, snuggled his neck briefly before placing her head to his. Albert watched in silence, awash with curiosity.

Bessimer remained still and simply waited. He didn't need to wait long. Seconds later Plebil left his neck and scampered back to his finger. Wearing a broad grin, he hoisted his arm and brought the little bird back level with his face.

'*You little beauty*!' he exclaimed, admiringly, 'that was absolutely *brilliant*. Thank you.'

'Dzorj,' she chirruped, contentedly. 'Dzorj love Plebil; Plebil love Dzorj.'

'What the heck are *you* grinning at?' Albert demanded. 'Did she whisper something? If so I didn't catch a smidgen. Come on, what's the drill? What the spiff's going on?'

Bessimer smiled and returned the Seetelbird to her resting place.

'Come on, you steaming, hard-faced ninja,' Albert snorted, 'out with it.'

'Image transfer, mind to mind,' Bessimer told him, still grinning. 'Can't think of a better way to describe it. Just like going to the pictures;

clear as a bell. Plebil relayed everything she saw out there. But for diving in and out of trees, I might have been flying in a helicopter.

'It's a good job we checked,' he added, ruefully, 'or we'd have blundered into a Brogtin. The trees to the right seem clear though. It's a good deal further but, hopefully, a darn-sight safer.

'But never mind the "how's, why's and wherefore's",' he went on, 'this isn't the place to loiter, it's far too exposed. High time we made a move. Fular could be watching and she's got Gimnal to do her bidding, don't forget. I vote we get cracking to lessen the chances of being spotted.'

'You betcher,' Albert agreed, and off they went, Bessimer taking the lead.

The first hundred or so metres downhill was one thing, progress through the indigenous brown verdure quite another. A mass of intertwined stems and twisting roots, most ankle-deep, the stuff reached almost to the knees with every dip in the ground. After a painful series of stumbles, they adopted a muscle-cracking form of high-step in order to remain upright. It was painful, tiring and frustratingly slow but, doggedly, the pals persisted.

Back at Fular's Keep, meanwhile, Gimnal had finally returned to face the wrath of his mistress. Brushing his apologies to one side and ignoring his desperate plea for clemency, Fular let rip.

'By Breethan shall Wegglar be held to account. They pair be close and threaten mine domain. Fular's bones doth tell and bones ne'er fail. Seek out and find this very instant,' she ordered, 'else wilt curse and consign thy carcase to rot in the dungeon from this day onward and forevermore.'

Gimnal blanched. For a freedom-loving grobbelin, the threat was far too terrible to contemplate. He quivered, shook his head, and began nervously backing away. Fular rounded on him, furiously.

'Stand still, thou doltish cockroach,' she screamed. 'Do as I say, or wilt flay thee alive.'

'Y-yes, Mistress,' the terrified manikin quavered, 'assuredly Gimnal shalt Weem.' Shakily, he managed to raise one leg and began to spin. The wall immediately changed colour, blurred and moving images quickly resolved; pictorial revelations that infuriated Fular the more.

'Drat, they wretched scallywags,' she screeched, practically apoplectic, 'I *knew* they be here…'

After thirty metres or so, espying movement some little way ahead, Bessimer stopped.

'What's up?' Albert whispered.

'Sh-s-sh, dunno. Keep quiet while I check.'

When several dog-sized herbivores hove into view, he heaved a sigh of relief.

'It's OK, it's only a bunch of "bunnies" – they're moving away already.'

'Thank goodness for that,' Albert wheezed. 'Can we please stop for a blow?'

'I suppose so – till they're out of sight. It'll be dark soon so we've little time to loiter.'

'Oh, gee, thanks,' Albert cheekily replied, and flopped gratefully to the ground.

'Come on, look lively,' Bessimer grinned, two or three minutes later, 'they've gone.'

Aroused from torpor, a thick-bodied reptilian with fearsome jaws came alert and sidled stealthily through the undergrowth, testing and tasting the air as it went. Nearing the forest margins and sensing potential prey, it came to a halt and waited, poised in readiness to strike.

The boys gained second wind, continuing to advance and making steady progress until within fifty metres or so of open ground. Inexplicably, Bessimer stopped again.

'What now?' Albert wanted to know.

'Precaution,' Bessimer told him. He tapped his pocket and pointed to the forest. 'Seek.' Unhesitatingly, the obedient little bird took wing and disappeared among the trees. Less than thirty seconds later she returned, nuzzled his neck and transferred her most recent images.

'Come on, Alby,' said Bessimer, grimly, with the Seetelbird safely back in his pocket. 'Plebil spotted a whopping great alligator-thing lurking inside the trees,' he reported. 'What's more, it knows we're here and probably fancies us for supper. Not perishing likely, mate. I vote we take her advice and give this chunk of woodlands a wide berth and head for the final stretch instead.'

Skirting the perimeter, they again set off, blissfully unaware the serpentine menace had already left the trees and was remorselessly and relentlessly dogging their each and every step.

It took a further half an hour to reach the third and final stand where Bessimer again dispatched Plebil to check and report. This time she gave the all clear and they made directly for cover, albeit a good deal later than Albert had earlier estimated.

Metres short of the tree-line, Plebil stirred. Unprompted, she re-emerged, deftly transferred to Bessimer's shoulder, nuzzled his neck briefly and silently flew away.

'Did you see that?' Bessimer exclaimed.

'See what?'

'Plebil upped and left's left; must be nearly night time. Quick, we'd better make a dash for it.' They covered the final metres at a run

– and barely made it. Just as they reached the trees, a distant flash and warning rumble sounded the knell of night, instantly plunging the forest into darkness.

'Better be careful, mustn't get separated,' said Albert, nervously grabbing Bessimer's arm.

'Yeah, stick close, why don'cher,' Bessimer frostily returned – but immediately relented.

'You're right, though. Keep hold; move when I do,' he directed. 'Reach out; feel for a tree.'

'OK,' his companion said, 'I've found one… ouch, blow it; stubbed my blinking toe.'

'Be more careful, then – and watch out for thorns,' was Bessimer's unsympathetic reply. Fumbling awkwardly, the weary pair unhitched haversacks and settled as comfortably as cold, unyielding ground would allow.

'I'm starving,' Albert complained. 'What wouldn't I give for some nice hot rabbit stew?'

'How about settling for a choccy bar – and half a can of coke,' Bessimer suggested, drily.

'You might fancy rubbish, but I don't,' Albert retorted, 'and why so frugal, all of a sudden?'

'We're low on crisps, down on choccy and almost out of lemonade, *that's* why. If we don't go easy there'll be nothing left for Connie. We did agree to save her some, remember.'

Albert muttered, but subsided.

'I'll take first watch, Alby,' Bessimer decided, 'while you get your head down.'

'What about a cloak of invisibility?' Albert countered, nervously. 'Before long there'll be animals on the prowl and *any* form of protection would surely be better than nothing.'

'Worse than useless in the dark,' Bessimer rejoined, sarcastically. 'Besides, pulling any sort of magic this close to Fular would most probably warn her of our presence.'

'I don't see why it should – as long as we don't oppose or in some way offer her a threat. In any case, she doesn't even know we're initiates.'

'Maybe not – and let's keep it that way. Pester as much as you like; the answer's still "no".'

Back at the castle, Plebil arrived to roost but before retiring, she reported to Wegglar. What she imparted had him frowning with concern. Tentatively, he reached out to Fular but her defences were far too powerful to penetrate. Night-time or no, witch's inviolate territory notwithstanding, his concern for the boys' safety far outweighed all other considerations. Scarcely giving the soured and selfish woman another thought, he summoned Bulgan.

'Hearken unto Wegglar, who needs thy special talents,' he began. 'Plebil dost reveal George and Albert art trapped midst trees nigh Bortzin; at risk beasts of the night; stalked by Zigron; perchance the wrath of Fular, who wishes Connie for her companion, regardless of consequence.

'Pray Weem right speedily, silent and unseen. Find, succour and assist – but return in an instant should'st either Zigron fangs or Fular's wrath give cause for imminent alarm. Wilt so do?'

'Yes, Master, at once.'

The loyal hominoid spun and disappeared... only to re-reappear almost instantaneously.

'Tis as feared, O Wegglar,' the manikin reported, agitated. 'Dzorj and Allbut art in mortal peril, yet canst not aid. Yon Zigron be monstrous; close to the trees making ready to strike.'

'Work thy magic and take us thence,' the wizard ordered, 'quickly, afore both are lost.'

'But wait,' Bulgan protested. 'Thou must first prepare… and dost not fear Fular, mayhap art also aware? My cousin, Gimnal, art also in Weem and doth observe from close nearby.'

'No matter,' Wegglar replied. 'No time for prepare. George and Albert art key to the future and canst never fall prey to Zigron, Brogtin or Brerb – nor suffer the wiles of Fular. For thus tis written; so too that Destiny shalt ever prevail.'

The humanoid's saucer-like eyes widened; 'eyebrows' uplifted in surprise.

The urgency in Wegglar's voice was unmistakable; Bulgan's reaction was immediate.

'If be so, then grasp my arm. Close thine eyes; remain still my count of three…'

The whispers, grunts, groans and whistles of the night ceased and, equally suddenly, every single atom of air became positively charged, the atmosphere electric. The hairs at the back of Bessimer's neck bristled. Sensing danger, he grabbed his haversack and scrambled to his feet. His movements alerted Albert.

'What's the matter? What are you doing?'

'Something's up.'

'Like what?'

'Haven't you noticed? Everything suddenly went quiet.'

'So it has, but what about it? What's going on? What does it mean?'

'Don't know, but something's up, you can bet your shirt on it. Grab your gear, quick. We'd better be ready to make a run for it.'

Albert felt for his haversack but stopped short.

'How the heck can we run anywhere? he snorted, derisively. 'It's practically pitch dark.'

'Not sure, but give me a moment. I'll try to think of someth——' He broke off, interrupted by sounds of movement somewhere close at hand. A dreadful whiff assailed his nostrils, vaguely reminiscent of the foetid breath of the Brerb.

'Watch out, Alby, something's after us,' he exclaimed, justifiably alarmed.

Deafeningly close, a blood-curdling scream of triumph rattled their ears. Not daring to move in the dark, the pals were completely at the mercy of whatever it was that threatened. Masked by night, the Zigron gathered its huge, sinuous body in readiness for the final charge.

'What the heck now?' Bessimer managed to gasp. 'Another rotten monster of some sort?'

'Dunno,' Albert muttered, uneasily, 'but it's a darn sight too close for comfort.'

'Too right – but shhhh, hang on a minute,' Bessimer replied, cocking his head.

At first barely discernible, they heard a rustle of leaves and the distinctive swishing of branches.

Disturbed and perplexed, the Zigron stopped dead in its tracks.

The sound intensified. An ethereal light gleamed from somewhere above the canopy and the darkness retreated, throwing the unworldly trees into sharp relief. Branches parted as if in deference, granting clear passageway to the skies above.

Her moment had come. The light cocoon flared, shrank and swooped through the canopy to alight directly in front of the striplings. Mouths agape, the boys watched helplessly as the manifestation resolved into the light-enshrouded shape of Fular, who immediately began to chant:

'*Move ye not, speak ye not, for here be Fular the omnipotent,*' she intoned.

Bessimer and Albert were instantly rendered immobile, incapable of neither thought nor movement, unable even to blink – much less make a bid to escape. Behind them, the ravenous Zigron roared yet again and prepared to charge. Gesticulating – almost casually, the witch waved her wand and again began to chant:

'Ziggedy, wiggedy, ye shall not feast, be gone I say, thou slavering beast.'

Equally casually, she waved her wand a second time and continued:

'Away we go, from jungle bold, back to mine fold, in truth be told.'

Amplified by night, the halo enlarged and blazoned into incandescent brilliance, forming an all-encompassing, impenetrable shield of light around the witch, the two boys and all their possessions.

Temporarily blinded, the monster crouched and screeched with anguish when, with an ear-splitting 'ker – boom', Fular, Bessimer and Albert were whisked away, with the clearing instantly reclaiming its former Stygian blackness. Shaking a dragon-like head, the baffled Zigron roared in frustration and slithered into the undergrowth, thoughts of supper abandoned; and in the jungle, normal night-time noises resumed…

Elsewhere and at the last possible moment, Bulgan aborted the rescue mission. He turned to the wizard, wringing his hands with dismay. 'O, Master,' he wailed, ''tis too late I fear. Fular didst arrive. She, Dzorj and Allbut be gone.'

Just for moment Wegglar seemed almost relieved.

'Fular most certainly hast rescued them,' he said. But as reality dawned, he changed his mind.

'Perchance hast escaped the Zigron, but might, nevertheless remain in danger. We must therefore follow – quickly now.' The hominoid expressed alarm.

'But what of Fular?' he protested. 'Is it not thou *dares* not follows?'

Wegglar hesitated, tugging his beard. Bulgan was right, of course; the witch's domain must remain inviolate, yet he was desperately anxious to protect his protégés. Eventually, however, logic and magical law prevailed and he was reluctantly obliged to concede:

'Magical code doeth indeed forbid intrusion upon another of the Arts, unbidden. Pray Weem alone whilst I remain. Go now, right speedily. Seek out George and Albert and return 'ere long – and woe betides Fular should harms befall either,' he added, darkly.

The manikin nodded dutifully, spun wordlessly to the ground and disappeared. Wegglar waited, fingers tapping anxiously. Five slow painful minutes ticked by before Bulgan finally put in an appearance but – and to Wegglar's dismay – the grobbelin was alone and unaccompanied.

'What news?' the wizard exclaimed. 'Did'st not manages to find George and Albert? Art they safe, unharmed?' The wizard's customary calm assurance abandoned, his agitation was plain to see; his beard positively bristled with anxiety.

Bulgan shook his enormous head. Orange tears welled; he seemed unusually incapable of speech. Wegglar became even more agitated.

'Come, Bulgan,' he demanded, peremptorily. 'Canst not inform what didst discover?'

'Woe unto me, oh Master,' the hominoid snivelled. 'Such powerful defence hast Fular, no Weem wilt ever penetrates nor Bulgan breach. Nor wilt my cousin disclose, so tis likely they be removed from danger, but canst not be sure.' Irrationally, he seemed perilously close to tears.

'Bulgan doth pray forgive,' he added nervously, even though personally blameless.

Touched by his distress, Wegglar realised he had gone too far and couldn't help but relent. Leaning forward, he reached out and patted his servant gently on the shoulder.

'There, there,' he soothed. 'Wegglar does not doubt nor doth Fular's power give shame to your loyalty. Memory serves that George and Albert art enabled mind-touch in dire peril but as yet hast not, therefore harms not to wait. Wegglar shalt approach Fular on the morrow and mayhap she wilt relents. Go now to rest,' he added, kindly. 'Wegglar also shalt retire for sleep.'

CHAPTER 11

Captive on the roof

Helplessly ensnared and snatched from the jungle, the friends were cocooned in impenetrable darkness, nauseously hurtling through the air; unable to determine whence they were going and for what purpose. Conversation was impossible, yet each remained aware of the proximity of the other; taking comfort from the knowledge. The journey was brief, however. After a short, uncomfortable period of time, movement ceased when they were deposited on a hard, flat, debris-free surface – no rocks, pebbles, twigs or the like, both instinctively felt about to be sure – with no idea of where they were or what next they should do – assuming they had a choice, that is.

Jungle noises were gone; the night hushed and serene. Strain as they might, there was nothing to be heard except the distant, barely-audible sound of running water.

Bessimer was first to recover his wits – as usual. Fumbling in the dark he located Albert and shoved a tentative forefinger in his ribs. The probing ministration, even if unwelcome, was instrumental in producing the desired effect. Albert groaned and protested, ruefully.

'Ouch,' he grumbled, 'do you mind? I ache all over, already.'

'Sorry,' Bessimer apologised, 'but at least we're safe and sound and still in one piece.'

'That's as maybe, but this isn't normal ground, so what is it and where the heck are we?'

'Give you one guess.'

'Um… somewhere near the witch's Keep. Right on top of it, maybe?'

'Reckon so.'

'And if we're not?'

'We'll cross that bridge when we come to it. There's nothing we can do tonight in any case so let's grab some shut-eye and resume searching for Connie in the morning – unless you've a better idea?'

'Course not,' Albert retorted, 'it's all that matters and the only reason for coming, isn't it?'

'Too right it is, but listen. There's more to this than meets the eye. Fular certainly saved our bacon back there – but why? OK, supposing we are sitting on top of her pad, why risk bringing us here? She knows we mean to rescue Connie. Why make finding her that much easier?'

'You tell me.' Albert shrugged into the darkness:

'Maybe she means to expel us from Skandos again, who knows? But I somehow rather doubt it. Let's face it, if getting permanently rid of us was within her power, she'd have been shot of us ages ago.'

'Could be she saved us purely to spite Wegglar? They don't exactly see eye to eye.'

'Maybe so, but it doesn't explain why she snatched us from the jaws of that monster, either. She's up to something, but what?' Albert took his time before grunting:

'*Your* guess is as good as mine.' Yawning, he retrieved his haversack and lay down.

'Cor, Penny Plinkers!' he muttered. 'The rotten surface is that hard I'll *never* sleep.'

'Dare say you'll manage,' Bessimer retorted, gaining a muffled grunt by way of reply.

He settled down himself, but before attempting sleep there was something he needed to try. Masked by night he screwed his eyes and tried to concentrate – sadly, to no avail. Gritting his teeth he tried again – yet more failure. Close to exhaustion after a long and stressful day, he was on the point of giving up but took a deep breath and decided on one last try. Gathering his last remaining strength, he again cast forth his mind exactly as schooled by Wegglar… and ten productive minutes later, smiling with satisfaction, Bessimer bade his sweetheart goodnight. Hard, uncomfortable surface or no, he was out to the wide in minutes.

CHAPTER 12

If at first...

Connie stirred in her sleep, sighed turned over and lay still. By and by a figure appeared, hazy at first but becoming clearer. At first she thought it was Albert and she sighed again. As if reading her thoughts, another figure joined the first and this time she smiled with pleasure and held out her arms... *Bessimer!*

She dreamt on; a stroll along the canal, hand in hand; a long, lingering kiss; a gentle caress. She slept a while longer, willing the experience to continue, but the moment passed. With it, the vision swiftly faded and so did her euphoria. A tear escaped her eye and trickled down her cheek. Still dreaming, she sobbed quietly but nevertheless slumbered on.

Out of the darkness from somewhere close at hand, a voice called, urgently: *'Connie! Connie!'* It seemed so real she awoke with a start and sat bolt upright, heart thumping mightily. With the dream still vividly fresh in her mind, she couldn't help but wonder... *Bessimer?*

By now fully awake, she got to her feet, peered uselessly into the gloom and felt about with her foot: sleeping furs, cold, hard floor. Clearly she was still in her cell-cum-bedroom and her heart sank on the realisation she had merely been dreaming... *Drat!*

Why then had she awakened? What if somebody really had called? Or had she simply imagined it? Then again, it could have been Fular, playing mind games... but then again, maybe not. She heard no sound nor could she detect the slightest suggestion of movement, yet felt buoyed by a curious sense of elation. Standing motionless, head cocked she listened again, only to confirm nothing whatever was to be heard, strain as she might. Disappointed and feeling a trifle foolish, she sank back down, hugged her knees to her chin, and tried to think rationally.

But then the voice came again: *'Connie, Connie,'* intense, loud, penetrating, causing Connie to jump. 'Who are you?' she gasped. 'Where are you? What do you want?' For a moment there was silence and then the voice again:

'Connie, Connie, concentrate. It's me; I'm calling with my mind. Can you hear me?'

Despite her astonishment, she recovered her wits and falteringly replied, 'Ye——es, who is it? Not Bessimer, I'd recognise his voice, and you're not in my room. So what are you, who are you and what on earth do you want?'

'It is me, Bessimer, sweetheart. I heard you that time so don't speak just listen and answer with your mind. To make this work properly you really do have to concentrate, although it does get easier with practice. Now, can you understand what I'm saying?'

Swiftly catching on, Connie kept her mouth shut tight and deliberately *thought* her reply.

'Yes, yes, yes, I can. Oh, Bessimer. Is that *really* you?'

And this time, amazingly, Bessimer picked up her response.

'It sure is. Now listen, Albert and I are holed up nearby – not sure exactly where – he's having a kip, by the way. We made it to the forest near Fular's Keep when night fell but the old bat upped and grabbed us – and in case you're wondering,' he added, with a meaningful chuckle, 'you're not dreaming and it isn't imagination, just a neat trick I learned recently. Tell you about it later, OK?'

'Oh, Bessimer, I just *knew* you'd come to the rescue. It's fantastic to hear you, even though your voice echoes and sounds ever so different. I've been really, really lonely and miss you terribly.'

'Me too, but don't worry, we'll soon be back home and together again,' he promised.

'I certainly hope so,' she thought back, and added, 'Goodness, I'm not dreaming. It's true; you really, really can hear me?'

'Sure can, sweet lips,' he chortled, 'but are you sure you're *really* OK?'

'I'm fine, thanks – and a jolly-sight better for knowing that you're around.'

'Brill, glad to hear it. You catch on quickly; jolly well done. But always remember, thought exchange doesn't work very well if you speak – apart from the risk of being overheard.'

'Don't worry, I'll remember,' she assured him. 'Gosh, this really is *fantastic.*'

'Thought it might come handy,' he said, matter-of-factly. 'Anyway,' he resumed, 'now that contact has firmly been established let's get down to business. First of all, where exactly are you?'

Striving to ignore dozens of questions which sprang to mind, Connie managed to contain her curiosity and responded intelligently with scarcely a moment's hesitation.

'I'm in Fular's Keep, locked in a room on the first floor,' she told him. 'It's down a long corridor, somewhere near the back of the place I think, it's difficult to be sure.'

'That'll do for now, gives us an idea where to make for once we get to you. Can't do a thing until daylight, though,' he declared 'so get some sleep while you can… and please, *please* don't try to contact me in case you're rumbled. Walls really do have ears, you know. Keep schtum, sweetheart, and I'll call you again tomorrow, OK?'

'Promise?'

'I promise.'

'OK, then,' she replied, happily,

'Night night.' 'Night night, honey-bun,' he returned, 'sleep tight.'

Connie snuggled back midst her furs, agog with excitement. So much so that sleep proved stubbornly elusive although she did, eventually, manage to drift into sound, contented slumber…

Unannounced, as usual, Skandovian dawn arrived with a bang. Not quite with its usual brilliance, perhaps the reason Bessimer was slow to awaken, yet still first to open his eyes. Blinking dazedly yet full of curiosity, he took a long hard, infinitely cautious look around.

Taking in something of the immediate, unprepossessing surroundings, memory came flooding back, and with it a stark reminder of the need for an urgent plan of action, for which Albert's full cooperation would be required. Soft snores and even breathing a metre or so away indicated his notoriously hard-to-awaken friend still slept; he therefore unceremoniously treated him to a none-too-gentle dig in the ribs. One good poke was sufficient; snores abruptly ceased.

Guessing the source of the offender and not bothering to open his eyes, Albert grumbled.

'Pack it in and let me be, George,' he groaned. 'Go find some other poor soul to pester.'

Not in the least contrite, Bessimer got to his feet and nudged the recumbent figure with his foot.

'Wake up, you grumpy little moaner,' he snorted, 'and shake a leg. In case you've forgotten, we were grabbed by Fular last night and we're in deep, deep trouble. Take a look; you'll see what I mean.'

Grudgingly, Albert climbed to his feet and for the first time, he too took a good hard look at their surroundings: a totally enclosed, limestone area some twenty metres by ten, backing onto sheer cliff enclosed by lofty sandstone walls on three sides – the nearest presumably the rear of Fular's castle. Having no obvious means of egress it formed an almost perfect prison – except for birds and other winged beasties, of course – or maybe a couple of trainee wizards, perhaps?… Hm!

Close to an outer wall, a bath-sized stone cistern equipped with a simple sluice straddled a shallow drainage channel running the full width of the enclosure, connecting with narrow slots chiselled through solid stone at either end. *Crikey, now that really is clever,* he mused.

'Unusual sort of set-up,' Albert aimlessly ventured. 'Wonder what it's intended for? Could be a thirties-style wash-area – or even an animal pen, I suppose. That cistern thing is obviously meant for water, so it could be some kind of horse-trough, though I know of no equine capable of flight – other than Pegasus, of course, but he's simply a myth. Why do you suppose the old bat had it built?'

'Give you just one tidgy guess,' Bessimer told him, dryly. 'Fular's bathtub, do you suppose? I'd be surprised if it was meant for anything else. Should your mythical Pegasus be in need of an imaginary drink, I doubt he'd much relish dirty bathwater – hers or anyone else's, for that matter,' he grinned. 'There's no apparent means of access either,' he went on. 'No doorway, hatch, stairs or whatever, so how mere mortals are expected to manage, I really don't know.'

Without a moment's hesitation Albert pointed to the towering ramparts and blurted:

'No problem. Transport ourselves up there, pick a destination and make a run for it?' he suggested, almost casually.

Bessimer reacted as though stung.

'What a stupid thing to say. What about our mission to rescue Connie? Having finally made it this far, why the heck would we scarper? In any case,' he hissed, 'it'd blow our cover. Fular would rumble us in an instant if we were to use the slightest hint of magic right under her very nose. For goodness sake, Alby, have you forgotten your training already?'

The reprimand was richly deserved: Albert was man enough to admit it.

'Sorry.' He flushed. 'I'll watch it in future. To put it another way: where do we go from here?'

'How about keeping quiet and waiting to see what fate has to offer?'

Albert scarcely nodded before a shadowy figure appeared as if from nowhere, resolving into the unmistakable form of Fular. She seemed extremely angry.

'Gimnal, mine Grobbelin, doth name thee Dzorj and Allbut. Which art Dzorj?' she demanded.

Wary of provoking the angry woman further, Bessimer hoisted his hand.

'It's *George*, actually, Ma'am,' he murmured, politely, 'and this is my friend, *Albert.*'

'No matter how spoke,' she snapped, peremptorily. Without pause for breath, she ranted:

'Tis no surprise you be here, thanks yon meddling wizard. How dare intrude my domain. If thinks take Konnee then shalt sorely be disappoint. Know not Fular could squash thee as maggots – aye, and with as little regard? What say thou?'

'I'm sorry if we've upset you,' Bessimer began, mildly, 'but we haven't come to take Connie but to protect and return her to her mother, who will increasingly be worried and missing her terribly.'

'Huff, stuff and balderdash,' Fular retorted, scathingly. 'You mean to have her for yourself. Tis no use denying, Konnee did tell me herself thee and she art both smitten.'

'It's true we are sweethearts,' Bessimer admitted, 'but we are *not* trying to take Connie against her will, only to escort her home – and that's the truth. Ask her, if you don't believe me.'

Perhaps impressed by the youth and his obvious earnestness, the witch visibly mellowed.

'Mayhap thou speaketh truth,' she allowed, reluctantly. 'Konnee assuredly doth speak kindly of thee. But no matter,' she hastened, sternly. 'Destiny didst move to heal the hurt in Fular's heart and brought sweet Konnee for comfort now and for many years hence. Who dares deny destiny?' she demanded. 'None,' she yelled, angrily, in reply to her own question. 'Neither naive striplings, nor yon meddling fool Wegglar, forsooth. Thus doeth Fular declare.' Having said her piece, she primly folded her arms and waited. The woman was domineering and positively oozed self-assurance but, unusually, seemed curiously to be inviting comment.

Albert opened his mouth to oblige but Bessimer silenced him with a glance. After all, as leader, it was *his* responsibility to take the initiative. Taking a deep breath, therefore, he began:

'Excuse me, Ma'am,' he began, timidly, 'I think I know what you mean and don't wish to contradict, but supposing destiny *also* sent Albert and me for the sole purpose of rescuing Connie? Please consider, for is it not written: "Destiny shalt always prevail"? That's what Wegglar said, and I'm sure he's right.' Fular had listened impassively, but her expression visibly darkened.

'Wegglar,' she snorted, derisively. 'What knows a mere stripling of Wegglar?'

'Well, *we* think he's a very nice man,' Bessimer began, 'and so should you. For one thing, he said you were beautiful – and so you are – and for another, he drove away an enormous Brogtin that was about to pounce. Not only that, he twice rescued us from the Brerb, and helped us on each occasion we ran into trouble. He's not been just kind, he's been absolutely *brilliant.*'

The witch eyed Bessimer up and down, speculatively. Her hard, black eyes softened.

'Did'st hears correct? Wegglar really didst call Fular "beautiful"?'

'Yes, he did,' Bessimer stoutly maintained. 'He also said you were of good heart and saddened by something that happened ages ago. He didn't say much, but was obviously fond of you then – and I reckon still is. It's not for me to judge, Ma'am,' he hastily added, 'but I'm sure he'd much prefer to have you for a friend.'

Fular seemed taken aback. She nodded wistfully, considered and apparently decided. Incredibly, given her previous anger, she smiled, fleetingly, lighting up her entire face.

'Mayhap for now,' she said, softly, 'thou shall stay whilst Fular considers.'

'Thank you very much,' Bessimer blurted gratefully. 'Oh, and before I forget. Thank you for saving us from that dreadful monster, whatever it was. Albert and I are both very grateful.'

Astonishingly, Fular threw back her head and laughed.

'T'was but a Zigron, of little moment,' she chortled, shaking with mirth. 'Fular's intent was to punish for trespass, what else dost ye supposes?'

'Maybe good old Destiny was taking a hand again,' Bessimer suggested, cuttingly. 'Can we speak to Connie, please?' he suddenly blurted.

'No, ye may not,' she frowned. 'Remain here; Gimnal shall attend your needs.' Abruptly, she turned towards the wall and with a single swirl of her cloak, lost substance and disappeared.

'Crikey Moses,' Albert breathed in awe, 'that was neat. How the heck did she do it?'

Bessimer crossed to the stonework to give it a good going over. He slowly shook his head.

'Don't know,' he admitted, 'but I'm certain it wasn't a trick. There's no sign of an opening, yet it seemed as if she actually passed through the wall.'

Dubiously, Albert scratched his head. 'Not even *Wegglar* could pull a stunt like that,' he scoffed. 'There's either a cleverly disguised doorway or Fular has an astonishing gift for illusion. On the other hand,' he grinned, 'and just supposing you're right, for a couple of greenhorn initiates we still have a lot to learn.'

Bessimer shot him a warning glance. Finger to lips, he whispered, 'Button it, you steaming twit, that's the second time you've forgotten where we are. Walls have flaming big ears, remember, especially those belonging to Fular – and her Grobbelin, or whatever.'

Albert reddened. 'Sorry, wasn't thinking,' he admitted, and hastily dropped the subject.

'I thought you did jolly well there, George,' he eventually ventured. 'I was beginning to think we were up the creek without a paddle. You must've struck a chord. Maybe the lady's human after all.'

'Don't count your chickens and stay on your toes,' Bessimer sagely advised him. 'We might have gained a small advantage, but we need all our wits about us if we're to complete the job we came for – and a whopping great dollop of luck into the bargain,' he added.

'Tee, hee, hee,' a familiar voice tittered, from a couple of metres away.

'Dzorj give Gimnal Choklit, Allbut give Gimnal Choklit?'

As if joined at the hip, the friends spun round, jaws agape. Albert sniffed:

'What do you want this time, greedy-guts?' he sneered. 'Apart from more chocolate.'

Pasting a facsimile grin across his unbecoming phizog, the optimistic manikin reached out both arms and greedily extended a grubby pair of clutching, six-fingered mitts.

'Give Gimnal lots, lots Choklit?' he whined. 'Gimnal help Dzorj, Gimnal help Allbut. Bring nice water for drink,' he grimaced, with a shudder, 'and lots more nice water for bathe'.

With Fular's words still ringing in their ears, it seemed likely Gimnal was just trying it on. Giving credence to the thought, Bessimer decided to bluff.

'Tell you what,' he artfully suggested. 'If you do as Mistress commands *and* help with some information, then – and only then, maybe we'll just think about giving you more chocolate.'

'Yes, quite right too,' Albert chipped in, 'you greedy little blighter. Go on, shove off.'

With the ploy failing, the grin departed and then, spiralling to the ground, so did the chocoholic hominoid – only to reappear seconds later bearing two earthenware jugs of water. Bobbing politely, he placed them at their feet. '*Now* give Gimnal Choklit?' he scrounged, ever hopeful.

Bessimer couldn't help but admire the creature's colossal cheek. Chuckling, he relented.

'First you provide bathing water and then tell us what we need to know,' he stipulated. 'Providing you speak truth, we'll give you some chocolate – but only one bar, understand.'

'Hokey, dokey,' Gimnal agreed – and, quicker the eye could follow once again he was gone. They made good use of his absence by taking a long swig of water from a jug apiece.

'Giving *him* chocolate is a bit like feeding strawberries to a donkey,' Albert remarked. 'Watch your step, George,' he warned. 'You said yourself we haven't much choccy left.'

'*I* know that; *you* know that, but *he* doesn't. We'd be well advised to "keep him sweet" – if you'll pardon the pun. A lot could still go wrong, Alby, and if it does we'll need all the help we can get. Gimnal proved useful in the past and so he might again. Let's face it, a bar or two of choccy is no big deal with Connie at stake. I doubt she'd complain even if we blew the lot.'

'You're right, of course,' Albert straightway acknowledged, 'I was only making a point.'

'Yeah, I know – and point taken,' Bessimer smiled.

Conversation ceased on the return of Gimnal, toting a pair of leather buckets brimming with water. Without speaking, he emptied both into the cistern and disappeared. He repeated the process twice more and returned a fourth time bearing two large drying cloths, rough-textured, but sufficient for the purpose. Handing one to each, he bobbed his head politely.

'After finish bathe, call Gimnal and Gimnal bring food. Is hokay?'

'Too right, a plate of steaming hot food is something we really *would* appreciate,' Bessimer said, eagerly, rubbing his rumbling tum. 'Thank you, Gimnal, thank you very much.'

Maybe his thanks proved overly complex for a creature of limited vocabulary, although Bessimer suspected the manikin understood far more than he pretended. Be that as it may, with a shake of his massive head, his 'eyebrows' lifted in puzzlement, Gimnal spun twice and vanished – yet again. As ever, the phenomenon never ceased to amaze.

'Crikey, I'd give anything to know how to do that,' Albert remarked.

'So would I,' Bessimer replied, fervently, 'and so, I suspect, would a good many others.'

'Maybe we ought to try finding out,' Albert said, hopefully. 'Gimnal might tell – for chocolate.'

'Waste of time asking. We've little enough as it is. In any case, not even Wegglar has cracked it and he's spent years trying to persuade Bulgan to cough up the mechanics. It seems Grobbelins are born with the ability but only achieve full potential on maturity. They don't penetrate the ground, either,' he continued, thoughtfully. 'Look where Gimnal was standing a moment or so ago. Not the slightest trace of disturbance. I've watched closely; that downwards spiral is deceptive. I get the impression he retracts his legs and compresses his body, making himself a whole lot smaller. Should that be so, what happens next, I wonder? Fact is only Grobbelins know. But just supposing they move from one dimension to another – a sort of space/time travel – and use it in conjunction with inborn ability to modify their bodies at will. It's only an idea, but it would explain how they can leave one spot and bounce back almost immediately.'

'Unlikely if you ask me,' Albert scoffed, forever dubious, 'but fantastic should you be right. He didn't use magic that's for sure, and there's no sign whatever of equipment. We've witnessed the trick before, but this time from really close at hand. It's no illusion so I suppose there *could* be something in your theory – but that still doesn't explain how the blazes it's done.'

'Easy, peasy,' Bessimer proposed, 'advanced mental ability, pure and simple. Take it from me, Alby, Grobbelins are nowhere near as dopey as they look.' Full of admiration and wonderment for the species, he allowed the subject to drop.

Apart from Gimnal's irritating addiction to chocolate, he was long viewed by the boys with admiration and respect, due in no small part to that astonishing ability to transfer himself and whatever load he chose from one place to another in an instant. What they had yet to discover, however, was that the incongruous, easy-going little humanoid possessed other, equally remarkable abilities, utilised and exploited in equal part by sometimes kindly, but often-demanding masters. One such talent, they were to discover, closely approximated the Seetelbird's talent for gathering and communicating information, even though achieved by differing, highly- specialised means. Returning to reality, Bessimer shoved the phenomena to the back of his mind.

'We'll achieve nothing by gabbing,' he said. 'Last one in buys the doughnuts.' Conversation ceased – temporarily, at least. Nearing the end of their ablutions, however, the subject of Grobbelins briefly resurfaced.

'Maybe they were taught by aliens from another planet,' Albert suddenly blurted.

Eyeing him askance, Bessimer spotted a golden opportunity to lay the subject finally to rest.

'Compared to where *we* come from, laddie,' he pointed out, quietly, 'this *is* another planet.'

CHAPTER 13

Connie plays a blinder

With the noisy arrival of dawn echoing in her ears, Connie awoke from slumber relaxed and refreshed. Memory of recent events still clear in her mind she sat with knees to chest and pondered. Although thrilled at hearing from Bessimer and hopeful of imminent rescue, his warning compelled her to realise that if he and she were able to mentally converse, it surely followed that thought might also be subject to interception. That being so, she pledged to heed his warning never to call first, and resolved not to dwell on the subject, content with his promise for further contact by the end of the day. She was roused from reverie by the sound of bolts being drawn – a morning chore invariably carried out by Gimnal since being permitted her daytime freedom. Anxious to pump him for news, Connie rushed to open the door. Quick though she was, however, she wasn't quick enough... *Bother, he's gone already... Oh well...*

The unusual rapidity of Gimnal's departure again set Connie thinking. It occurred that touting for information might easily have proved catastrophic. After all, what questions might she have posed without arousing suspicion? In all probability Gimnal came pre-warned to be on his guard and reveal nothing. Generally talkative and friendly, he was also a servant who would undoubtedly report back to his mistress if instructed. *Maybe this time I got lucky... Whew!*

Still thinking about Gimnal, she recalled her initial fear; wondering whether his talents went further than the amazing scenes projected on Fular's wall. She considered his complex, cringing relationship with an often bad-tempered mistress and the evident power she exerted over him, his subservient cringing and unswerving loyalty despite suggestions of cruelty and beatings.

Nowadays, Connie had quite come to like the quaint little humanoid and regarded him with amused affection. She no longer sought to avoid him and rarely missed an opportunity for a chat. Far more intelligent than appearances would suggest, and although his pronunciation still left much to be desired, much of his improved vocabulary and command of English was probably a direct consequence of their frequent exchanges. But she suspected he would never dare betray his mistress and could not, therefore, be depended upon as a friend… or could he?

Still wondering, she tidied her quarters and slipped easily into the routine of the day…

Once dry and dressed, the ravenous duo felt more than ready for breakfast. They exchanged hungry glances: it was time to put Gimnal's invitation to the test.

'Gimnal, oh Gimnal,' Albert called, hesitantly, 'please bring hot food, we're starving.' They waited and when nothing happened he tried again – this time louder… but still nothing!

'Oh, blow it,' he exclaimed, glaring at his grinning companion. 'You blooming well do it, smarty-pants.' Bessimer merely chuckled, vividly recalling the summoning of Bulgan.

'Gimnal, come hither,' he called. 'We're ready.'

'Hokey, Gimnal come,' a sing song voice from nowhere announced. 'Bring food.'

Almost at once the humanoid materialised, stooping to place a wooden tray at their feet.

'Well, if that doesn't beat all,' Albert moaned. 'What the heck have *you* got that I haven't?'

Bessimer artfully tapped the side of his nose and grabbed a share of a not-so-hot breakfast – four small oatcakes and a pitcher of ice-cold water.

'Is that all?' Albert gasped. 'Blow this for a joke. I'm absolutely *famished*.'

'Two for Dzorj, two for Allbut,' Gimnal proudly piped. 'Not hot but very good. Call when finish' – and promptly vanished.

'Stone me,' Albert gasped, 'the little blighter. He *did* hear but only responds to you.'

'Well, at least he heard you. Don't get your kecks in a twist, maybe breakfast wasn't ready.'

'Humph,' Albert grudgingly grumped, 'if you say so, I suppose.'

'I certainly do say so… fancy topping up with a bag of crisps?'

Once breakfasted, Bessimer left Albert to open the sluice and drain the cistern, leaving him free to inspect the extremes of their enclosure, seeking evidence of concealed openings or signs of weaknesses. Although he drew a blank, he thought it a wise and necessary exercise. Needing Albert on board, he placed a finger to his lips for hush. Bending his head, he whispered:

'Careful, we mustn't be overheard.'

Catching on, Albert whispered back:

'Can't we mind touch then?'

'Absolutely not, I've a feeling we'd risk being overheard.'

'Innermost thoughts intercepted? Nah, you're pulling my leg.'

'I'm not, you know. Anything's possible in this place; no point taking chances.' Albert shook his head, anxious to pursue the matter, but Bessimer doggedly pressed ahead.

'And speaking of mind touch,' he whispered, with a grin, 'I hooked up with Connie last night and we had a pretty decent chat. I even managed to find out roughly whereabouts she is.'

'Crikey,' Albert gasped, 'she's had no training. How on earth did you manage *that?*'

'Not without difficulty,' Bessimer admitted. 'It took umpteen tries and a great deal of effort, but we're pretty close and I guess that helped. She's fine and perfectly OK, by the way.'

'Good, that's something – but I thought you said mind touch was risky.'

'Yes, I know, but it was a risk I just had to take, given the circumstances.'

'Fair enough, we did need to know. Where exactly is she, by the way?'

'In a first floor room, somewhere down there', – indicating with a jerk of his chin.

'Can we get to her, do you reckon?'

'I've no idea; mostly depends on Fular, I suppose.'

'What now, do you reckon?'

'Sit tight, give nothing away and just wait.'

'OK.'

Wordlessly, they drew apart, needing time to consider. Alert to the possibility of eavesdropping, conversation became desultory and all but petered out. After an hour or so with nothing to do but stare at grim, looming sandstone, Albert began to fidget.

'Steady up, old chum,' Bessimer murmured, gently, 'no point fretting.'

Albert glared, moodily, but made no comment, continuing to sulk in silence.

'How much longer are we going to be stuck in here?' he suddenly demanded.

'Until Fular decides otherwise,' Bessimer replied, 'we've no alternative but to live with it.'

'There must be. We were brought here by Fular, so she could take us out. I tell you, I'm sick to death of just hanging around doing nothing. Surely there's *something* we could do.'

'Well there jolly well isn't so blooming-well can it,' Bessimer told him, bluntly; 'We're nearer to Connie than ever before. That's surely progress, old chum, so be satisfied with that, at least for the time being. I know I am.'

Accepting the reprimand, Albert offered what he considered a more practical suggestion.

'Why not try summoning Fular, or ask Gimnal to pass a message?' he suggested.

'No, trust me; it's not worth jeopardising everything by needlessly rocking the boat.'

Bessimer's clear-thinking finally won the day; Albert grudgingly conceded…

… and yet more, long, incredibly boring hours ticked slowly away…

Connie was halfway through ablutions when Fular appeared in the doorway, smiling and nodding, knowingly.

'Thou art still but child,' she declared, wonderingly, 'yet so soon becomes a woman.' The girl flushed brick-red. Snatching a cloth to preserve her modesty, she let rip:

'What the heck do *you* want? Can't a girl have a bit of privacy?'

'Fular begs forgiveness,' the witch said, though clearly unrepentant, 'didst not mean to intrude.

'When done, pray partake alone; food doth lay ready on thy platter…' and she was gone.

Still annoyed, Connie nevertheless went in search of breakfast. After helping herself to a couple of oatcakes, she cast about for something to do, and although Gimnal was responsible for cleaning she had often lent him a hand… it seemed the perfect solution.

Adhering to her self-imposed resolution, she closed her mind to anything other than the task in hand, as she busily washed, swept and dusted for most of the morning. And as she worked; she sang, trilling through many of the timeless melodies from the wonderful *Sound of Music.*

Unfortunately, and despite the fact she frequently cleaned, such unusual industriousness aroused the curiosity of the witch. Totally engrossed, Connie neither noticed Fular reappear, nor that she stood watching a few short metres away. Nearing the end of a corridor still sweeping merrily away something – sixth sense or plain old-fashioned intuition – triggered a feeling of being observed, and she paused to glance round. On seeing Fular so close, Connie jumped, almost guiltily.

'Oh, it's you again,' she cried. 'For a moment you quite startled me.'

'Why so?' the witch replied. 'Hast not seen Fular afore this very day?'

Connie glared, propped her broom, and muttered: 'Sorry, I just didn't hear you.'

'Drat the girl,' Fular tut-tutted, impatiently. 'If not Fular, then whom else might I be?'

'Nobody,' she flushed, 'except Gimnal, perhaps. But *he* doesn't creep up on me – and anyway, I can mostly hear him coming.' The barb struck home; Fular immediately snapped:

'Why dost so mightily labour, unbidden? And for what reason art unusually joyful?' Her attitude was icy; her black eyes gleamed; the question smacked of third degree.

Connie's blood ran cold, but her nimble mind whizzed into top gear. *Bother, she's suspicious. It* might *be down to me – or was she eavesdropping? Oh, dear, what* have *I done? Quick, what shall I do? Play for time, of course, but tell her nothing.* It seemed so unfair. She'd borne kidnap and imprisonment; fought homesickness; suffered a total lack of affection – and now this; and with dearest, darling Bessimer finally on the doorstep.

Connie's heart sank, tears started to well and her lower lip trembled… but gave her an idea. *Should* she? *Could* she? If Fular *had* intercepted that amazing conversation, she might not only have ruined Bessimer's plans but be labelled a scheming hussy into the bargain. Risky admittedly, but a risk she was prepared to take. Enough was enough and it was surely time for action. Nor should it prove unduly difficult; those embryo tears were real, her misery genuine. Screwing her eyes, she puckered her face and began to cry.

'What's wrong, don't you *like* to see me happy?' she snivelled. 'If you don't like what I do, then take me home, I w-want my mother, anyway. And I miss my sweetheart *ever* so much – and then there's our friend, Albert…' She tailed off, dabbing her eyes in misery.

'Do you know where they are?' she begged. 'I suspect you do; they were in those pictures on your wall. If you *do* know, then please, *please* tell me. I really do need to know…'

It was a heartfelt, impassioned plea, delivered with all the sincerity at her command. But was it sufficient? With bated breath, Connie waited to find out.

During the ensuing silence, Fular's dark eyes softened; her stern look melted.

'Come, Konnee,' she murmured, tenderly, 'distress no longer. Come, come to Fular.'

Recent events; a lack of meaningful affection; the meagre diet – it was all too, too much. Impulsively, Connie threw herself into the waiting arms, sobbing softly. *Have I done enough?*

At first, the witch hesitantly patted Connie's shoulder and then, when Connie responded by snuggling closer, switched to a comforting, full- bodied hug.

'There, there,' she soothed. 'Don't cry, Konnee, else Fular doeth cry herself.'

It was better than Connie could have hoped. She disengaged and looked the witch squarely in the eye. It felt right: it was time to put her cards firmly on the table, once and for all.

'I'm really sorry, Fular,' she began, dabbing again, 'but I feel so unhappy and alone. Sometimes you're kind – and I know you want me to stay, but you're often cross and I spend far too much time on my own. It feels as though I'm being punished though I've done nothing wrong. I'd love to go home, of course. But most of all I want my boyfriend back. Can you help me? *Will* you help me? Please.' Fingers crossed behind her back; again she waited, anxiously scanning the witch's face.

Fular seemed hesitant. At one point she seemed about to speak, but remained frustratingly silent. By now Connie was on tenterhooks: *Come* on, *missus, get a flipping jerk on!*

Maybe the girl's earnest entreaty caused Fular twinges of conscience; though whether she in any way regretted Connie's kidnap would remain forever in doubt. What was becoming clear, however, the harridan was beginning to view her captive in an entirely different light.

A few nail-biting moments later, Connie's patience was finally rewarded.

Again the sorceress smiled. 'In truth thy love be strong,' she declared. 'Forgive Fular who does thee grave injustice, thou art indeed no longer child; but brave of heart, loyal and deserving. Tis true,' she went on, 'Fular *dost* know and will aid; ye shall see thy beloved this very day. But beware,' she added, sharply, 'tis no promise lightly made.' Her beautiful face darkened.

'Dzorj and Allbut didst befriend yon wizard, liar, turncoat and coward,' she scowled, 'and for that shalt assuredly atone.' Shaking her fist, angrily, she went on to screech:

'Neither patience try, nor liberties attempt; for none shall go free till penance be served.' Once again her expression lightened, and she asked, anxiously:

'Art now happier, Konnee? Wilt smile again, hug and be true?'

She held out her arms invitingly, and not for one second did Connie hesitate…

CHAPTER 14

Sweethearts reunited

For all Bessimer's wisdom, he too found tedium increasingly hard to bear. After lazing around for an hour or so, he got to his feet and began pacing from one side of the compound to the other and back again, twenty-three paces one way and twenty-three the other, pausing occasionally for a breather, then resuming a short while later. Albert, however, chose to while away *his* time by simply lazing about lolloping, dozing fitfully from time to time.

He was leaning with his back to the cistern, watching through narrowed eyes as Bessimer approached, still stumping up and down, when from the corner of his eye caught a glimpse of movement; a shadowy shape close by the wall, where it hovered briefly – and simply disappeared.

'What the deuce was that?' he asked aloud, jerking himself upright.

'What was what?'

'Something moved over there – a bird or something.'

'Where?'

'There, over by the wall.'

Bessimer's eyes followed the pointing finger. He pursed his lips.

'Nothing there, go back to sleep.'

'Wasn't asleep, wasn't dreaming. *Something* was there, I tell you.'

'Nuts, you're imagining things.'

'I'm not you know,' Albert retorted, grumpily.

Without warning, the light dimmed; dense thunderheads rolled in from nowhere, transforming an already leaden, purple-hued sky into an intense, sickening plum-like colour.

'It looks like as if a storm's due any sec,' Bessimer remarked, casting around for cover.

'Quick, over by the cliff,' he added, already halfway there.

Albert nodded and he too made a dash for it, crouching to join Bessimer beneath a small overhang.

It didn't amount to much, but it was better than nothing especially, as within seconds a tropical storm let loose: fork and sheet lightning darted and flashed, ever closer. Thunder synchronously roared and rumbled, *crack*, *ker-bang* and *crack-crack*; echoing and reverberating. With it came screeching winds and driving rain, heavy and torrential, blindingly wet, cold and penetrating. The overhang gave some protection but they were completely drenched in minutes despite bomber jackets. And as if that were not enough, the overloaded drainage channel overflowed, rendering the unyielding enclosure ankle deep in water.

Shouting to be heard over the din, Bessimer roared, 'Where the heck did *that* lot come from?'

'Dunno, you tell me,' Albert yelled in reply, 'but let's get the blazes out of here.'

'Can't, what about the witch?'

'Blow the witch; we're soaked to the skin.'

As quickly as it arose the wind abated and the storm eased; dark clouds lifted and disappeared. Emitting an unearthly gurgle, the final millimetres of laying water finally drained away.

'Crumbs, that was soon over,' Bessimer remarked, 'but *what* was that about Fular?'

'She here,' announced a deep contralto nearby. It was a voice with which the pals were all too disagreeably familiar…*Fular!* They looked, and there she was, standing beside the cistern, arms akimbo and – to their absolute astonishment – she was actually *smiling.*

Albert was on his feet in a flash. Fast as he was, however, Bessimer was milliseconds faster, grabbing Albert's arm in order to restrain his sometimes impetuous friend.

'Steady up, old son,' he murmured in an aside, 'better leave this one to me.'

'Yeah, but just look at her,' Albert muttered darkly, 'all lovey-dovey – *and* as dry as a bone.'

'Shhhh, give it a rest.' Crossing the intervening space, Bessimer calmly addressed the voice's proprietor.

'Hello, Ma'am,' he began politely, 'it's nice to see you again. We've been waiting all morning hoping to have a word. We desperately need to speak with Connie and need your help. Right now though, we're soaking wet through… Could you… would you?'

Forbearing to answer, Fular began looking them up and down, her smile widening to a grin. It looked suspiciously as if she found their bedraggled appearance amusing. Eyeing them more closely her amusement was fully justified: long scruffy hair plastered flat against their skulls; soggy wet clothes and woebegone expressions, they were enough to make a cat laugh. Sheepishly, they both smiled back and then, unpredictably and to their astonishment, she burst out laughing.

'Just look,' she chortled, shoulders shaking. 'Like two drowned rats in a barrel. Methinks Gimnal didst attend in vain. Mayhap fate conspires to bathe thee again – still in thy raiment?' She positively cackled with merriment. Holding her sides she guffawed – again and yet again.

'Oh, mercy me,' the witch chortled, 'if art not the funniest sight in many a long year.'

Still with a twinkle in her eye, she switched expressions, and became serious again.

'First you must dry and Gimnal will assist, but quickly now afore Fular dost relent; perchance Konnee grows anxious,' she said, smiling at Bessimer.

'Gather thy goods together,' she instructed. 'Return hence and stand by me…'

Throughout the raging storm, Connie sheltered within a cloister flanking an inner cobbled courtyard, watching the Skandovian equivalent of Mother Nature let loose in all her fury. At the height of the tempest she jumped each time a particularly brilliant flash of lightning slashed a searing pathway across the gloom: winced at the accompanying boom-crack-crack of thunder.

Reflecting on Fular's astonishing turnaround, she hugged herself, agog. She tried hard to contain her excitement, not to appear overly triumphant, but her heart performed a delighted back-flip; something Fular would never have failed to notice. Scarcely able to credit her success and amazing change of fortune, she continued to be almost beside herself with joy. Providing the witch was true to her promise she was soon to be reunited with darling Bessimer, a prospect more appealing than just chatting inside her head, exciting though it had been.

'Wh-*what* did you say?' she had stammered, unsure. 'Does that mean you're *really* going to help me and I'll be seeing George and Albert again?'

Smiling at the girl's incredulity, Fular nodded.

'Most assuredly Fular didst mean, Konnee,' she replied. 'What is more this very day.

'Conclude thy chores and prepare,' she smiled, 'for soon t'will come to pass.' With that the witch walked away, leaving Connie to finish her task in blissful anticipation.

Once finished, she washed away the dust of her labours and vigorously brushed her hair. An occasion like this called for a change of clothes, but there was no option other than make do.

Soon ready she waited in Fular's parlour – until the storm rolled in, when she went to the cloister to watch. As soon as the storm passed, however, she straightway returned.

Time passed while Connie waited – and waited – and waited. There was no sound; no sign of the witch nor, unusually, anything to be seen of her familiar. At least an hour ticked slowly by during which time the poor girl grew increasingly impatient. *Where's Fular? Where's Gimnal?*

'…and today's the day I'm supposed to be seeing Bessimer,' she grumbled, bitterly. Was Fular for real, or was the stingy old curmudgeon playing silly games? To compound her disenchantment, a rumbling tummy suggested lunch was overdue. Breakfast was long in the past; the evening meal far into the future… it really wasn't fair.

'Gimnal!' she shouted, peremptorily. 'I'm hungry. Bring me bread and soup.' It wasn't so much an order, more a cry born of frustration. The last thing she expected was an answer, although Gimnal would sometimes put in an appearance should he be summoned. Today, however – in the shape of an apology from thin air – the response was immediate.

'Gimnal begs forgive, Mistress Konnee,' a disembodied voice replied….*Corks, another talent?*

'Fular tell Gimnal; she say help Dzorj, help Allbut, so Gimnal help.

'Promise brings Konnee grub-grub very soon, hokay?'

Whilst conversing with Bessimer in her mind had been weird but strangely comforting, a two-way chat with an invisible Grobbelin bordered on the ridiculous. *This place gets crazier by the minute.* Connie came close to cracking up. She pulled herself together, however; resisted an impulse to giggle and, despite feeling incredibly foolish, forced herself to reply to an empty room.

'*What's* that about George and Albert? What help? Tell me, what's wrong?'

'No wrong. Mistress says Dzorj wet, Allbut wet. Tell Gimnal help to dry.'

'Oh, I see,' Connie said, mollified and at the same time hugely relieved.

'Well, OK then – but don't be long.'

'Hokay.'

'What…?' Connie began, but changed her mind. *That* question she would keep for later…

Having rejoined Fular, each was grasped firmly by an elbow and effortlessly propelled skywards at a blistering rate, across the roof and down to a front courtyard, thence an open portal and a long corridor, halting in front of a heavy timber door which obligingly swung open on their approach.

'Enter and wait,' the witch commanded, treating both to a helpful shove. The instant they were inside the door slammed shut to the sound of retreating footsteps.

'Oh corks, we've bought it,' Albert exclaimed. 'Trapped! She's got us at her mercy.'

'Stop moaning – and don't jump to conclusions,' Bessimer warned.

'This isn't a prison, anyway,' he opined, 'just a plain old ordinary living room.'

And plain it most certainly was, a quick glance around confirmed. They were in a spacious chamber – comfortably warm despite a bare stone floor – sparsely furnished with a solitary rough-hewn table and a couple of odd chairs. There were no windows – light entered via slits just below ceiling height – and there was no apparent means of egress, other than the door by which they entered – a door that actually wasn't locked, as a quick check confirmed.

Further discussion was cut short by the re-appearance of Gimnal, bearing four super-sized versions of the by-now all-too-familiar drying cloth, proffering one apiece.

'Remove apparels, give Gimnal,' he squeaked, with a bob of his head.

'Fular says assist dry, and then take to Konnee… Give Gimnal Choklit?' he added, hopefully.

'Maybe chocolate later,' teased Albert, grabbing a cloth and shucking his clothes.

'Brrr,' he shivered, towelling vigorously. 'That was some storm. I'm absolutely frozen. But at least it's dry in here and a jolly sight warmer – thank goodness,' he added.

'That's for sure,' Bessimer agreed, hurriedly shedding his own gear.

As soon as they were done, the humanoid handed them the remaining cloths.

'Put on body for warm,' he suggested, stooping to gather their wet belongings.

'Gimnal back soon,' he chirruped, rotated and disappeared.

'Back soon? He'll be lucky,' Bessimer remarked, parking on one of the chairs. 'Those togs were saturated; they'll take ages to dry so we may as well be comfortable.'

'Yeah, I reckon,' Albert grumped, following suit.

'Ouch!' he huffed. 'This chair is so hard I've corns already. Serves me right for lounging around all morning, I hear you say.'

Bessimer grinned: 'The thought never even entered my head,' he lied. 'But I tell you what I *do* think,' he offered, 'if you're interested, that is?'

'Course I'm interested. Fire away.'

'Well, you remember the way Fular seemed to pass through solid wall?'

'Naturally, of course.'

'I've been comparing that with how she whizzed us from the roof, stopping outside the door.'

'What of it?'

'No skulduggery, no gimmicks, just plain ordinary transportation.'

'What the blazes are you getting at?'

'I was wrong. In retrospect I think there probably *was* a doorway in that wall, after all.'

'*You* looked and couldn't find one.'

'I know, but I was seeking the conventional, whereas doorways can really be any old shape or size. Pound to a penny there were hairline cracks…' *Drat. If only I'd looked more closely.* Albert shook his head, far from convinced.

'Supposing there *was* a door, for argument's sake. She couldn't have used it without us noticing.'

'Ah, but maybe she could. Remember my Grobbelin theory? What if she's mastered the knack of suspending time – milliseconds would be sufficient. Remember that flickering shadow? Now *that* was a dead give- away, if ever there was one.'

'Maybe,' Albert replied, dubiously. 'An interesting theory – except that it doesn't quite gel.

'You said Wegglar spent years trying to winkle the secret from Bulgan, so what makes you think Fular could possibly succeed where he couldn't? Sorry, I just don't buy it.'

'I'm not asking you to,' Bessimer retorted, irritably, 'although it seems perfectly logical to me.'

'Have it your way, if you must' Albert retorted, 'I'll believe it when I actually see it.'

'But you *have* seen it,' Bessimer insisted. 'Think: it's the only possible explanation.'

Challenged, Albert pursed his lips and, grudgingly considered.

'Maybe you're right – up to a point,' he eventually conceded. 'Anything's possible in this crazy place… but that isn't to say Fular can manipulate time,' he quickly added.

'It's equally within the bounds of possibility that she managed to hypnotise us.'

'Rubbish——' Bessimer began, cut short by the re-appearance of Gimnal.

'Tee hee hee,' the engaging little humanoid tittered, less than a metre away. 'Behold, Gimnal dost return.'

'C–crumbs,' Bessimer stuttered, taken aback. 'Where the skingy did *you* spring from?'

Raising a single eye-flap, the Grobbelin contrived to appear both hurt and puzzled.

Placing neatly-folded clothes in front of their respective owners, in a distinctly human-like manner, he tapped the side of his nose.

'No skingy. No spring,' he declared, waggling a single, trombone-like lughole.

'Gimnal promise bring dry, Gimnal *bring* dry.'

'I know,' Bessimer replied, 'but are they *properly* dry? You weren't away long and they were absolutely soaking. Drying thoroughly that soon simply isn't possible.'

'Try and see,' the humanoid retorted, annoyed at being doubted.

'Maybe quick here,' he protested, grumpily, 'but not quick there.'

What a strange thing to say, Bessimer thought. *What* does *he mean?*

'Mine are absolutely bone dry,' Albert piped up, already buttoning his shirt.

'So are mine,' Bessimer was forced to admit, climbing into his trousers.

Apparently still upset, the humanoid turned bright pink and stamped a six-toed foot.

Recognising warning signs, Albert hastily stepped into the breach.

'You did *splendidly*,' he assured the manikin, 'but so quickly you took us by surprise.' He fished in his haversack, produced a bar of fudge and proffered it.

'Gimnal like chocolate?' he suggested, soothingly. 'Reckon you've earned it.'

Annoyance forgotten and true to form, two black lips parted, the Grobbelin spread wide his capacious maw, at the same time reverting a more normal shade of green. Simultaneously and in a single, surprisingly fluid motion, he grabbed the delectable sweetmeat and whistled it out of sight. He beamed, sighed, burped – and, artfully, tried his luck again.

'Lovely glub – maybe Allbut give Gimnal more?' he wheedled.

'Maybe later,' Albert half promised, shrugging into his jacket. 'We shall see.'

'Hokey, please remains here. Now art ready, Gimnal shalt inform mistress.' He bobbed his head, turned, and rocking comically he shuffled towards the door. Once there, he opened it and paused to call over his shoulder:

'Dzorj and Allbut stay here,' he warned, 'else Fular become *exceeding* angry.' He waddled out and as the door closed, Bessimer nudged Albert in the ribs.

'What, no Weem? Still, intelligent little chap,' he remarked. 'Did you notice his vastly-improved command of English? He's streets ahead of Bulgan.'

'Yes, now you come to mention it. Maybe he's taking lessons.'

'Now there's a thought.'

But before Bessimer could elaborate, the door flung open and there, in the opening, wearing the broadest of grins and with Fular close behind, stood the delightful figure of the girl they so earnestly and diligently had striven to rescue...*Connie*! Bessimer's heart performed an almighty somersault!

With a glad cry the girl launched herself with outstretched arms. Looking deep into his eyes, she put her arms round his neck and delivered a lingering, full-blooded kiss on the lips. The expression on Albert's face reminded her they were not alone and she blushed to the roots of her hair. Hastily, she pulled away and made do with holding Bessimer's hand. At this point, Fular came fully into the room, wearing a strangely enigmatic but wistful smile.

'Enough,' she declared – but not unkindly. 'Pray follow, tis time to eat.'

Gleefully recalling a scrumptious rabbit stew, Albert rubbed his tummy.

'Yes, please,' he chortled, 'I'm absolutely ravenous.'

Fular led them out of the door down a long corridor and into another, much larger room equipped with several rough-hewn chairs and a matching table set with pitchers of water, drinking mugs and a platter of oatcakes. Drawing up a chair, Fular sat down and signalled them to join her.

'Pray eat,' she invited. 'Tis little enough, yet better victuals hast none.'

Eager anticipation turned to abject dismay. Albert for one couldn't contain his disappointment.

'Stone me,' he moaned, 'is that *all*? Cor, Penny Plinkers, I'm absolutely *starving*.'

'Yes, so am I,' Bessimer felt bound to agree.'

'Fular doth truly regret,' the witch quickly apologised. 'Mayhap wilts fare better the morrow.'

She sat back as the trio began to eat. Of the seven on the platter, six cakes rapidly disappeared, leaving just one for Fular – or so they supposed. Yet several minutes later and umpteen sips of water still it remained.

'Is that one yours?' Bessimer politely inquired, no longer able to contain his curiosity.

Smiling, the witch shook her head and, somewhat pointedly, replied, 'Fular hast already eaten, mayhap Allbut would'st like?'

Albert blushed brick-red and stuttered, shame-facedly.

'N––no, th––that one's yours. I––I've really had sufficient, thank you.'

'Oh, take it,' she replied, testily, 'for hast not thy hunger declared?'

'Ye––s,' he began but, thinking better of it, quickly subsided.

Guiltily, he grabbed the cake and practically swallowed it whole. Rudely, he pulled a wry face and rubbed his stomach, denoting extreme hunger in *any* language. Bessimer frowned; Connie's hand flew to her mouth whereas Fular, looking distinctly frosty, simply rose to her feet and stalked from the room, looking neither left nor right.

'You blithering idiot, why on earth did you do that?' Bessimer scolded. 'Fular is obviously offended. You had your share then scoffed the one intended for her. What got into you?'

Albert was immediately contrite. 'Sorry, didn't think, but I was just so hungry. She said she'd already eaten – yeah, too right she had. Beautifully cooked, steaming hot, plate piled high and absolutely delicious,' he darkly declared. 'All we got was few measly oatcakes. I didn't think it fair.'

'It's your manners that weren't fair. She *realised* you were still hungry, you twit, *that's* why she claimed to have eaten so *you* wouldn't feel embarrassed. You'd better apologize at the earliest opportunity – or I'll do it for you, then you really *will* be embarrassed.'

'Okay, okay, 'nuff said,' Albert huffed, 'I'll say sorry first chance, OK?'

'I should jolly-well think so. She's been kind enough to let us see Connie and you upset the applecart the moment we seemed to be making progress. Alby, I'm surprised at you.'

Albert visibly shrank; the shamed miscreant put up his hands in surrender. He'd most *definitely* got the message!

Neither was it long before he was able to fulfil his promise when Fular reappeared. Noting that Bessimer and Connie were still holding hands, her sunny smile reappeared.

'Er, um, excuse me, Fular,' Albert stammered, 'I was very rude earlier and I'd like to say sorry.' Her smile deepened – she really was beautiful; even a blind man couldn't have failed to notice.

'No matter,' she assured him gently, in the sweetest imaginable tones. 'T'was clear ye hungered mightily; mayhap thy stomach didst rule thy head. Tis of little moment, Fular doth understand.'

'But come,' she went on, briskly, 'tis time to view thy quarters. Pray, follow Fular.' She glided from the room, towing three hugely relieved youngsters in her wake.

Halfway down 'Connie's' corridor, Fular stopped, opened a door and motioned Albert and Bessimer inside. She waited while they inspected the interior, and her expression lightened when both nodded – even laughed gently when Albert performed a little jig.

'It's *very* nice,' Bessimer declared. 'Thank you, Fular.' They now had comfortable-looking trestle-beds with furs for bedding, a substantial window – high in the wall but adequate for the size of of the room, providing plenty of light and ventilation – plus a scattering of rugs. It seemed luxurious by any standards and couldn't be faulted.

'Beats hard, lumpy ground,' Albert confirmed, clearly delighted.

'Tis well, Fular art pleased,' said the witch, extending her hand. 'Come, Konnee, now for thee.'

Connie was conducted to her old room, now much improved. She too had a trestle bed, for example – a huge improvement, a couple of chairs and a scattering of rugs. Connie smiled, appreciatively; she too had no complaints…

Her door was also left unlocked.

All were free to wander where and whenever they chose and soon set about making full use of the privilege; exploring the Keep was a must. Apart from Fular's personal quarters – tactfully avoided – within a couple of days there remained few places with which they remained unfamiliar.

Unsurprisingly, Connie and Bessimer contrived to spend time together as much they could but never, they were careful to ensure, at Albert's expense. Having left him to his own devices once, the consequences of isolating him would never be forgotten. Friendship was infinitely more important than personal pleasures, no matter how desirable they might be.

And what of the ultimate goal – getting back through the barrier and returning home. Bessimer cheerfully accepted it as his responsibility and set about broaching the subject. Casting about, he began. 'Right, you two,' he whispered, when all three stood admiring the view from the battlements – a perfect observation platform, proving spectacular views over a wide panorama of Skandovian countryside. Alien it most certainly was but at the same time incredibly beautiful. From here, the high tor marking the lair of the Brerb was clearly visible.

'How and when should we set about getting home?' he began, but warned, 'Keep your eyes peeled and voices low. We mustn't risk being overheard. You first,' he said, nodding to Albert.

The Keep provided superb protection, virtually impossible to approach unobserved. Bessimer's admiration for Fular grew in leaps and bounds. How a practically defenceless young woman had managed to build such an impressive, carefully thought-out citadel in alien surroundings was almost beyond imagination. She had single-handedly achieved all this with nothing but her own two hands, whatever local labour she managed to muster, ambition, intelligence and exception magical ability – incredible.

Albert had no doubt, opting for what seemed the simplest solution.

'Collect our things and meet back here. Explain to Connie how transportation works, link arms and scarper – easy, peasy.'

'Hang on,' Connie protested, indignantly. 'For one thing, Bessimer says we can't use magic, and for another, you're not suggesting we buzz off without consulting Fular – especially after everything she's done?'

'Why ever not?' he replied, seemingly puzzled.

'It wouldn't be fair, that's why not.'

'What's fairness got to do with it? If she knew, she'd stop us. I for one don't fancy another dose of locked doors, filthy temper and everything that goes with it. You don't seem to realise just how rotten she can be. It would surely be far better to consult her first? Where's the harm in that?'

'Connie's right, you know,' Bessimer soothed. 'I vote we simply tell her we want to go home. Don't pretend you're not homesick too,' he added. 'Should Fular agree then maybe she'll help; surely that's preferable to getting her hackles up and then doing her level best to stop us.'

'I suppose – but don't say I didn't warn you.'

'I wouldn't dream of it.' He turned to Connie, to murmur:

'We'll do it your way, the sensible way. You can open the batting but please be careful. I know you and Fular have become close, but just remember she has a nasty side as well. She most certainly isn't your Mum.' She smiled agreement, squeezed his hand and moved to rest her head on his shoulder.

Deciding she should be accompanied by the boys, Connie nervously informed the witch of their intended departure. To their utter astonishment and not at all as expected, Fular failed to explode, quite the opposite in fact.

'I doubt the journey possible,' she replied, amazingly gentle considering her well-known temper. 'Skandos be dark, fraught with danger and impossible to escape from,' she went on. 'Fular has so attempted a great many occasions,' she sighed, 'and so too, you may be sure, hast Wegglar.' Her expression became curiously wistful at the mere mention of his name… strange!

'Then again,' she continued, 'dost not recall that Destiny doth bring Konnee to Fular, and that Destiny wilts ever prevail? Konnee wilt stay. *Thee* remain or leave as you please,' glaring at the boys. 'But *should* you somehow escape,' she added, dramatically, 'darken not my doorstep again. Thy departure wouldst assuredly break Konnee's heart, that which Fular couldst ne'er allow.' It seemed she knew nothing whatever of Bessimer and Albert's newly acquired abilities…

'So that's that,' Albert remarked later. 'What now, I wonder?' Connie smiled wanly.

'I'm so sorry,' she confessed, softly, 'you were right, I should have known better. You go, I stay, and maybe Bes – er, George too. There's no way she'll ever let *me* loose.'

'*Don't* be sorry,' he replied, 'you were right but the question needed to be asked; it was the right thing to do. Fular has treated us really well recently and is aware of our position, whilst we in turn know exactly where we stand. Don't you agree, George?'

'Yup, couldn't have put it better myself. But what now, do you reckon?'

'Seems we've no alternative,' was Albert's crisp reply. 'We up and scarper. Can't we use magic and just scram?' he added, hopefully, 'if so, how soon can we go?' Bessimer gave him a withering look and lowered his voice:

'Are you *completely* off your trolley? Use magic, right under her nose? She'd be on to us in a flash. How far do you imagine we'd get – the first stand of trees? Well, possibly, but only if we were very, very lucky. Forget it, Alby. Try again – only *this* time, apply a little of that superior intellect you so fondly imagine you possess.' The sarcasm was intentional; Albert *must* learn to *think* before blurting the first thing that came to mind – his life (and theirs) might one day depend upon it.

Albert bridled but, perhaps wisely, held his tongue.

A long silence followed; there was a great deal to think about.

Eventually, alert to his responsibilities, Bessimer steered them back to reality.

'I don't know about you sorry-looking pair,' he chirped, cheerfully, 'but it's been a long day and I for one am ready for a spot of kip – anybody else care for a smidgen of bye byes?'…

At breakfast the following morning, three hungry individuals were confronted with a very difficult choice – ice-cold water and a couple of tasteless oatcakes apiece – or go without! All were manfully munching away when Fular entered the room. Unprompted, the boys rose in deference. She smiled graciously and waved them be seated.

'Fular doth regret such miserable fare,' she began, 'but in truth tis all canst offer. Howsoever,' she hastened to add, 'mayhap for just a short while longer. For Fular hast, this very morn, joined mind with Wegglar.' Incredibly, her smile deepened as she continued, 'Just as we he, alas, hast vittles a-few, and also needs renew.' She positively radiated as she concluded, 'Therefore, this very day, wilts reunite a-purpose clear. Thus all may feast again.' She turned towards the door and paused, adding, 'Gimnal shall attend thy needs, wilts not be alone. Prithee no fear, Fular shalt return ere long. Fare thee well.' And she was gone.

'Well, blow me,' Albert exclaimed. He rushed to the door and checked the corridor. 'All clear,' he announced. 'Opportunity doeth knocks,' he sarcastically misquoted. 'What now?' He eyed Bessimer, expectantly, who took his time before answering:

'Well,' he began, 'Fular made perfectly clear her intentions regarding Connie. Equally obvious, she's not bothered whether we stay or not – isn't it nice to feel wanted?' He came to a decision:

'She cares deeply about Connie's welfare, there's little doubt of that. She's prepared to have us as guests because of Connie; otherwise we'd be out on our ears in a flash. Be that as it may, we're equally determined to get home together and nothing; repeat *nothing* is likely to alter that. So, once we're certain the coast is clear, how long will it take us to grab our gear and meet up again?'

'What about Gimnal?' Albert wanted to know. 'He'll be under instructions to keep the gates locked and he's completely under her thumb. I'll stand corrected if I'm wrong.'

'Chocolate,' Bessimer replied, succinctly, 'the ultimate secret weapon. Bribe him to leave the gates unlocked so we can hop it. As far as we know neither she nor Gimnal have a clue we've magic at our disposal, which gives us a very real advantage.' Albert whistled.

'You mean, push off using conventional means and keep *that* little gem up our sleeves?'

'Precisely,' Bessimer said, tapping the side of his nose, artfully.

'I like it,' Connie exclaimed. 'You really *are* clever, sweetheart, (Bessimer blushed) but what's all this about chocolate?'

'We brought loads with us – some meant for you, but forgotten about until now. It was to sustain us when we got hungry – quite often, as it happens, so there's not a great deal left – more especially since we discovered Gimnal absolutely *adores* the stuff, which came in jolly useful when a spot of bribery was called for. Unless you would prefer to keep the residue, it might come equally handy again.'

'Don't worry about me,' she assured him. 'Use it as you will. I've managed perfectly without until now; a little longer certainly won't bother me.'

'Thank you, sweetheart, it's more than generous of you.' And this time *Connie* blushed.

'When you two finish gabbing,' Albert rudely interrupted, 'why are we still hanging about? I can be ready in five minutes – how about you?'

'Not so fast. First make sure Gimnal keeps schtum. Once that's sorted, we'll leave by the front entrance and leg it for the trees. I think we have a *reasonable* chance of reaching them before the little twerp realises what we're up to and blows the whistle… Now, I'm open to suggestion.'

'You came up with a purler,' Albert reminded him. 'Use chocolate!

'Yes, let's,' Connie agreed. 'Con him. Pretend to be going out to sketch flora.'

'Brill,' confirmed Bessimer. 'Give me ten minutes.'

'Right you are,' said Albert. 'By the way, have you ever seen a grobbelin eat choccy?' He directed his remark to Connie, who shook her head, looking puzzled.

'Boy, are you in for a treat,' he sniggered, but declined to explain.

'What *does* he mean?' she asked Bessimer.

'Well, they're terribly greedy and scoff the bar whole still in the wrappers.'

'That doesn't sound particularly polite.'

'No, I suppose not. We were horrified at first, but it's just the way they are.'

The ploy worked faultlessly. Gimnal accepted the bribe and, true to form, scoffed it in a flash – spun and vanished, re-materialising with a wad of crude drawing paper and a selection of coloured sticks resembling crayons, but formulated from something other than wax.

Minutes later, the trio strolled unhurriedly though the entrance and crossed open ground to the first stand of trees unchallenged. As protection, the boys wore trousers and bomber jackets and carried satchels. Connie opted for the same jeans and top she wore when abducted, now bleached shades lighter by sun and continuous laundering.

Once in the trees out of sight, they crossed a small clearing to find themselves confronted by a forest of close-packed spiny trees and tangled undergrowth bearing innumerable quantities of vicious-looking thorns, rending passage extremely difficult if not practically impassable, totally alien for Connie, never previously confronted by such awful-looking terrain. But they were bound to press ahead if they were to succeed in making good their escape.

'Take great care,' Bessimer warned. 'Most of those thorns are poisonous.'

Progress was difficult, but with Bessimer's help and encouragement, she bravely battled on. An hour later, panting and soaked with perspiration, the trio made it to the far side of the stand without serious incident. Once there, they paused to take stock and snatch a well-earned breather.

'That was tough,' Bessimer remarked, unnecessarily. 'The next trees are some way off and we're far enough away from the Keep to try a spot of magic.' He took Connie's hand and tucked her arm securely under his. 'Don't worry,' he soothed, noting her look of alarm. 'It's a really neat trick we learned recently. It's quite good fun when you get the hang of it, you'll see.

'Albert will do likewise,' he explained. 'Link arms and clasp hands in front of you, you'll be perfectly safe. We'll take to the air and make for those trees, the nearest cover. It's a bit like flying, similar to the way Fular brought you to Bortzin, but nowhere near as fast. Don't be frightened and don't panic. We'll take jolly good care of you.'

Alas it was not to be. They emerged from the shrubbery to be confronted by a distinctive figure barring the way. There she stood, arms akimbo, scarcely the caring, friendly woman last seen little more than an hour ago. Three faces fell, reflecting alarm, dismay and disappointment.

'Gimnal, the slimy little twister,' Bessimer hissed, in an aside. 'He scoffed our blinking chocolate then grassed us to Fular. Fifty pre-war yen to a rusty deutschmark he's been following our each and every move and reporting back.'

'Place a bet with you? Not flaming likely,' Albert retorted, swallowing his disappointment. 'Go find another sucker. Everyone knows you *never* gamble – except on gold-plated certainties.'

Overhearing, Connie giggled, privately in agreement. But the matter was serious.

'Stone me, what a waste of effort,' she gasped, 'the old curmudgeon knew exactly what we were up to and where we were heading. Look out, gang, we're in for a right old earful.' But instead of lecture, punishment and perhaps imprisonment, her reaction was totally different.

'Come, children,' she bade, serenely, 'hold together thy hands and be still. Prime victuals doeth await. Needs must return right soon, or supper wilts assuredly grow cold.'

Lost for words, the miscreants sheepishly obeyed. Fular made sure all three were linked and in the twinkling of an eye propelled them skywards at a blistering rate. Soaring high above the tops of the trees and back towards Bortzin, in moments swooping down through the gates, they slowed to walking pace to land in Fular's courtyard with scarcely a hair of the beautiful woman's hair out of place. The witch calmly directed them to their respective rooms with instructions to freshen up before eating.

Throughout a plentiful and truly delicious supper, Fular uttered not a single word of reproach. After the meal and as was her custom, she rose to her feet and moved towards the door. Today, however, instead of leaving, she stopped and turned.

'Fular bids thee sleep well,' she said, 'this day forethought, good fortune and mine faithful grobbelin didst ensure thee suffered no harm – yet take heed,' she warned, 'Skandos art ever fickle, unpredictable and exceeding dangerous. Further adventures canst freely embark, have little doubt; yet pray first advise Fular.' She smiled sweetly and continued on through the door. Astonishingly, it seemed, they were to remain free of restraint, able to come and go as they chose.

'If that doesn't beat all,' Albert felt bound to remark. 'We pull a stunt like that and she doesn't so much as turn a hair. It's uncanny, unnatural and surreal; what on earth has got into the woman?'

Nobody argued when Connie perceptively suggested, 'Dunno, maybe she's in love.' Bessimer stood up, stretched and yawned. He reached for Connie to give her a kiss.

'Night, night, honey; don't know about you, but I'm bushed. I'm off to try one of those comfy-looking beds. Bags I the one nearest the door,' he told Albert – and was gone. For a couple of days, life at Fular's Keep was pleasant, full of interest and incident free…

The witch had built wisely, taking full advantage of the location to maximise security. Great for exploring, the building was extensive with a great many rooms, although relatively few were in daily use. A delightful, plentiful and varied menu seemed now to be the norm. Fular invariably hosted, although conversation was often desultory, rarely more than pleasantries and the occasional inquiry regarding health and comfort. Gimnal had taken to appearing at the mere mention of his name, anxious to please; servile – and willing to be of service in any way possible… Choklit?

Fiercely independent, Connie was busy with laundry one afternoon while the boys went exploring. In a remote part of the Keep, curiosity guided their feet to a disused room where Albert amused himself examining some old papers.

Bessimer's attention was drawn to a dimly-lit corner, where an ornately-carved oak chest caught his eye. It somehow 'rang a bell' and, drawn by something other than idle curiosity, he crossed for a closer look. Quality of workmanship was immediately apparent. Now desperate to look inside, there seemed to be no lock yet the lid stubbornly refused to budge.

At that point, Albert looked away from his papers, spotted Bessimer and was instantly curious. 'What are you up to, over there?' he called.

'Nothing much,' Bessimer replied. 'This chest reminds me of another I came across in Wegglar's castle. That one also had no lock and a lid which refused to open, it's a bit strange.'

'Don't see that it much matters,' Albert shrugged, 'but hang on, I'll give you a hand.'

'Don't bother,' Bessimer replied, shortly, 'just carry on with your papers, I can manage.'

'Nah, I've seen enough,' Albert replied. 'I'll come over anyway.' He crossed the room and peered at the chest: 'Pretty dusty,' he observed, 'looks ancient, probably not worth much.' Bessimer resumed his examination without speaking. Suddenly, he straightened:

'Hold it,' he exclaimed, 'I remember now. The other one's lid was stuck same as this, but it opened when I tinkered around with a pair of loose bosses – much like these.'

'Go on, you're having me on, 'Albert pooh-poohed, 'but go on, why not give it a try?'

Bessimer didn't reply, but pressed first one and then the other and then, when one moved, he simultaneously and instinctively manoeuvred both sideways and pressed. There was a loud click and the lid swung open, remarkably like the one in Wegglar's castle.

'The other one had a goblet of some sort inside,' he remarked, 'decorated with pretty pieces of glass and stones…' He stooped, reached inside and produced a wrapped bundle.

'Eureka!' he chortled. 'Bet you a fish supper to a tadpole we've found another.'

Trailed by Albert, he moved to a nearby window to examine their find.

'Wow!' Albert whistled, as the wrappings fell away. 'It's absolutely *beautiful.'*

'Sure is,' Bessimer said. 'Seen in this light, I'd say it's made of gold and those are real jewels.' Swiftly, he replaced the wrappings, returned the goblet to the chest as found and closed the lid.

'Why all the hurry?' Albert wanted to know.

'It might be there for a purpose, it's probably valuable. Exploring is one thing but it wouldn't do for Fular to discover we've been prying,' Bessimer explained, shortly…

Life carried on but it couldn't continue in idleness: Bessimer was fast becoming restless. A couple of hours into day three following the thwarted escape bid, he seized the first available opportunity to again raise the subject of going home… after all, it *was* his responsibility. High in the battlements – a favoured lookout location, he addressed his companions:

'Now listen, gang,' he began, 'we've something of a problem – a real conundrum, if ever there was one. We have Fular's permission to depart Bortzin whenever we choose – providing we serve due notice. We tell her when we are going and by what means so she can intercept and haul us straight back. This is ludicrous; pure, plain potty. Yeah, go pull the other one; surely we can do better than that! We just *have* to if we're ever to escape and go home. No matter how many attempts we make, all are doomed before they've even begun. Freedom of movement or not, effectively we remain prisoners. Thinking caps, comrades; meet here same time tomorrow. All ideas to the vote; first with a majority wins.'

They duly met as arranged: Albert opened the batting.

'I *still* reckon we should make a run for it,' he stoutly maintained. 'If we concentrate hard; magically transport as fast as we can, ducking and weaving then maybe, just maybe, we might then make it.'

Bessimer was justifiably sceptical.

'You're forgetting something,' he argued. 'Our combined powers are barely sufficient for two – we're only novices, after all. What might we achieve with the added burden of Connie? Just minutes at a time at best. We've flown alone until now, managing a third could be beyond us. I propose a modicum of caution. Escape remains an overriding priority, but flying would be difficult, challenging and extremely dangerous.' He turned to Connie. 'It's a no from me, I'm afraid. What about you, sweetheart?'

'I strongly agree,' she affirmed, 'far too risky.'

'Suggestion vetoed,' Bessimer announced. 'Sorry, Albert, try again.'

'We need to be especially careful,' Connie murmured, as an afterthought. 'Fular is unlikely to view future attempts quite so favourably. Loss of freedom would be the least we could expect.'

'That's true,' Bessimer replied, 'and if she locked us in, escape would become virtually impossible – unless you've an idea to the contrary? Well, have you?' Sadly, she shook her head.

'Afraid not, I'll tag along with whatever *you two* decide. You're the ones with experience; after all, you managed to make it safely here. Fact is,' she chuckled, 'I only came for the ride.'

'Chit-chat won't do,' Albert snorted to Bessimer. 'Surely *you* can come up with something?"

'Yes, I've an idea, but need time to properly think it through. Be patient; watch this space.' The friends dispersed, still mulling the question: how best to escape, stay free and return home?

Delicate, cautious yet persistent, as fine as the thread of the tiniest of new-born spiders, the tenuous mental tendril probed gently but insistently, urgently seeking attention. In moments, the approach was detected by alert mental receptors and the response was immediate:

'Welcome, O Bez Mer, most assuredly. Why so? Doest danger loom or art sorely troubled?'

'Greetings, Wegglar. We are in urgent need of your help, but fear being overheard.'

'Fear not, tis possible but rare, for unless minds attune, thoughts art secure,' Wegglar assured. 'Yet how so, doth Fular maltreat again?'

'No, she has been very kind, but again thwarts our sworn determination to rescue Connie.'

'Verily, didst meet with Fular recent for vittles to procure,' he mused. Fleetingly, Bessimer sensed a hint of affection, but the wizard continued. 'She didst assure ye were safe, well and free from harm. However, pray open thy mind to Wegglar, then needs no further explain.'

Bessimer obeyed and within the space of a single sigh, the wizard was in possession of every single detail. Explicit instructions were passed and the connection broken. Bessimer now knew precisely what he must do.

As usual after breakfast the following day, the friends reassembled.

Two pairs of expectant pairs of eyes focussed on Bessimer and this time he cheerfully delivered.

'You were right all along, Alby,' he admitted, ruefully, 'we've simply no other choice.'

Albert grinned, smugly, but managed to resist an impulse to gloat, '*I flaming-well* told *you so*'.

'We leave at the first opportunity,' Bessimer confirmed. 'Can either of you suggest a way to distract Fular for long enough to gain a head start?' Connie was anxious to help but shook her head. Albert opened his mouth to speak but, thinking better of it closed it again. He too shook his head.

'Right, then,' said Bessimer, 'I'll see if I can come up with something. Either way, we scarper from here same time tomorrow. 'See you later, Alby.' He turned; 'Come on, Con, let's go and explore for a bit.'

Nothing resembling an idea presented itself however, and having gained the wizards blessing the previous evening, Bessimer covertly signalled his compatriots to assemble as arranged…

'Are you two ready?' he asked. Connie nodded, nervously. 'Yup,' Albert confirmed.

'Don't forget,' Bessimer cautioned, 'as quickly as possible, keep going, no matter what.'

'I thought we couldn't use magic so close to "you-know-who"?' Albert whispered.

'Element of surprise,' he was informed, sotto voce. 'We'll be gone before she knows it, by which time it won't matter. Wegglar says so and he should know.' He turned to Connie.

'Don't be scared, honey, just hold on tight. Right then, Alby, let's go.'

Chorusing an appropriate incantation and effortlessly, despite the added burden of Connie, they sailed clear of the battlements, across the intervening ground to reach the first trees – and at twice the speed previously attained. Bellowing to be heard, he roared:

'Keep going, Alby, we're doing fine. Don't go straight; head for the forest over to the right. Fular won't be expecting that.'

A grave mistake, he was later to discover. Once a course was set, to change it whilst airborne would invariably interfere with the original incantation. However, by altering course, this time they effortlessly attained the new objective and were soaring high above the canopy, when catastrophe struck: screeching, howling gales from nowhere, buffeting, thrusting, catapulting, first this way and then that. Higher and lower, hopelessly out of control; little could be seen because of blinding, torrential rain. Lighting streaked, ball, sheet and fork; ceaselessly assaulting the senses; thunder crashed and rattled – ker-ack, ker-boom and crack-crack.

Poor Connie, her terrified cries could clearly be heard, despite all the kerfuffle.

'Don't worry, Con,' Bessimer bellowed, 'everything will be OK, just hang on in there.' She ceased screaming, but remained terrified. Bessimer strove for control but neither he nor Albert's efforts seemed to make the slightest difference. He called frantically for help:

'Wegglar, Wegglar, art sorely afraid. We are still in the air, but midst tempest and storm, lost and know not what to do. Please, please, come to our aid.' There was no reply.

After battling on for what seemed an eternity, Bessimer was fast becoming desperate.

'Hey, Albert,' he roared, close to despair, 'it's no use, try making for the ground.'

'OK,' Albert shouted back, 'here goes.'

Bending every effort, they gradually inched downwards until they suddenly plunged, careering helplessly through trees and undergrowth, landing heavily in a tangled heap, surprisingly unscathed, apart from a few odd scratches and a bruise or two. It may have been coincidence, but it was almost as if a celestial switch had been thrown. Wind, storm and torrential rain abruptly ceased; tranquillity immediately restored. But where the blazes were they?

Picking himself up, Bessimer left Albert to fend for himself in order to help Connie.

She threw herself into his arms crying with relief. 'Oh, Bessimer,' she sobbed, 'I thought we were goners. What happened, do you know? And where on earth are we?'

'Tropical storm – I suppose,' he replied, 'just one of those things.' Privately he thought rather differently. His suspicions were not entirely correct, but neither were they entirely wrong. His failed attempt to contact Wegglar seemed strange but not particularly worrying; the wizard may well have been otherwise engaged. He nevertheless felt uneasy. What if Fular knew of their escape and was aware of their location? He shrugged. They would cross *that* particular bridge if and when they came to it.

'As to our whereabouts,' he continued, 'I haven't a clue. Important thing is that we seem to be more or less intact.'

'Speak for yourself,' moaned Albert. 'I'm black and blue, ache something shocking and spiked all over by stonking great thorns. It feels as though I've been flattened by a steamroller,' he lied.

Bessimer smiled. 'Sounds good to me,' he said, 'you could just as easily have snuffed it. Be grateful for small mercies, as my mother used to say.'

'Humph,' was the disgruntled reply.

'How about you?' he asked Connie, solicitously. 'No broken bones or anything?'

'Nary a one,' she smiled. 'A couple of lumps and one of Alby's thorns, nothing to worry about.'

'Thank goodness for that,' he said, much relieved. 'But it does leave us with something of a problem. Water we can find, but apart from choccy we've nothing to eat. Nor have we the slightest inkling of where we are. On top of that, we're not too bad but Connie's soaked to the skin and needs to dry out, what's more we need to find shelter for tonight… all in all a bit of a tall order.'

'Ask a flipping policeman,' Albert growled, sarcastically, a remark which passed unheeded.

'Come on, you two,' Bessimer told them, cheerfully, 'less of the gab; we've work to do'. Leading the way and hoping to increase the distance between themselves and Bortzin, he led his companions into the undergrowth. Dishevelled, perspiring, huffing and puffing, the trees and undergrowth eventually thinned and they emerged to be confronted by rock- strewn slopes rising to a lowering, overhanging tor. Glancing up, he spotted some sort of cave-cum-grotto and climbed higher for a closer look – was it an animal lair, perhaps?

'You two wait here,' he said. Approaching the cave with caution, he saw nothing out of the ordinary and carefully checked the entrance, peering inside. It seemed empty but he ventured several steps inside to be sure.

'OK, all clear,' he called, 'what a stroke of luck. Come on up.' They complied. Once safely inside, soaked and shivering, Connie turned to Bessimer pleadingly.

'I badly need to get dry, but how?' By way of answer, Bessimer gallantly shucked his jacket and slipped it round her shoulders.

'Drying shouldn't be a problem, the weather's quite warm,' he said. 'Use the back of the cave and keep my coat for as long as you like, Alby and I will manage. We're nowhere near as wet as you – and neither of us is likely to peep,' he assured her, 'no need to feel shy.'

'Oh, I wouldn't mind if *you* saw me,' Connie whispered, archly, 'but Alby…?' She smiled and blushed, delivered the kiss she thought he deserved and inched her way to the rear of the cave, where she removed her outer togs and most undergarments and spread them to dry. Immediately regretting her bravado, she screened herself as best she could with Bessimer's jacket and, to avoid further embarrassment, remained as close to the rear and as far from the light as possible.

'What now?' Albert wanted to know.

'Take stock, shove rocks across the entrance for protection and sit tight until morning.'

'I suppose… but a warm fire and a nice plate of grub wouldn't go amiss.'

'You know full well there's no chance of either. We've no food and nothing out there will be dry enough to burn – even if we had something to light it with, which we haven't.'

'I was only saying…' Albert began, but tailed off. Bessimer grimaced, but noting Albert's crestfallen look, partially relented.

'Cheer up, it's not all bad,' he declared. 'For one thing, we haven't got Fular breathing down our necks and for another I've learned that mind touch can generally only be intercepted by those mentally attuned, so eavesdropping, whilst theoretically possible, is extremely rare.'

'Oh, yeah, smarty-pants, then *how* do you know?'

'Wegglar told me.' Despite further questioning, Bessimer refused to be drawn further.

In the warmth of the cave and to her relief, Connie was able to slip back into her more intimate garments quite quickly, although it took a further hour for her jeans to dry sufficiently to wear.

Approaching nightfall, the refuge was dark and gloomy and she reached instinctively for her sweetheart and drew him to the ground, where they lay side by side in a comforting cuddle. Protected from the elements, the cave was dry and comfortable and when night came – abruptly, as usual – three tired and hungry travellers settled down and did their best to sleep.

Whilst waiting for blessed oblivion, Connie inexplicably began to giggle. Her gentle, tinkling trill caused Bessimer to smile. Curious, he squeezed her hand and whispered, 'What's tickling your fancy that strikes you as funny? Come on, I could do with a good laugh.'

'Nothing really,' she replied. 'I was thinking about Mum. If she knew I was sleeping with a boy she'd be absolutely horrified.' Hugging him close, she giggled even louder.

'Go on with you,' he chuckled. 'She knows I love you and would never do you harm. She also trusts you implicitly and with very good reason. I fancy you something rotten and I know you fancy me. But we're both too young and far too sensible to take things any further. But just you wait until we're married,' he promised, mischievously.

'Ooh, you say the nicest things,' she said. 'Er, do I take that as a proposal?'

'Not really,' he laughed. 'I haven't bought a ring – but one of these days?'

By way of reply, she kissed him again, sighed and snuggled yet closer and soon, lovingly entwined, they drifted into relatively contented slumber.

As for Albert, several feet away, sleep proved infuriatingly elusive. In attempting to get comfortable, he continually shifted hither and thither until, eventually, he too slipped into uneasy sleep. Soft breathing, sometimes heavy; infrequent snores and occasional incoherent muttering combined to emphatically confirm that all three at last were now completely out to the wide.

The watching entity knew it was time to strike and drifted silently into the shelter on invisible wings. Muttering incantations, she caused the sleeping youngsters to move apart and made ready to strike. A hand flashed to clamp firmly across the girl's mouth, stifling an instinctive attempt to scream. Within moments, victim clutched firmly in an immensely powerful grasp, the intruder soared out of the cave, up into the night sky and sped westwards.

As often the case, Bessimer was first to awaken. Groggily, memory returned and he instinctively reached for Connie. Still barely awake, he patted, first this way and then that, encountering nothing. His eyes sprang open and he became fully alert. Jumping to his feet, he glanced around anxiously… no sign of Connie! *Maybe she went outside; perfectly feasible.* But no, the rocks piled across the entrance remained undisturbed. *Maybe she clambered over?* Unlikely;

she would surely have sought his assistance. He applied his toe to Albert's ribs.

'Hoy, Alby, wake up.' Albert barely stirred. He tried roaring in Albert's ear.

'Hey, time to get up. **Al-bert. Wak-ey wak-ey!**' This time Albert groggily responded:

'Go way. Wossa marra? Warra yer want?'

'Quick, come alive, it's urgent. Connie's gone!' At which Albert sat bolt upright:

'What do you mean, she's gone? Gone where?'

'You tell me, she's nowhere to be seen…. Do you think – Fular?'

'How could she? Surely we'd have heard something.'

'Easy, web of immobility, even *we* can do it.'

'The artful, shameless, scheming old harridan. What do we do now?'

'Go after them, what else? Come on, up on your feet, look lively.'

Albert obeyed, rubbing his shoulder to restore interrupted circulation.

'Do you suppose she was behind that storm that forced us down?'

'Pretty much a certainty, I'd even bet *your* last nickel on it.'

'Yeah, you wouldn't risk yours,' Albert grinned. 'But that surely means she's realised we've acquired sorcery skills of our own. We couldn't have transported all three of us here otherwise.'

'She'll have blamed Wegglar, hopefully. Explains the wind, thunder, lightning and all that.'

'Let's hope so.' Striding to the entrance, he began frantically tossing rocks to one side.

'What's the hurry?' Bessimer moved to assist. 'Toilet,' replied Albert, shortly. 'Me too,' came the admission. They bent to the task and swiftly cleared a passage, completing their ablutions in double quick time.

By this time, Albert could contain himself no longer.

'If Fular really *did* grab Connie, where do you suppose she's taken her?'

'That blooming Keep of hers at Bortzin, where else?'

'Are we going after her?'

'Too right we are. Our purpose is to rescue Connie and that's exactly what we'll do.'

'It's proving a lot more difficult than we thought, though,' Albert remarked.

'Even more reason for not giving up,' Bessimer countered, firmly.

'OK then, which way?' Bessimer indicated the tor summit with his chin.

'Nip up there and check it out.'

There was no need to climb far. Scarcely above the forest canopy the unmistakable outline of Bortzin hove into view, dark, mysterious and ominous.

'OK,' said Bessimer, 'assuming you're ready, let's get going.'

'Now?'

'Yes, why not?'

'No reason. How far are we going in one hit, the whole of the way?'

'Not quite, just as far as the last copse of trees. I've an idea I'll tell you about later.'

'Now, are you ready?'

'Yep.'

Linking arms as commended by Wegglar, Bessimer intoned:

By Breethan, by Zildus, fain let us go
from here to Bortzin, thus will it be so.

They shot into the air and whizzed skyward, making a beeline for their destination. In no time at all, Bessimer yelled, 'Slow down, drop lower, quick. If we overshoot she's sure to spot us.'

'OK,' Albert shouted. Acting in concert they swooped, slowed and settled gently into a clearing, a few metres short of the tree line.

'Whee-ee-ee,' Albert whooped, gleefully, 'that was fun. What now?'

Bessimer smiled and nodded, feeling bound to agree.

'Well, the drawbridge is closed so how about a cloak of invisibility and slip in via the roof. If that fails, we wait until the signal for impending nightfall.'

In the event and after several failed attempts, they were obliged to hunker down until nightfall was imminent. Emerging from the trees at the first warning rumble of thunder, they took off and sailed effortlessly across the open ground, up and over the battlements to land safely on the roof, unchallenged.

'So far so good, what now?' Albert whispered.

'Make for the stairway and down to our room. We'll nip inside and hole up till morning – providing the door isn't locked, that is. If it is, we'll come back here and rough it. We'll not only surprise Connie tomorrow, but give old Fular the shock of her life into the bargain. If she doesn't already know we're here, that is,' he added, sagely.

'Hm, well, maybe. What's that brilliant notion you were on about?'

'Sneak in without being spotted, what else?' Bessimer replied, innocently. Albert kept his peace and headed for the stairway.

Minutes later they were back in their room, safe and sound. Heaving a sigh of satisfaction, Albert dived for his bed – but immediately complained:

'I'm absolutely starving – and practically dying of thirst.'

'Can it. We wait until breakfast, final word.'

The following morning, contrary to form, Albert was first to awaken. Abandoning his normal pre-breakfast lethargy, he hopped out of bed as if following an urgent, pre-determined plan.

'A-ha,' he chortled, gleefully, viewing the nearby recumbent figure with satisfaction. He pounced, pulled back the furs and with a whoop of glee, applied his foot with gusto, shoving his unsuspecting victim completely out of bed, landing heavily with a loud 'whoof' of expelled air.

'What the heck…?' Dazed and disorientated, Bessimer scrambled to his feet – only to be confronted by his tormentor.

'Gotcha!' Albert hooted, falling about with laughter. 'Wakey, wakey, sleepy-head,' he chortled. 'Come on, George, shift yourself. Come, come, little one, it's time to rise and shine,' he cackled.

Ruefully rubbing his bruised rump, Bessimer smiled despite himself. 'Touché, Alby,' he allowed, 'but one of these days, mister smarty-pants, you might just have cause to regret that…'

Making no attempt to move quietly, the pair completed ablutions without detection – as far as they were aware – and casually strolled into dining room to find Fular and Connie already seated. Fular made no comment, merely smiled and gestured them be seated. Connie's hand flew to her mouth; her eyes widened and sparkled with joy.

Bessimer smiled, outwardly calm but inwardly dismayed. Just as suspected, Fular had been aware of their movements *and* the means by which they returned. Their cover was blown; their secret a secret no more, but how? Gloomily, he realised there was only one possible answer: Gimnal! He glanced at Albert, questioningly. Albert nodded; he'd arrived at the self-same conclusion. The matter needed debating at the earliest opportunity.

'Do you really think so?' Connie gasped, beset with dismay.

'Afraid so,' Bessimer told her. 'I was watching as we strolled in; she was far too calm and collected. If she'd been the least bit surprised, well, I'm pretty sure I'd have noticed.'

'That makes you dead right again, blow it,' Albert exclaimed, 'so what now?'

'I'd no idea so I tackled Wegglar,' Bessimer replied. 'He made no bones about it; our only remaining chance is to make a run for it *without* the use of magic and to avoid being spotted. I asked for his help but he declined. Said it would only cause friction and achieve nothing – he won't oppose Fular in her own domain, magical law forbids it. I guess we're on our own, gang. I've done my bit for starters, so maybe it's time you pair put your thinking caps on.'

Albert was curious. 'Did you discover why he failed to answer during that blinking storm?'

'He couldn't, he was away with Fular collecting provisions. Oh, and by the way, that storm was perfectly natural and had nothing whatever to do with either of them.' He lapsed into silence. Several minutes passed without a single suggestion. Sensing defeatism, Bessimer prompted:

'Come on, guys, surely one of you has *something* to suggest. What about you, Alby?'

Albert shook his head. 'Beats me,' he admitted, 'seems we haven't a prayer. Daren't used magic; most likely be spotted going through the doors, much less making it to the trees – although that might be possible given a bit of luck, but what then? Sweat buckets trekking through those rotten trees and undergrowth – just to find ourselves back here? No, thank you, what's the point?'

Shifting his attention to Connie, he smiled at the girl, invitingly. 'Well, we've tried the obvious as well as the not-so-obvious,' she mused, thoughtfully, 'so maybe it's time to try something different. Instead of going forwards and outwards, how about going up? Forget magic, use shanks' pony. Do the unexpected, like up over the mountain, across the hills and as far from here as humanly possible.

If we escape immediate detection, it might then be safe to employ magic. We might even call upon Wegglar, for that matter.' Bessimer smiled.

'I always knew there was more to you than just a pretty face,' he told her, admiringly. 'It's obvious, when you consider the options carefully, but why didn't either of us come up with it?'

'Too close to the problem, maybe?' she murmured, modestly.

'Someone had to sort you out.' She chuckled, delighted to have been consulted. 'We girls are nowhere near as thick as people imagine.'

Bessimer raised a submissive hand. 'Right, motion carried,' he said. 'Take your time; each to examine possible routes without giving anything away… stay cool, be cautious and ultra careful. The slightest hint could give the game away and put us straight back to square one. Meet here in the battlements same time each day to compare notes. Let's see what we can come up with.'

CHAPTER 15

Into the unknown

Having the benefit of uncluttered frontal approaches and virtually impregnable from the rear, Fular chose the location for her Keep wisely and with extreme care. Built within an eighty metre recess backed by sheer cliffs, the building abutted living rock to three elevations. It follows, therefore, that not only was it protected against potential intruders, but was virtually impossible to escape from. Had it been located in the world without that may not have been entirely the case – hot-air balloonists or experienced climbers would be a couple of feasible possibilities.

But this was Skandos, the world within, harsh of climate, alien in terms of both flora and fauna; peopled by two distinct species of hominoid; superior cave-dwelling grobbelins, masters of hyper-spacial movement, the other – smaller in stature but no less talented – subterranean-dwelling gnomes, expert mining engineers – the elite of gnome society, lesser quarrymen, labourers and stone-cutters and, latterly, two magically endowed humans from the world without together with, more recently, three younger members of the same race albeit considerably smaller in stature.

'Seems to me there's only one possibility,' Albert ruefully concluded, 'and that calls for agility practically the equal to that of mountain goats – and I'm not being facetious, either.'

'Normally, I'd agree,' Bessimer replied, equally seriously, 'but that gulley does seem to offer a possible way out. I've weighed it up carefully and it's the only viable exit route, as far as I can see, everywhere else is either perpendicular or else sheer with overhangs impossible to ascend except, perhaps, for monkeys or highly-trained, experienced and well- equipped mountaineers.'

'Well, we're none of those and it frightens the life out of me to be honest,' Connie admitted. 'I've shinned up many a tree in my time and I'm not particularly fazed by heights, but I'm nowhere near as strong as you guys and to me that mountain seems nothing less than impossible.'

'Ah, but it's not all bad news,' Bessimer declared, 'and reckon I could make it to that gulley without *too* much trouble – but it'd take a good strong rope to get you two up there safely. Given that we had some, I'd secure it and drop it back down for you. It'd make things a whole lot easier.'

'Theoretically worth a try,' Albert agreed. 'Better still, find a suitable peg to take with you – and a decent-sized rock to bang it in with. Trouble is I've seen nothing resembling rope around here – or in Wegglar's castle either, for that matter.'

'What about washing line – or maybe something similar?' Connie suggested.

'Too thin to grip properly,' Bessimer decided, 'has to be rope – good, strong sisal, preferably. But where in the world would we find anything like that – or even long enough, for that matter?'

'Wouldn't be a problem back home,' Albert snorted, 'but this isn't home, it's Skandos. Don't suppose anybody here even knows what rope is, much less leave yards of it lying about.'

'Fular does,' Connie retorted. 'Fitted to the drawbridge, it goes round pulleys and that dirty great windlass thing inside the front entrance. You must have seen it.'

'Yes, now you come to mention it. A length of that would be just the ticket. I dare say Fular keeps a spare, in which case where it is likely to be?' Bessimer chanced a glance at the gully, estimating distances. 'Hm,' he grunted, 'around twenty-five feet – eight metres. The drawbridge arrangement is easily that. All we need is to locate the old bat's store. OK,' he said, 'everybody get cracking. Find it: no need to tell you what depends on it.'

Anticipating trouble, Albert got in first. 'We need to be extremely careful poking about,' he lectured. 'It wouldn't do to arouse Fular's suspicions – or that nosy little grobbelin's either,' he was quick to add. Nobody bothered to reply.

Twenty-four hours later they reconvened. 'Any luck?' Connie chirped, hopefully. 'Nope, no sign anywhere,' Bessimer sighed, none too pleased. Albert pulled a face and gloomily shook his head.

'Dig further,' Bessimer exhorted, but had an idea. 'Tell you what,' he suggested to Connie, 'how about telling Gimnal you're missing your skipping exercises? He'll be puzzled, but you could easily explain by going through the motions. Tell him it requires a metre of rope – draw a diagram, if needs be. You know how helpful he likes to be. If he comes up trumps, invent a story: tell him one length is not enough; it soon wears out. Eight times as long would be perfect; you could cut a piece off whenever necessary. If that works, kiddo – Bingo, we'd be back in business.'

'What a brilliant wheeze,' she grinned. 'Just leave it with me, I'll give it a whirl.' Their paths crossed a short while later but as 'walls have ears' – especially with Gimnal around, she made do with a grin and a nod to tell him the ploy had worked, postponing details until they next met at the rendezvous.

'Tucked out of sight under my bed,' she announced. 'No idea where he got it – I didn't ask.'

'Did you remember his chocolate?'

'Sure did. He had his hand out shouting, "Choklit" the moment he turned up.' Bessimer grinned.

'Good *girl*,' he said, approvingly. 'Come here, wench, and get yourself thoroughly kissed.' She didn't quarrel on *that* score. Albert averted his gaze, pretending to be embarrassed.

'What sort of rope did he get?' Bessimer asked, when they came up for air. 'It can be thick or thin, smooth or rough – whatever, but strong and substantial enough to grip.'

'I think it is, but I thought I heard Fular coming and had only seconds to whizz it from view. But it *is* proper rope,' she assured him, 'although I haven't a clue where he got it. Gimnal's a right hog for chocolate but wouldn't dare risk Fular's wrath if it turned out to be hers.' Wordlessly, Bessimer kissed her again. Albert exploded.

'Why don't you two give it a rest?' he snorted. 'All you ever seem to do is gab, gab, gab, smooch, smooch and yet more smooch. Surely scarpering is far more important? I'm sick to death of this rotten place and you two lovebirds are getting on my wick – boring, boring, boring.'

'Go boil your bucket,' Bessimer told him. 'Has nobody ever told you about your snoring?'

'What's snoring got to do with it?' Albert retorted, defensively. 'Your feet stink something rotten; have you ever known *me* to complain?'

'Maybe not, but we're going nowhere till I've checked the rope and only then when I'm good and ready, most probably in the morning. Now can it.'

'Don't be *too* hard on him,' Connie murmured, soothingly. 'He does have a point, you know.' Bessimer held her at arm's length. 'You surely don't mean that?' he spluttered.

'No, course not, but I hate it when you two disagree – especially over something so trivial.'

He burst out laughing. 'We weren't the least bit serious, honey, just pulling one another's legs.'

'That's right,' Albert grinned, much amused. 'Er, was I right? Do his feet *really* smell?'…

'Today's the day,' Bessimer announced the following morning, once Fular had departed. 'To give me a head start and help allay suspicion, you two stick around for half an hour where clearly visible then make your way – unhurriedly, of course, to "you know where" where the rope should be dangling, ready and waiting. You go first, Con, with Albert following in case you need assistance. Is the rope still where you put it and can I nip in to get it on the way?'

'Certainly is, I checked before I left,' she replied, 'and of course you can, just make sure nobody spots you – and mind how you go,' she added. 'A broken arm or leg wouldn't be of much help.'

'Nor a broken neck,' he chuckled. 'Don't worry, I'm not given to taking chances.' With a smile and peck on the cheek for Connie, a brisk nod to Albert and he was gone.

'Fancy a spot of exercise?' asked Albert, a moment or so later.

'What, just as we're about to leave?'

'Just an idea,' he grinned. 'George said we should make ourselves visible. How about a game of tag in the middle of the courtyard? Couldn't be more visible than that, now could we?'

She groaned. 'We women have to do *all* the blinking work. I still ache from yesterday, but as it's a pretty nifty suggestion let's give it a go'… and several joyous scampers later, Albert called a halt.

'Phew, that'll do, I'm puffed – oh, look, there's the rope, just touching the parapet. It's out of sight at the top, so is George. The gulley must change direction. Quick, up you pop, I'll follow.'

Perched on a narrow ledge some eight metres above their heads, Bessimer was not entirely confident his makeshift anchor would hold, therefore the moment the rope twitched he made a grab for it to take the strain. Within minutes the adorable, smiling face of Connie hove into view.

'Give us your hand,' he urged and assisted her to the ledge. 'Where's Albert?

'Just behind – or so he said,' she sniffed. 'I didn't fancy holding back for *that* old slowcoach.' She smiled, giving him a kiss. 'Tell him he should take a lot more exercise in future.'

'Don't be so rude,' Albert huffed, puffing into view. 'I was making sure we weren't followed.'

'Sure you were,' she giggled, scarcely breathing heavily, 'I was only teasing.'

'You'd better watch out for that one,' Albert puffed, 'she went up that rope like a monkey.'

'I'll manage,' Bessimer chuckled, coiling the rope: 'Pretty stout stuff,' he remarked, 'wonder where good old Gimnal whistled it up from?'

'Ask no questions, perhaps…' Connie suggested: 'Are you going to leave it here?'

'I had intended to,' Bessimer admitted, 'but you never know, maybe it'll come in handy.'

'Good idea,' she said. 'I'll carry it while you path-find,' she offered. 'Here, give it to me.'

'The gulley wasn't as straight as it first appeared,' Albert interrupted, 'the parapet is completely out of sight.'

Bessimer nodded. 'Good. If *we* can't see the parapet, then nobody on the parapet can see *us*. At long last, it looks as if we've flaming-well made it.'

'Don't count your chickens…' Albert warned, ever cautious. 'We're not out of the wood just yet.'

'Maybe not,' Bessimer conceded, 'but well on the way. The ledge seems wider to the left, so let's make tracks that way and see where it goes. It's dodgy underfoot and narrow in places, so we need to be careful not to slip.' He peered over the edge, whistled and grimaced.

'One direction is as good as the other, I suppose,' Albert grunted. 'OK, lead on, McDuff. You next,' he suggested to Connie, 'and I'll bring up the rear.' Indicating the rope on her shoulder, he remarked, 'You won't be skipping so why bring that with you? Won't it get in the way?'

'Precaution,' she said. 'No point leaving clues lying around apart from the fact it'll probably come in handy – and no, I don't see that it should. Anything else troubling you?' she murmured sweetly, taking position behind Bessimer as he moved off.

Shaking his head and muttering something unintelligible, Albert fell in behind.

Swirling mist rolled in and it started to rain. Negotiating the ledge proved far more difficult that Bessimer at first had thought. Narrowing from time to time, occasional vagrant rocks and loose shale merely added misery to worsening visibility; passage was not only uncomfortable it was becoming downright hazardous. Almost too narrow to negotiate in places, it was only possible to continue by sidling sideways, hand in hand, backs to rock and with nothing to grab at but thin air. Rising steadily for the most part, the ledge nevertheless levelled out here and there. After an eternity of struggle, Bessimer decided enough was enough and came to a halt.

'I don't like the look of this,' he told them. 'We're getting wet, it's jolly hard going and I for one am bushed. Progress is becoming more and more difficult and the ledge continues to narrow. The idea of spending the night clinging on by our fingertips doesn't exactly appeal. Something tells me I should climb lower for a look-see while there's still sufficient light, and that's exactly what I intend to do. Albert can be anchor man, so you two back up to where it widens and exchange places. Meanwhile, I'll knock in the peg and get everything secured in readiness.'

Albert returned to take charge of the rope. Connie peeked around his shoulder.

'Careful,' she exhorted, anxiously.

'No worries and don't fret,' Bessimer replied, 'I won't be long.' Swinging his legs over the edge, he took a deep breath and disappeared from view. The rope moved as if alive but suddenly – and inexplicably, it went slack. Albert stiffened, white-faced, puzzled – and understandably alarmed.

'What on earth's the matter?' Connie cried. 'Is B… er, I mean George, is he OK?' Albert tugged at the rope anxiously; he was plainly relieved when Bessimer promptly tugged back.

'Nothing to worry about,' Albert reassured her. 'Most likely the rope snagged momentarily.'

A couple more tugs and it again fell slack. Albert swore. What in blazes was Bessimer up to? As if mind-reading, Bessimer shouted, 'Keep your cool, chaps, I'm coming back up.' After another tug and a couple of pendulum-like swings Bessimer duly reappeared.

'Don't gawp, give us a hand,' he grunted, red-faced with exertion. Albert was happy to oblige.

Questions flew, thick and fast: 'What were you doing?' 'What was happening?' 'Thought for a moment we'd lost you, you'd fallen or something.' Then Connie added her own six penny worth:

'I thought something had gone wrong but then Alby said you were OK, thank goodness.

'I was getting really worried, to be honest. Oh, Be-ss-, er, George, I mean, do please be careful.'

'I told you not to worry, didn't I?' he smiled, 'and *'Bessimer'* will do fine. Now listen, I've no idea what prompted me, but it's a jolly good job I followed my hunch and went down for a look. None of us would have guessed, but around four metres down, there's a cave – a big one. Not immediately below, I had to swing to the left to reach it but it seemed interesting so I nipped in for a look. Real stroke of luck: it's dry, uninhabited and an ideal place to hole up in for the night. Alby, you go first to help Connie inside and I'll follow.'

'Sounds good,' said Albert, cocking his leg over the edge, 'but what about the peg – will it take your full weight, unsupported?'

'Should be OK,' Bessimer replied, 'hasn't moved so far,' testing with his foot to confirm.

'What about recovering it? You never know, we may have need of it.'

'What would we use to get back up with?' Bessimer countered. 'Better leave it where it is.'

'Yeah, I suppose.'

Transferring from rope to cave proved relatively incident free, relative being the operative word. No sooner had Bessimer begun to swing for the entrance than the peg pulled free. Lunging for the safety of the cave, he just made it – in time to see both rope and peg go snaking past, disappearing through swirling mists and down into the abyss beneath.

'Corks, that's torn it,' Albert gasped. 'We're stuck. Without rope we've little hope of escape.' Connie paled; eyes wide with alarm. Bessimer instinctively hastened to reassure:

'Don't fret, hon, something'll turn up – if all else fails, we can fly.' She smiled, wanly.

'Oh, Bessimer, what shall I do? I'm freezing and soaked to the skin. I need to dry out.' Gallantly, he whipped off his jacket and slipped it around her shoulders.

'Here,' he said, 'take this. Tell you what, slip back there out of view – not that either of us would peek. Anyway, you've done it before. Shuck your togs and spread them to dry; shouldn't take long, it's quite warm in here. How does that suit?'

'Oh, yes, thank you,' she said, gratefully. 'I certainly will. Whatever would I do without you?'

'It's nothing, really,' he modestly declared, 'it's the obvious thing to do, to my mind.'

Connie regarded him with awe, treated him to a peck on the cheek and disappeared. Bessimer was right. Although dark and gloomy, it was pleasantly warm. Scattered rocks made ideal drying platforms and she was practically hidden from view – Bessemer's jacket helped spare her blushes in any case. After just twenty minutes, the flimsiest garments were sufficiently dry to put back on, although the jeans were still a bit damp. She was, nevertheless, able to rejoin her companions in relative comfort in something less than an hour – and not a moment too soon.

With no warning other than a distant flicker of lightning, the gloomy interior was instantly plunged into darkness. Almost unannounced, night time in Skandos had arrived.

'That's torn it,' Bessimer exclaimed. Feeling for Connie's hand he edged cautiously further into the cave, taking her with him. 'Don't move an inch,' he warned Alby. 'Stay exactly where you are.'

Albert chuckled, clearly amused. 'What for? I'm perfectly safe where I am.'

'You're too close to the entrance, that's why. Move towards me – slowly, be careful. Follow my voice. I'll keep on talking – eenie, meenie, minie, mo—'

'Give over, you big soft Nellie,' Albert interrupted, in Bessimer's ear. 'I'm here, right beside you.'

Bessimer jumped, but taking no offence, he mildly replied, 'Good, get down on the floor and stay put until daylight.' Still holding Connie by the hand, he guided her to the floor, hunkered down beside her and took her into his arms. They shared a long, lingering kiss preparatory to settling down for the night.

The sound of Albert's breathing changed to a slow, rhythmic snore – asleep already!

Connie cuddled closer and inexplicably giggled.

'What's so funny?' he asked and wheedled, 'Come on, do tell. I could do with a laugh.'

'Well,' she murmured, 'it's not that funny, really. I was thinking about my Mum.'

'What about her?'

'I still miss her, of course but can't help wondering what she'd say about us sleeping together. It's becoming something of a habit – and I like it,' she giggled, 'but it's getting a bit risky, don't you think?'

'Not really,' he assured her. 'As I've told you before, we're far too sensible to take things to another level but better watch out,' he laughed, 'one of these days I might just change my mind.'

'No, you won't,' she replied, confidently. 'Once you promise something you mean it. I've never once known you go back on your word, one of the reasons I love you so much.'

Connie guided his hand to her waist and snuggled closer. Quite soon, both were fast asleep. By and large, they enjoyed a relatively peaceful night whereas Albert fared less well, feeling rather isolated, apart from cold, hard, lumpy and totally unforgiving ground.

Unheralded, dawn in Skandos eventually arrived. Albert was first to awaken. Stiff, sore and uncomfortable, he creaked upright, moaning and groaning. Realising Bessimer and Connie still slept, a fiendish grin appeared on his face. *Gotcha, you rotten blighter,* he cackled to himself. Stooping across Connie's recumbent figure, he bellowed, right in Bessimer's ear:

'Avast, ye lazy toe rag, let's be having you. Wakey wa-key, rise and shine!'

Connie woke with a start, dazed, bewildered and disorientated. 'What's the matter? What's happened?' she gasped.

Bessimer merely opened one eye and muttered, sleepily, 'Sharrup, Alby, you silly berk. Buzz off and leave us in peace.'

Nerves shattered, Connie was justifiably indignant.

'That wasn't nice,' she told Albert, reprovingly. 'What on earth do you think you're playing at?'

The miscreant grinned. 'I owed him, if you must know. What's with you anyway, why all the fuss?'

'Time you grew up,' she scolded, 'you're old enough to know better.' Turning to Bessimer, she helped him to his feet. 'Childish twit,' she sniffed, scornfully, 'for two pins I'd give him a slosh.'

'Don't worry about it,' Bessimer chuckled, 'his turn will come… every doggy has his day.' Sketchy ablutions over, the trio breakfasted on crisps and a small piece of chocolate apiece, washed down with a couple of swigs of water; hardly satisfying but sufficient to keep them going.

'What now?' Albert asked, patently unimpressed by their surroundings.

Still annoyed, Connie pounced, doubtless still smarting at his needless and totally unwarranted attack.

'Explore, what else, you twit?' she snorted. 'Supposing there's a tunnel around here leading directly to the barrier and we missed it, simply because nobody bothered to look. Curiosity may have killed pussy, mister, but there are precious few moggies in Skandos, as you very well know.'

Taken aback, Albert flushed.

'What the heck are you ranting about? Have a go at Albert day, is it? Give it a rest, can't you?'

'Don't speak to Connie like that,' Bessimer intervened, sharply; 'and it wouldn't hurt for you to keep a civil tongue, either,' he scolded the girl, reprovingly. 'Now pack it in, the pair of you.'

'Sorry,' she said, clearly not sorry at all. 'He started it… but never mind that,' she said, hastily changing the subject. 'Isn't it time we set about looking around?' Bessimer nodded.

'Yes, it certainly is,' he agreed. 'You've been to the rear already, so you might just as well begin there. Albert and I will take a side apiece and work towards the centre – which gives us a far greater area to cover.'

'That's all very well,' Albert suddenly remarked, 'but what exactly are we looking for?'

'To be perfectly honest I haven't a clue,' Bessimer admitted, 'but as we're likely to be here for some time, the more we know about the place the better; besides, we need a source of water.'

Connie pulled a face. 'Yuk,' she grimaced, 'stuck here in this dump? What we really need is a way out, surely.'

By tacit agreement, the search began and after barely ten minutes she called to her companions:

'Hoy, you two. Come and look. We may be on to something.' Both responded with alacrity.

'Well, what is it?' Albert demanded, irritably. 'I can't see anything.' He seemed disappointed.

'What is it, love?' Bessimer asked. 'I see nothing but rocks, rocks and yet more rocks.'

'Nor I,' she retorted. 'Feel, not see. There's a draught coming from somewhere, can't you feel it?'

Bessimer tested the air with a damp forefinger, first one way and then the other, and whistled.

'Crikey, you're right; it's coming from somewhere but where exactly?' Connie sighed.

'Over there,' she said impatiently, 'a narrow crevasse right in the corner.'

Bessimer investigated. 'So there is. Who's a clever girl then?' He squeezed past jagged rocks and felt about inside.

'Come on in,' he called, 'seems worth investigating – anybody care to join me?'

'It's tidgy-widgy and pitch dark,' Connie complained, hard on his heels. 'Is it safe?'

'What's to lose?' he replied over his shoulder. 'We can always back out again. But before we go further,' he decided, 'we'll see what Alby has to say.'

Predictably, Albert had few doubts. 'Wherever you go I go,' was his immediate response. 'Hang on, I'll go fetch the haversacks. It'll be hot, thirsty work creeping about in here, we'll be glad of a drink.'

With Bessimer leading, Connie following and Albert bringing up the rear, they set off. Initially narrow, the crevasse widened in places, but for the most part was little better, or even a trifle narrower than at the beginning. Despite steady progress, Bessimer was tempted to turn back on several occasions, but the enticing breeze, coupled with the possibility of finding an exit persuaded him it was worth continuing. Eventually and after what seemed an eternity, he was on the point of abandoning the struggle when he spotted a distant pinpoint of light. Stopping to rub the dust from his eyes he looked again to confirm it was still there – and it was.

'What's up, calling it a day?' Connie asked, to which he replied, 'Not exactly, there's a spot of light up ahead which might indicate a way out – can you see it, or am I imagining things?' He moved his head to one side, allowing her an unimpeded view.

'No, you're not imagining it,' she replied, excitedly. 'I see it too – sort of pale primrose.'

'Are you *sure*?' Albert doubtfully grumped. 'I can't see a thing and I very much doubt you can, either – and let me tell you this,' he ranted, 'I've just about had enough of this rotten tunnel. It's hot in here and I'm tired, dirty and thoroughly fed up. I vote we pack it in and head back for the cave.'

'No, not yet,' Bessimer said, decisively, 'you go if you wish, but we're carrying on, right, hon?'

'Too right,' she said. 'Spend another night in that horrid cave? Not likely, at least not while there's a possibility of finding an exit.' She was backing Bessimer, pretending indignation. He grinned in the dark. 'All in favour say "aye". Right, vote carried.'

They trekked wearily on – until, several minutes later, Albert finally blurted, 'Crumbs, you were right. I can see it now.'

With revived vigour and enthusiasm, the trio pressed ahead. As they plodded onwards, what began as a distant, barely perceptible pinprick of light gradually became larger and brighter, transforming what began as a half-hearted venture into a collective determination to penetrate the crevasse to the bitter end – or as far as they were able.

As so often in the past, Connie reprised Bessimer and Albert's friendship. Take Bessimer, she mused; he was cute and delightfully dishy, intelligent, thoughtful, far-sighted and decisive, a born leader and she loved him with all her heart. Albert, almost as intelligent, equally humorous, questioning and, occasionally, downright cantankerous, was nevertheless sharp-witted and utterly loyal, a perfect foil to Bessimer's leadership. Both were good company and discounting her relationship with the latter, she felt honoured and privileged to consider them both as friends.

As they progressed, the light steadily brightened and changed colour. What originally appeared pale primrose, moved gradually through the spectrum to pink until, as the tunnel widened on approaching the exit, it appeared a distinctive red – not just any old red, but the deepest of reds, almost the colour of blood. As they emerged into the open, it transpired the sky itself was red, virtually the same observed from within the tunnel. Seeming extraordinarily bright after so many hours in darkness, they blinked and stood rubbing their eyes, anxious to discover whatever it was that lay beyond the mountain they had come to know as Bortzin.

Advancing cautiously several paces, an ominous rumble from behind was followed almost immediately by a tremendous explosion – not unlike that of thunder, but a thousand times louder – stopping all three dead in their tracks. What the blazes?

'Get down, *now!*' Grabbing Connie's hand and taking her with him, Bessimer made a dive for the ground followed a split second later by Albert, galvanised into action by noise and aided by the lightning-fast reflexes of youth.

After a second or so, Bessimer cautiously raised his head but clouds of choking dust, and debris whistling dangerously by sent him hurriedly back to the ground, arms raised for protection. Sensing Connie's terror, he manoeuvred his back to the mountain, so as to shield her from debris to the best of his ability.

'Don't worry, honey,' he yelled, 'I'll look after you.'

Meanwhile, back in Skandos, shortly after dawn, Gimnal entered Fular's bedchamber bearing the witch's customary morning water.

Jiggling across the room, he part filled the basin to her liking but instead of departing as normal, he hovered anxiously by her bedside, wringing his hands and rocking from side to side. After several minutes and the witch still had failed to stir, he fearfully shook her shoulder until, eventually, she grudgingly grumped, 'Whatever art ye matter? Why fore distressed? Speak, Gimnal, art thou ill?'

Fearful of punishment and painfully aware of the witch's temper, the manikin began to cry.

'Gimnal dost take water as bidden, first Konnee then Dzorj and Allbut too. But, alack and alas,' he snivelled, 'none were present nor anywhere else couldst be found.'

Leaping from her bed, she screeched at the top of her voice:

'Art bereft thy senses? Look again – and ensure art more thorough this time. Return to Fular ere long,' she told him, grimly, 'else fear for thy skin tenfold, for patience Fular now hast little.'

By the time the grobbelin did eventually return, Fular was finishing breakfast. She looked up.

'Well?' she demanded. 'No doubt hast found? Where were they hiding? Now, explain.'

The terrified manikin shook his head, 'Gimnal regrets,' he tearfully announced, 'hast still not found. Didst search both high and low; rooms, closets, passageways, nooks and crevices from battlement to dungeons, inside and out. Have pity, mistress,' he sobbed, 'tis no fault of Gimnal, who hast done everything mistress didst instruct.'

Having been compromised into providing the humans with the means to escape, the last thing he dare do was to admit it. But did Fular know already? Trembling, fearful, and arching his back in anticipation of the first blow, the terrified little creature cringed and waited.

'There, there,' Fular artfully murmured, 'distress no longer, tis no fault of thine. Perchance we shall search together,' she suggested.

'Mayhap thy cousins wouldst assist?' Clutching his arm, she paused to collect her broomstick from its resting place and fairly dragged him back to the entrance.

Fearful of her intention, inwardly rebellious but unable to refuse – Grobbelin code expressly forbade disobedience – the little humanoid did exactly as instructed. One day, he promised himself, an opportunity for revenge would arise – and when it did… but, for the time being, he subserviently acquiesced, immediately and without question.

Once through the portal, the witch straddled the broomstick and tightened her grip on his arm.

'Come,' she said, 'come fly with Fular.' For timeless hours – or the local equivalent – the ill-matched pair travelled the length and breadth of the witch's domain, searching for the slightest clue, anything that might possibly lead them to the whereabouts of Connie and her companions. Obliged eventually to concede defeat, she returned to the Keep, frustrated, dejected and sorrowful.

Fearing for Connie's safety, she decided to approach Wegglar in a last- ditch bid for assistance. Once contact was established, she began. 'Oh, Wegglar,' she cried, "tis bad tidings. I fear Konnee, Dzorj and Allbut hast departed,' she sobbed. 'Fular knowest not where nor by what means. Compared thy knowledge and wisdom Fular art but child. Wouldst thou perchance, assist?'

'Of a certainty,' he replied, 'but didst not guard and protect thy charges as thou should?'

'Yay verily,' she declared, 'to Fular and mine Grobbelin's diligent and most earnest endeavours.'

'Then shall Wegglar attend this very instant,' he declared, 'for needs must most urgent discuss.'

He arrived at her portal a short while later to find Fular waiting to greet him. She invited him to her parlour, bade him be seated and summoned Gimnal. The little humanoid materialised, bowed subserviently and piped, comically: 'Pray tell, how may Gimnal serve?'

'Wegglar doth kindly agree to assist,' she told him. 'Canst bring refreshments, perchance?'

'Yes, mistress,' the servant said. 'Greetings, oh Wegglar,' he added, gyrated once and vanished.

Wegglar motioned Fular to a chair. 'This matter art far more serious than dost realise,' he told her, 'the Advent of Bez Mer itself is at risk, for "Dzorj", as ye know him is, in reality, Bessimer – Bez Mer, to be precise. Connie art his beloved and Albert his squire. Sworn to return Connie the world without and to counter thy vile ministrations, Wegglar hast installed Bez Mer and Albert as Sorcerer Initiates. Albert shows promise but Bez Mer – born of wizardry ancestors – hast learned quickly and well, exceeding expectation for one so young. Methinks,' he chuckled, 'Bez Mer art far smarter than didst allow. How so else?' he demanded. 'Couldst escape thy clutches unseen, unheard and disappear. And yet, all is not lost, for Wegglar will, perchance and with thy aid, achieve and mayhap safely return. But first,' he said, 'what actions hast thus far done?'

In detail and whilst the wizard listened, silent and unmoving, Fular explained how Gimnal came to discover the trio had disappeared. That he had twice searched the keep without discovering by what means or their current whereabouts. She told him of her own exhaustive search in company with Gimnal and knowing of his regard for the boys and that he had taken them under his wing, it was right and proper she should turn to him for assistance, in the hope he would permit the search to be extended to include areas into which she was neither magically empowered nor dare venture without first obtaining his approval.

'You see, dear Wegglar,' she concluded, 'Fular canst do no more and fear they children couldst encounter mortal danger and mayhap be lost forever.' Her eyes filled with tears.

'There, there,' the wizard soothed, 'pray, dry thine eyes and do not distress, for Wegglar most assuredly wilts assist and together shalt depart to search, mayhap soon, this very morn.'

True to his word, Wegglar took Fular by the hand and together they left Bortzin to continue searching throughout the length and breadth of Skandos, including places never previously entered but without finding the slightest trace of the missing youngsters. En route back to Fular's Keep, the couple called at Wegglar's castle to enable the wizard to question Bulgan, his grobbelin.

Totally open, Wegglar informed the hominoid about the missing youngsters and explained that he and Fular had concluded a wide-ranging search without success. Before leaving Bortzin, Fular had asked Bulgan to request his cousin, Gimnal, to contact as many relatives as possible and pass on any information in their possession concerning the whereabouts of Dzorj, Konnee and Allbut, and in particular how they had contrived to escape from Fular without anyone noticing.

The hominoid bowed, comically. 'Tis verily so,' he said. 'Gimnal didst so inquire but none couldst admit any such knowledge or information. None couldst assist, alas, therefore art Bulgan fearful and desolate, my master.' Bowing obsequiously, the little manikin made his exit.

Fular dabbed her eyes. 'Tis such sorrow,' she sobbed. 'Fular doth miss Konnee dreadfully.'

The wizard snapped, 'Thy selfish desires are root cause these problems.' He frowned. 'Were it not, mayhap wouldst be returned from whence we came, for so 'tis written. What dost thou say?'

The witch was momentarily silent and then said, slowly and wistfully, 'Fular dost regret, but didst always long for children. Once when we were united, Fular didst passionately long for a child. T'was but thy refusal didst drive us apart. Fular hast never or ever couldst forgive nor forget.'

This revelation upset Wegglar and he appeared positively stunned.

'What dost say?' he roared, once recovered of breath. 'Knowest not Wegglar hast also yearned a son for many a long year? How then, dost Fular believe otherwise?'

Her expression changed, from frustrated longing and despair to one of astonishment, disbelief and, finally, to one of hope.

'But, Wegglar,' she protested, 'whilst we were together, Fular doth clearly recall suggesting a child, but thou didst remark, "Tut, Fular, doeth not dream, be practical, pray. We must study, study and study again, else sorcerers wilt ne'er become. Bother not about children, thou silly wench, back to thy books, I say."' It was now she who waited.

Wegglar pondered long and hard until, eventually, his face cleared. He sighed and then declared, 'Never once didst Wegglar say nor intend wouldst *never* have children. T'was but until studies be done and we couldst be married. Wegglar didst love thee then – aye, and loves thee still. At last tis clear; forsooth, so many bitter, misunderstood and wasted years – well, Fular, shame upon you.'

Her eyes widened but, wisely, she made no reply. The wizard took further moments to consider.

Astonishingly, it seemed Fular's desperate longing for children had been the sole, underlying reason for her long-standing moodiness, irascibility and soured personality. The beautiful, affectionate young woman with whom he developed an intense and loving relationship transformed into an irascible, frustrated spinster who perpetually spat venom and rarely missed an opportunity to vent spite on almost everyone with whom she made contact, and all because of an imaginary grievance magnified out of all proportion and left to fester over so many years.

Fular remained indisputably beauteous and he realised he loved her still – despite her foul temper and the cruelty openly displayed towards her hapless familiar. Having kidnapped an innocent young girl to satisfy her own selfish desires, she had done her best to thwart the girl's would-be rescuers regardless of consequence. She tried repeatedly to have them evicted from Skandos – even delivered them by the lair of the Brerb! But could he yet – in spite of everything – take her unto himself and again love her unreservedly? Remarkably, he thought it might still be possible – but did she, he wonder, really love him? Despite her assurances, he still couldn't be sure and decided to put it to the test.

Rising to his feet, he offered his hand – and waited. Fular hesitated, and with a sob of joy, rushed forward and threw her arms around his neck… But it was too much and far and away too soon.

Wegglar gently disentangled himself and returned her to her seat. And yet he needed her cooperation, without which Bez Mer and his companions would remain at risk and out of reach. Any form of rescue would be fraught with difficulty and Fular in particular would require careful handling. The wizard knew that one false step on his part could render rescue that much more difficult, or – perhaps – downright impossible. He eventually came to a decision:

'Mayhap all wilt be well, dearest Fular,' he told her, tenderly. But first we must jointly strive to restore our young friends to Skandos or else forever fail to realise the Advent of Bez Mer.'

CHAPTER 16

The world beyond

After what seemed like hours but was in reality mere minutes, noise ceased and the wind abated. Stiff, sore, bruised and battered, Bessimer climbed painfully to his feet and glanced nervously about him. There, right behind was Albert, apparently unscathed, mooching about disconsolately.

'You OK, pal?' Bessimer asked him.

'Yeah, more or less,' the unhappy youngster soulfully replied. 'Corks, what a mess.'

Indeed it was. The immediate area looked as if a bomb had gone off; rocks and rubble were strewn just about everywhere. The cause of the explosion had yet to be determined, but the aftermath was immediately apparent – the mountain had collapsed within itself, completely blocking the crevasse – the only possible route, so far as they knew, for any possible future return to Fular's residence or indeed to Skandos itself.

The rift from which they emerged opened onto a narrow plateau some three metres wide, roughly midway beneath towering cliffs on the one hand and dun-coloured plains far below on the other, stretching into the distance for almost as far as the eye could see. The violence of the implosion, coupled with the blood red sky raised another distinct possibility – had they inadvertently passed from one parallel earth – or time zone – into another? Were they, perhaps, no longer in Skandos? It was a disturbing thought, but what other possibility was there? None that Bessimer could think of. He resolved to keep the theory to himself, for fear his companions would worry needlessly. Good grief, Albert – and *Connie!* He almost panicked until, almost as if a switch were thrown, a voice broke into his reverie. *Thank heavens*, he thought, it was the love of his life, firing question after question.

'What are you thinking about? What's going on? What on earth was that dreadful noise? Don't stand there gawping, help me up.'

In hastening to comply, he realised he was stiff and sore, bruised and battered, no doubt a consequence of flying debris, unnoticed at the time. How might Connie have fared had he not protected her? He shuddered to think. Brushing dust from his jacket, he succeeded in hoisting the girl to her feet and asked whether she was OK.

'Fine,' she replied, 'apart from an odd bruise or two. With a hunk like you looking out for me what else would I be?' The look in her eyes was unmistakably one of admiration and love.

Much relieved, he just hugged her and then, holding her at arm's length, suddenly burst out laughing.

'What are you like?' he chortled. 'Covered in dust, black as nougat's knocker and as mucky as a dustbin lid. It looks as if you've been dragged through a hedge or three backwards.'

'You've little room to talk,' she retorted. 'Were you to swop clothes and plonk a banjo, you could easily pass for an old-fashioned minstrel. To make things worse, your eyes look like buttonholes in a cast-off cardigan.' She giggled helplessly at the thought.

'Give it a rest, can't you?' Albert rudely interrupted. 'Just look at the sky, it's very nearly black. The light's fading, it'll soon be dark. Night is far too slow coming for this to be Skandos, and if we're not in Skandos, then where in blazes *are* we?' His concern was palpable.

'I noticed,' Bessimer admitted, 'but didn't choose to mention it. No point in needlessly worrying either of you. I've no more idea of what's happened or where we are than you have. At best, I could only hazard a guess.'

'Well, guess away, what *do* you think? Surely we've a right to know.'

But then Connie intervened. 'I agree with George, no point guessing; nothing we could do would change things, anyway. Wait until we know more about it, we'll be better equipped to make an informed judgement.'

'Point taken,' said Bessimer. 'But, changing the subject, we need somewhere to camp for the night. Close to the cliff should provide at least a modicum of protection – remember the Brerb?'

Selecting an area adjacent to the blocked-off crevasse, they swept a space clear of rubble and settled down, backs to rock for support and huddled together for added safety. Exhausted by the events of the day, they soon fell asleep, despite extreme discomfort. Snuggled close to Bessimer, Connie fared rather better than her companions.

As they slept, oblivious, darkness intensified, filled with the distant howls, wails and screams of hunting carnivores. Unseen and unheard, seven shadowy figures departed the plains below, creeping ever upward by means of sucker-like extensions, attracted by the scent of carbon dioxide to signal the presence of live animals upon which they depended for food. Slithering over the rim, the curious-looking carnivores anchored themselves to await daylight and a rare opportunity to gratify an almost insatiable craving for mammalian flesh.

Awakened by heavy breathing, Connie opened her eyes and glanced around – Albert! She might have known. Less than a metre away, lolling comically with his back to the cliff, head on his rhythmically rising and falling chest, he was obviously deep in the land of Nod. She grinned, sorely tempted, but reluctantly decided this was neither the time nor the place and that retribution for his earlier mindless stupidity would keep for another day.

Bessimer also slept. Trying not to disturb him, she raised his arm and gingerly wriggled free. Clambering to her feet, she was greeted by clear blue skies, with a golden sun beginning to rise behind distant mountains above which several vulture-like shapes were lazily circling. Judging by distance, however, they seemed larger than any sort of bird she had ever heard of or read about.

'Oh corks,' she gasped, in a moment of dawning perception. 'This isn't Skandos – it can't be!' Frantically, she shook Bessimer's shoulder. 'Quick, Bessimer, wake up, we could be in trouble.'

'What's up? Oh, hi, honey, whatever's the matter?' he asked, rubbing his eyes.

'Look,' she said. 'The sky isn't purple, it's blue. And look at those enormous birds the other side of that plain. We can't possibly have moved out of Skandos, surely?'

'It's hardly likely,' he admitted, 'although it does seem vaguely similar to home. Maybe we've stumbled on a way of bypassing the barrier? If so it might be the best news yet.' Connie, however, was by no means sure. She seemed a trifle upset – annoyed, even.

'Rubbish,' she declaimed, 'this isn't a bit like home, not in a million years. Besides which,' she tutted, 'I was getting really fond of Fular and you and Alby think the world of Wegglar. Even if we never see them again,' she pouted, 'it would be nice to have said goodbye.'

'You're right,' he said, thoughtfully. 'Early days, though. We shall have to wait and see.' He moved away, leaving Connie attempting to clean her face with a moistened handkerchief.

As she scrubbed – rather ineffectively, she glanced towards the rim and noticed that several enormous objects had mysteriously appeared overnight. Whatever they were, she had no idea, but they certainly weren't there before; it would be impossible not to have noticed. Even in poor light and worsening visibility the previous evening, they would have stuck out like king-sized pelicans on a parson's nose. Curious though wary, she advanced for a closer look. Mottled grey, unlike anything she'd ever seen, reminiscent of giant artichokes – or even cauliflowers at a pinch, there was something about them that made her uneasy; the more she looked, the more uncomfortable she became. Opting for discretion in favour of valour, she turned away and retreated. Turning for a final look, she was horrified to witness the nearest object peel back a leaf and peer balefully in her direction. Startled, she called to Bessimer,

'Quick, we've visitors.' Instantly alert, he at once replied, 'What's up, hon? Visitors, you say, where?'

Connie seemed unusually agitated. 'There, right there, over by the edge.'

He followed her pointing finger – and spluttered, 'What on earth…? There was nothing there last night; I'd stake my life on it.'

He grabbed for Albert's shoulder and shook him awake.

'Alby,' he shouted, 'wake up, we've visitors.' Albert mumbled but failed to budge. Bessimer tried again. 'Come on, you lazy ha-porth, shift your tail.'

Reluctantly opening his eyes, Albert huffed, 'Alright, alright, keep your shirt on. Now, what's the matter?'

'Visitors,' Bessimer told him, 'animals of some kind, over by the rim. They don't appear to pose much of a threat but Connie caught one watching her. It scared her stiff and I don't much like the look of them myself, they could be dangerous. Come on, see for yourself.'

Albert grudgingly complied… not a moment too soon. Triggered either by voices or by movement, the entire group reared up on short, stumpy legs and began moving towards them, humping and slithering and brandishing long, scything mandibles. Their intensions were obvious: huge slavering mouths wide open in menace, row upon row of fearsome teeth; these creatures were unquestionably alien and anything *but* friendly.

Bessimer snapped an order, as decisive as ever: 'Come on, those animated veggies definitely mean business. We'd better leg it, and quickly.'

Albert needed little prompting. Grabbing his haversack, he yelled, 'Which way?'

'Left, the plateau that way is quite a bit wider and stretches way into the distance.'

'OK,' he said, and was away like a shot, followed by Bessimer and Connie side by side. Running flat out for several hundred metres soon took its toll, however, and when a nasty stitch compelled Bessimer to ease back, Connie was obliged to slow too.

Glancing behind and noticing the others falling back, Albert switched to a trot and waited until they drew level before shouting, sarcastically: 'What's up? Running out of steam, are we?'

'Not exactly,' Bessimer said, winking at Connie, 'taking a breather, actually. We're streets ahead of those things so let's rest for a bit. No point wasting good energy now is there?' Having made his point, he forthwith drew to a halt. 'No objections, I take it?' Albert shook his head.

'No, OK by me,' he confirmed. Breathing heavily, he was obviously of no mind to disagree. 'But I tell you what I do think,' he panted. 'How about a spot of magic? Be a jolly sight easier.'

'I dare say,' Bessimer replied. 'Oh, come on then, let's give it a go. Don't be too ambitious, try for that big rock just up ahead – it'll do for starters.' Linking arms, with Connie in between, he chanted an incantation – but nothing happened. Again he tried and again they failed to move.

'More or less as expected,' he admitted, sadly. 'I had a funny feeling magic wouldn't work.'

'Why ever not, pray? It's always functioned before.'

Bessimer shook his head. 'I tried to mind-touch Wegglar last night, that's why,' he said, 'and couldn't raise a whisper.'

'What's mind touch got to do with it? Surely transportation is completely different?'

'Not so different really, both rely on magic. I've not the slightest idea where we are, but wherever it is, magic just simply doesn't work.'

'Curious. Why on earth not?'

'Too far from source, I reckon. Magic stems from the ancients, according to Wegglar, and we draw on those powers and mysticism for every rite and incantation we make, without which no magic could ever work. Sorcerers and witches would be utterly powerless and cease to exist.'

'How come it worked perfectly well in Skandos then?' Albert wanted to know.

Bessimer pursed his lips. 'Through Wegglar, I guess. Fular too, to a lesser degree. Distance also plays a part – Skandos adjoins our world whereas this place is clearly much further away.'

'Yet apart from slavering cauliflowers – and nothing whatever to eat, it does resemble home in a funny sort of way, the place we've known and loved for most of our lives,' Albert said, wistfully. 'Have we *really* ended up in yet another different world, then?'

Bessimer nodded. 'Looks that way, I'm afraid. I may be wrong, of course, but besides the colour of the sky, there are other things which seem to point to it. Those unearthly creatures, for one thing – and look how dull and featureless the landscape is. On top of which, magic doesn't work which just about clinches it. But cheer up, Alby,' he said, 'and don't be worrying. We found a way here so there has to be a way back – stands to reason. All we need is to jolly-well find it.'

'Watch out,' Connie interrupted, sharply. 'Those disgusting things are catching up.'

'Crikey,' said Bessimer, 'so they are. We'd better get moving.' He broke into a trot. Alternately running and walking helped them to draw further and further ahead and after an hour or so their pursuers had fallen so far behind they had long since disappeared from view.

The effort was taking a toll, however. Despite themselves, lack of food and insufficient rest, coupled with stress and the fear of attack brought them almost to the point of exhaustion and they desperately needed rest. Having gained a satisfactory margin, it seemed perfectly reasonable they should take time out for a decent break.

'Right, that'll do for now,' Bessimer decided. 'We'll have a bit of a breather.' But he fidgeted uncomfortably, sensing they were being watched but – not for the first time – failing to spot black-rimmed, distinctly humanoid eyes peering balefully from one of many concealed peepholes scattered along the cliffs. Despite aching limbs, all three tried to relax whilst sharing a bag of crisps washed down with water. But after ten minutes or so, Bessimer had failed to shrug away the same persistent sense of unease and got to his feet.

'Come on, let's get moving,' he said, brooking no argument and set off again, followed by Connie and Albert – albeit reluctantly – dropping easily into an energy-saving jog.

They continued for about a kilometre when the pace involuntarily quickened at the sound of running water from somewhere up ahead. And as they grew nearer, water it most certainly was, a waterfall. Rushing and gurgling, flashing and falling, cascading from somewhere high in the mountains, down to and across the plateau, plunging down to the plains below, doubtless to join an unseen river flowing ever onwards and into a distant sea.

The friends watched, mesmerised, as the water glistened and scintillated in the afternoon sun. Albert started forward but Bessimer stopped him. 'Hold it, I'll check it out first,' he cautioned. 'You too,' he told Connie, who seemed about to follow. 'We can't afford risks,' he explained, 'that water might not be quite as pure as it seems.' Albert laughed. 'Go on, you're having us on.'

'Of course I'm not,' came sternly. 'Could be caustic soda – or even cyanide, for that matter.' He strode forward, cupped his hands and sniffed, moistened his lips and tasted, and then turned, with a grin. 'What the hell were you worried about? It tastes fantastic; cool, sweet and as fresh as a daisy. Come on, kiddiewinks, fill the bottles and then, for heaven sake, wash your filthy faces.'

At the base of the fall, through many thousands of years' relentless pounding, a half-metre deep pool had formed. The flow was fast, constrained within a narrow channel running the full width of the plateau, yet by linking arms, the adventurers waded across with little difficulty.

Once there, Connie gazed longingly at the cascading water – a shower! *Should she, could she?* She turned to Bessimer, appealingly. How could anyone – much less Bessimer, possibly refuse?

'Course you can, you scruffy little ha'porth,' he smiled, 'you could do with a wash.' She smiled gratefully, but huffed, 'If you think *me* dirty, you should see what *you* look like.' Obviously her indignation was pretended, for clearly she was delighted.

'Just one small thing,' she pleaded. 'I'll need to strip off. Any chance of some privacy?'

'Course. Goes without saying – but listen, without a towel how will you dry yourself?'

'Don't worry, I'll manage.'

'OK, Albert and I will go the far side of that prominence. It's not far and we'll still be well within earshot. But don't be too long. I'd like us to swop places so Albert and I can have a good slosh before moving on, particularly as we've still some distance to go before dark. OK by you?'

'Brilliant,' she grinned, sealing the bargain with a kiss.

The boys had been in position barely five minutes when they heard a terrified shriek: *Connie!*

'Help,' she cried. 'Those horrid creatures have caught up. Quick, come now – it's all right, I am decent.'

The boys set off at a run and were approaching the pool some twenty seconds later by which time she had wisely retreated and was already in the process of slipping on her shoes.

'Oh, darling,' she sobbed, flinging her arms around Bessemer, 'thank goodness you're here. Look, there they are, right close to the water. How the heck did they get here so quickly?'

'I've no idea. Strewth, seen from this close, they're even bigger than I thought.'

'Yes, they are,' she shuddered. 'I was getting dressed, looked up, and there they were, reaching out with those dreadful feeler things trying to grab me. They scared me half out of my wits.'

'Never mind,' he soothed, 'you're safe now. But hurry. Let's get out of here – and quickly.'

'What's all the rush?' Albert wanted to know. 'I've been watching and they haven't budged. Could they be afraid of water, I wonder? And if so, what else might they be afraid of?'

'To answer your first question, it's possible and as for the second, I've no idea,' Bessimer admitted, 'but regarding your observation, Alby, spot on and well done, but why, do you suppose? Maybe they're unable to swim, and if so, we could camp here in perfect safety. But we badly underestimated their speed, I'm afraid, they can obviously travel a lot faster than we supposed.' There was no way Bessimer could have known, but not only were the hybrids terrified of water, but although mobile during the night, were physiologically incapable of feeding in darkness.

'Maybe they can fly,' Connie sagely suggested, albeit nervously.

'Positively not,' Bessimer averred, 'they'd have nobbled us right at the very beginning.'

'They still haven't shifted,' Albert said, 'may even have drawn back a little. Look, they're retracting feelers and closing those huge cakeholes. Whatever can they be doing, I wonder?'

'Dunno, to be honest,' Bessimer admitted, 'but we'll keep a close eye on 'em. Move back a bit and be ready to scarper.' He stood poised, ready to act at the slightest suggestion of threat.

'They could be getting ready to pounce,' Connie suggested. 'They have to be up to something.'

She was right, for even as she spoke, the creatures visibly shrank. The trio watched, fascinated, as the beings swiftly reverted to the same cabbage- like shapes first encountered. All that remained to suggest they were anything other than giant vegetables were seven pairs of glaring, red- rimmed eyes — until they too disappeared, concealed behind the last leaves to re-furl and seven unbelievably obnoxious and highly dangerous plant- animals finally became still.

'Well, blow me,' Albert exclaimed. 'Looks as though they've given up and calling it a day. What do we do, get going, or chance it and stay till morning? I desperately need a shower.'

'What?' Connie screeched. 'Stay all night with *those* things for company?' she shuddered, 'Not on your Nellie, mister. You stay if you want to, I'm off – and so is Bessimer. The more distance we put between ourselves and those disgusting monsters the better. What say you, sweetheart?'

'I'm inclined to agree and I'll tell you why. They conned us into believing they were slow movers but the moment we were out of sight they upped a gear and almost caught us napping. Were it not for water and Connie's shower, it's likely they'd have had us for tea instead of breakfast. It proves they are intelligent and capable of rational thought, so who knows what else they may be capable of. They arrived during the night, unheard and unseen. Where did they come from and by what means? Only they could answer that. Can they climb? Have they some other means by which they might get at us without crossing water or by flying? Again, who knows?'

'Stop,' said Albert, 'you've said enough. I'm convinced. Blow it, I'll forego the shower and have a wash instead. My grubby old carcase will have to wait. I wouldn't trust those caulies any further than I could throw a wet elephant. It may seem they've given up but that could easily be a ruse. The sun is well past zenith; it'll be dusk in three or four hours by which time it'll be too dangerous to continue. 'Those things pursued us aggressively, and it's unlikely anything as innocuous as a puddle of water will force them to give up. It would be nice to think we've seen the last of them, but we really ought not to count on it. I think we should get as far away from here as possible and as fast as our legs will carry us. I for one would feel a whole lot safer, anyway.' Bessimer declared, 'Vote carried. Come on, but don't push too hard. We need to conserve energy in case of further emergencies. In this place, let's face it: one never can be sure.'...

Having exhausted all material means at their disposal, Wegglar and Fular were obliged to turn elsewhere in order to locate their protégés and return them to safety, agreeing it made sense to pool their respective resources and concentrate every effort on this one objective. To avoid unnecessary travel to and from residences, Wegglar placed a room at his castle at Fular's disposal, making it clear it was solely to enable them to concentrate on the task in hand, rather than for personal reasons. Her concern was clearly as great as his, although he was perfectly aware she was biased in favour of Connie rather than either of the boys. Astonishingly, for one well-known for verbosity, she managed to hold her tongue, knowing that to find one would result in finding all three. Besides, her long-standing desire to secure the handsome wizard for herself seemed latterly more likely to succeed after so many wasted years of loneliness, frustration and bitterness.

Delving deep into magical archives long into the night and after endless studying of respective portfolios of mystic spells and incantations, Wegglar and Fular settled on three courses of action, any of which, theoretically, would lead to pinpointing the whereabouts of Bessimer, Connie and Albert. The first involved further deployment of Plebil. She had already concluded her own search of Skandos and found nothing, but might be prepared to travel over the mountain and into the unknown beyond, although to do so would be highly dangerous and might even mean losing her life. He knew she was fond of Bez Mer, loved being in his company and was extremely loyal, but even so, might not be prepared to take such an enormous risk, sensible and far-sighted little bird that she was.

The second – and more likely – plan involved a complex succession of potent incantations which would need careful programming and optimising of individual components' implementation. The third possibility required full cooperation from both Bulgan and Gimnal, but the well-known Grobbelin reluctance to venture outside Skandos rendered that course of action decidedly unlikely.

Requests to accompany himself and Fular on food-hunting forays had always met with flat refusals, after all. Wegglar knew with reasonable certainty Bez Mer was at least still alive and kicking and although he had made strenuous efforts at personal contact without success he had, nevertheless, twice detected traces of tenuous mental probing that could only have originated from his youthful protégé. On each occasion and to his dismay, the tendrils were far too weak to latch on to and disappeared again almost as quickly as they had appeared. He kept these happenenings and possibilities to himself, however, not yet trusting Fular sufficiently to take her fully into his confidence… but one day soon, perhaps? He mused.

The wizard shrewdly suspected Bortzin to have figured largely in the youngsters' escape. They almost certainly were no longer in Skandos, nor was it likely they could have reached and passed through the barrier without detection or having left a trace of some kind somewhere along the way. Again he kept his reasoning to himself and as none of the possibilities could be pursued until daylight, both he and Fular retired to their respective rooms to rest for a few hours.

Unburdened by the presence of his irascible mistress, Gimnal diligently conducted his own unique brand of search, Weeming hither and thither, disappearing and re-appearing a second or so later, seeking to establish the likeliest route taken by the escapees, or at least some clue as to their whereabouts. In no time at all he spotted a rope lying at the bottom of a ravine and recognised it immediately. He descended to retrieve it and Weemed to replace it in Fular's store so as to avoid the terrible consequences its absence would inevitably have brought… he shuddered at the thought. Tilting his misshapen head, it took but a second for the intelligent little manikin to pinpoint the cave from where it had either been dropped or discarded and, almost directly above, a ledge along which the young humans were most likely to have travelled, stretching as far as Fular's Keep and for quite some little distance beyond.

He spun twice and vanished, reappeared at the cave entrance and went inside. An empty crisp bag tucked into a niche confirmed his suspicions and within moments he located the entrance to the rift and knew beyond doubt just how they had escaped and their likely current whereabouts. He considered mounting a single-handed rescue, but having been impressed from an early age *never* to venture beyond Bortzin where nothing existed but barren lands and voracious giant ogres – who regarded grobbelins as little more than tasty morsels, besides various species of carnivorous creatures constantly searching for prey, he hastily thought better of it. Fearing for the safety of the escapees in such a dreadful place, his eyes flooded with tears and he wept copiously and at some length. Awash with sorrow, he ventured no further, remaining entirely unaware of the rift collapse deeper into the mountain. Had he known he might easily have assumed the worst and abandoned the earthlings to their fate, not daring reveal his suspicions to Fular for fear of retribution – even though personally blameless. Immensely proud of his success and unable to contain his excitement, he buttonholed his cousin Bulgan and related the details of his discovery in full...

The friends fell into a jog and maintained the same comfortable pace for a kilometre or two without incident until the plateau dramatically narrowed to little more than a shelf, obliging them to slow to a walk. Exercising caution, they pressed on for a while, but the shelf continued to narrow yet further until Bessimer wisely concluded it far too dangerous to continue.

'That's torn it,' moaned Albert, what now?'

Bessimer hesitated. 'Off hand, I'd say we have two options,' he said, slowly. 'With care, we could press on for a bit but who knows for how long? It'll be dark in an hour or so and the idea of spending the night perched on a cliff-face is none too appealing – who knows, the ledge might become impassable or even cease altogether; alternatively, we could simply bite the bullet and stay put. But before deciding, let's weigh the situation individually and put suggestions to the vote. I've an idea in mind but I'd like to mosey around and weigh the possibilities myself. I don't know about you, but a rest wouldn't come amiss either. So, unless either of you objects, let's get on with it.'

Neither did, so leaving them to their own devices, Bessimer began to survey the cliff, criss-crossing from high to low and from side to side to side, seeking a route up which they might climb. Finding none, he peered downwards over the rim and repeated the process, again without success.

'That's it, I'm afraid,' he declared. 'No scalable way up or down as far as I can see. It looks if we're stuck for the time being – unless either of you can come up with a viable alternative?'

'Not really,' Connie replied, after Albert had shaken his head. 'We've already agreed it would be dangerous to continue,' she said, 'and we daren't go back because of those dreadful animals.'

'Perhaps we could,' Bessimer disagreed. 'I doubt they're night-feeders else they'd have nobbled us while we were asleep. If they haven't shown by nightfall, it's doubtful we'll see them again before daylight and until then, I reckon, we should be as safe as houses.'

An innocent enough remark, but a remark scarcely further from the truth, as subsequent events were to prove. Bessimer seemed almost decided yet still hesitated.

'I suppose we should call it a day and stop here – unless Alby thinks differently, of course?'

Albert pursed his lips and scratched his chin before finally replying.

'Guess not,' he shrugged, 'but didn't I hear you mention something you had in mind?'

'Yes,' Bessimer said, 'it's an outside chance, but I'd like to try a different sort of mind-touch. I've tried to contact Wegglar twice without raising a toot, but if we link minds and work together, as I'm sure we could, our combined mental output might just do the trick. Fular is bound to have told the wizard we've scarpered and he's probably out there somewhere right now looking for us. He will probably have had the same idea himself, perhaps joining minds with Bulgan – or even Fular, for that matter. I wouldn't be surprised to discover Wegglar planted the idea in my mind in the first place; he has more than sufficient capability. What say, who's up for giving it a go?'

Two nods confirmed acquiescence. 'Good,' Bessimer said, 'unanimous. Let's do it.

'Remember, concentrate hard, don't speak or it won't work.' After a few minutes practice, the trio successfully linked minds and, thus reinforced, Bessimer renewed his efforts to achieve that all–important first contact.

'Wegglar, O Wegglar,' he called, 'it is I, Bessimer. We have travelled through Bortzin and are lost beyond Skandos. Danger lurks and we badly need food. Please, can you help?' Several times he tried, each with no response. Disappointed and desperately tired after an extraordinarily stressful day, he was eventually obliged to concede defeat – temporarily at least.

However, combined mental energy had proved Bessimer's theory – in part, for although too weak to elicit a response from Wegglar, their efforts were intercepted much nearer to hand…

'I don't know about you two,' Bessimer gasped, 'but I'm bushed. What say we rest and try again tomorrow?' Both nodded, and he cast around to eventually settle on a nearby recess in the cliff.

'That seems reasonably sheltered,' he remarked, 'it'll do for the night. I'll take first watch.'

The friends shared a bag of crisps, made do with water and lost little time making themselves as comfortable as possible on lumpy, cold, hard and totally unforgiving ground.

CHAPTER 17

King of the Gnomes

Night had yet to arrive and his companions were already settled when Bessimer was alerted by soft thrumming immediately to his rear. His head swivelled and he gasped with disbelief as a section of cliff shimmered alarmingly, became translucent and dissolved to reveal an orifice a metre high by little more than half a metre wide. He scarcely had time to blink before a solitary, squat humanoid appeared, closely followed by others of similar size and appearance, chattering excitedly in a strange tongue whilst pushing and shoving as if for a better view. Bessimer gaped.

'Oh heck, that's all we blinking-well need,' he groaned. 'Must be some of those horrible gnomes that Gimnal was on about.'

Despite being half asleep, Albert quickly picked up on his remark.

'Gnomes, you say? Ugly little blighters,' Albert managed to sarcastically remark. Jerking back to reality, he gave the newcomers a quick once-over to discover they were short, with powerfully-built bodies, muscular arms and legs, large heads and curiously darkened, decidedly unlovely features, uniformly clad in two-part gear comprising doublet-type tops and pantaloon bottoms, woven from brown, rough-textured, sack-like material remarkably similar to Grobbelin attire, and with feet similarly clad in plain leather sandals. He whistled.

'What's going on, what's the blinking racket?' Connie wanted to know, but Albert merely grunted. Both came alert, however, when a gruff voice barked a single command, 'Grillop' (apparently to quieten his followers, as chatter abruptly ceased).

Regarding the three balefully, the leading hominoid beckoned a stubby forefinger.

'Come, follow,' he declared, in unworldly, guttural tones.

'*Oops a daisy,*' Bessimer muttered. '*Watch out, my boy, this lot look more than a trifle dodgy.*' His first thought was for the safety of his companions.

'Run for it,' he yelled. 'I don't like the look of this little lot.'

Assuming a refusal the hominoid snapped another command and in a trice, he and the entire group emerged from the opening at a run to throw themselves on the trio and effectively pin them to the ground. A third order followed and their arms were pinioned with crude but effective bindings and a fourth saw them ignominiously half-carried, half-dragged head-first through the opening and into a long, dimly-lit tunnel.

As they progressed, their captors resumed chattering, oblivious to vociferous protests. Behind them the entrance quietly closed and the external cliff-face resumed its former appearance. Seven frustrated carnivores emerged from a deep crevasse, humped and slithered down to and across the plateau, disappearing over the ledge en route to the valley below to seek for sustenance elsewhere.

Finding themselves tightly pinioned and borne headfirst in semi-darkness to an unknown destination was pretty scary stuff and Connie in particular was frightened. Desperate for reassurance, she called twice to Bessimer, but realised she must raise her voice in order to be heard.

'Help, Bessimer!' she cried, wriggling ineffectively. 'Help me, please, I'm frightened.'

'Sorry, hon,' he called back. 'I can't move myself. But don't worry – either of you,' he added for Albert's benefit. 'We'll discover their intentions soon enough, but I don't believe they mean us harm. Keep still, give over resisting and try to relax, if you can.' It was sound advice, given the circumstances and all three ceased struggling.

From almost total darkness, visibility gradually improved as they became accustomed to the gloom, until it was possible to see that the tunnel appeared man-made, hewn through solid rock, softly illuminated by patches of fluorescing green moss set in niches at regular intervals. The tunnel remained narrow and seemed to lead ever downwards but eventually the roof increased in height when, barely audible above the din, they heard the leader snap yet another command. The group stopped, lowered their charges to the ground and removed their bonds.

'No speak,' the leader growled, gesturing them to rise.

Unwilling to re-inflame the situation, Bessimer signalled acceptance by slowly getting to his feet, cautiously eying the roof as he did so. Noting it was high enough to stand without stooping, he rose fully, closely followed by Connie and Albert. Prompted by unintelligible commands, umpteen prods and nudges, they were persuaded onwards, but in a manner rather more dignified and considerably less stressful. Progress continued for what seemed an eternity, until the tunnel opened into a high-roofed, vaulted cavern where their captors again stopped.

Whilst they travelled, Bessimer had made it his business to examine their surroundings as best he could and it has to be said that little escaped his sharp-eyed scrutiny. Glistening black in the semi-gloom, he supposed the tunnel followed the path of an ancient coal seam, presumably excavated by the gnomes for reasons he was unable to guess. It was pleasantly warm, twenty to twenty-two degrees Celsius, he supposed – and the air smelt pleasantly fresh and earthy, the tunnel well ventilated by a gentle, barely- perceptible breeze. He was no expert, of course, but assuming the gnomes were responsible for everything – tunnel, cavern and ancillary works – an undertaking of such magnitude represented a pretty impressive achievement by any standards, rendering Gimnal's apparent revulsion of gnomes difficult to understand. Was it because grobbelins occupied cave systems close to the surface, whereas gnomes resided very much deeper, perhaps giving grobbelins a lofty sense of superiority? It was certainly a possibility.

Had he realised just how far those tunnels penetrated, he would have been astonished, more so had he been aware an intricate network of the self-same tunnels ran the full length and breadth of the mountain and beyond, comprised of never-ending caverns, extensive food production and sleeping areas, coal recovery and coke-producing facilities to name but a few… he simply had no idea. If he had, he may have connected the rift collapse with subterranean tunnelling and mining, a possibility other than natural causes – a shifting of tectonic plates deep underground and associated tremors, perhaps?

He reckoned they were around a kilometre into the mountain, therefore little doubt they were deep below ground – almost claustrophobically so. At this point, a voice interrupted his reveries when the leader rapped yet another gruff order, dismissively waved his companions to one side, and turned his attention back to the friends.

'Come, follow,' he again instructed, addressing himself primarily to Bessimer.

'Why? Where and what for?' he immediately wanted to know.

'For sleep,' he was curtly informed.

'Do you mean me, or all of us?' he asked, unwilling to abandon Connie and Albert. The diminutive little hobbit pointed again, first Bessimer, then Albert and then Connie.

'All,' he huffed, grumpily, and stalked off without as much as a backwards glance.

'He's a man of few words,' Albert observed impishly, as they fell in behind.

'Seems like it,' Bessimer agreed. 'Maybe he doesn't speak much English.'

'Reckon you're both right,' Connie confirmed, adding her own small change. 'He's uttered barely a dozen intelligible words since he and his mates turned up.' Neither replied, no doubt busy taking in something of their surroundings… not that there was a great deal to see.

Arriving at the far side, their guide pointed to a pile of furs in a two metre by two metre alcove: no door; no curtain; no privacy. So this was to be their 'bedroom' for the night? And so it was.

'Here sleep,' the grumpy little gnome grunted, turned on his heel and departed.

'Well,' said Bessimer, 'that wasn't very polite. He didn't even say good night.'

'Maybe he meant to but didn't know how,' Connie offered, rather more charitably. 'I vote we make the most of it and see how things go. Who's for kip?' Albert grinned.

'That'll do for me,' he chortled, and made a beeline for the furs. He grabbed a sizeable pile, fashioned a makeshift mattress and dived on top with a blissful grin.

'Ah, this is the life,' he said, with a wicked little snigger.

'Help yourself, why don't you?' Connie snorted. 'There's plenty to go round anyway.'

'Now don't be at it,' Bessimer warned. 'Keep schtum while I try to mind-touch Wegglar.'

When several attempts met with failure, he gave up. 'No go,' he reported, glumly, 'not a peep. We're still too far from Skandos,

I guess. But maybe it's time to try a little magic?' He withdrew his wand, selected a granite splinter by his feet and directed it to move. Stubbornly, it refused to budge. Connie sighed at his disappointment and attempted to console him with a kiss.

'Never mind, honey, better luck next time.' She smiled, but Bessimer shrugged her away.

'Hang on, it's entirely my own fault,' he was honest enough to admit. 'I didn't try hard enough.' Wegglar's words of wisdom came crashing to mind: 'Always remember, magic cometh from the heart', and Bessimer recognised his lack of effort. Pulling himself together, he marshalled his energies and pointed the wand again. This time and to his delight, the shard shot across the floor and glanced from the far wall with a resounding 'ping'. Anxiety dispelled, his face relaxed into a delighted grin.

'There you go,' he said with a smirk, 'cracked it. We're nearer Skandos than I thought.'

'If that's the case,' Connie questioned, 'why on earth couldn't you contact Wegglar?'

He shrugged. 'No idea, to be perfectly honest, maybe otherwise engaged. Mind Touch isn't guaranteed, you know. Bit like visiting; no use knocking if there's no-one at home, so to speak.'

'Oh,' she said, wonderingly, and let the matter drop. But not so Albert, singularly unimpressed.

'Why don't you two button it for a change? Gab, gab, gab; all you seem to do. Get some flaming shut-eye, for Pete's sake. It's been a long, hard day and I for one am knackered.'

'Sorry, Alby,' Bessimer contritely said, 'you're right, of course. But magic works again; that's good news, surely?' His apology remained unanswered; the only reply a gentle snore…

Cushioned from hard, unyielding floor, all slept soundly for the first time since leaving Fular's Keep. First awake, Bessimer crawled to the extremes of the alcove and clambered to his feet. Despite subdued lighting, a check confirmed no signs of movement; not a single gnome in sight.

Squinting, he could just make out the tunnel by which they arrived and, diametrically opposite, a further tunnel seemed to beckon; the only route, perhaps, for making good their escape. Returning to his companions, he gently shook each awake:

'Come on, Alby, you too, Connie,' he whispered, urgently. 'There's nobody about so let's do a runner while the going's good.' Predictably, perhaps, Albert immediately demurred.

'Oh, give it a rest, I was sound asleep. Anyway, where's to go and what the heck for?'

'Anywhere away from here – except the way we came, of course – and I'll tell you why. Do you remember Gimnal's reaction when we once mistakenly called him a gnome?'

'Yeah, went absolutely potty, what of it?'

'He rates gnomes the lowest of the low, that's what. But for some reason they snatched us from the plateau out of reach of those cauliflower things – why is anybody's guess. Fact is they did, and for that we should be grateful. On the other hand, maybe they intend holding us to ransom – who knows? But whatever the reason, it would be daft to hang around for long enough to find out… All in favour?' he asked. 'Motion carried. Grab your gear – and all the furs you can manage, and let's get out of here.'

'Hang on, we haven't yet decided which way to go,' Albert protested.

'Oh, but we have,' Bessimer chortled. 'Out there there's a tunnel roughly opposite the one we came by. Theoretically and with a bit of luck, it'll lead us back to Skandos. Happy?'

'I suppose,' Albert muttered. 'I was only asking.'

Connie made no comment. Perfectly happy in Bessimer's company, she was content to follow wherever he chose. Be that as it may, however, although the cavern appeared deserted, Bessimer deemed it prudent to take precautions:

'Let's go for a cloak of invisibility,' he suggested, 'better be safe than sorry. Alby, do you fancy doing the honours?'

Albert grinned broadly, clearly delighted with an opportunity to demonstrate and practice something of his recently-acquired capabilities.

'Sure, why not?' he replied. 'Keep close and I'll give it a whirl.' He withdrew his wand, circled the air around each of their heads in turn and began to chant:

Stream and river, ocean and sea,

Screen from view so none shall see—he stopped short, as a veil of transparency spread from his fingers and into the air, swiftly enveloping them in a blanket-like shroud of mystical anonymity. 'There you go, fixed,' he said smugly, 'just like that.'

'Well done,' Bessimer applauded, 'right first time. Guess you must be improving. Quick, grab those furs and leg it for the tunnel – but remember, keep in contact.' Aided by dim light and apart from miniscule flickering each time they moved, invisibility was virtually absolute.

Emerging from the recess, the pals sprinted for the tunnel as fast as they were able, making little noise. Soon inside, they slowed for Albert to lift the spell. Leaving him in charge they resumed at a trot going left at a tee junction after three or four hundred metres. Reaching yet another junction – triple branched – they stopped to confer. Baffled, Albert had no idea which to take.

'Which way?' he groaned. 'Left, right or straight on?' Bessimer made a calculated guess.

'Right,' he decided, 'we'll be heading in the general direction of Skandos, I reckon. If not?' He shrugged. 'Who knows?'

Albert sniffed. 'All very well,' he said, 'but what about something to eat? I'm as dry as a bone and absolutely famished – bet you two are as well.'

'Yes, point taken,' Bessimer was obliged to agree, 'we'll stop for a breather.'

Breakfast was miserly – two sips of water, their last bag of crisps split three ways – and a disconsolate, hungry Albert, predictably, perhaps, grabbed a heaven-sent opportunity to let rip.

'Cor, Penny Plinkers!' he groaned. 'We should've asked for food before having it away on our toes. What difference would ten minutes or so have made?'

Connie sniffed, pointedly. 'Can it, you old moaner,' she told him, affectionately, 'this could be our one and only chance of escape, as you very well know, and Bessimer was right to grab it while the going was good.'

Albert snorted, but conceded to logic. 'Yeah, but I'm *still* starving,' he huffed.

'Aren't we all,' she told him, sternly. 'Come on, get going; we've distance to cover and those tidgy little men might already be on to us – and nowhere near so willing to untie us as last time,' she added.

Bessimer grinned broadly, more than a little amused.

'Good on yer, kiddo,' he chuckled, 'that told him.' Still chortling, he turned to Albert.

'Makes a change for somebody else to tick you off,' he grinned. 'I'd better watch out, next thing she'll be taking over and I'll be redundant.' Albert pulled a face, embarrassed.

'Go on,' he said. 'I only sounded off because I felt like it; didn't really mean to offend.'

'No offence taken,' Bessimer assured him. 'Anyway, all is forgiven.' He got to his feet. 'Come on, let's get this show on the road.' And Connie added, 'We've still ground to cover.'

The friends set off but after barely a hundred metres they encountered yet another junction, a multiple with no less than four branches. It was confusing to say the least and Bessimer felt obliged to confess to being lost.

'Blessed if I know which,' he grumbled. 'Tell you what, Alby, this time *you* choose.'

Albert scratched his head. 'Where's the flaming signpost?' he protested, ruefully. 'Oh, go on, then,' he said, 'I'll take a stab at that one,' pointing to the second from the right.

No-one was of a mind to argue and for a third time the trio resumed. Minutes later they huffed, puffed and panted their way into a vaulted chamber and were half-way across before the penny dropped. Too late! With no time to collect their thoughts or to scoot back for the tunnel they found themselves surrounded by scores of the little men who appeared as if from nowhere.

'Oh, crikey, that's torn it,' Albert groaned, 'we're back to where we flaming-well started from.'

Two minutes later, that's exactly where they were, pushed and jostled, back to the self-same niche of the previous night. Unbidden, the gnomes silently dispersed, leaving three frustrated adventurers to their own devices.

Bessimer spread his hands. 'Now what?' he wondered.

Clearly fed up, Albert slowly shook his head, Connie seemed equally unsure. But before either had time to fully collect their thoughts, a veritable phalanx of gnomes appeared at the entrance, the leader dressed spectacularly in vivid blue pantaloons, scarlet doublet and a claret-coloured, gold-edged cloak, in stark contrast to the garb of his companions – brown, mundane, ordinary. Even his manner set him apart, confident, regal and quietly dignified. He stood surveying the trio for several moments before stepping forward and posing a rather remarkable question:

'Why dost leave and return again before first eat and drink?' he asked, curiously. The friends exchanged glances; mixed metaphors, but perfectly understandable: three rumbling tummies versus a leap into the unknown? No contest! It might be supposed that escape could be temporarily consigned to the back boiler, but wily Bessimer had other ideas:

'We'd like food, to be sure,' he quickly responded. 'Having hardly eaten for a couple of days, something hot would be lovely. But what can we have and where do we go to get it, please?' A question for which the gnome was obviously prepared.

'Most gnome food art not for thee,' he regretfully replied, 'but could'st provides hot gruel aplenty – more to thy liking, perchance. If indeed be so, then Graldug shalt surely arrange.' Albert seemed about to intervene but desisted following a warning glance from Connie. Continuing with his spur- of-the-moment plan, Bessimer hastened to accept:

'That sounds lovely, thank you.' He gratefully smiled. 'Hot gruel you said. But gruel is made from oats and oats only grow in fields, I believe, so where on earth did yours come from?'

The gnome nodded. 'Thy belief art true,' he replied. 'From fields of course, just as yours. Many moons ago, my brothers didst provide much stones in return for gold and provisions from the world without. We received none of the gold promised, although didst get oats a-plenty.' Grimacing, he went on. 'Oats not to my people's liking, alas, therefore goodly amounts remain.'

It was Bessimer's turn to nod. 'A further question – if you don't mind, that is,' he added. 'Would you mind telling us who you are?'

The newcomer sighed and slowly spread his hands. 'Of a certainty,' he said, 'I am Graldug, King of the gnomes. By what names are thee and what dost wish to know?'

Shocked by the revelation, Albert and Connie glanced helplessly at one another, unsure of how best to respond. Unusual for one normally vocal and eloquent, Bessimer also struggled, but eventually managed to recover his voice.

'I'm George, this is my friend, Albert, and this is my beautiful girl- friend, Connie.'

'Graldug pleased for acquaintance,' the hominoid carefully and gravely responded.

'Crumbs, you speak English jolly well,' Connie chipped in, accompanied by a little curtsey.

'Pingol good teacher,' was Graldug's immediate but bewildering response.

'Pingol! Who the heck is Pingol?' Albert rudely demanded.

The gnome hesitated as if puzzled, but after a moment his chiselled features creased into something approaching a smile.

'Tis clear art truly unaware,' he replied, 'therefore Graldug shalt explain.' He glanced at each of the pals in turn, but nevertheless directed himself principally to Bessimer.

'Pingol art Gnome-speak for wizard, who art Wegglar, our niggardly mentor, who cometh from the world without many, many sleeps ago,' he announced. 'Wegglar didst teach Graldug man-talk when but young gnomelet.' Three pairs of youthful eyebrows shot skywards.

'W-wegglar!' Albert stuttered. 'Wegglar the magical Wizard? You actually know Wegglar?'

'Indeed so,' the King replied, 'and for many long years. Wegglar once very good friend.'

'Well, blow me down,' Connie remarked. 'Now *there's* a surprise if ever there was one.'

Bessimer couldn't stop himself – he began firing question after question after question.

'We also know Wegglar; he looked after us in Skandos. What do you mean once good friend? Have you spoken to him recently? Does he know we are here? Where is this place? How far is Skandos? Why were we kidnapped?'

The king's friendly demeanour abruptly changed.

'Graldug not speak Wegglar for many moons,' he replied, 'not since refusing gold for stones, and thou art *not* kidnapped,' he snorted, testily, 'but rescued from vile, flesh-eating monsters from the world beyond, poised above yon portal in readiness to pounce.'

'Rescued?' Bessimer exclaimed. 'Does that mean we're free to come and go as we please?'

'Thus t'was my intention,' the King replied, albeit a trifle angrily, 'but if Wegglar truly be your friend, mayhap wilt not until he and Fular doeth pay their dues. What else did ye suppose?'

'What dues?' Bessimer asked, puzzled. 'We know of no dues, nor is it fair you should hold us to account. In any case, it certainly feels as if we are prisoners, having been pounced on, tied up and bundled into your tunnel without so much as a "by your leave". What else were we to think? Nobody bothered to tell us otherwise.'

The gnome king pursed his lips before replying.

'No time, creatures were close,' he explained, 'and few of my brothers know man-speak.

'And as for this place,' he hurried on, 'thou art in my kingdom, the Kingdom of Gnomes, which *hath* no name. And as for dues (he frowned), Wegglar didst promise gold in return for fifty-two score stone blocks and more but hast not paid.' He was clearly extremely indignant.

'Oh, I see,' Bessimer lamely replied. 'In that case I suppose we ought to apologise on his behalf, but there must have been some sort of misunderstanding. Wegglar simply isn't the sort of person to renege on a promise. We got to know him very well.'

'Mayhap tis little your concern,' the King allowed, 'but a debt is a debt and must be paid.'

He broke off and summoned his nearest aide, giving the fellow a string of instructions, with much finger-wagging as if to emphasis their importance. Nodding his head, the little manikin eventually scuttled away and the king returned his attention to the friends.

'Come, 'tis well past time to eat,' he snapped, suddenly and inexplicably impatient. Raising his hand as if in farewell, he turned and strode away, closely followed by his retinue.

Bessimer made as if to follow and signalled his companions to do likewise, but contrived to hang back until the manikins were a good twenty paces ahead, then stopped.

'What now?' he whispered. 'Should we make a break for it – or hang on for something to eat?

'In any case, Wegglar's so-called debt has nothing to do with us,' he quickly added. 'Well, what's it to be?' He glanced from one to the other, anxiously.

'Grub, you daft wuzzock, what else do you suppose?' hooted Albert. 'I'm absolutely *starving*.'

'Me too,' Connie felt bound to admit. Unsurprisingly, after little by way of sustenance since leaving Fular's domain, three rumbling tummies were fairly screaming for food, compelling Bessimer to hesitate no longer.

'OK,' he agreed, 'grub it is. Come on, chaps. Better step lively before it's all gone.'

Without further ado, the trio hurried to catch up and fell in behind as the group entered yet another enclosure obviously set out for dining – rough-hewn tables, benches and so on. Obeying the King's gesture to be seated, they were soon tucking into steaming-hot gruel, washed down with ice-cold spring-water served in crude tankards by several surly-looking gnomes – and, needless to say, the hungry pals set about stuffing their faces until none could eat no more.

Engrossed as they were, faint movements by the far wall passed unnoticed, not even when the rocky surface became opaque, shimmered briefly and then silently returned to normal. A couple of minutes later the phenomenon appeared for a second time, again vanishing as quietly and mysteriously as the first.

CHAPTER 18

A magical rescue

Throughout the time the friends remained missing, Wegglar and Fular were united in effort to find a means by which the youngsters might safely be returned. Every conceivable magical formula was explored, every possible avenue pursued, all without success. Shortly after their whereabouts had finally been established, Wegglar had even suggested Gimnal and Bulgan should make available their special talents to enable a rescue to be mounted, but the very thought had both Bulgan and his cousin reduced to quivering wrecks, terrified of the dreadful horrors they might encounter should they venture into the world beyond. It was fear thoroughly ingrained through childhood indoctrination and impossible to ignore, on top of which, they pointed out, there was also the possibility of losing the ability to Weem beyond Skandos. Faced with abject fear and vehement opposition, Wegglar and Fular had no alternative other than to abandon the suggestion in favour of magic, although unable to transport themselves through solid rock without considerable difficulty. It soon became apparent sorcery was unlikely to be of much use either. It wasn't until the youngsters were breakfasting underground that Wegglar's trusted familiar and confidante appeared at his master's elbow, positively agog and clearly impatient for attention.

'What dost thou want now?' Wegglar demanded, curtly, brow furrowed with worry. Unabashed, the little man regarded his master with the grobbelin equivalent of glee.

'Tee, hee, hee, oh master,' he chortled. 'Glad tidings I bring. My cousin doth reveal that Dzorj, Allbut and Konnee at long last art found.' A look of revulsion flickered across his face.

'But tis not all delight, alas, for hast been captured by accursed gnomes who demand gold afore wilt release, claiming it the king's rightful dues.' He paused, studying Wegglar's face expectantly, clearly disappointed when the wizard stroked his beard and his frown deepened.

'Glad tidings indeed – in part,' his master eventually replied, 'but no more than could'st expect, for once blocks for Castle and Keep were delivered in return for provisions, the artful curmudgeon demanded gold even though neither I nor Fular agreed or couldst afford.'

Wegglar had every reason to proceed with alacrity but also with caution: gnomes were notoriously greedy, opportunistic and devious, manipulative, aggressive and untruthful. He shook his head sadly; no wonder the species were vilified as a whole and universally despised.

'But wait,' he said. 'Wegglar must first engage mind-touch with Bez Mer.' Dutifully, Bulgan stepped back and waited.

Bez Mer, O Bez Mer, the wizard mentally intoned. *Wegglar hast learnt thou art returned from the world beyond. Dost thou hear?* Time and again the sorcerer sought contact, each to no avail.

Sighing with disappointment, he returned his attention to Bulgan.

'Tis no use,' he sadly remarked. 'Bez Mer doth not hear.' He scratched his beard. 'Now where were we?' he muttered. 'Oh yes, Graldug, the scallywag, didst ask to learn 'man-speak', as he called it, in recompense for building blocks to which Wegglar didst eventually agree. It required a great many hours over countless days before sufficiently proficient, when didst agree the so-called debt to be cleared. Howsoever, tis no great surprise he thinks to try again,' he ruefully added.

Bulgan elevated his eye-flaps and his look of abject disgust actually strengthened.

'Vile creatures, gnomes,' he declared, 'the lowest of the low. All doth cheat 'tis but their nature. But yon rogue Graldug be worst of all, mayhap reason he be king.'

Wegglar merely shrugged and reverted to his more normal brisk, decisive self.

'Hush, whilst confers with Fular,' he bade the grobbelin. 'Must needs acquaint and agree what actions should be done.' He closed his eyes and successfully engaged mind touch with the witch, knowing his servant would patiently await further instructions. During the minutes he conferred, the lines on the wizard's forehead faded and for the first time in days, relaxed and became visibly at ease, much more his customary self. Moments later, his eyes snapped open and he smiled.

'Tis agreed,' he told Bulgan, cheerily. 'Fular shall join us presently. Meanwhile wilt not negotiate nor pay ransom, especially not gold. King or no, Graldug shalt surely feel the winds of displeasure whistle his burrows whilst we remove Bez Mer, Allbut and Konnee from his greedy grasp and return them hither – aye, afore he hath time to blink. Hasten, find them and return right speedily to Wegglar.'

Without further prompting, the obliging little man spun twice and departed, reappearing a split-second later, his cakehole agape in the grobbelin equivalent of a broad grin.

'All art safe, happy and well,' he gleefully reported. 'Taking gruel in a central cavern, barely one league hence. What is thy pleasure, oh Wegglar?'

It was an invitation the wizard found impossible to resist and he pounced.

'Mayhap couldst Weem thee and me and all could'st return as one?' he artfully suggested.

The grobbelin was aghast, his demeanour changed in an instant. His colour flashed from green to pink, then to gold, black and back again.

'Wouldst if Bulgan could but cannot and dare not, oh Wegglar,' he declared, emphatically, arms akimbo.

Despite himself, Wegglar frowned yet again and drew himself up as if to let rip, whereupon the grobbelin hesitated, and then blurted, 'For certainty t'would hastens the death of thee!'

Despite a great many refusals to teach the wizard how to Weem, for the first time Bulgan had voiced a valid reason, taking Wegglar completely by surprise. His beard jutted in annoyance.

'Why not explain afore?' he demanded, angrily. 'Dost not fully trust thy master?' Bulgan's eyes filled with orange tears which promptly overflowed and cascaded down his cheeks.

'Bulgan begs forgiveness,' he snivelled, 'but couldst not countenance thy displeasure to find all things not possible for thee. Know that Weem be for Grobbelins alone, who canst not when small until grown and schooled, fain certain death all others.' He looked at his master, beseechingly. The little creature's distress was obvious and Wegglar melted, his eyes softened and, dangerously close to tears himself, he slowly nodded his total understanding.

'There, there,' he soothed, 'prithee upset thee not.' Patting Bulgan on the shoulder he drew him into a gentle embrace. 'Please forgive Wegglar for failing to realise…' he choked.

'But come,' he continued, more briskly. 'Fular doth come and we must unite together to move Bez Mer, Allbut and Konnee to safety – aye, and afore this very day art done.' He dismissed Bulgan with a single wave, who discreetly made himself scarce just as the entrance door opened and closed. Wegglar, thinking on his feet, turned to intercept the witch, already crossing the room.

'Greetings,' he smiled, as they exchanged a brief embrace. 'We have much to do but thus Wegglar doth propose.' He put forth an outline suggestion which met with enthusiastic approval.

'Tis just such a plan as Fular wouldst engage,' she smiled.

'Good,' he replied, simply and recalled Bulgan.

'Yes, oh master,' the little fellow chirped, popping up an instant later.

'Go thou unto Bez Mer,' the wizard ordered. 'Remain close at hand out of sight, whilst Fular and I follow.' Bulgan nodded, spun once and vanished. Turning to Fular, Wegglar offered his arm.

'Come,' he smiled, 'let us proceed together.'

A moment or so later, still arm in arm, they sailed effortlessly into the air and soared towards Bortzin and a known entrance giving access to the gnome kingdom. Touching down at the threshold, the wizard's cloak flared and swirled from his shoulders until both he and the witch were fully enveloped. Having previously used the entrance, Wegglar knew both opening and tunnel were far too low to accommodate his frame; uncomfortable for Fular too, for that matter. Drawing the cloak tighter, he began chanting and soon their bulky outline started to oscillate and gradually diminish until all that remained was a heap of clothes topped by two distinctive forms of headgear. The pile moved and a brace of twitching noses wriggled free as two small creatures emerged, apparently supervising as clothes and hats separated into two piles and deposited themselves in dense undergrowth on opposite sides of the tunnel. Heedless of terrible danger, a pair of beady-eyed little animals resembling field mice scuttled side by side into the entrance and passed from view…

Meanwhile, all was not going quite as Bessimer might have hoped. Whilst Albert was polishing off the last of the gruel, a group of about twenty dubious-looking gnomes appeared, eying the friends menacingly from a couple of metres away, muttering among themselves.

Replete almost to bursting, Bessimer still managed to haul himself to his feet, motioning his well-stuffed companions to do likewise. 'Come on, gang,' he said, 'I don't much like the look of this little lot. We'd better get moving and find a way out of here.'

Not without difficulty, the other two obediently heaved themselves off their tails but the instant all three were on their feet, they were immediately surrounded and jostled by the newcomers.

'Hoy, what the spiff?' Bessimer spluttered, indignantly. 'Get off, you little twerps. What do you think you're doing?'

His protests fell on stony ground as both he and his comrades were roughly frog-marched out of the dining area, across the cavern into a previously unnoticed tunnel along which they were propelled to a darkened recess and ignominiously shoved inside. A succession of iron bars rammed home, they were well and truly trapped: the tramp of feet diminished into the distance and they were alone – or were they? From out of the darkness a voice softly called:

'*Hist, hist, Bez Mer, canst hear?*' Bessimer jumped.

'Corks, what was that?' he gasped.

'What was *what?*' Albert sarcastically snorted.

'I thought I heard somebody call me.'

'Well, I didn't hear anything.'

'And neither did I,' echoed Connie. 'Could be imagination,' she added.

'No, I definitely heard a voice – sounded a bit like Wegglar, come to think of it. Hang on a sec while I check it out.' He closed his eyes, switched into thought mode and gave it a try.

'Wegglar, oh Wegglar, can you hear?' he called. 'It is I, Bessimer.' He waited. There was no reply so he tried again. And this time the distinctive boom of the wizard's voice came loud and clear inside his head. 'Greetings, oh Bez Mer, it is I, with Fular and Bulgan nearby. Bulgan shalt Weem this instant and guide us to thee. Art thou ready?' Bessimer's heart leapt with joy.

'You bet,' he chirped, ecstatically. 'The sooner the better. We're ready and waiting.'

'Guess what?' he announced in a whisper. 'Wegglar. Fular and Bulgan are with him and they're coming to get us shortly – *don't* make a fuss and risk giving the game away.'

Wisely heeding his warning to keep schtum, the friends hugged one another, just as the cell brightened by the appearance of a pale green spot of light, increasing in intensity to transform into the blurry but unmistaken outline image of a Grobbelin. A split-second later the image cleared and stabilised, and there stood the welcome figure of Bulgan glowing in the dark, huge gob agape in the widest of grins. 'Tee, hee hee,' he chortled, 'art pleased?' he asked, rather needlessly.

'We certainly are,' Bessimer told him, patting his shoulder affectionately. 'How did you find us? How soon will Wegglar and Fular arrive?' The grobbelin nodded, sagely.

'Weem, what else?' he declared. 'But my cousin Gimnal didst first find,' he admitted. 'Gimnal tell Bulgan, Bulgan tell Wegglar – but not Fular for fear she be angry.' He hesitated.

'No tell Fular?' he implored, appealing from one to the other. Bessimer smiled reassuringly.

'Of course not, you old rascal, don't worry – but what about Wegglar and Fular?'

Bulgan was clearly relieved and his grin reappeared. 'Soon, soon,' he replied, 'very soon.'

He fell silent, and Bessimer saw an opportunity to examine their surroundings. Bathed in Bulgan's nightlight the cell was about three metres by three with a floor to ceiling height of around two – unusually high for gnome habitat. Far too small for three strapping teenagers, the niche was stark and windowless, bereft of furs or furnishings of any kind. In view of previous treatment, it seemed unlikely it was intended to accommodate them for long. Bessimer nodded, thoughtfully.

'Looks promising,' he said. 'No furs or what-knots. We won't be staying here, not even for tonight.' For once, Albert seemed to be in total agreement. 'Yup,' he said, 'sure looks like it. But in any case, good old Wegglar is due soon.'

Guided by Bulgan and hard on the heels of Albert's optimistic words, two little quasi field mice came scampering down the tunnel and skidded to a halt. Peering through the bars, they hopped through stopping in the centre of the cell, whiskers a twitch.

Connie shrieked, petrified. 'Eek, eek,' she squealed. 'Mice, mice, I'm frightened of mice.'

Grabbing her hand, Bessimer hastened to reassure. 'Worry ye not,' he chuckled, 'it's only Wegglar and Fular in disguise.'

Relieved, Connie quickly subsided, looking – and feeling, no doubt – suitably crestfallen.

Untroubled by Connie's discomfiture, the pseudo-mice returned to the bars, reared to their haunches and began squeaking in unison almost as if singing a duet. Sizing up their likely intention, Bulgan waved the pals back so as to create plenty of room.

'My master and Fular art casting spells,' he whispered. 'Bez Mer, Allbut and Konnee be still.'

The squeaking abruptly ceased as, working as a team, the pair rubbed each of the bars in turn with a wet nose. Stepping backwards, they watched intently as each bar dissolved into dust and fluttered silently to the floor, rapidly dispersing and scattering until nothing was left. Turning their attention to three gob-smacked youngsters, the so-called rodent duo produced an entirely different bag of tricks. Whilst one looked on, the male version again sat on his haunches, rummaged under his fur with a claw that seemed remarkably like a human hand and pulled forth a tiny piece of stick. Pointing it at each in turn, he began to chant, this time in high-pitched but distinctly human-like tones, waving what looked suspiciously like a miniature wand, starting with their heads and circling completely to their toes and back again. Further squeaks and Bulgan, the friends and two so- called rodents winked from view and the cell appeared empty. A loud whooshing sound not unlike air escaping from a ruptured balloon swiftly ensued – and empty indeed the cell was!

Travelling at breakneck speed cocooned in an invisible, totally impregnable magical capsule, three dazed earthlings, accompanied by an accomplished wizard and his equally qualified female counterpart were finally on their way back to Skandos, guided by markers laid down moments earlier by Bulgan, Grobbelin of Skandos, already at his destination. Slowing perceptibly, the cocoon came to a halt just beyond the tunnel entrance, allowing Wegglar and Fular to revert to human form and recover their apparel in privacy. A kiss and a hug of appreciation followed.

The capsule dissolved and three pairs of eyes blinked open, shedding tears of joy under the relative brilliance of a Skandovian sky after suffering the gloom of Graldug's kingdom for so long. Arms intertwined, the five took to the sky and soared towards Wegglar's castle, where they landed safely a few minutes later.

CHAPTER 19

The Bez Mer Chalice

The moment they landed, unshed tears glistened as Wegglar hugged each of his protégés in turn and bade them welcome. Not to be outdone Fular spread wide her arms and drew the girl into a welcoming embrace.

'Tis wondrous thou art safe returned, dearest child,' she whispered, planting a kiss on Connie's brow. 'Fular has missed you – oh, so very much,' she added, dangerously close to tears.

'I've missed you too,' Connie truthfully replied, 'but I haven't bathed lately and I'd give anything for a nice cold shower – I've started to pong, and badly in need of a change of gear.'

'Pooh, art easily rectified,' the witch told her. 'Come; fly with me to Fular's keep and both shall instantly be yours.' Bessimer couldn't help but overhear. He gave Connie an adoring look.

'I guess we're all in the same boat, hon, but you look good enough to eat as you are. Still, Alby and I could also do with a bath so you cut along and we'll see you later.' He turned to the wizard:

'Is that OK with you, O Wegglar?' he asked, formally, to acknowledge who was really in charge.

'Of a certainty,' the sorcerer boomed, with a smile, 'thou must forever heed the wishes of thy beloved, else risk incurring the wrath of a woman denied her female rights.' It was a bittersweet remark from a man speaking from personal experience and the barb struck fully home:

'Tis a lesson wouldst do well to remember,' the witch acidly scolded him, but then smiled. 'But thou art truly forgiven, dearest Wegglar,' she said, happily, 'thou art really a softie at heart.'

And so it transpired: Connie and the witch soared into the air in the direction of Bortzin leaving Bessimer and Albert to conduct well-overdue ablutions at the wizard's castle. And later that day, after a much refreshed trio were reunited, they were treated to a slap-up feast in company with their saviours, lovingly prepared from freshly acquired ingredients from far and wide by Wegglar and Fular, working happily and contentedly side by side for the very first time since entering Skandos.

During the course of the meal, the subject of the gnome king accidentally cropped up. Greedily eying the remains of a tasty stew while still busily scoffing a delicious pudding, Albert idly remarked, 'It's great to be here, but those perishing gnomes will have missed us by now. Really neat the way you whizzed us out of there,' he said, glancing from Wegglar to Fular admiringly.

'I'll bet Graldug was – still is, for that matter, absolutely furious,' Bessimer remarked, sagely. 'They must all be scratching their heads.'

Unusually, Wegglar permitted himself a satisfied smile.

'T'was nothing, really,' he said modestly, 'just a little magic. Fular be equally responsible.'

'Well, we're etremely grateful to you both,' Connie said, not to be denied. 'I think you're both wonderful and make a lovely couple.'

Fular blushed, whereas Wegglar hastily changed the subject.

'Wilt visit Graldug the morrow,' he announced, firmly. 'Didst rescue and treat thee well and art deserving of compensation. Wegglar shalt therefore pay him five gold pieces as reward.'

'Canst afford, dearest Wegglar?' the witch asked, anxiously. 'Fular has little enough left.'

'Mayhap riches remaining art little enough,' he slowly and actually fibbed, 'but a goodly deed needs be acknowledged and cannot pass unremarked.'

At this, Bessimer's ears pricked up. 'You could always sell your gold cup,' he suggested, 'probably worth a king's ransom.'

Wegglar's expression said it all: *What on earth was the boy on about?* Clearly, he had no idea.

'What gold cup?' he demanded to know. 'Wegglar doth possess no such object.'

'You really don't know?' Bessimer gasped, scarcely believing his ears. 'It's tucked away in an oaken chest in a room the other side of the castle. I stumbled across it when Albert and I were exploring one day. Been there donkey's years, judging by the amount of dust. Sorry,' he meekly added, 'I was just curious and didn't mean to snoop.'

The wizard swiftly recovered his composure. ''Tis of no great moment,' he said, casually. 'If tis true art destiny and destiny shalt ever prevail. But come,' he went on, with a smile, 'if art finished mayhap wouldst accompany Wegglar hence.'

'It's true alright,' Bessimer replied. 'I'm stuffed and couldn't eat another thing. I'm ready if you are,' he said, rising to his feet.

'Wilt return anon,' the wizard told Fular and Connie, as he and Bessimer left arm in arm. Whilst readily recalling the room – he built it – the chest presented something of an enigma, however. It was not one he made himself, nor could recall seeing before. He fleetingly wondered where on earth it could have sprung from. But when Bessimer confidently manipulated the lid mechanism, the point paled into insignificance and he decided it unworthy of comment.

Five minutes later they were back, Wegglar bearing an ornate gold drinking vessel which he placed on the table for all to see.

Fular and Connie sat for a while, staring in astonishment at the gorgeous, heavily-jewelled artefact. Seen in daylight, the treasure was incredibly beautiful and the witch lost little time in saying so. 'Tis wondrous to behold,' she murmured, picking it up for a closer look. 'Fular has never in her life seen the likes afore.'

'You should have,' Bessimer remarked, sharply, 'cos you've got one just like it. It's tucked away in a chest in one of your cellars just like this one was. Were you keeping a secret, or something?'

The revelation earned him shocked disbelief and an instant reproof. Fular glared at him, angrily.

'Dost imply Fular be telling untruth?' she screeched. 'Fular assuredly *hath* no such possession.'

'But,' Bessimer helplessly spluttered, 'yes, you have, I've seen it for myself. I mean neither harm nor disrespect,' he swiftly added, 'I'm merely trying to help.'

The witch went ballistic. Practically incandescent with rage she appealed directly to Wegglar.

'Dost thou not believe me, either?' she demanded, eyes full of resentment.

With the benefit of personal experience and therefore well qualified to judge the sort of mischief she was capable of, the wizard hastened to pacify the furious woman.

'Hist now, dearest heart,' he soothed, 'upset not thyself. Bez Mer doth express surprise, not disbelief. Mayhap like Wegglar, tis destiny thou should'st also possess a golden cup. Be thou grateful Bez Mer art possessed of long, pointy nose,' he sternly admonished, but with a twinkle.

'Forsooth he should give up wizardry and hunt instead for truffles,' he artfully added. Remarks calculated to remove the sting from the situation — and they did.

The witch instantly subsided and burst out laughing. 'Lawks a mercy me,' she chortled, wiping tears from her eyes to examine the trophy more closely. 'To think art also possessed of such beautiful treasure and knowest not,' she breathed. 'Perchance Bez Mer shalt accompany Fular on the morrow to guides the way?' she begged. Never before had she addressed him by the name Wegglar so strenuously insisted was rightfully his, a fact Bessimer was quick to acknowledge.

'I'd be truly be honoured, ma'am, I've never flown with you before,' he accepted. 'But I'd rather you called me "George", just as before. It's the name by which I'm usually known and the one I feel most comfortable with. I'm not really "Bez Mer", you know. Thank you anyway.'

'Yet Konnee doth always call thou "Bessimer",' she protested, seeming puzzled.

'Connie is my girlfriend and very special,' he informed her.

'As you wish,' the witch replied, absently. She rose to her feet to begin clearing the table but Wegglar hastened to intervene.

'It's been a long, busy day, my dear,' he solicitously said, 'and you seem tired. Why not leave the dishes to me and have an early night?'

She smiled gratefully and kissed his whiskery cheek.

'Thank you, dearest heart, methinks I shall,' she replied. Crossing to Connie, she affectionately kissed her, bade her good night and turned to face Bessimer. Her face creased into a friendly smile.

'Goodnight, dear Bes – er, George,' she corrected herself. 'Fular shalt see thee on the morrow.'

'OK, sleep tight, Fular,' he replied, as both he and Albert got on with assisting the wizard.

The Skandovian night passed peacefully enough and shortly after breakfast the following morning, the witch duly buttonholed

Bessimer and led him to the battlements. 'Fular knowest thou canst already fly,' she told him, 'but stand still and leave everything thing to me.'

Confident he could easily recover should anything go wrong, he obediently complied. Gripping him by the arm, she muttered an incantation and shot into the air, dragging Bessimer with her. She was astonishingly strong.

Whizzing though the skies at an impossible rate brought tears to his eyes. *Yes, I can fly,'* he thought, *but nowhere near as fast – with the return journey still to come!* Ah, poor Bessimer! But landing safely at Fular's Keep minutes later, he soon cast lingering concerns from his mind.

Leading Fular unhesitatingly to the chest in which the vessel was secreted, he twiddled the bosses and the lid sprang open. A quick glance confirmed it still there, apparently undisturbed, and he retrieved the package and handed it to the witch unopened. Moving to better light, she removed the cloth to examine the item more closely: 'Art really mine?' she breathed. Not seeking an answer, she replaced the wrappings and led the way back to the roof.

Still no broomstick, Bessimer casually noted. *No room for two anyway,* he supposed, reminding himself she took to the air perfectly well without, yet gritting his teeth in readiness for takeoff. To his surprise and despite being every bit as fast, the return journey proved as smooth as silk and not in the least bit frightening.

Half an hour later a pair of jewelled gold drinking vessels stood proudly on display side by side on Wegglar's living room table. Seemingly identical, both were absolutely beautiful.

'May I?' Bessimer asked, timidly and when nobody objected, picked one up for a closer look. He turned it, first one way and then the other, upside down and back again. Replacing it on the table he subjected the second to an equally thorough examination. 'Which one belongs to you?' he asked Fular.

'That one,' she replied, pointing to the nearest.

Looking puzzled, Wegglar chipped in. 'As far as can readily be seen,' he observed, cautiously, 'art nothing to distinguish one from the other.'

'Except for one small thing,' Bessimer murmured, at pains not to appear unduly triumphant. Confident he could distinguish one from the other, he upended both and pointed to the bases.

'Look a little closer,' he said. 'You'll see they're actually male and female. The one belonging to Fular has concaved grooving just inside the rim whereas yours has matching protrusions.

'Blessed if thou art not right,' the wizard exclaimed, peering closer. 'Why then should'st thus be so?' he wondered, stroking his beard, thoughtfully.

'Tis surely of little concern,' Fular suddenly snapped, tiring of what seemed to her to be nothing more than needless nit-picking.

Bessimer suspected he knew the answer. Wordlessly, he gingerly offered the base of one to the other – and it entered readily. Gentle pressure, a turn and a twist gave way to a loud 'click' and the pair became locked together. He attempted to reverse the process but neither half would budge. Frantically, he tried but again without success.

'Oh, corks,' he muttered, half under his breath, 'now what do I do?'

Nobody answered. Painfully aware four pairs of eyes were watching his every move, keenly aware one half belonged to Fular, the other to Wegglar, he took a deep breath to give it one last shot. Straining with all his might and red-faced with effort, he twisted, turned, pulled and shoved – yet failed miserably.

Two separate drinking pots of incalculable worth now seemed irrevocably connected. What should he do? But were they truly identical? He determined to find out. Firstly he placed the conjoined pair on the table Fular side up and studied the result, reversed them and carefully checked again; no apparent differences that he could tell, apart from the hidden connection system. He sighed: time to face the music. In trepidation and with thundering heart, he crossed his fingers and addressed the watchers over his shoulder, none of whom had uttered a sound throughout.

'Sorry, folks, seems like they're stuck,' he said, almost casually. 'Don't suppose it matters much, though, they seem virtually identical – apart from the way they connect, that is,' he added. 'Maybe you'd like to try to part them, O Wegglar?'

In the absence of a response, he turned to face the wizard's wrath – only to discover him down on one knee holding the witch's hand whilst looking deeply into her eyes. Fular for her part appeared mesmerised by the intensity of his gaze. Albert merely looked on, silent and uncomprehending, mouth agape.

Didn't anybody care he had a potentially serious problem on his hands? Bessimer huffed. 'What the spiff?' He glanced down sharply.

The artefact seemed to have become animated of its own volition – alive, almost, right under his nose. There was an impression of light shining from somewhere deep within. The precious metal gleamed as if freshly polished. Every single jewel glowed, sparkled and flashed; a myriad stars against a burnished background. Not for the first time, Bessimer felt a curious sense of familiarity sweep over him; it was almost as if he's been here before. A feeling of euphoria seemed to permeate every atom of his being; the very air seemed charged with electricity, coinciding with the very moment Wegglar chose to speak.

'Dearest Fular,' he began, 'Wegglar doest love thee with all my heart. To thee I pledge my troth and beg for thy hand in marriage.' Producing a magnificent diamond ring acquired many years ago towards the end of their courtship, he slipped it on the third finger of her left hand. Gazing intently into her eyes, he nervously begged, 'Wilt thou marry me?'

The witch shrieked with delight and fairly leapt to her feet to fall helplessly into his arms. The long-suppressed chemistry between them was palpable.

'Yes,' she cried, 'yes, yes, of course I will!' Her face literally shone with joy.

During the ensuing silence while they kissed, for Bessimer the penny suddenly dropped. Fanned by the flames of inner conviction, he realised these were never designed to be matching goblets, beautiful though they undoubtedly were, but united together as a single spectacular chalice, identical no matter whichever way up. It seemed obvious now; the cup would become the base one way or vice versa. Further attempts to separate the haves would be futile; they clearly belonged together. He sighed with relief; he was off the hook, there'd be no recriminations, after all.

He glanced at Connie to catch her eye. It wasn't difficult, she was already watching him, lips parted provocatively and looking more desirable than ever he remembered. Not even thinking about it, he rushed into her welcoming arms and they kissed – and they kissed – and they kissed.

'Hoy, give it a rest, can't you?' Albert suddenly blurted, flushed with embarrassment. 'First those blinking two, now you pair snogging like there's no tomorrow. Has the world gone mad?'

Bessimer and Connie immediately separated – but far from apologetically, it must be said. Still holding his sweetheart by the hand, the enamoured youth faced squarely up to his responsibilities.

'Sorry, Alby,' he said, even if not in the least contrite. 'I suppose there's a time and place for everything, but Connie and I are so much in love we really couldn't help ourselves. Something in the air, I suppose. But listen, one day we'll be married and I'd like you to do me the honour of becoming my Best Man? How do you feel about that?'

Irritation forgotten, Albert beamed with pleasure. 'Just you try and stop me, mate,' he chortled… Problem solved!

Disturbed by the chatter, Wegglar and Fular finally – and reluctantly, it seemed – pulled apart.

To Bessimer's astonishment, the wizard again fell to one knee, this time facing the bemused boy, whilst bowing his head obsequiously. Fular started forward, stopped by a warning glance from her recently betrothed. Connie and Albert merely looked on, both appearing puzzled.

'Tis the Advent of Bez Mer,' the wizard declared, almost reverently. 'Thou are truly Bez Mer as often hast said, come to Skandos to remove the magical bond that didst bind and compel Wegglar and Fular to forever remain in Skandos. An ancient Symbol of Togetherness now stands before us and commands lovers and those at variance to cast aside their differences and unite. It is written. At last we are free and therefore Wegglar shalt serve thee faithfully and be in thy debt forever. What now is thy command, O Bez Mer?'

'Corks,' said Albert, totally flummoxed.

'I just knew it,' Connie cried. 'I've always loved you and always will.'

Bessimer grinned sheepishly, stepped forward to assist Wegglar to his feet. 'Aw, shucks,' he blushed, 'if you say so, then fair enough, I suppose. But you really are most welcome – both of you,' he added, smiling anxiously at Fular.

Previous wariness permanently swept aside and positively radiating happiness, the beautiful raven-haired sorceress dropped a curtsy, smiled gratefully and acknowledged her own debt to the deeply embarrassed boy.

'Fular dost truly regret doubting,' she began. 'Wegglar, my beloved, art right, thou art indeed Bez Mer, seed of Zildus, master magician of the ancients, come to Skandos as long foretold. Fular doth therefore bow her head and wilt faithfully serve and honour thee as rightfully should'st. Canst thou – *wilts* thou forgive the past sins of a lonely, sad and bitter old woman?'

Not for one instant did Bessimer hesitate. 'Of course I will,' he said warmly, 'not that there's anything to forgive – and you're certainly not old,' he quickly added, 'far from it. You only did what you thought to be right and there's nothing wrong with that.' He moved to help her to her feet, but was forestalled by the wizard, who grabbed the witch's hand and answered for her.

'Thou art both generous and kind, O Bez Mer, for which art grateful,' he declared, then produced a bombshell of his own. 'As dost know, Wegglar and Fular art soon to marry – as one day so shall ye,' he said, with a smile for Connie. 'Pray tell, what art "Best Man"?'

Bessimer quickly explained.

'Aha.' The sorcerer slowly nodded. 'Wegglar doth understand. Then mayhap Bez Mer wouldst truly honour Wegglar and be *his* "Best Man"?' he asked, anxiously.

'Of course I will, goes without saying. I'd be delighted,' the boy replied. Despite himself, Bessimer just couldn't resist a mischievous grin. 'You two lovebirds make a lovely couple.'

CHAPTER 20

The homecoming

Packing a few necessities, Fular closed her Keep, magically secured against unwanted intruders and took up residence at Wegglar's castle, where the couple intended to spend their honeymoon and visit as and whenever they chose. Wegglar privately decided never to abandon the much-treasured and beautiful castle he had so diligently built and lovingly equipped over time, but to preserve and maintain it for holidays far into the future.

The flight to Nantwich was simple, fast and uneventful. Sailing effortlessly through the air, the quintet crossed the Skandovian landscape to reach the barrier in minutes which, although still very much in evidence, no longer presented a hindrance. Touching down beside the canal, it was agreed they should cover the remaining distance on foot. They therefore separated, Albert strolling unhurriedly in the direction of town, taking in something of the green and pleasant surroundings he so well remembered, now strangely alien after so many days in Skandos, leaving two deeply enamoured couples to follow in his wake.

Connie and Bessimer were anxious to be home, but far too wrapped up with one another to take in much of the scenery.

Fular and Wegglar, however, gazed about wonderingly, chattering excitedly about almost everything they saw, the blueness of the sky, oak, elm, ash, elder and lime trees, green, verdant pastures dotted with cattle, birds going about their daily business, rabbits, a badger, an occasional squirrel, and even a curious vixen.

But even though they took their time, all too soon they found themselves knocking on Connie's front door. Her mother answered.

'Oh my goodness,' she shrieked, 'Connie, Bessimer, Albert, where on earth have you been? We've been worried sick. What's wrong with your mobile?' Then realising they were not alone: 'And just who, pray, are these two people?' she demanded. 'But never mind all that,' she gabbled on, scarcely taking breath, 'you're home safe and sound, that's the main thing.' Grabbing her daughter, hugging, kissing her and almost beside herself with relief, lovingly smoothed the girl's hair and kissed her, again and yet again. 'Well,' she demanded, 'aren't you going to introduce us?'

Connie laughed. 'Oh, Mum, you do go on. Meet two very good friends who've been looking after us. This is Wegglar and this is Fular. We took turn a wrong turn and they kindly came to our rescue – and my flipping battery upped and went flat, if you must know,' she added, offering the instrument as proof.

'Pleased to meet you, I'm sure, but come on in, don't just stand on the doorstep.'

Connie's simple explanation regarding their seven-day absence was accepted without further question. The full facts and time spent beyond the barrier were scarcely credible, anyway. And later, after chatting over a cup of tea, five oddly matched people knocked on Albert and Bessimer's respective doors, gaining remarkably similar receptions. Neither the tall, distinguished-looking gentleman nor his beautiful companion elicited comment, adverse or otherwise, despite their unusual dress and distinctive headgear.

Nostalgically homesick, Wegglar revisited his former residence in Makklis (now Macclesfield), and promptly reversed his former decision to leave his Skandovian residence where it was, and instead to purchase suitable nearby land and one day relocate his castle, block by block. On informing Fular of his decision, she cheerfully abandoned her one-time ill- informed objections and agreed it should one day become the marital home. She made a similar visit to *her* former home at Than-Gol (now Llangollen). Approaching the front door it swung open as if by magic and there, lying on the mat addressed to her, a legal-looking document proclaimed her the legal owner, having been bequeathed the entire estate by the late Zildus.

Albert and Bessimer remained the firmest of friends, jointly accepting Wegglar's suggestion they should continue their magical studies under his guidance and tutelage free of charge right through to graduation. 'Tis right and proper,' the wizard remarked, 'Wegglar dost owe thee a great deal more. Besides,' he went on, 't'would be waste if not so, art already well advanced, O Bez Mer, and thou art not far behind,' he told an astonished but delighted Albert.

Normal studies were resumed. Reluctant to be parted from the girl already familiar with mind-touch and of whom she had grown extremely fond, Fular undertook to school Connie in the ancient arts of witchcraft.

Financially, both witch and wizard fared better than Fular once supposed. Wegglar's carefully nurtured stock of gold guineas dating from the Middle Ages were now worth many times face value and virtually priceless. One sold at auction proved sufficient to sustain them for more than an earthly year.

Time passed. Fular and Wegglar were duly joined together in wedlock, with Bessimer proudly officiating as the wizard's Best Man and Connie fulfilling the role of Fular's Chief Bridesmaid.

Although touching and joyful, it remained a quiet yet beautiful ceremony and whilst fancy dress wasn't specified, a surprising number of guests sported swirling black cloaks and tall, pointy hats. Few elicited much by way of attention, however, although a couple of dumpy cartoon-like characters wearing green and pink grease paint and sporting orange- coloured, trombone-shaped ears did attract a few amused glances. It was rumoured some guests secreted miniature broomsticks about the person, although *that* peculiar notion remained entirely unproven…

CHAPTER 21

Togetherness

Despite their youth, Bessimer and Albert both graduated with honours, became fully qualified wizards at seventeen and were duly elected into the profession, news which created something of stir throughout magical circles, never before achieved by one so young, never mind by two. Indeed, one grizzled veteran went so far as to voice his concerns over the net, but hastily retracted when challenged by Wegglar to publically pit his own skills against either.

Connie also excelled in witchery, but as witches are judged purely on ability, she was not subjected to any form of examination, at liberty to practice as and when she chose virtually without restriction, always providing ancient limitations were never exceeded.

In the fullness of time and just after turning eighteen, Connie and Bessimer also became husband and wife. Still very much in love and rarely apart, Connie realised the fulfilment of a long-standing dream and for Bessimer the satisfaction of having finally secured the love of his life; the gorgeous girl he had fallen for, hook, line and sinker during a simple afternoon's fishing on the Weaver when just thirteen. *Who claims thirteen to be unlucky?* He chuckled to himself.

Just as promised, Albert fulfilled the role of best man – brilliantly, delivering a well-prepared, touching and humorous speech to a captive but enraptured audience, with Wegglar an honoured guest and Fular in attendance as Connie's Matron of Honour. A wonderful reception at a posh hotel followed — a wedding present from the wizard and his wife — including a tasteful, well-planned meal towards the end of which Albert rose to his feet and called for order.

'Ladies, gentlemen, honoured guests,' he began, 'thank you for your attention. As many of those among you, I feel honoured and privileged to include Connie and Bessimer among my oldest, dearest and closest friends, two delightful people I have known and loved for much of my life. We have shared many an adventure together. Some fun, light hearted and interesting, a few downright dangerous but none ever boring, all faced with intelligence, courage, humility and fortitude, throughout which their love for one another has never once dimmed nor for an instant wavered. I thank and salute them from the bottom of my heart,' he concluded.

'Please be upstanding, raise your glasses and join with me in a toast to the happy couple.

'To Connie and Bessimer. May you enjoy a life full of happiness with many joyous and fruitful years together. Good luck, good health and may Breethan look upon, guard and protect you. God Bless you both.' He concluded by saying: 'To Connie and Bessimer,' echoed by the guests: 'To Connie and Bessimer,' sitting down to rapturous applause and a standing ovation.

Two years later Connie presented her darling husband with a beautiful bouncing boy. Their happiness was complete. Bessimer junior was greatly loved and thrived, seemingly always healthy, suffering never so much as a runny nose. Comfortably meeting milestones well in advance of expectation, he was on his feet at ten months and toddling happily soon after.

Strolling through the park one chilly autumn day, when Connie and Bessimer were taking turns pushing the buggy, a much-treasured teddy bear (a present from Wegglar) shot out and went hurtling through the air, landing a good twenty metres away. Sighing, Bessimer patiently retrieved the toy and firmly replaced it, this time at the bottom, well out of reach. Two minutes later, out it came again, this time travelling much faster and for twice the distance. His puzzled parents peered inside only to discover their mischievous offspring cooing away happily while still cosily wrapped in his blanket.

'You naughty little boy,' Bessimer scolded, but with a chuckle, 'leave Teddy be, you little stinker, or I'll jolly-well give you a tickle.'

'Ted-Ted goes fly, Dada,' the infant innocently replied.

Bessimer threw back his head and laughed. 'Cor, Penny Plinkers,' he exclaimed to his wife, 'catches on quickly, doesn't he?'

'Just like his brilliant Daddy,' she proudly smiled.